Praise for

AMERICAN BY DAY

"Ingenious. Humorous. Wonderful."

—Lee Child, "May's book recommendation"

"Sure Derek Miller's novels are smart and full of heart and savvy and hilarious, but even more than all of this, he's *fun*. He's as dedicated as any writer I know to the proposition that readers should enjoy themselves, should delight in the experience of life and language. If our hearts get broken along the way, so much the better." —Richard Russo

"[An] outstanding crime novel . . . Leavened throughout with Miller's wry reflections on Norway's 'chronic sense of discontentment,' this incandescent exposé of European and American mores profoundly entertains and provokes disturbing questions about personal and societal values." —*Publishers Weekly*, starred and boxed review

"If Tocqueville had written a police thriller, it might look something like this engrossing and wryly humorous but also deeply serious work. [*American by Day* is] for fans of Miller and his previous works (e.g., *The Girl in Green*), which were deservedly acclaimed."

—*Library Journal*, starred review

"What lifts this well above average are the characters, notably Sigrid and Irv, and their relationship and discussions, ranging from the investigative process to the characteristics of their respective countries, as they determine to what extent they can work together to achieve their desired goals. Miller offers a slightly different spin on Scandinavia-set crime fiction, wrapping a thriller plot around the character-driven substance of literary fiction to produce a hybrid that is compelling from any angle."

—*Booklist*, starred review

"Like his acclaimed debut, *Norwegian by Night* (2013), Miller's highly enjoyable new book is a solid mystery wrapped up in musings about individuality and freedom, grief and sadness."   —*Kirkus Reviews*

"A superb novel on all levels."   —Marcel Berlins, *Times* (UK)

"Not to be missed ... A subtle crime story peopled with beautifully drawn characters."   —*Daily Mail* (UK)

Praise for

NORWEGIAN BY NIGHT

"Has the brains of a literary novel and the body of a thriller."
          —*New York Times*

"One of those books that completely transcends its genre and offers us one of the most memorable characters—Sheldon Horowitz—that I've encountered in years."   —Richard Russo

"*Norwegian by Night* shifts along like an inquisitive wind, with a voice so confident you would follow it into a leaning house. Generous with its wit, dazzling in its cultural and historical reach, it is the kind of sweep-you-up tale a reader always wants but rarely finds, the kind where you stand in the bookstore reading the opening pages and whisper, *This is the one*."
          —Leif Enger, author of *Peace Like a River*

"An unusual hybrid: part memory novel, part police procedural, part sociopolitical tract, and part existential meditation."   —*Kirkus Reviews*

"Have you ever lucked into one of those novels so taut and suspenseful that you can't turn the pages fast enough, yet, at the same time, so magnificently written and psychologically incisive that you find yourself unable to turn those same pages *slowly* enough? Such novels are as rare as great comets. *Norwegian by Night*, I'm happy to report, is one."
          —Jonathan Miles, author of *Dear American Airlines*

"Both an exciting chase thriller and a poignant story about a man who comes into his own again in his dotage . . . The many admirers of Scandinavian crime novels will enjoy this bighearted first novel."

—*Library Journal*

"No brief plot outline can do justice to a book that deserves to find a place on a few best-of-the-year lists. Sheldon is a brilliantly imagined character, a true mensch, made of Greatest Generation stuff . . . Miller joins the ranks of Stieg Larsson, Henning Mankell, and Jo Nesbø, the holy trinity of Scandinavian crime novelists."

—*Booklist*, starred review

"An outrageously intelligent thriller, and its philosopher-sniper hero, Sheldon Horowitz, is a character who'll stay in your brain for decades. You might come for the guns and the ruckus, but by the last page, you'll be crying at all the goddamned beauty and love in the world."

—Patrick Somerville, author of *This Bright River*

"Truly a page-turner . . . *Norwegian by Night* is about past wars and present-day ethnic strife, family, grief, guilt, and, ultimately, redemption. Korea (and phantom Koreans), Vietnam, the Holocaust, ethnic identity—Serb, Norwegian, Muslim, and yes, Jewish—these are the true characters of the novel . . . Funny, moving, and thoroughly gripping."

—*Jewish Week*

"One of the most surprising and unusual novels to emerge in recent years . . . Miller takes readers down many paths, commenting thoughtfully on war, family, country, identity, and the personal as political, yet never loses the tension or propulsion of his story. Thought-provoking, evocative, and wry in the best way, *Norwegian by Night* is a remarkable novel."

—*Shelf Awareness*

"Ostensibly a Scandinavian thriller yet recalls Saul Bellow and Philip Roth's more cerebral creations . . . At once a rich psychological study, a political parable . . . and a moving story of an old man's last chance to slay his demons."

—*Sunday Times*

"A stunning examination of how our lives shape our character, and how our allegiances shape our destiny."

—*AARP*, "12 Summer Reads for 2013"

"A rare comedic gem that is so special . . . Dark, moving, meaningful, absolute fun to read, and a thriller to boot."   —*Psychology Today*

AMERICAN
BY DAY

Derek B. Miller

Mariner Books
Houghton Mifflin Harcourt
BOSTON   NEW YORK

First Mariner Books edition 2019
Copyright © 2018 by Derek B. Miller
Q&A with the author copyright © 2019 by Derek B. Miller

For information about permission to reproduce selections from this book,
write to trade.permissions@hmhco.com or to Permissions,
Houghton Mifflin Harcourt Publishing Company,
3 Park Avenue, 19th Floor, New York, New York 10016.

hmhco.com

Library of Congress Cataloging-in-Publication Data
Names: Miller, Derek B., 1970- author.
Title: American by day / Derek B. Miller.
Description: First U.S. edition. | Boston : Houghton Mifflin Harcourt, 2018.
Identifiers: LCCN 2017045332 (print) | LCCN 2017051669 (ebook) |
ISBN 9781328876737 (ebook) | ISBN 9781328876652 (hardcover) |
ISBN 9781328585080 (pbk.)
Subjects: LCSH: Women detectives—Fiction. | Missing
persons—Investigation—Fiction. | BISAC: FICTION / Literary. | FICTION /
Action & Adventure. | FICTION / Humorous. | FICTION / Mystery & Detective /
Women Sleuths. | GSAFD: Humorous fiction. | Mystery fiction.
Classification: LCC PS3613.I5337 (ebook) | LCC PS3613.I5337 A84 2017 (print)
| DDC 813/.6 —dc23
LC record available at https://lccn.loc.gov/2017045332

Printed in the United States of America
DOC 10 9 8 7 6 5 4 3 2 1

For Sheldon

AUGUST 2008

THE RIGHT QUESTION

SIGRID ØDEGÅRD'S HANDS rest on the unopened blue folder as she stares out the window of her office. The seal of the *Politi* is embossed on the front in gold, red and black, meaning that someone decided to break out the good stationery for this one. It displays no author or title but she knows what it contains and she is in no rush to read it. Only two short months ago, in June, the entire city of Oslo, Norway, was trimmed with lilacs. Sigrid's father had once told her that the early summer flowers were her mother's favorite, and when the season was at its peak in Hedmark, their farmhouse was filled with them: a bouquet in each bathroom, a vase on the kitchen table. Their errant petals, he said, would drift through the house after her family as they journeyed its hallways stirring them up and scattering them in their wake. This collective movement—this collective memory—however, was thirty-five years ago. Sigrid was five years old when Astrid died. Sigrid wonders, looking out over the park with its August sunbathers and running children, whether those memories are even hers. They might have been given to her by her father. And if the memories are not hers, are they less precious or, perhaps, more?

She turns her attention from the window to the blue folder.

This, she's been informed, is the final report and verdict about the events last month that resulted in the shooting deaths of four hostage-takers at a summer cabin near the Swedish border in the village of Glåmlia. She was the commanding officer and had made the decision to utilize the emergency response force—the *Beredskapstroppen.* Their assault killed three of the perpetrators. Sigrid, herself, killed the fourth.

Conscious of being watched through the glass by the prying eyes of her department, Sigrid flips open the cover but doesn't read the words. She should have closed the blinds after she'd received the folder from the young cop who'd knocked on her door to deliver it. He was blond and looked worryingly pale despite it being late summer. She'd found his boyish face immediately annoying.

"Thanks," she'd said, and started to close the office door.

"You're welcome," he'd said and then—oddly—extended his hand.

She couldn't think of a reason why he'd do this but she shook it to make it go away.

He seemed pleased with this and walked off.

During the past month the internal affairs department has been studying the events leading to the shootings in accordance with standard procedure. The report was standard procedure, though, only in the sense of being formalized; it was hardly common. The last time a Norwegian cop had fatally shot anyone was two years ago, in 2006, and before that it had been . . . forever. A decade? It simply didn't happen in Norway. Violent crime was very low, murder rarely happened, and when it did it was usually between people who knew each other, and most often between lovers. The man was always to blame.

Their training, at the academy, had been focused on how to deescalate a situation and gain a measure of control over it rather than rush in and encounter it. This is not what happened last month.

It was still the right call, she thought; they had taken a man, woman and child hostage. Under her fingertips, though, was the institutional wisdom of her department on the same topic. It may, or may not, be the same as her own.

They had chosen to deliver the file to her today, on Friday. Without reading it she'd never know whether the decision was sadistic or gracious.

The summer house where the shootings took place was deep in the woods behind a small field. It was a little larger than a standard *hytte*. It was a place intended for serenity. A hunting lodge. An escape for lovers. A moment after she had sprung from the police car with her colleague Petter, a young man emerged from the cabin—a man she had never seen before—and he ran in her direction.

To her? Toward her? At her? He was in motion, that was all she understood. His motive was opaque. Her fear and his direction, however, were not.

As she watched him she'd half expected him to stop. People usually change their behavior when seeing a police officer. They drive more slowly. They become more aware of their actions. They drop the weapon. They raise their arms.

He kept running. She called for him to halt. He kept running.

She saw the carving knife in his hand immediately. It seemed less dangerous than it did incongruous. There they were, in that beautiful season when the natural world was at its most expansive; the moment Norwegians wait for and dream about all through the dark winter so that its arrival is both blessed and wistful for being so short. And there he was, silently running toward her with a knife designed to slice meat.

If she'd delayed he'd have been on top of her. So she shot him. And then she shot him again.

"Screw it," she mutters in her native language and starts reading the file.

His name was Burim and he was from Kosovo, apparently. His family fled to Norway as refugees from the war in the 1990s. His father had died of health complications after being freed from a Serbian internment camp. The report attributes the death to malnutrition and damage to internal organs likely caused by beatings at the camp. Young Burim, fatherless, had fallen into the wrong crowd in Oslo as he failed to assimilate into Norwegian culture. His immigrant experience and his behavioral patterns in Norway—concluded a forensic psychologist—suggested immaturity rather than malice or ambition. That was who she had killed.

However, the report continued to explain that the legal findings about her own guilt or innocence in the matter were based on a study of the facts of the case, and the circumstances of the encounter between the assailant (him) and the officer on the scene (her). She reads about the events that were in part described through Petter's own testimony as he had eyewitnessed the shooting from his side of the patrol car.

The report contains a narrative account of the shooting. To Sigrid it reads like historical fiction. It is a story about a woman with her own name but this fictional character is clearly not Sigrid herself because the author of this story wasn't at the cabin when all this happened. There was no video and other than Petter no witnesses. How could anyone possibly know what she'd really been doing let alone thinking?

Sigrid flips to the next page and reads on.

On what basis does this bureaucratic reenactment draw its claims and attributions of cause and effect? Who is this writer who drew conclusions about what happened at the moment Sigrid pulled the trigger on her weapon? And who is this forty-year-old Norwegian police officer named "Sigrid Ødegård" who shot the man and instead of rushing over to care for his wounds, ran instead to the eighty-two-year-old American man who had tumbled out of the cabin, his neck slashed with a knife?

The report does not mention the gentle and soft hand of the old man reaching up to touch her face, leaving his own fingerprints in blood on her cheek. It does not mention how she did not see those fingerprints until later that night when she returned to her own apartment in Grønland, alone, and looked in the mirror. Why was that not in the report if this writer knew her so well?

By page twelve it is clear that both Sigrid and her literary doppelgänger have both been exonerated.

• • •

Sigrid raises her eyes to see whether any of the junior staff are watching her with the file.

As none of them are looking at her it is clear that, moments earlier, all of them were.

She returns to the report, increasingly attentive to its fictions and assumptions; false premises and confident rhetoric.

And the more she reads past its bureaucratic surface and its misplaced certainty, the more Sigrid can sense a higher firmament of truth. Somewhere, beyond her sight but not her understanding, she can hear a different story; an untold story about a confused Kosovan refugee with no violent record, fleeing from a bad choice rather than making his way toward another. His lethal mistake was not his decision to hurt her but rather running in her direction and not speaking Norwegian well enough to understand the words she had called out twice: "Halt or I will shoot."

In this story, everything is the same but the meaning of everything is different.

She pictures the events again. The green grass. The red cabin. The blue sky. The running man and his auburn hair. His wide brown eyes.

Sigrid reads on, ever more bothered by the casual ease of the writer. After page twelve, when the verdict is made clear, all other descriptions of the event seem reverse-engineered back to the conclusion. The author is reading into the events whatever is needed so that the findings become better illustrated rather than challenged. It does not seem to be—as best Sigrid can tell—entirely conscious or even deliberate. It is only that the pieces are all easy to explain once the final explanation is provided. In fact, by the end of the report it seems to Sigrid the chief that this fictional Sigrid character was destined to pull the trigger. That it was not only justified but even inevitable.

Not only does the report legally vindicate her, but somehow she is not even considered responsible for the shooting. And there, finally, is the disturbance. Because for the past month she has been tormented over the consequences of her very deliberate and not at all predestined decision.

She was tormented precisely because none of this was inevitable. It was a decision. A decision Sigrid needs to understand and one that can perhaps best be understood by taking apart the definite elements and replacing them with something new—something unexpected.

At her desk, her eyes closed, Sigrid engages in a technique she often uses in her own investigations. She turns summer to winter. She strips out the green grass between the patrol car and the cabin and replaces it with a snowy field. She turns the red summer house into a brown mountain cabin. She fades out the azure sky and replaces it with an iron canopy that presses down from the Arctic.

And across that snow, still holding a knife, and approaching at the same speed, comes the man. But not the same man.

This man is a blond Norwegian.

In this version he is Bjørn—not Burim—and he rushes at her through fresh powder snow with the determination of a Viking. Here is a counterfactual world. A new model. A new set of relationships. Here, in this scenario, everything is familiar but estranged. And it is in the blue eyes of that charging man that Sigrid finally finds the question that the report has not thought to ask. The question no one could imagine asking or, perhaps, no one dared.

It is, however, the question she has been looking for. The one that dismantles the institutional presumptions of cause and effect and inevitability. It is the question that calls everything into doubt and makes space for new truths to be known and, ultimately, acted upon:

Would she have shot him twice in the chest—she can now wonder —if he had been a native Norwegian?

A WEIRD PLACE

SIGRID SPENDS SATURDAY binge-watching American TV shows on a streaming service recently introduced to Norway. Her friend Eli insisted she subscribe.

"It's better than a cat," she'd said.

"Who mentioned a cat?" Sigrid answered.

"You don't have a boyfriend."

"Which is why I need a TV subscription?"

"Exactly," said Eli.

It was easier, she'd reasoned, to pay the seventy kroner a month than to untangle that knot.

Sigrid soon learned that the streaming service had a function that caused the next episode in a television series to begin only fifteen seconds after the conclusion of the previous episode, thereby saving the subscriber the calories that might have been burned pressing the button. This simple function produced a new kind of restive anxiety that seemed to call out for a name.

The dull flicker of the television and the semi-satisfying stories are helpful at first but after watching for six straight hours she starts to ignore the story lines and instead indulge in spells of curiosity.

Why, for example, is overacting preferred in situation comedies but not in dramas?

Why doesn't acting more dramatically result in more drama?

Why are American TV actors so . . . shiny?

British actors don't appear to reflect light off their skins in quite the same glossy manner as American actors do. How can it be that with all the skin colors available in American society, each one comes with the same glossy finish and never matte?

Could it be something they're eating? Or . . . not eating? Are Americans naturally glossy or . . . unnaturally?

Which would be scarier?

The television shows are terribly unrealistic but she is not bothered by this. It is in that space between divine truth and humanity's fumbled efforts to make sense of it that Sigrid finds comfort in knowing she is not alone.

By eight thirty at night she has reached a broad conclusion about America. It is not an especially sophisticated conclusion, nor does she suspect that it is original, but it is satisfying to think so deeply about something for a long time and finally hit bedrock. It goes like this: "What a weird place."

On Sunday she wakes to a Scandinavian summer sun that is so intense it threatens to turn her to dust. It is seven a.m. but the sun is high enough in the sky for the day to burn as noon. Sitting up in bed she realizes that her stomach aches from the bag of sour cream and onion potato chips she devoured last night. Neither the stomachache nor the guilt compare to the taste in her mouth that the toothpaste couldn't defeat.

After a shower and coffee she tries, briefly, to hide inside the television again, but it has lost its magic. Without a sign of rain to encourage further isolation, she finally succumbs to her Norwegianness and accepts that she has to go outdoors.

She and her older brother, Marcus, had regularly been tossed outside by their parents, whatever the weather, based on a deeply held if unspoken Norwegian belief that any child who does not spend at least three hours outdoors every day might actually die.

Without her parents to compel her, or a child of her own for a surrogate, Sigrid forces herself outside. She spends the warmest part of Sunday alone on a small beach called *Bygdøy sjøbad* wearing an extra-large T-shirt over green bikini bottoms that have mysteriously grown smaller since last summer. The thin straps cut into her hips.

She has brought a book written by an American humorist. It is called *When You Are Engulfed in Flames*, and she bought it solely for the title. On the beach, leaning against a stone wall, she spends most of her time not reading it but watching small children run along the crescent-shaped bay, finding starfish and small crabs, and holding them up in delight and terror for their parents to see. Her father has been asking whether she wants children. She looks at the expressions of the parents on the beach for an answer.

That night, as Sigrid and her sunburn recline on the cool sofa across from the television, her father calls. It is not scheduled but it is not unexpected.

Sigrid puts the television on mute and watches an American police car with poor handling chase another car with poor handling though an urban environment, endangering the lives of hundreds.

"Hi, pappa."

"You didn't call me with the results of the report."

"Sorry."

"I take it the findings were favorable."

Sigrid switches ears. "Why?"

"Because I know you. You wouldn't have shot a man unless you thought it was necessary."

"Maybe I shouldn't have thought it necessary. That's the part the police department is ignoring."

"You made a choice, not a mistake, in a situation where any reasonable person would have experienced danger. You're free to return to work?"

"Yes."

"Come home instead," he offers. "We'd be happy to have you."

"We?"

"Me and Ferdinand."

"Who's Ferdinand?"

"The duck. I could have sworn you'd met."

On Monday morning Sigrid reports to the office convinced that her hair still smells like her compatriots' oversexed flesh, their barbecued pork, and the tropical suntan lotion that no one needs this far north. As she enters the building she nods to the smokers by the door, their faces turned toward the sun like so many sunflowers past their prime.

Inside, the light is weaker and the air colder. She passes through the halls of the building that make the days bleed into each other by design. In uniform, she seats herself outside her commanding officer's door. At precisely 9:15, and on schedule, he opens it and waves her in.

Sigrid stands to adjust her tie but does not step forward into his office. She wants to avoid signaling that this might be a long conversation. "I'm taking leave," she says immediately.

"You don't have to," her CO says, standing with his hand on the door lever. "You're cleared. The report was definitive. You rescued the hostages and took out a criminal network. You might even be up for a medal."

"I'm going to take leave."

He nods as though he understands something, though Sigrid can't imagine what that might be. "There's counseling," he says.

"I'm going home."

"You won't mope around your apartment, I hope."

"My father has a farm."

"How long will you go on leave?"

"Until I'm back."

HOME

S HE DRIVES NORTH to Hedmark with one suitcase. There is traffic on the E6 as she leaves the city, but it thins out and she settles into the drive, following signs for Trondheim.

The farther one travels by car from Oslo into what Sigrid thinks of as Norway—Oslo not being a part of it—there are fewer speed cameras. She always feels that as the speed cameras disappear so too does the state and its central control. Her breathing becomes freer, the air a little sweeter, and the tension in her shoulders releases. When she watches American Westerns she wonders if this was how they felt with their horses, six-shooters, and the view of the horizon.

Her father likes to insist that the cameras are not really speed cameras at all but part of a complex troll-detection grid set up around Norway's most populated areas. From the bar atop the SAS Radisson in the center of Oslo, where she has on occasion had a drink, this theory might seem preposterous, but out here, on the highway, there is no denying that the farther she leaves the city behind, the more she feels the essence of the woods, the weight of the shadows, and the flow of a million small waterfalls that spill from cracks in the plunging fjords.

When traveling south into Roman Europe on vacation, Sigrid feels antiquity. But as she journeys north into Norway's forests, what she feels is ancientness.

Maybe there are trolls.

There were never any trolls in the woods behind the house in 1973 when she was five and Marcus eleven. There was, however, a graveyard by the small church adjacent to their property. That is where their mother, Astrid Ødegård, was buried that year. Sigrid can only remember the four of them as a perfect family. Her earliest memories are of two enormous horses at the farmhouse, three stuffed animals she used to play with—a blue dragon, a pink one, and a panda bear—and her parents sitting in the living room reading at night by a fire. She can smell *kanelboller.*

The memories are mismatched, separated by time, and unlikely to be reliable. Sigrid has never tried to concoct a story to connect them or question what feels most authentic about them. What is important, she has always believed, is how the memories make her feel. And they make her feel happy. The heart is one of the few places where facts and truth may be separable.

When her mother died, though, that happiness ended. The family broke apart. Marcus was angry at his father for his mother's death and became—in Sigrid's view—irrationally unwavering in his certainty that it was Morten's fault and then, later, his own. Neither made sense to her. The consequence of Marcus's anger was that their daily life—getting him off to school, doing his homework, managing their activities, surviving the intensity of weekends—became impossible.

And yet, this is not how she remembers her brother. Her enduring memory, her enduring feelings, are of how much she loved him. How much fun he was. How they were inseparable. How she would abuse him and make him cry and he would take it because there was no meanness to him, no revenge, no cruelty.

Morten explained to Sigrid, much later, that the year after Astrid died proved to him that Marcus was not going to forgive and was not going to heal unless a new approach was taken. Morten was devastated by his inability to turn the situation around while grieving for his wife and trying to be a support to little Sigrid. Morten ultimately succumbed to the recommendations of doctors and extended family that life would be better for everyone if Marcus moved in with Astrid's sister Ingeborg, who lived in a village by the Hardangerfjorden and ran an apple farm with her husband, Jakob. They were childless, loved Marcus very much, and were desperate to help.

Astrid had died of cancer. When Sigrid became a police officer she checked the death certificate and even asked for the medical records. She had not been suspicious, but her access to the files made them impossible to avoid. They were as expected and exactly as her father had explained. What was not in those records but was true nevertheless was that her parents had loved each other. She learned this from the stories of neighbors and the comforting words of family and friends whose memories never conflicted. Her feelings, she knew, were not a lie. Her memories were youthful and incomplete but they were not wrong. So why Marcus blamed Morten and himself for Astrid's death was never clear, even though she asked, and even pressed him, as they grew up.

The family would reunite on holidays and vacations, but Marcus never reconciled with Morten. Not entirely. Sigrid, however, adored her father, and so the difference in her brother's stance toward him resulted in an emotional breakwater that kept the strongest emotions — good ones and bad — from reaching either of them. She tried, as they grew, to replenish what they had had, but she and her brother had irreconcilable feelings about their childhoods. It was a hard foundation for an adult relationship.

When Marcus moved out Sigrid had her father mostly to herself from the age of six to eighteen, when she left for the university. And until recently, she has mostly had him to herself in her adulthood, as he never remarried and she never married at all. They keep each other company. Not that he was alone. He also had his library, of course. After Astrid died he filled the void of words unspoken with the new silence of books unread.

He built the library in the dining room after Marcus moved out. The urban hip would say he "repurposed" the room but Morten would have scoffed at the inaccuracy, as the room evidently hadn't been serving any purpose at all.

Morten lucked upon a small municipal library in Elverum that was refurbishing and therefore dispensing with their gorgeous oak bookshelves at a very reasonable take-them-away-please price. He paid a few young men in town a fair wage to collect the shelves and directed the boys to place the units so they covered all walls but the windows. There was enough space remaining to place two of the long shelves in the center of the room, thereby creating "stacks" around a long table between them, which he and Sigrid used for studying. They spent as much time in there, together, as they did in the adjacent kitchen.

It was, perhaps, an affectation, but her father had placed a bronze-finished green banker's lamp on the table; it warmed that already darkened wood and pushed away the hurried, the ephemeral, and the radical notions that come from direct sunlight. When Sigrid moved out and went to the Big City to study at the police academy, Morten placed an easy chair in the corner of the room too, which was as good for the nap as for the read itself. This room became his primary sanctuary.

She had argued with him, many times, to be more social, but he scoffed at her, saying that she didn't understand the term. Time alone, he explained, need not be wasted or lonely. Yes, there are men who turn inward and reclusive when their wife dies and children move off. Depression and alcoholism are common. Norway is not alone in this regard, he said, though it has perfected the art.

He is not a candidate for this, he said. She shouldn't worry.

"We're only a three-hour drive away from each other in a country that is twenty-five hundred kilometers long," he'd said to her. "Marcus is only five hours away. This is nothing. And although you have moved out, you haven't really moved away. We talk almost every day. I'm not lonely. And if I become lonely . . ." he'd said, "I'll get a pet."

For the twenty intervening years Sigrid kept herself convinced that her father was happy enough. Now, unhappy herself, her optics have changed. She cannot tell whether she is seeing him more clearly through this new understanding or whether she's projecting her feelings onto him. Either way, she has no place being a police investigator right now.

Early evening, Sigrid rolls her car across the packed earth of the farm's driveway. The last time she was home the hills were covered in snow between her front yard and the Arctic. Now everything is green. The sun is still high. Night will not properly come. Dusk, at this time of year, only merges with the dawn.

Sigrid heaves the suitcase from the car and trudges across the driveway, dragging it into the hall. She parks it by the empty umbrella stand with its upturned mouth gaping like a carp's.

Her father is in the kitchen and he does not interrupt his task to welcome her. He is adjusting a hinge on the back door that opens to the barnyard with its tractor and the few remaining animals. He is on his knees, which rest on a neatly folded towel. He wears a flannel shirt and old jeans with the washed patina that young people covet. His pharmacy-bought reading glasses perch on the end of his nose and he studies the hinge as if it's an ancient text.

Morten is sixty-nine. His arms look thin to her. She watches him work.

"Planning to stay for a while, I take it," he says, not looking up.

"What makes you think so?"

"The sound of your suitcase being dragged like a body across the pebbles."

"It might do both of us some good."

Morten sits back for a moment to study his handiwork.

"I'm using a lubricant to loosen the joint because it squeaks, but I've applied too much, and one of the defining characteristics of lubricant is its ability to attract grit, which creates friction, which creates the very problem I'm trying to solve, and that makes the entire process too ironic to tolerate. It's this sort of thing, at a grander scale, that will eventually cause the universe to collapse back in on itself."

"How about a napkin?" Sigrid says, and collects one from the kitchen table and hands it to her father.

He takes the napkin and cleans the hinge, saving the world.

"That was close," she says.

Sigrid removes a bottle of Farris mineral water from her bag. She unscrews the blue top and pulls heavily. Her father scowls. "We have the finest water on the earth flowing through the taps. Why are you paying for that?"

"Convenience."

"Save the bottle, then. Fill it with real water."

"It came with water of its own. I wasn't going to dump it out on principle."

"What did you bring me?" he asks, rolling off his knees and joining her at the table. He rests a hand casually across his knee and for a moment he looks younger and strong.

"In the car. Supplies from civilization."

"Is that what we're calling Oslo these days?"

"You mentioned on the phone something about a duck. Where's the duck?"

"Doing duck things. I don't pry."

"Is it a pet?"

"A pet?"

"You once said . . ."

"What?"

"Forget it."

Sigrid takes two cans of pale ale from the refrigerator and pours them into glasses while her father places dark bread, cheese, and sausage on the table.

Sigrid looks at the distant hills across the farmland, their tops shorn by time as with everything old. She had forgotten how good silence can sound in the company of others.

"It's good to be home," she says as she takes her place at the table across from her father. "I feel like I could stay forever."

"That's too bad," her father says, after taking a long pull on his beer, "because you can't."

"Why not?"

"Because you have to go to America tomorrow. Late afternoon."

Sigrid does not understand the joke but laughs anyway. "Why would I do that?"

"Because your brother is missing. And you're going to find him."

QUE SERA, SERA

THE BEER IS not enough, so her father places a bottle of aquavit on the table between two small decorative glasses that have served the same purpose for a century.

"Aquavit is for Christmas," Sigrid objects.

"It's also for Christmas," he says, pouring a glass for each of them.

"*Skål*," Sigrid says.

"*Skål*."

They each drink the full measure.

After a pause Sigrid says, "Fine. Out with it."

"As I said, Marcus is missing."

"He's in America teaching a couple of university courses as an adjunct on conservation or something. You've been corresponding."

"That's right," Morten says.

Letter writing is an old-fashioned and obsolete form of communication they both prefer, he explains. Letters on paper are penned deliberately and read without interruption. Also, there is a timeless pleasure in walking to the mailbox in anticipation. The Romans did this, he says.

"And?" she asks, not yet interested.

"A slow and deliberate conversation was good for us."

"That isn't what I meant."

"I didn't like something in the tone of his last letter," Morten says. "And they stopped coming after that."

"That's the mail for you," Sigrid says, pouring them each another drink. "I'm assuming you've called him."

"His last letter was sent a week ago," says Morten. "I received it only three days later. I called immediately. No answer on his home phone and his mobile has been disconnected. I called the university but he doesn't teach during the summer, so they don't know anything. I tried the hospitals, too. Nothing."

"And the police?"

"I called you."

"Again . . . not what I meant."

"I want you to talk to the police. You'll know what to say."

"You're a father concerned for his son. You provide his name and address and last working number. You explain where he might go and . . ."

Morten shifts in his chair.

"What?" she asks.

"I want you two to see each other."

"Why?"

Sigrid and her father are close, but long speeches and discussions are typically rare. The simple pleasure of company has served as a worthy substitute for the words not spoken. Sometimes, though, words help.

"Pappa . . . why?"

"For a while it felt like Marcus was going to come home."

"That's wishful thinking, pappa. You've been saying that since he moved in with Aunt Ingeborg."

Morten stands and leaves the room, returning soon after with a bundle of letters. He removes them from a shoebox that bears the name of a company long since out of business.

Her father places the small stack of white envelopes with their exotic American stamps in the center of the table. There are scenic vistas, national park scenes, famous citizens, and ducks.

"Ducks," she says.

"Ducks are universal," says Morten, untying the bundle. He takes the letter from the bottom of the pile and the letter from the top and places them on the table, facing Sigrid. Side by side they are identical aside from the stamps themselves and the dates they were franked by the U.S. Postal Service. They have the same addresses, to and from. The same handwriting.

Morten taps the oldest letter but does not open it.

"Seven months ago he wrote to me. I was surprised. I was worried when I found it in my mailbox. I assumed—I feared—it would contain startling news of some kind."

"Like what?"

"Everything a parent worries about. An injury. A financial crisis. An unwanted pregnancy or child. A wanted one that something happened to. I came in and read the letter and I was indeed startled, but only because of how unexpected it was. He seemed happy. He had taken the position at the university—this 'adjunct' position you mentioned—and even though it lacked prestige or payment and any other obvious career path, he was putting that old master's degree to use, as well as some thirty years of professional experience in agriculture. There was little personal in the letter, per se, nothing emotional, nothing too confessional, but it opened the door for casual conversation. And there was a mention of a woman's presence in his life. Lydia. He didn't say much. Only mentioned weekend trips to interesting spots. He shared some vivid memories of hiking and rock climbing. Nothing personal, though. Nothing about her. Nevertheless. It was a letter written by a fully living person. I was . . . delighted."

Morten places his right hand, with his wedding ring, on top of the stack of letters.

"I knew you two were writing but I didn't know much about it."

"I suppose," he says, "I wanted it to remain between Marcus and me for a while. I wasn't trying to keep it a secret from you. I just felt . . ."
—he stops for a moment to consider what feelings he might have

had—". . . that you and I have had so much time together, alone, that perhaps I owed it to Marcus to do something apart. Just the two of us."

"It's fine."

"He's forty-six."

"I know," she says.

"I can't come to terms with all the time that's passed."

Morten drinks another aquavit. Sigrid refills both glasses.

As close as she and her father had become, there was little joy in the house. Intimacy and love, she learned, did not coincide necessarily with happiness or pleasure. The absence of her mother created a strangeness to the world, as if the palette of the sky had inexplicably shifted and the mind never became fully accepting of that new condition. Her father was not a successful guide, and together they treated what was lost as though it had merely been misplaced—as if, on some off-chance, Astrid might return. It did not startle Sigrid, as a little girl, to learn that her mother died as much as it baffled her that her mother would continue to be dead each morning and repeatedly not return.

"I'll need to read these," Sigrid says, reaching over and patting the stack of letters.

The sun is finally behind the western hills. Though the sky is still blue, the kitchen grows darker and much colder. Morten stands and closes the window above the sink. He lights four candles on the kitchen table.

She actually needs an answer to a more pressing question.

"So. You were joking about America. We'll make some more calls tomorrow."

"I bought you a ticket. Even put a tour book in your room. Read the letters on the plane."

"I'm not going to fly to another continent without a valid and considered reason. We have not, by any stretch, exhausted our options from here."

"Two possibilities," Morten says. "He's fine. Like when this was sent. In which case, you have visited your brother after years apart and you rejoice in each other's company while you use the opportunity to talk through the fact, my daughter, that you recently killed a man, only to have another die in your arms moments later."

She begins to object, but he raises a hand. He is not finished.

"A reunion is long past due. Your circumstances alone warrant this. But if, by chance," says Morten, shifting the second letter forward and pulling the first back, "he needs your help, which is the other possibility, you'll be there to help him. There is no downside. It is the right thing to do. And it's all better than you moping around the farm."

"I wanted to come home and relax."

"Do this instead."

"America's weird," she says with confidence.

"And wonderful. It's both. Or so I'm told. I've never been. They're having an election in under three months where they might vote a black man into the White House. Go be a part of history. Your plane leaves tomorrow. Icelandair to Montreal. You'll pass through customs and then take a small plane to a town called—unimaginatively—Watertown. I figure you can rent a car from there or take the bus to your final destination. You don't need a visa from Norway. You can stay for three months as a visitor. Go. Have an adventure."

"In upstate New York?"

"Adventures are mostly about the people," he conceded. "You should know that his letters took a dark turn about two months ago. Something happened. He didn't mention what. I tried to draw him out further but he wasn't forthcoming with details. I suspected that his romance ended harshly, and perhaps on her terms. I don't know what I did wrong that both of my children should be in their forties and not have a spouse and children."

"Not this again, please," Sigrid says.

"Women think they can wait forever these days. It's an illusion. You know the rate of miscarriages after the age of . . ."

"I'm not waiting for anything, pappa. I'm living my life, which will be what it will be."

"Ah . . . the Doris Day approach to planning."

"I don't know who that is."

"No. Why would anyone anymore."

Morten empties the glass of aquavit and Sigrid reaches to fill it again, but he covers the glass with his palm.

"How's your head?" he asks her.

"Fine. How's yours?"

"Five weeks ago you were hit on the head by a criminal who popped out of a closet. How's your head?"

"How's your duck?"

"What is it with you and that duck?" her father asks.

"You named it."

"Ferdinand. He has personality."

"He has nutritional value. Which he is likely to lose if he has a name."

"I watched a film recently about a farmer who trained a pig to be a sheepdog. There was a duck in the film. He was very funny."

"We're going to eat that duck, pappa."

"It'll be much harder now that he has a name."

Sigrid leaves her father alone at the table shortly afterward. She kisses him on the forehead and wishes him a good night as he packs a Danish pipe with Cavendish tobacco and disappears into a cloud of aromatic smoke. Sigrid retires to her room with Marcus's letters and the intention of trying to take seriously the idea of traveling to the United States of America on a plane leaving tomorrow for an adventure to reunite with her brother in order to please her father.

The suitcase from Oslo contains only one nightgown, and she slips into it and then under the soft white bed sheets that protect her from the itchy but warm woolen blanket on top. Under the reassuring weight of the blanket she switches on the reading lamp to her right and opens Marcus's final letter.

It is typed—not handwritten. It looks as if it has actually been produced on a mechanical typewriter. She runs her fingers across the back of the page and feels the subtle embossing produced by the type hammer striking the page.

The paper is American-sized, eight and a half by eleven inches, rather than the nearly universal A4, which runs a bit narrower. She's read a piece in *Aftenposten* about how America is one of three countries left in the world retaining imperial measures rather than adopting the metric system. The other two are Liberia and Myanmar.

"Weird place."

The letter reads:

> Dear pappa,
> It happened again. You told me the first time that I didn't understand. That I misunderstood everything. Well, I'm a grown man now and it happened a second time and this time I understand it all too well. And more than that. It has forced me to see it all with a line of sight unobstructed by the years and the events and the decisions in between. What I now understand is that it was my fault. It was also yours but you, I forgive.
> Your son,
> Marcus.

SIDE EFFECTS

S IGRID FLIES OUT of Oslo's Gardermoen Airport on an Icelandair Boeing 757. Her father had upgraded her to "Saga Class," either generously or because he couldn't resist the term.

Traveling internationally is still fresh and she admits to herself a certain excitement when boarding the plane and turning toward the left—the business class—when being handed the headphones. The steward, very handsome, smiles at her for her good fortune and good taste at paying for a wider seat.

She has attended a few European conferences that have aimed to link academics with policymakers on matters of organized crime, cross-border cooperation, interagency workforce guidelines, new findings on smuggling routes, and the confusing overlap between criminal and terrorist activity. Three trips to Brussels. One to Geneva. But rather than exchanging ideas, the academic and policy practitioners were more likely to exchange fluids. Little was produced by such events aside from bastard children, misunderstandings, and heartbreak, so she stopped going when she had the choice.

More interesting and applicable to her job is Norway's 1,600-

kilometer border with Sweden, which has made smuggling and illegal immigration more of a problem since Norway joined the Schengen Agreement in 2001. That agreement opened the borders for freer movement of goods and people. It also created new undercover opportunities in Sweden in cooperation with the police in Gothenburg and Stockholm. She liked her Swedish police colleagues, aside from their stuffiness, and working undercover helped her rise more quickly in the ranks. But there were no planes in those jobs.

The first flight is only a few hours. There would have been enough time for a movie, but she opts for music and reverie. She chooses classical; a selection from the Budapest Festival Orchestra, who are playing something by Vivaldi. It is a solid choice as background noise to blot out the engines.

Norway disappears below her and exposes proof that there is a wider world. It looks like fresh air outside but it is separated from her by layers of plastic.

The latte-colored seat beside her is empty, and she stretches out by filling it with the correspondence between her father and brother, a bottle of water, the in-flight magazine, and that book by David Sedaris she'd failed to even start reading on the beach. It was one of two books she'd brought along. As the sun breaks through the clouds she feels momentarily hip and up to date. She opens to the copyright page. The cover art, she learns, is called *Skull of a Skeleton with Burning Cigarette* and is an oil on canvas piece by Van Gogh, sheltered in Amsterdam. Sigrid is no expert on these things, but the style seems to have more in common with Elvis on black velvet than *The Starry Night.*

The only reason she'd been at a bookstore at all was because Eli had insisted she start reading again. This was after Eli's victory with the television streaming service, and—strangely—she didn't find the two contradictory at all.

"You want me to start reading again because I don't have a cat?" Sigrid quipped.

"What does a cat have to do with it?"

She returns the book to her bag for a second time because the author's chipper tone disrupts her angst about finding Marcus.

The second book—insisted upon by Eli—is about yet another alcoholic male cop with a secret past unable to get along with authority. For no logical reason, though, he's taking point against a serial killer in a Nordic country with one of the lowest crime rates in the history of the world. The murders are so ghastly, they should have made global headlines but instead only rattle the tranquility of a small town from which no one ever moves away or thinks to worry.

After an hour she is bored. As a professional investigator herself, she would have liked—just once—to have seen something of her own experience at least obliquely referenced inside a book that professes to be about her own life. Instead, the fictional investigation proceeds on instinct, character, happenstance, natural talent, and coincidence. It is a world without procedures, rules, templates, investigation strategies, analytical frameworks, resource allocation plans, time lines or punch clocks. It is uninformed by the realities of police work and does not acknowledge the existence of women unless they are the source of sexual tension or else have been physically dismembered.

She flags down a stewardess, who has been wearing the same smile since takeoff, and orders a Bloody Mary with a slice of lemon.

The letters demand her attention but she's not ready to read them. Sigrid opens her iPad and creates a simple spreadsheet, which she populates expertly with the dates franked by the U.S. Postal Service on each letter. She builds a chronology that results in time series data about when the letters were sent. She has no questions or hypotheses now. She is simply setting up the frameworks that will allow for patterns to emerge from the data. From these, observations will be made that should lead to questions derived from the facts of the case. This is "terra firma." Observation first. Questions next. Interpretation last.

Was any of this going to be productive and give her insight into Marcus, his life, and—if necessary—his whereabouts? Who knows. That's how it really works in police investigations. No wonder no one writes about it.

Taking a break, she flips from the music selection to the films.

One involves robots beating each other up. It looks promising. Unfortunately there is no time left to watch it all; she'd hate to miss the third act.

"Ma'am?" comes a man's voice.

Sigrid looks up. A handsome man is smiling at her and she can't think of a good reason why.

"Yes?"

"You're working quite intensely," he says in English.

"Is that a problem?"

"No. I . . . was wondering if you'd like a drink."

The man is wearing an outfit provided by an airline, they are not in a bar, and he's leaning in for an intimate and yet completely unthreatening personal conversation in the way that only gay men can. But for a brief, awkward, and mentally unhealthy moment she registers none of this and basks only in the blinding light of his generosity.

"Sure," she says.

"The same?"

"Sure," she says.

"What are you working on?"

"A Bloody Mary."

"I meant the document."

"Oh," she says, looking down. "I'm looking for emergent patterns in the data using a grounded approach in order to advance a missing persons case."

"Wow."

Mistaking his surprise with interest, she continues: "It's really about ordering my thoughts at the beginning of the investigative process. Getting my hands into the material. That's all. The fact is, all scientists—and investigators, too—know that most spontaneous insights happen only when you're steeped in the data. I like to think that intuitive sparks are a function of creativity and analysis rubbing against each other."

She smiles at him and in that moment a crystallizing chill runs through her body. In its wake comes adrenaline and clarity. What she sees is a young man smiling back at her with a look of absolute pity. He places her second Bloody Mary on a square napkin in front of her as one might provide mush to a moron at an asylum. In watching his gesture it dawns on Sigrid that she might never—not metaphorically but for real—*ever* have sex again.

The thought makes her both terrified and strangely relieved.

"If there's anything else you need," he says, "just ask." Sigrid smiles at him gently, knowing that he is, at that moment, her primary caregiver.

Sigrid passes through Reykjavik without incident or interest, boards the second plane, and tries to sleep part of the way to Canada. They are chasing the sun by flying west during the daytime, and so, like at home, night never comes.

Her friend Eli always has solutions to problems that aren't her own. In this case, when Sigrid sent her a brief email from the farm telling her about the unexpected trip to the U.S., Eli recommended a drug for jet lag called Ambien, which is called Stilnoct in Norway. She swore by it and insisted that Sigrid buy some at the pharmacy before leaving for America. Her husband, a doctor, could send the prescription to the local pharmacy.

Eli often traveled to Los Angeles because she works in the film industry doing something called "development," which Sigrid has never understood and does not take much interest in either. Eli's time in L.A. has clearly contributed to her view that drugs can help with any naturally occurring problem.

In the morning, while packing, Sigrid looked up the drug on the internet. It is American, so she checked with the U.S. Food and Drug Administration, which states, "AMBIEN may cause serious side effects: After taking AMBIEN," it began, before changing the typeface to bold, "you may get up out of bed while not being fully awake and do an activity that you do not know you are doing. The next morning, you may not remember that you did anything during the night." To ensure it was not misunderstood, the FDA provided a bullet-pointed list of things you might do during the night that you wouldn't remember, including these:

- driving a car ("sleep-driving")
- making and eating food
- talking on the phone
- having sex
- sleep-walking

This was not a theoretical list made to be illustrative. Rather, it was a list of things that had "reportedly happened."

Sigrid decided not to buy Ambien at the pharmacy and instead take her chances with jet lag.

She arrives in Montreal having slept almost three hours. She passes through customs and collects her rolling luggage. She is stopped by a small border control beagle with floppy ears and brown eyes. It sniffs her bags and crotch for drugs, bombs, and cheese.

It is early evening, local time, and well past midnight back in Norway. She transfers to yet another gate for her third airplane; this one to Watertown, New York, USA. On that plane she does little more than hold on to the arms of her tiny chair and hope that the propeller plane —possibly borrowed from an Indiana Jones film—doesn't crash.

When she arrives she is pale, constipated, and tired. The summer evening is colder than she'd expected. The taxi that collects her is a monstrous American sedan not sold in Norway. She sits small and low in the back seat as the driver silently delivers her to a Holiday Inn close to the airport. It is properly dark when she checks in. The carpeted hallway smells of mothballs and lemon. She opens her hotel room door by inserting a white plastic card. A light turns green; the future is open.

Sigrid removes her shoes and parks the suitcase by the dresser knowing she will not unpack. She washes her hands and face in the bathroom after being shocked by the unflattering glow of the fluorescent bulbs.

In a small black refrigerator she finds tiny bottles of Johnny Walker Red. The price may be high by local standards, but it is far lower than what she'd pay at a bar in Oslo. And this is closer. She takes two.

Barefoot, Sigrid pads down the hall to a blue room with an ice-maker and vending machines filled with chocolate and chips. She places the bucket on a plastic grate and presses the button above it. Ice is hurled into her bucket as though by something trapped and angry. She freights a small mountain of ice back to her room.

Strutting toward her in the narrow hallway is a dark-skinned girl too young for a bra and wearing jeans that are too tight for her age.

"Hello," Sigrid says.

The girl eyes her quizzically and strides by as if Sigrid has made a lewd remark.

Back in her room, she tries to connect to the internet on her tablet. It costs $12.95 for four hours. She decides to pay, only to learn she can't because the software does not allow her to enter a non-American address.

Sigrid opens her suitcase for a nightgown and realizes she didn't bring one. What is inside, however, is a book with a faded cloth cover that is so worn, the golden lettering has flaked off. There is a hand-written letter from her father folded and placed inside the cover with the title page.

"Sigrid: This book was published in 1835 in French. In 1838 it was published by Adlard and Saunders in New York in English. Mine's a later reprint, of course. It is called Democracy in America by Alexis de Tocqueville. He was sent to the United States by the French government when he was twenty-six years old to study prisons, which, at the time, were thought to be among the world's most progressive and humane. You can read it on the plane over. There's a new edition with an introduction by the wonderful Daniel J. Boorstin but I don't have a copy of that. In any case, this book will put your head in the right place."

"Oh, pappa," she says, tossing the book back into the suitcase.

In bed, trousers off, she drinks her whiskey on the rocks; she uses the ice liberally. The TV is on a sideboard across from the foot of her bed. As she's looking straight down her body, it appears as though she's standing on its gray and bulbous screen. She wiggles her toes to the left, and then to the right, and then whatever way she wants, dancing on the little glass moon. Her body is under her complete control but she has no idea how. Her imagination, however, might not be.

Sigrid spreads her legs a little wider and tries to feel—for a fleeting moment—what a tryst in a place like this might be like. She pictures the kind of man who would probably be here with her. It is not the best way to start a fantasy. She might as well have picked the steward from the airplane because he was beautiful but her own sense of hyper-realism intervenes and produces a more appropriate lover: A man, eyes closed, up on his elbows, old enough to be concentrating on his own orgasm rather than hers, wears an expression of someone trying to hump a refrigerator up a flight of stairs. On her back, the gravity pulls her own cheeks taut, making her appear younger and thinner from his perspective. Unfortunately, from her perspective, that same gravity slides his old and thinning skin down his cheeks, creating jowls. His lips have fallen away from his teeth, turning his mouth into a black orifice from which something scarier than a groan might emerge. His face becomes redder for all the pumping and straining, and underneath it all is Sigrid, who is looking at this man from the same angle that the toilet sees the drunk.

She crosses her legs at the ankles, shifting her attention to something more productive like wondering who Marcus's girlfriend might have been and what had happened to them as a couple. In one letter she caught the first name: Lydia. But no last name. No details.

What kind of woman would attract Marcus? What kind of woman would be attracted to him? Did both of these things even happen?

Sigrid imagines Lydia with dark hair and brown eyes. She's attractive but no model. They spend weekends in a rustic cabin two hours from the university, out in the woods by the Canadian border. Not by a lake. They wouldn't have that kind of money. This place is more simple; a retreat. The walls are covered in books and board games, with blankets on the sofa and logs for a fire that are dry enough to light with a match. Lydia's smile is more maternal than saucy. It would be no mystery to either of them—smart as they are—that Marcus is attracted to Lydia both for who she really is and who he needs her to be: the mother he lost. The lover he craves. The feel of home that envelops him like a scent and is all-encompassing but also proves elusive and ephemeral.

Why would it have ended? Sigrid lies there and wonders. The obvious answer would be that Lydia wanted to be more than a projection of Marcus's needs. She would have been happy to fill that void for him also, but not only. She was too mature, too much of an adult, to assume the role of savior or mother. She would have known, and perhaps even said, that she didn't need a forty-six-year-old son. At her age—at Sigrid's own age—she would have treated time as precious. And even if she were resigned to not having children, she would not have dismissed a chance at long-term happiness founded on a mutually appropriate relationship. Sigrid surmised that it would have been Lydia who raised the topic. Gently, perhaps, but with certainty. Marcus would only be truly attracted to a smart woman. And if she was smart, she would have taken seriously the obstacles rather than try to overcome them with romantic ideals and short-lived passions.

And now, Sigrid thinks, Lydia is gone. Maybe she works at the university too. If she does, it means that every day she passes by his window on campus. He possibly glimpses her—purposefully, to hurt himself—at the café nearby where she likes to grade papers at a round table in the corner that no one else likes because once you sit there you're stuck. Lydia, though, finds the crowd comforting.

Sigrid places the spent whiskey glass on the end table by the ugly lamp. Really, she concedes: Who knows? She has nothing to go on. As far as she knows Lydia is a blond trucker shaped like a turnip.

Sigrid falls asleep on top of the blanket without brushing her teeth.

NOT HOME

COPERNICUS KNEW THE world was round. So did Galileo.
Ferdinand Magellan actually circumnavigated the earth. But
none of these men ever experienced jet lag. Not one. They
couldn't have possibly imagined it.

Brussels and Geneva are both in the same time zone as Oslo: no jet
lag. Sigrid also made two trips to Britain, which sets its clock a mere
hour earlier than Europe. But a six-hour time difference after a day
flight and a nearly sleepless night filled with whisky? This is something new.

Sigrid wakes at four a.m. and, instead of feeling tired or hung over,
is wide awake, her mind revving up like a motorbike.

The hotel room is hot. She looks to the wide ivory air conditioner
mounted near the ceiling; it's producing noise but neither moving nor
cooling the air. The curtains are hanging still, and a thin shiv of pre-
dawn light cuts the fabric.

For twenty minutes she pretends she might go back to sleep and she
does try before suffering defeat.

The shower is powerful and hot but the water itself is too soft and leaves her hair limp. Raw and steaming, she dresses in civilian clothing; no badge, no tie, no identity, no authority. It is the same as being naked.

Breakfast is not served until seven and she doesn't want to wait. The man at the checkout desk—a man with the right character to nightshifts—does not ask her about her stay. He processes her without looking up.

It is shy of five in the morning as she walks the gray, perpendicular streets. This is not small-town America or even a city. She is in the outskirts. On every corner is a franchise. Each rises from the concrete in its own corporate colors and logos, architecturally oblivious to those around it, not unlike the train sets that Marcus would build when he was ten. She remembers how each one of them was a microcosm of happy people working at some establishment: a gas station, a police station, a fire station, a freight mover, a hospital.

Here, at full scale, are the same institutions only grittier. As she pulls her suitcase behind her, lights are coming on at the places that serve coffee. Arby's, Roy Rogers, Dunkin Donuts. None of these exist in Norway.

Dunkin Donuts sounds familiar, as she'd passed one once in London. She also knows what a donut is because they sell them at the co-op supermarket near her apartment in Gamle Oslo. Whoever Roy Rogers might have been, his fame hasn't crossed the ocean. And Arby, absent a family name, sounds too casual in his approach to food.

She crosses the empty street to a parking lot where a pickup truck squats long and empty beside an eighteen-wheeler with too much chrome.

Inside the white, orange, and pink dream of the donut hall, a fat man in a nylon jacket silently eats at a table affixed to the floor while a black girl pours cooking oil into a vat from a plastic jug almost too heavy for her to lift.

"With you in a minute," she says, not looking over.

"Take your time," Sigrid says.

The girl places the jug below the deep fry and flicks some switches over the donut display, illuminating a palette of Disney-colored frostings.

The girl does not look any sleepier than Sigrid feels. She must be accustomed to these hours.

"Latte with sugar," Sigrid asks. "And whatever he's eating." It is something with eggs and a bread product. It looks hot.

"That'll take five minutes."

"Got a newspaper?"

The girl takes Sigrid's money. "Down the block on the right. Otherwise, I think someone left one here last night on that back table there. I'll call ya when the food's done."

Sigrid sits herself at the table with the Sunday edition of the paper dated 10 August, which means no one cleared the table Monday, Tuesday, or this morning, either. She reads old news about Russia and Georgia going to war and one hundred and forty people being crushed to death in a human stampede at a Hindu Temple in Northern India; at least forty of them were children. Leading the headlines, though, is the U.S. presidential elections. Many are saying that Barack Obama will win. This strikes commentators as extremely important.

Outside, fed and caffeinated, Sigrid pulls her luggage behind her and over the pitted streets as the first light of dawn rises behind the neon lights of the pawn shops and check-cashing offices. Trucks in the westbound lane pass her bearing Canadian plates. That country is even more of a mystery to her. Her only association is with Katarina Witt winning the figure skating Olympics in Calgary in '88. As a young woman Sigrid thought that she'd never have a body like that; grace like that; be beloved like that. They were the thoughts of an adolescent. They turned out to be right.

The bus station smells of urine. The ticket counter is closed, so Sigrid sits alone on a bench beside Gate 4. There is a taste in her mouth from the food or the milk that isn't going away. Something she's eaten since arriving has made her feel bloated.

Two men approach and sit on the bench and Sigrid watches them. One wears beige trousers and a shirt that could never have been white.

The other is late middle-aged and wears shorts and sneakers and a gym T-shirt over skinny shoulders and a round stomach. They don't engage with her or each other. They didn't look at the gate number or check their tickets. Their motion is routine, learned, and performed in the muscles. When they stop moving they look painted into place.

The bus arrives. It halts with a hiss and shuts down so thoroughly, it becomes immediately derelict; the engine doesn't even crackle from the heat.

The driver looks like rotting fruit. Sigrid can tell she is in the last job she'll ever have. She leaves for her break.

More people arrive. Ten minutes later the driver is back looking twenty minutes older. She fires up the bus, which rumbles to life with the enthusiasm of an old man passing gas. The hydraulic doors seem to suck the passengers inside; a giant vacuum it clears the platform and removes all traces of humanity except the lingering smell.

Sigrid, together with the accompanying passengers, sits like a convict looking out the window at places she hadn't known existed before and even on seeing them, somehow, still doesn't believe that they actually do.

The bus ride lasts thirty-five minutes. She arrives with the sun flooding through her window, glinting off the step as she descends to the sidewalk. The morning is up now. The day is on. There is a glare from the map she will follow to Marcus's home to find whatever might be waiting there.

As far as she knows, Marcus has never had any real money. He didn't come from it, didn't respect it, and hadn't pursued it. He has no special head for business and he considers the stock market a seductive playground of legalized gambling. He always rented an apartment or house and generally wasted any financial cushion he built from years of steady work on long periods of unemployment or underpaid idealistic efforts. He was not against material pleasures but he had no space for them in his life. Everything came and went. There was no point in becoming attached to a cup, to a vase, to a painting. Sigrid has always suspected that a steady relationship with a sensible woman might change all that—both by contributing to the household and also by holding him accountable for acting in a mature manner.

Sigrid tried to be that sensible woman, if from a distance. She was more than prepared to vacate the position for a fresh candidate.

It wasn't that she didn't want to help him. They corresponded once a month or so and spoke a few times a year. The tempo never increased, though, and the easy talk of their youth never returned. Yet she persisted because she loved him and because the strained relationship between Marcus and her father meant she must ensure their cohesion.

If he married, Sigrid reasoned, all that might change. She could befriend the wife and a new alliance would form of adult women managing their childish men. It was a popular model.

Now it's a broken one.

These days, Marcus is earning meager pay from the state university and he is subsidizing this new life choice with prior savings. As a financial strategy it is a death spiral and there is no indication about how he plans to turn this around. Sigrid doesn't see a path for Marcus, middle-aged and without a doctorate or a list of published books and peer-reviewed articles, to a stable academic career. And if this is not his aspiration by working as an adjunct lecturer . . . what is he doing there?

He had sent photos of his house to her by email about two years ago when he moved to teach the courses. She called him when the pictures arrived.

"Why don't you come home?" she'd asked him immediately.

"You don't like my new place?" Marcus had asked.

"What are you doing over there? It's been . . . how long?"

"Eighteen years."

"You were planning to go for three."

"I got stuck."

Reaching the house from the bus stop involves a charmless walk over roads of rubble and stone, cigarette butts and beer cans. The houses lining the streets look condemned. Many have boarded windows and graffiti tags that are as indecipherable as hieroglyphs. Most of the children in the neighborhood are black and Latino, which she hadn't expected from upstate New York, but then . . . she knows nothing of the place. This is a poor neighborhood that is adjacent to a better one, which abuts the state university—so says the map. She is being given odd looks as she drags the suitcase behind her. None seem threatening, only curious; as though her presence might portend something.

Sigrid arrives on the corner near Marcus's house and it is as bad as she'd feared. It is not the sort of place one is meant to stop because it is not the sort of place one is meant to be at all. This is a place you scurry past like a mouse hoping not to be noticed.

As best as she can tell, the house was once white, but any proof of its original color has been covered over or long since flaked off. It is an achievement in ugly, whether by intent or negligence. The front is too narrow and the sides too wide. The slope of the roof is too severe and the windows are small and don't align. The entire structure sits awkwardly on its own lot—not facing forward, as such, because there is nothing left to face.

The house has no immediate neighbors. Sigrid suspects that the other owners sold their land to developers or the city and only this guy had held out for the American dream, which is always one business deal away.

Is this indicative of his state of mind and the condition of Marcus's life? Is he inhabiting someone else's failed dream? Or it is a waypoint —a stop to catch his breath before settling someplace where life could settle into a new permanence? Marcus has encamped, in this case, in a place where the streets and buildings around it clearly don't *want* the house anymore. Whatever neighborhood it had once belonged in is now gone. A gray and concrete world has been erected around it, oppressing it, as though the city itself is a circling beast and is preparing for a slow kill.

"Everything has potential," Marcus had insisted when she questioned him about the house.

"Well . . . to change, sure," Sigrid had answered, "but not necessarily improve."

Having come this far, though, Sigrid has no choice but to approach it. As she pulls her black suitcase a small stone from the sidewalk wedges into the well between the top of the wheel and the frame.

"Oh, no you don't," she says to it in English, as it's an American stone.

Sigrid half rolls, half drags the luggage behind her. Reaching the curb, she makes an effort to dislodge the pebble by first backing it up the other way—with the expectation that it might fall out—but on seeing how this does not work, she opts to assert herself by picking up the whole damn thing and thumping it on the ground. This works. However, it's more abuse than the beast can take, and the suitcase surrenders the wheel along with the pebble.

She drags the handicapped luggage, now irreparable, behind her as she approaches the house; the shade from the nearby overpass blocks the sun and bathes her in semidarkness.

Sigrid yanks the suitcase up the three steps to the front door, raps loudly, and then waits.

As she waits she cannot help but look at the house. It is truly awful. It is also big; More than one person needs. But how do you split something like this? And with whom? A local motorcycle gang? Surely they'd have parked on the lawn.

Sigrid bangs the crap out of the door and hollers in Norwegian.

"Marcus, wake up. It's Sigrid."

She stands back and waits for the door to open.

It doesn't.

Leaving the suitcase on the doorstep, she hops down the steps and crawls over browning bushes and around the corner of the house to see inside the first window she can reach.

There is some kind of steel mesh in front of the window—something she's never seen before. It makes it very hard to look inside. Through its rust and the crust of cobwebs she half expects to see gangsters, drug mules, and cockroaches playing cards while sipping Budweiser.

Sigrid has raided places like this before. Nothing good has ever opened the door.

He isn't inside. Nor is anyone else. No need to loiter in the bushes anymore.

Turning to pull herself out of there, Sigrid accidentally snags her purse on a branch. Had she been in a more forgiving mood she might have stepped forward to remove the strap from the twig and better navigated the minor inconvenience. But this is not what she does, because her mood does not permit it. That mood has been shaped by the house itself and its surroundings, by Marcus and his choices, by the bad breakfast that has left her fat and greasy, by the jet lag, by China's trial-and-error approach to the manufacturing of consumer goods. And in such a mood, she tugs at the bag to teach the twig who is boss.

The twig proves stronger than expected and the purse more slippery. This transforms the twig into a catapult and her purse into a missile. In flight it glides through the air with a sleek Italian elegance; on impact, though, the fancy is ended and the bag splits like a severed head, splattering its contents all over the road.

Sigrid surveys the results of her choices and swears in the choice language of a seafaring nation.

As Sigrid continues her auto-rant, a woman from across the street emerges from the shadow of the off-ramp. Sigrid, on seeing her, stops swearing.

"He ain't here, ya know," she says in an accent that seems more southern than northern, but Sigrid is no real judge of these things.

"Who?" Sigrid asks.

"Marcus? You said Marcus like twenty times. I'm saying: He. Ain't. Here."

She is a hooker. She has to be. No matter the country, hookers dress the same. The only logic Sigrid can find to this universality is that they are meeting men's expectations of what hookers are supposed to look like. But men have learned this from the hookers themselves. Could it be that everyone wants it to stop but no one can turn it off?

Her miniskirt is made of purple sequins. Her stomach is exposed to no positive effect. Her tank-top presses so tightly against her enormous chest that the wires of her bra have become smiles beneath her boobs—each with an unblinking eye above; they sit there, together, like demented cyclops twins.

"Who are you and how do you know that Marcus isn't here?" Sigrid asks.

"I'm just sayin'," the woman says.

Sigrid says nothing and the woman—being American—fills the lull:

"He hasn't been here since he moved out. He's gone. He ain't comin' back."

"What do you know about it?"

The woman crosses her arms and takes a defiant stance. "Who the hell are ya, anyway?"

"I'm his sister."

"Oh yeah? Where you from?"

"Earth," Sigrid's mood answers. She regrets it the moment she says it, but the pleasure was undeniable.

"He's foreign. If you're his sister, you'd know."

That is true. The woman has made a valid point.

"Norway," says Sigrid as a reward for reason.

The prostitute's face softens through the industrial putty of her makeup.

"Look," she says, defensively. "He gave me his key. Said I could stay there when he was gone. I asked when he was coming back and he said he wasn't sure if he was ever coming back and I said, Well, what about your shit? He said none of it was worth a damn but the guitar and books. He said I could keep the books and I made a face like he was fuckin' with me—cuz, what? I'm gonna read 'em?—and he said I could burn 'em in winter if I wanted, but I ain't burnin' no books whether I'm gonna read 'em or not and I asked if he wanted to fuck and he said no and I asked if it was on account of that woman who died. He said it was, which seemed kinda sad. In my experience, fucking is the sixth stage of grief but no one ever asks me about it, though I am an expert. Now I'm staying here, which is totally legal and above-board and I don't want any crap about it, OK? But if you've come for his stuff you can have it. I ain't no thief."

"Died? Who died?"

"That fancy woman he was seeing. Talked about her all time. Loved her something fierce."

"The woman Marcus loved died?"

"You've got that echolalia or something? I seen a woman like you on *Oprah*. Kept repeating the last thing anybody said. Echolalia."

"Echolalia?"

"Yeah, you got it bad," the woman says. "You a little retarded? Autistic or such?"

"I'm foreign," says Sigrid, refilling her purse.

The woman seemed to accept this as a reasonable synonym. "Yeah. Marcus's girl. She up and died."

"Died?"

"Yes, died," she says, starting to laugh. "Fuck me, how do you get through your day? Say this: 'Dude, where's my car?'"

"How did she die?" asks Sigrid.

"Oh well . . . yeah, I don't know. He didn't say. But it broke his heart and he decided to pack it all up and take off. And now . . ." she says, opening her arms for dramatic emphasis, "here we are."

"I need to get in and look around."

The woman looks at her wristwatch. It's sized for a man and made of gold-colored plastic.

"I don't have much time," the woman says.

With her purse full again, Sigrid walks around the corner of the house and back to the steps by the front door. The woman follows her. As she does, she pulls her skirt down after every third step, fighting its inclination to become a cummerbund.

At the door the hooker removes a rabbit's foot key ring from her purse and opens the lock. The stale smell of shag carpet hits Sigrid and gives her pause before she steps in.

"Where's my suitcase?" she asks.

"What suitcase?"

"Black. Cheap. Broken wheel."

"How the hell should I know?"

"Has anyone else been here?" Sigrid asks.

"Wait a second. You left your suitcase on the steps. Here?"

"Shit."

"Earth, huh?"

THE DEFINING
CHARACTERISTICS OF GUM

DESPITE BEING ON a tight schedule, the woman in the midmorning sequins wants to talk to Sigrid. "What do you want in here, anyway?"

"Do you know where Marcus is?"

"I told you. He's gone."

"I understand that, but do you know where he went?"

"I figured he went home."

Sigrid does not reply.

"To your home," the woman clarifies. "Norway."

"I checked there."

Sigrid resists the impulse to take off her shoes because she doesn't want to prompt a new round of intercultural conversation, but she is careful about where she places her feet. Taking her smartphone from the scuffed Italian purse, she snaps pictures.

"You a cop or something?" the woman says.

"I'm on vacation," Sigrid says, clicking away liberally.

"You act like a cop."

"I'm trying to find him. I don't know all the right questions to ask yet. I'm collecting information broadly so that later, when I do build an investigative strategy, I'll have material to consider, informed by a framework."

"That doesn't sound like what they do on TV," says the woman.

"It's not."

In the course of her career as a beat cop and later an investigator, Sigrid has been inside many homes. Most adults are invited into the homes of friends and neighbors and family, but that is a limited social and economic range of homes, and the frequency curve on new locations flattens out the older people get. The simple fact is that most adults seldom enter new spaces on a regular basis. Cops, though, are in new places all the time. Domestic disturbances, abuse, murder, missing children . . . they are all invitations to the wider world.

The house does not look like the typical bachelor homes she often saw in Norway during her time as a beat cop. Then, she used to visit drunks or occasionally drop them off at home. One apartment after another was filled with IKEA furniture bought from the discounted corner near the cashier for being damaged or having pieces missing; the disposable income spent on a TV too big for the room and placed like a god in its center; video game consoles with white and black cords intermingling like interracial robots; Grandiosa frozen pizzas in ordered stacks in the freezer; boxes of wine sorted like ammunition in the pantry.

Marcus's living room does not look like this. He has placed two brown three-seater sofas across from each other and a large wooden coffee table between them as though for a summit of some kind. The crumbs and detritus under the cushions, however, prove that he always sat alone and in the same spot; a spot that does not face a television. Instead, and nearby, is a teetering stack of books piled with the spines facing in all directions.

"Was Marcus depressed?" Sigrid asks, running a finger across the windows and wiping the dirt on the upholstery of the sofa.

"He was sad."

"I don't know if that's different," Sigrid says.

"Me either," the woman whispers.

Upstairs the woman guides Sigrid through the two bedrooms. In the master, she explains how she'd put everything of Marcus's that looked valuable or useful into the same boxes she'd used for the move. Sigrid decides not to ask where she moved from because it seems tangential. The number of boxes tells Sigrid that she has taken the move seriously and is intending to stay for a long time; the same length of time she expects Marcus to be gone.

Her name is Juliet McKenna; it is printed in capital letters on every box in purple marker.

"They got my name on 'em," she explains unnecessarily. "That's why the cops didn't touch 'em."

"What cops?"

"The ones who came here with a warrant and looked around. Didn't we talk about this already? No. Well . . . Irving. Irving the cop. And that little sidekick who follows him around? I forget her name. They were trying to find Marcus. I didn't tell them anything, though. I told them not to touch my shit unless my name's on the warrant. And it wasn't. That backed them off."

"The police were here looking for Marcus?"

"I can't tell if you're summing up or trying to catch on."

"When and why?"

"A week ago. Listen, you can't just pump me for information without . . ."

"Are you telling me that Marcus was seeing a fancy woman, that the woman died, Marcus disappeared, and that the cops came here with a warrant looking for him, and went through his stuff?"

"You're repeating shit again."

"Who's Irving?" Sigrid asks.

"Irving Wylie," she says. "Irv."

"OK."

"The sheriff."

"You're joking, right?"

"About what?"

"Sheriff Irving Wylie? You have sheriffs here?"

"Police station. Center of town. Can't miss it." She looks at her watch and says, "Oh shit, I've got a date. Don't fuck up anything while I'm gone."

Juliet leaves Sigrid in peace, and she takes the opportunity to not only see her surroundings but try to feel them. The bedroom is furnished in earth tones and shadows, with the single window facing the busy off-ramp of cars. The kinetic energy of the world outside underscores the static space of the room, and the absence of whatever life has previously been experienced here.

Juliet has already removed most of Marcus's clothes from the closet and stuffed them in her JULIET MCKENNA boxes. Sigrid sees how unceremonious her efforts had been once she opens them with the Buck lock-blade knife she finds on the dresser and decides to keep, as it must have been Marcus's.

The contents are mostly balled-up casual clothes, though she does find a good blue suit and leather shoes tossed in with the rest.

In the third box Sigrid finds a sling bag—the kind with one strap that cuts across the chest and is popular with bicycle messengers—and decides to keep that. She has no clothing now with the suitcase gone, but there may be enough here to help her make do until she can visit a store.

She had been hoping to stumble on something of Lydia's, but there is nothing. Given the state of the house, that doesn't surprise her, but there is a good chance that the condition of the apartment has deteriorated over the past month. Maybe Lydia had come here during better times.

Marcus has always been taller than her, and while he isn't particularly athletic he does have a lean build. He never had much of a belly. Everything he owns, however, is decidedly too big for her. Nevertheless, she finds a slim black T-shirt that will work, a gray sweatshirt she can sleep in, some sweatpants, a pair of gold-rimmed aviator sunglasses, a mobile phone, and a dated but seemingly functioning iPod. Most important, though: an orange hard drive that has been rolled up inside a Rush T-shirt that displays the word SIGNALS above a photo of a Dalmatian sniffing a fake red hydrant on a tuft of Astroturf.

She flips the bag across her chest and heads downstairs.

In the kitchen Sigrid checks the fridge and freezer. In the living room she flips through the books—a collection of novels, environmentalist textbooks, popular nonfiction, and biographies. Nothing particularly personal remains, and the house is devoid of the small knickknacks and memorabilia that tend to accumulate around the aged, sentimental, or lazy.

There is one sign of life, though. In the corner of the living room, a meter to the left of the boarded fireplace, is Marcus's acoustic guitar. It is the same one he played as a teenager. Sigrid does not know much about guitars, but this one is easy to recognize by its color. It is made of a beautiful mahogany and the headstock says MARTIN AND CO. EST. 1833. She bought it for him, used, the Christmas of 1981, when he turned nineteen and Sigrid was thirteen. The money came from a summer working at an adventure-tourism outfit, rigging ropes and cables from trees so that urban people could test their fear of heights and trust in one another.

The guitar is leaning at an unnatural slant on its stand. Scanning the room, she finds its hard case with its assortment of stickers from Marcus's favorite bands and visited cities, as well as from airline security. Marcus wasn't a particularly good guitarist but he wasn't that bad either; he could strum a tune and carry a song. There has always been a warmth and sincerity to his voice that allowed him to find and share the simple melody at the center of a song and make the moment more complete. He played alone in his old bedroom when he came to visit. She would sit in the hall and listen, eavesdropping to feel closer to him.

Sigrid puts the guitar in its case and locks it. This is coming too.

Geared up, Sigrid steps outside into the shade and noise to find Juliet walking toward her while slotting cash into a wallet.

She's chewing a piece of gum.

"Wouldn't you prefer mouthwash?" Sigrid asks.

"I got gum."

"Yeah, but . . . gum's defining characteristics are that it doesn't dissolve and it retains flavor."

"What's your point?"

"Marcus's girlfriend was named Lydia," Sigrid says. "Did you ever meet her?"

"No."

"See her?"

"No."

Juliet chews away and Sigrid cannot help but visualize what must be happening between her molars. All those tiny white heads—exploding.

"Do you want to help him?" Sigrid asks.

"How?"

"I'm alone over here, and I suspect Marcus is alone wherever he is, too. And something I'm sure about is that it's almost impossible to do anything hard all by yourself. I might need help at some point. I'm going to give you some money in case something comes up. The idea is, I pay you now for help later. I'll give you my number. What do you think?"

Juliet takes the money.

"Which way is the police station?" Sigrid asks.

SHERIFF IRVING WYLIE

A T THE POLICE station, a few miles down the road from Marcus's house, Sheriff Irving Wylie is yelling into his phone at Roger Mandel. He is yelling because he likes to, because it is morally justified, and because he can't help himself. Or he probably wouldn't be able to help himself if he tried, but since he likes to yell at Roger he'll never really know for certain whether he could have stopped or not.

Roger calls himself a journalist at WRGT, a local ABC news affiliate. Irving isn't prepared for the word "journalist" to be so elastic as to stretch to Roger Mandel.

Irv is two years into his second four-year term as a Jefferson County, New York, state sheriff and he would have thought, by now, that he'd have trained the local journalists about what kinds of questions he is willing to answer and what kinds will get them ridiculed, humiliated, embarrassed, or yelled at by their producers, spouses, or mothers.

It still tickles Irving that these morons call him, time and time again, trying to get quotes about cases that are either ongoing, outside his jurisdiction, or ones he's simply not in the mood to talk about.

Law and order, he has explained during lucid rants, doesn't mean the draconian oppression of the population or the cynical manipulation of public opinion to create a condition of tyranny. No. The simple idea is this: You follow the law to produce the order. That's the part he likes. That's why he took the job. That and the title. And the boots. And the pea shooter.

Irv says as much: "That's why I took the job, Roger."

"Yes, Sheriff," says Roger.

Irving is sitting at his desk at the police station with his snip-toe cowboy boots, crossed and steady, up where they shouldn't be. Roger does not require all of Irv's attention, so he uses the reserves to tear open a white packet of sugar while balancing a phone in the crook of his neck. It occurs to Irv, as Roger rambles on, that only a person of a certain age would even try to cradle a cell phone in the crook of his neck. It's an interesting exercise, though, at least compared to listening to Roger Mandel.

"I was elected to enforce the law, not make the law, Roger," Irv yells into the phone. "You talk to the state legislature if you want to know where laws come from. They will surely give you a guided tour of their own assholes. There's always room in there for one more. Meanwhile, I cannot, will not, and don't even want to talk about the Simmons case, which isn't even a case anymore, as the judgment came in months ago. And I would like to remind you that the death of Jeffrey Simmons took place on the other side of an invisible jurisdictional line that the American people, in their infinite wisdom, have established, thereby turning what looks like one place into two places, so they can have someone else in charge over there who isn't me. So go back to your rock, Roger!"

"But there's a family connection between the Simmons case and Lydia Jones case, Sheriff. And the Jones' case is in your jurisdiction. So what happened over there might have had an influence on what happened over here. There's got to be a link."

"Not a legal one."

"Surely you've got an opinion, Sheriff?"

"Police work, Roger, is not a matter of opinion. In the name of the good Lord Jesus Christ, if I ran an investigation on the basis of opinion and ideology and not facts I'd be breaking the Ninth Commandment—God's law itself—by, de facto, bearing false witness against my neighbor—or, more accurately—by bearing witness against my neighbor that I could not, in all good consciousness, swear was not false because I don't have the facts. Do you see my point? What I'm saying is that I cannot be a good Christian and swear on His name without data. Science is not antithetical to the Christian spirit, Roger. It is the means by which we enact the justice that God has commanded of us to perform unto our fellow man. Why am I the only one who gets this? I remind you that I ran on a platform of 'excellence through knowledge' and I'm six years into repeating myself and if I wanted to be repeating myself ten times a day I'd still be married. Why do you keep calling me? Are you lonely?"

Irv pours the packet of sugar into his coffee, not dropping a grain to the ground.

"I got papers on the left side of my desk, Roger, that have to be moved all the way over to the right side. You think they're gonna get up and move themselves? I'm busy here. Go do your Hunter Thompson thing someplace else."

Irving hangs up.

He shouts his views to Melinda and Cory in the next room.

"You know why they want opinions? Because it's cheaper and easier than finding the facts. Whatever happened to the days of Bartles and Jaymes or whoever the hell took down Nixon?"

Irving looks up from his coffee mug—World's Most Average Dad —and finds he is alone in the office.

"Where the hell is everyone?" he mutters under his breath.

"WHERE THE HELL IS EVERYONE," he shouts at the top of his lungs.

Cory Liddell pops his head into the main station room from the adjoining waiting room—christened the Green Room on account of people there waiting to "join the show"—and explains that everyone is in there.

"Well . . . why? It's past eight. We're supposed to be . . . working."

Cory says it's James's birthday today so they were having ice cream cake, which is why everyone is in the other room.

"At eight in the morning?"

Cory says the freezer is on the fritz again so they have to eat it now.

"Well . . . that's perfectly reasonable then," Irving said. "Just remember, you're all on duty. And you're getting fat. I don't like fat cops. Nothing more pathetic than a fat, wheezing cop trotting down a road after a perp, holding his belt up. There's a video series on the internet now of all kinds of hoodlums filming the fat cops who are chasing them. Wheezing and puffing and turning bright red. At least the black cops don't turn red. Still fat, though. God I hate seeing that. I can run a ten-K in fifty-two minutes and I'm forty-eight years old."

Irving Wylie checks the local news, the state news, the national news, and they are all talking about a black man with a foreign-sounding name who may soon be elected president of the United States in November. Irving is a big John McCain supporter, and considers the senator—much like himself—among the last of the Real Republicans, but when McCain chose that reason-impaired bimbo from Alaska to be his running mate even Irv had to get off the GOP elevator. That doesn't mean Irv is ready to jump ship and become a Democrat—because really, what is a Democrat?—but it does mean he can pretend it's all not happening right up until the excruciating and bitter end, and by then, hopefully, the election will be a *fait accompli* and his vote won't matter anyway.

McCain, though, is getting pudgy too, and he hates to think of Palin being one cholesterol-saturated heartbeat away from the presidency. The good news, he figures, is that elections couldn't possibly get any weirder than this one.

The sheriff's station—at Irving's instruction—has a bell over the door so that people who come inside will be announced and feel like welcomed customers. Most find it disconcerting but he's holding on to it. This morning when the bell rings, Irving looks across his coffee mug and watches a middle-aged, slightly disheveled, semi-OK-looking blonde walk in wearing aviators and carrying a motorcyclist's messenger bag and a guitar case; all of which is incongruous enough to be suspicious.

The woman scans the police station like the Terminator, locks on to Irving, and proceeds to his desk.

"Are you Irving Wylie?" she asks.

"That pleasure is mine," Irving says without conviction.

"I'm here to report a missing person," she adds.

She is foreign. He can't place the accent, though. The three most common foreign accents up here are French Canadian, Mexican, and Brooklyn, and she doesn't sound like any of the three.

"I can help you with that," he offers.

"Are you the police chief?"

"I'm the sheriff."

The woman does not reply.

Irv removes his feet from the desk and sits properly. He reaches for a pen and clicks it open a few times for effect. It clearly has none, so he continues:

"I'm Irving Wylie, duly elected second-term sheriff, at your service. You can call me Irv. What's in the guitar case?"

"A guitar. You were elected?"

"Well . . . it wasn't a coup or rigged or anything, if that's what you're wondering. What kind of guitar?"

"Acoustic. You elect police officers in America?"

"We elect sheriffs in much of America and specifically here in Jefferson County. Ma'am, are you on any medication?"

"No."

"Are you supposed to be?"

Irv can't recall the last time a blonde made him nervous. Redheads, obviously, but not blondes.

Well, actually, there was the odd Nazi or two, and there has been some minor trouble with white supremacist gangs, but those were all blond men. Not women. This woman is clearly not a gang member either. She isn't a drug user, a heavy smoker, a chronic drinker, nor does she have any obvious tattoos. She isn't wearing anything to concern him, like gang colors, swastikas, or One Percenter icons. Still, something about her unsettles him. He wants to put his finger on it, give it a name.

"Why are there no chairs in front of your desk?" she asks.

"There's a birthday party in the next room and they needed the chairs. We didn't expect the morning rush we're having right now. Can you slowly open the guitar case, please?"

Sigrid opens the guitar case, removes the guitar, and plays an E chord, which is all she knows.

"That was lovely. Would you like a chair? I can arrange that."

"I'd like you to find my brother. He's missing," she says, returning the guitar to the case.

"Maybe we can do both; let's see if we're up to the challenge." Irv stands up, brushes some breakfast crumbs from his shirt, and pops into the Green Room to emerge moments later with a steel-legged office chair with a drab olive vinyl seat. He places it in front of his desk and taps it two times for effect.

Sigrid removes the shoulder bag and sits down.

"I know what it is," he says.

"You know what what is?" she asks.

"You're very composed. A cool cucumber."

"I'm not sure what you're talking about," Sigrid replies.

"Doesn't matter. Lay it on me," says Irv in a warm and deep voice.

"My brother lives here and he's missing. I visited his home this morning and found that he's been absent for about two weeks. He allegedly told a local prostitute she could stay in the house and that he was leaving. I have no proof of that but I believe her. What's unclear are the circumstances in which he left, his motives, whether he was coerced, and . . . of course . . . the fundamental matters of his whereabouts and well-being. The prostitute's name is Juliet McKenna. And she says you have been to his house and you're looking for him too. Which I take to be good news, but it makes me wonder who filed the missing person and when."

Irving was attentive at his desk with his elbows resting and fingers locked. "That was well presented. Are you a cop?"

"Yes."

"Not from around here, you're not."

"I'm from Norway."

"Norway?"

"It's a country in northern Europe—"

"I know where it is. How long have you been in America?"

"Since yesterday."

"Can you prove that?"

Sigrid does not answer.

"Did you understand my question?"

"I'm thinking about the answer." Sigrid is silent for another moment and it makes Irv fidget.

"Yes. There's a stamp in my passport. Here it is." She hands it to him and he examines it.

"Can you prove you're a cop?"

Sigrid removes her ID from her wallet and hands that to him too.

It is a hard plastic card with her picture on it, a code in hi-viz yellow letters and numbers on a black background and across the bottom it says POLITI. Irv flips it around and holds it up to the light, illuminating the numerous security codes and holograms. The name on the badge matches the name on the passport, which matches the face of the woman with the calm demeanor in front of him.

Sigrid remains sitting across from Irv as he searches the internet for images of Norwegian police ID cards. They look like this one.

"OK, you're a cop," he says to her, handing back the card and passport. "And it does sound like your brother is missing or something like it. What's his name?"

"Marcus Ødegård," she says, hoping the full name will help.

"Marcus?"

"Yes."

"Man, you really buried the lede, didn't you?"

"I don't know what that means. English isn't my first language."

"We know Marcus Odegard," he says, pronouncing it with an atrocious accent. "We're already looking for him, and your English sounds superb."

Sigrid sits back in her chair. "Yes. I heard you were at his house. What can you tell me?"

"What I can tell you, Ms. Odegard, is that your brother Marcus is wanted in connection with the death of Professor Lydia Jones. Which, in our view, is why he's missing."

CORINTHIANS 13

S HERIFF IRVING WYLIE removes a folder from his drawer and invites Sigrid to follow him through a door behind his desk, down a narrow gray hallway, and into a large room containing two holding cells, both empty. Irv steps casually into the closest one, sits on a long bench to the left, and starts unpacking the contents of his folder.

Sigrid lingers at the entrance to the jail cell and looks at the open door.

"Well, come on in, don't be shy," Irv says, not looking up.

"Why are we sitting in a cell?"

"The Green Room is occupied and the interview room is being painted. The smell gives me a headache. I like it better in here." He nods toward the barred windows. "There's fresh air and a hint of lemon."

Sigrid follows him inside and sits on the bench opposite his.

"Is this jail new?" she asks.

"Why, because it's so clean?"

"They usually smell bad."

"We don't use it much. We prefer to take people out back and shoot them."

"I see."

"Now, the dumpster . . . that smells terrible."

"OK."

"So," says Irv, crossing his legs and placing the file on his lap. "Your brother is missing and his girlfriend is dead and you've come here to find him, and to do that, you've been to his house and—not finding him—you've come to the police. How am I doing so far?"

"You haven't found him, so . . . not so well, Sheriff."

"It's a process. What can you tell me?" he asks.

"About Marcus?"

"I'm sure not interested in Norway."

"My father corresponds with him. Marcus stopped writing. Pappa became worried. He tried calling and emailing. He thought it would be best if I came to look for him."

"He wasn't overreacting a bit?"

"It was a good time for Marcus and I to see each other anyway, and I have some leave. I heard wonderful things about upstate New York."

"I doubt that."

"Your turn," Sigrid says.

"Fine. Professor Lydia Jones, Ph.D., thirty-nine years old, never married, born in Syracuse, New York, and moved here for a university position seven years ago. Made tenure in the department of philosophy specializing in . . . Wait a second." Irv removes some bright red reading glasses that are more suited for a woman, puts them on, and continues, saying ". . . the politics of race and the history of identity politics in America. That's some pretty heavy and sophisticated stuff. She wrote three books—two academic and one for a popular audience—seven peer-reviewed articles . . . all of which have colons in the titles, so they must be important . . . and she died by defenestration at Eighty-Six Brookmeyer Road two weeks ago. Autopsy performed. Toxicology negative. Small rip on the right shoulder of her sweater, demonstrating a struggle—forensics insists it was incompatible with a mere snag for some fancy reason—and there were traces of skin under her fingernails. Always a popular touch. We have a DNA match between those samples and your dear brother's, which we collected at your brother's house with a warrant. We have issued an APB—that's an all points bulletin in our vernacular—and we are still looking for him. But now that you're here," Irv says, removing his glasses, "I think we have a much better chance of bringing him in without anyone getting hurt. So welcome to the show."

"May I see the file?"

Irv hands it to her. She takes it and does not immediately open it. She wants to hear the story from Irv first. This will give her a basis for comparing interpretations, which is crucial for undermining his confidence in his own case.

"Any eyewitnesses? Video?"

"As a matter of fact, we found a guy named Chuck who saw your brother exit the building Lydia fell from, run to her body, check it, call 9-1-1, confess, and then run away. So I'm feeling pretty good about things, but I'm always open to scrutiny and abuse."

"That's it?"

"What's it?"

"Your case against Marcus. That's it?"

"I'm not making a case, but yes. An eyewitness and a confession. Two of my favorite things. It feels pretty solid. Or at least a good start until we talk to him."

"Nine-one-one's the emergency number in America?"

"Yes. They route the calls and send fire or police or EMTs."

"How do you know Marcus called it?"

"We have the recording, we have the witness saying he placed a call for a matched duration at a matched time. And if that isn't enough, I plan on using you to ID his voice, under oath. And that ought to square *that* circle."

"What did he say?"

"'She's dead. She's dead. She's dead. I did this. I did this.' You're welcome to hear it, of course. In fact, you'll be required to."

"He said, 'I did this' twice?"

"Yes."

"What else do you have?"

"I have trace elements of his skin under her fingernails, which is a nice example of Locard's Law playing itself out."

"You're referring," says Sigrid, "to Locard's 1904 piece on scientific method and criminal cases?"

"I'm referring to something a guy named Howard says about transfer always happening. I was repeating it in an effort to impress you, which has backfired."

"We don't know if there was a criminal act," Sigrid says. "Locard's Law may be an illusion. Transfer of physical evidence between the victim and perpetrator does often happen as Locard theorized, but for all kinds of reasons. That's where we've made advancements since 1904. The general can never be a substitute for the particular."

"Huh," Irv says.

"You have a witness to a phone call," says Sigrid, "Marcus's skin under her nails but without any sense of how it got there, and an ambiguous message on an emergency call."

"I also have him running away from the scene."

"What else?"

"And away from the police."

"What else?"

"And his family."

"What else?"

"What do you mean, 'what else'? I have Marcus running away from his job. From his apartment. He left everything behind to an opinionated hooker."

"So it isn't exactly open and shut."

"We have not decided to arrest him for the charge of murder yet, no. I admit that it is circumstantial, but the golden triangle of motive, means, and opportunity is starting to form a nice equilateral shape that I find pleasing."

"That's a heuristic. It's not an algorithm for proving causality," says Sigrid.

Irv smiles at her. His face brightens immediately and all sense of seriousness and weight is not only erased but seems to have been part of another past. He looks to Sigrid as though smiling is his natural state, and it is only by rallying his small reserve of adulthood and maturity that he can appear stern and focused.

"Why are you smiling at me?"

"I like the way you said that, especially for a woman for whom English is not her first language. No, it isn't a conviction machine. I—for example—have motive, means, and opportunity to kill most journalists in this town and yet I don't, I won't, and if they end up dead it doesn't mean I did it. It does mean, however, that it would be perfectly reasonable to suspect me of doing it if one had been hurled from a window. Right now, your brother is the only one inside my golden triangle. So I need to talk to him. And I am under some serious pressure to do so. And quickly. You don't know the politics around here. You are a foreigner in a foreign land with foreign ideas and a laminated piece of plastic. Back to you. What do you want to share with me next?"

"I'm not going to help you catch my brother."

"Now, now, Ms. Odegard. Cop to cop—we wouldn't want to be obstructing justice or becoming an accessory after the fact, now, would we?"

"I think there's a hard line to be drawn," says Sigrid, "between aiding a fugitive and not working for you for free."

"You're smart," says Irv, pointing at her and nodding his head. "A smart cucumber."

Sigrid says nothing.

"And quiet. Do you have Asperger's or something?"

"No."

"You're a quiet one," he says quietly.

"I think Americans can't abide silence."

"You only got here yesterday."

"The pattern is robust."

Irv puts his finger back in the holster and leans back against the bars to his cell. "What kind of cop are you?"

"I'm a section chief in Oslo."

"Oslo's the capital."

"Yes."

"How big is it?"

"The city is around six hundred and fifty thousand and the urban area is closer to a million."

"So you're a capital-city cop with a serious job. And you're how old?"

"Forty."

"You've been promoted pretty fast. You must be talented or have good connections. What does your father do?"

"He talks to ducks."

"Are they police ducks?"

"No," she says. And—worried she might be falling into the rabbit hole of pointless American banter—adds, "We're a farming family. Marcus stayed in agriculture generally and I went off to the big city to fight crime."

"So we'll go with smart and talented for now. You seen much in your time on the job?"

"Yes."

"That face, right there? See, that's interesting," Irv says, pointing at her again. He uncrosses his legs and leans forward. "You're quiet but you've got an expressive face. I'm guessing you've been through something. And recently. Which is why none of this fazes you. Your bar is set higher. Not just in your heart," he says, tapping his chest, "but in your soul."

Sigrid leans back against the bars to put a little more distance between herself and Irv's analysis. She glances at his cowboy boots and he notices.

"Like 'em?" he asks.

"No."

"They'll grow on you."

"Do you really have time for all this?" Sigrid asks. "This useless talk?"

Irv taps out a bongo solo on his knee and scrunches up his face. "It's only useless if you don't know how to listen to it. Meanwhile, we've looked in all the usual places and some exceptional ones to find Marcus and we can't; every place Tommy Lee Jones would have us look, we've looked. But . . . you know . . . this is a very, very big country that is very, very easy to move around in. At the moment we're watching the credit cards and stuff, but it's quiet. What you could do is help us collect him. If he's innocent, he walks. If not—it's best no one gets hurt as we determine that, right?"

"We're at cross purposes, Sheriff."

"It's family and you obviously believe in him. I get it. I'm not that cop in all the action movies who doesn't get it. But he does have to come in and talk to us. He was the woman's lover and there's an eye-witness putting him at the scene of her death. So consider this," Irv says, leaning forward again and resting his arms on his knees, "just in case you decide to get clever and try to find him on your own. I've got local police, state police, and FBI if I need it. I was born and raised here and I know this land and these people. You're a foreigner. You don't know anyone and you're traveling alone. There is no way that one foreigner in an unfamiliar land can outfox the local police."

"I've seen it done," says Sigrid. And she adds, "Recently."

"Against someone as smart as me?"

"Too soon to tell."

"OK. But consider this. If we work together, and we find him to-gether, you are guaranteed to be the first one in to talk him out. But if you go off on your own, and you don't get there first? All bets are off."

"You haven't called her death a murder yet."

"You don't miss a thing, do you?"

The case folder is still on Sigrid's legs, and for the first time she turns her attention to it. She knows that Irv isn't wrong, and if she were in his position, holding this same file, she would have made a similar appeal—though with fewer words.

In truth, it would be better if Marcus came in. Whatever happened to Lydia Jones, it wasn't caused by Marcus. He never exhibited an ex-plosive personality, was never enraged, was never abusive to women, and has never been in a fight even as a boy, as far as she knows. His flaws run the opposite direction. He is too sensitive, too vulnerable. Her father used to say that he suffered from perspective. His view of the world is too broad to permit attention to the banal but otherwise necessary activities of life. In her two decades as a police officer, Sigrid has never once arrested a person like that for violence.

She opens the file and what she sees startles her.

During the past month she has reviewed hundreds of photos from the assault on the summer house in Glåmlia. When the emergency response team engaged the criminals inside, they had ascertained that they were armed, they were dangerous, and the hostage situation was fragile. They opted to go in shooting, which Sigrid supported. When it was over there was paperwork. She's been looking at dead bodies all month.

It isn't Lydia Jones's contorted and bloodied body on the sidewalk that surprises her. It is that Dr. Lydia Jones was black.

"She was black," says Sigrid.

"You didn't know that?"

"No. I hadn't had time to look her up or . . ." Sigrid stops short of saying "finish reading Marcus's letters and look through his hard drive," because it wasn't necessary for Sheriff Irv Wylie to know about the letters. Or the hard drive.

"Or . . . what?" asks Irv.

"Hmm?"

"You said, 'or' and I said, 'or what'? You were about to add something."

"Brush my teeth," Sigrid says.

"What does that mean?"

"It's a Norwegian expression. Hard to translate."

Irv looks doubtful. "What's your plan, Sigrid?" he asks.

"I'm working on it."

Sigrid watches Irv stand up and walk into the main room, where he calls to someone named Melinda and asks her to join them in the holding cells. When he steps back inside he speaks quickly:

"There's a Motel Six down the road," he says. "Sixty-three ninety-nine a night plus taxes. Puts you at seventy bucks a night or so with taxes. But there's no kitchenette, so you're looking at twenty dollars a day in fast food and another couple for coffee and oddities. Add in the public transportation and a few cabs and you're looking at at least a hundred and ten a day to stick around here, assuming you never go to the movies or have a drink. Now, I don't know what they pay cops in Oslo, but if I can guess, that's a painful bite if you're here for a few weeks. It would be for me. And you already said your family's in farming, and probably not the Big Agro type. So here's what I think."

Melinda arrives and loiters by the door to the jail. She is a white twenty-something cop in uniform wearing a Beretta nine-millimeter in a black holster. She moves with it comfortably. That would put her in the job for at least a few years.

"Melinda, this here is Sigrid Odegard."

"Ødegård," Sigrid says, correcting his pronunciation.

"What she said. She is the sister of Marcus . . . of the same family name. She's come here from Norway looking for him. She's gonna stay with you for a while so we can lend her a helping hand in that noble effort."

"OK."

"Why would you do that?" Sigrid asks.

"Because the sheriff asked me to."

"Not you. You."

"So we know where you are and can more easily follow you around."

"Right. But I don't know where he is."

"I believe you completely," says Irv. "And I think your intentions are just and true. But I also suspect that you are going to track him down like one of those little sniffer dogs. You know the little sniffer dogs?"

"Yes."

"Like one of them. Maybe a beagle. Or a schnauzer."

"I can't imagine why you think I'm going to be more successful. You just delivered a speech about how I can't possibly find him by myself in a strange land."

"Not against us, no. But with us? Absolutely. And here's why: We always have to leave the possibility for individuation during investigations. To us he's an amalgam. A profile. A typification. But not a person. You, however, know him. You know what makes him . . . distinct.

That means you have the edge on knowing how his personality might manifest as behavior. Also, I think you see the world differently than I do, Ms. Sigrid. I believe we, at the sheriff's station, are seeing your brother's world through a glass darkly, which is why we can't find him. But through your clear blue Norwegian eyes we're going to learn to see him face to face, and you know why? Because love never fails. And I believe you love your brother. So: Corinthians Thirteen. Who knew it was actually a foundation for a solid investigative strategy in a murder case."

THE GENERAL OPINION

OFFICER MELINDA POWELL is from Buffalo, New York, where she grew up with her mother, Lisa, and her father, Albert, in a white house with black shutters that was close enough to school so she could walk there, which was really nice because some of her friends had to take the bus every morning and the kids on the bus could be sort of mean, especially this wild kid named Benny whose parents got divorced when he was really young and no one ever seemed to talk him through it so he was crazy angry at everyone, and that made walking much better because in the winter she got to see all the snowmen people put up in their yard, with the coal and the carrots and the whole deal, and obviously no one pulled her hair or started her day off in a bad mood, which can mean a lot when you're a teenager especially, and it all made growing up really nice even though it was sort of near the city and it had crime and stuff but not too much in her area, so really, she's not exactly sure why she became a cop but she did and she just loves it because it feels like she can make a difference, and Sheriff Irv is just the greatest and he's such an original thinker and straight shooter she knows she can learn a lot from him.

Sigrid learns all this between the time she leaves the police station and the time she enters the passenger-side door of Melinda's prowler. She wonders how much more she might have learned from Melinda if she'd actually asked a question.

Melinda eventually asks Sigrid where she wants to go first and Sigrid—in an effort to blend in by bonding—says, "I think we should try Marcus's secret hideout. Have you looked there yet?"

Maybe the delivery was too dry, because Melinda says, "No. That's a great idea! Do you know the address?"

Sigrid has read someplace that culture is all about language. It seemed reasonable when she read it. Now that she is speaking English she should have been transformed into an American of sorts. But clearly that is not happening and she isn't fooling anyone. There must be something deeper going on.

"I was telling a joke," Sigrid explains.

"Really?"

Melinda pulls out into traffic. Sigrid has no idea where they are going.

Or maybe Sigrid has it backwards. Maybe Melinda is a comic genius.

"Wait. Are you joking?" Sigrid asks.

"No. Are you joking about me joking?" Melinda asks.

"No," says Sigrid. "I'm being serious."

"When Irv said you're from Norway, did he mean, like, your heritage? Minneapolis or St. Paul?"

"No. The actual country."

"Huh. So . . . why do you think your brother killed that woman?"

"Your name is Melinda, right?"

"Yes, ma'am."

"Melinda, there is a difference between what we call the investigative question and the interview question. The first one is what you secretly want to know. The second one is what you ask in order to learn it. They are seldom the same question. That's the science. The art is engaging your subject into revealing information you want to know through indirect questioning. If you're treating me as an interviewee here, and you want me to reveal information, you're going to have to try harder. I won't blame you for doing it, but you're going to need to raise your game if you want to win. OK?"

"I don't remember this coming up in the police academy."

"They were probably teaching you to shoot instead."

"Huh?"

"Nothing. Where are we going?"

"Where do you want to go?"

"You first."

"Nowhere, really," Melinda admits. "I was just driving around hoping to ask you a few questions."

"OK. I need to buy some clothing. Mine were stolen."

"That sucks."

"That's the general opinion."

"I'll take you to Target, where you can 'expect more and pay less.'"

"That sounds ideal."

The prices at Target are so low that Sigrid feels a momentary pang of guilt for the abducted and enslaved children who surely weaved the clothing with their tiny little fingers. It is unsettling, though, how quickly that feeling fades as she holds up a pair of not-half-bad-looking jeans being sold on sale for twelve dollars: the price of coffee and a muffin in Oslo.

Melinda stands, bored, like a little sister being dragged around town. "They stole your suitcase?" she asks.

"Yes."

"You're gonna need a new suitcase," Melinda concludes.

"They have suitcases here too?"

"They got everything."

Sigrid's shopping is partly a solitary affair and partly a team effort because Melinda is obviously under orders not to leave her alone for too long. She does, however, leave her alone long enough for Sigrid to snag the few items she is going to need to carry out her own work in parallel to that of the police department. Luckily, these items are small enough to slip under the clothing in the cart.

Melinda follows Sigrid toward the bathrooms and waits at the end of the short hallway for her to return.

Five minutes later, on reemerging, Sigrid says to her, "I'm still here."

"We're all on the same side," Melinda says, neither convincingly nor enthusiastically.

"Of course we are," Sigrid agrees.

At the cash register Melinda eyes over the purchases Sigrid isn't hiding from her in the bag at her feet. "Good haul?" she asks.

"I can't complain."

She might have complained, though, because the cashier tried to stack the returned coins on top of the slippery receipt rather than handing over the coins first. They slid off and fell to the floor.

"Sorry. That happens all the time," the girl says.

"So why do you keep doing it?" Sigrid asks.

"What?"

On the plus side, Sigrid bought a suitcase and new wardrobe for less than the price of the suitcase alone in Oslo with its twenty-five percent sales tax.

The parking lot grew crowded while they were inside. Sigrid looks at her surroundings as they place the suitcase and its contents into the trunk of the police car.

It is a rather desolate place, Sigrid notes, but no worse than certain areas of Oslo that are really an embarrassing knot of roads, roundabouts, warehouses, and sprawl. Areas like Økern. Adding to the general mood of disrepair and neglect is a shack-turned-bar tucked behind the Target that may have once been a homestead in the 1800s and remains standing only because it refused to sell out or fall down. It is the kind of structure that looks to be propped up by spite.

"What's that?"

"Biker bar. The Inferno. Mean place."

"You ever break it up?"

"They're like hornets. They just come back again later."

Melinda starts the car and switches on the police radio. Unlike in Oslo, where there is constant chatter, here it is mostly quiet.

As Melinda pulls out of the parking lot Sigrid decides to level with her. "You realize I'm going to have to shake you at some point and carry on alone?"

"I've been told to follow you but not get in your way," Melinda says, not taking her eyes off the road.

"Were you supposed to tell me that?"

"Irv said it wouldn't matter what I tell you."

"You realize that I'm a section chief and a twenty-year veteran of a police force with one of the highest education levels in the world, right?"

"Yeah. Irv looked it all up on Wikipedia. He said none of that would matter either."

"You both sound a little cocky to me."

"The thing about Irv," Melinda says, "is that he always seems to find the angle on things that no one else has ever thought of before. You should ask him about God sometime. He's even got that all figured out."

IT'S CONTAGIOUS

THE STATE UNIVERSITY campus is as flat as a pond and as
green as its students. Sigrid and Melinda roll through the main
gate, which proudly announces the name of the school on a
black plaque with gold lettering. There is a long road to the primary
visitors lot and it is empty. They park close to an old brick building
that squats incongruously alongside a massive modern glass and steel
structure housing a new science and engineering center.

It being mid-August, the campus is desolate despite the fine
weather. Melinda knows where she is going. She's been here before.

"It's the middle of the summer vacation," Melinda explains. "I
doubt anyone's even going to be there, but . . . it's your investigation." She walks like a cowboy with her thumbs hooked into the black
leather of her police belt. They cross between the Frederick Douglass
Building of Government and some kind of administrative building.
Sigrid notices that all the buildings have names and identities and how
the newest and most expensive buildings are for the natural sciences,
computer sciences, and career center, whereas the more quaint buildings of neo-Gothic design are for the humanities.

They cross into an enormous field that Melinda calls a "quad" though Sigrid can't see how it is a fourth of anything. It is a lovely and inviting manicured lawn, the center of which boasts a flaccid American flag atop a massive white flagpole.

"It's worth the visit," Sigrid says. "What did you ask the last time you came?"

"We were here because of Dr. Jones," Melinda explains. "The sheriff wanted us to look past the eyewitness and see what else might come up. He said your brother was the obvious suspect but our job was to understand the relationship between him and the victim."

"So you were focused on establishing a motive for Marcus?"

"Well," Melinda says, without conviction, "I'm not sure it was that specific. All he said on the way over was that when you see a picture of a running man you can't know from looking at it whether he's running toward something or away from something or just going for a jog."

"What did you learn about Marcus?" Sigrid asks.

"That he loved Lydia and he loved working here."

"That doesn't sound like a motive for murder," Sigrid says.

"Not right off the bat, no, but the sheriff says that whenever there's love there's a universe of possibility."

"He's quite the philosopher, your sheriff."

"He used to be a Bible scholar or something back before he became sheriff. Smart, smart guy."

When Sigrid signed up for an MA in criminology a lifetime ago, she lived in an apartment in Bislett, in Oslo, with three other friends who split the rent. Most of her classmates were from Oslo and so lived at home with their parents. The University of Oslo is a city university with no campus to speak of, at least from an American point of view. There are clusters of buildings off Ring 2, but the students don't make it their home in the way they do in American dorms. This place—Sigrid thinks to herself, strolling through the picturesque campus—is a universe unto itself. She can see why Marcus would be seduced by it.

She imagines the conversation she would have with him:

You have found a place to hide after all, she would have said to Marcus if he'd been here right now.

"With girls and sunshine," he'd reply.

"And they pay you for this?"

"Barely. It's below minimum wage if you run the numbers."

"Why do you do it?" she'd want to know.

"Look around, Sigrid," he would have said. "The students are hungry. The hunger is everywhere. For knowledge, for companionship, sex, solutions. They even want the complications. They want it all. Everything they haven't experienced or thought yet. They want it to flood in. And yet for all that hunger and need, they are exactly where they want to be, doing what they want to be doing. They are hungry and satisfied at the same time. It's an unnatural state of being that is somehow perfectly stable. That sense of impossible balance is what defines the place. Like them, I'd pay to be here if I had to."

"You're being exploited."

"I know. And yet, look at this late summer day and tell me where else one is supposed to be on this earth?"

She and Melinda finally arrive at a building that reminds her of the zoological museum in Oslo in the botanical gardens. It houses the Department of Earth Sciences, which includes agriculture and environmental studies—according to a large directory inside the main hall.

Their footsteps echo as they walk up the stairs.

"His department head is Dr. Ernie Williamson," Melinda says.

"You met him?"

"Yeah."

"Do people know that you suspect Marcus as having played a role in Lydia's death?" Sigrid asks.

"You mean that we think he murdered her?"

"Yes, that's my question."

"Oh, no. That's not public. They only know he's missing."

"How would you describe Dr. Williamson?" Sigrid asks.

"If I used the phrase, 'straight out of central casting,' would you know what that means?"

"No," Sigrid says.

"I won't use it then."

Dr. Ernie Williamson is in his late fifties. He's a white man with straggly hair and glasses that do not fit correctly on his face; their bridge sits too high across his large nose, producing a gap. It is not the sort of eyewear selection a man would make if he'd been accompanied by someone else.

Sigrid looks to his wedding finger—remembering that the Americans wear it on the left hand, not the Norwegian right. He doesn't have one, and there is no tan line. His desk, like his glasses, allows for a gap—this one between the skirt of the desk and the floor. Poking out from the slot are black shoes designed for comfort, which signal a loss of interest in human sexuality.

He waves Sigrid and Melinda into his office with informality and sincerity.

"Come on in. Come on in. You're . . . Officer . . . don't tell me."

"Melinda, sir."

"Melinda. Nice to see you again. I heard your footsteps in the hall and my first thought was . . . zombies. I mean, who else would be roaming these halls on a day like today? It's so beautiful out there. So beautiful, there's nowhere to go but down."

"Just us local police, sir," Melinda confirms. "No zombies. None we noticed, anyway."

"Well, come on in. What can I do for you? How are things going with Lydia's case? We're all very shook up about it around here."

Sigrid watches Melinda move, without hesitation, to the farthest of two chairs across from the professor's desk, suggesting that she sat there last time. People tend to fall into patterns of that type quite naturally. Melinda sits down while introducing Sigrid: "This is Marcus's sister, Sigrid. She's from Norway. When I was here last time we talked about Marcus and Lydia and their relationship. As you may know . . .

Marcus is missing. So we're looking for him. And we're hoping you can help."

Professor Williamson places his hands on the desk. He stretches out his fingers. "Yeah. He's a quiet one, your brother. Doesn't surprise me in the least that he'd be looking for some solitude after something like this. Didn't tell you where he was going, huh?"

"No, he didn't. Professor," asks Sigrid, "when Melinda and the sheriff were here last time, what did they ask you? We discussed it of course," Sigrid lies, "though it's always helpful to hear it from another perspective."

"Well, let me see," says Dr. Williamson, placing his fingertips together to create a sort of pulsing organ the size of a human heart. "He asked how Marcus and Lydia knew one another, but I didn't know how they met. As I explained, Professor Jones worked in a completely different department. So I didn't know her well. She and I were both on the CARE committee—that's Compliance, Accountability, Risk, and Ethics—which met for two hours a month. We didn't socialize, though. And with Marcus, though he's a lovely man and a good teacher, he is only an adjunct, and since I'm head of the department we don't engage with one another much either. So I wasn't very helpful."

"Anything else you all discussed?" Sigrid asks.

"The sheriff asked about the subjects Marcus teaches and whether the students like him."

"Do they?"

"Oh, yes, very much. He really talks the students through the differences between conservation and preservation. He has a good theoretical understanding of the places versus spaces distinction and—because he's a foreigner—he can make very interesting comparisons with his native Norway. I don't see how any of this will help you find him, though."

The office walls are lined with textbooks and photographs of plants and stretches of land that must mean something, because Sigrid can tell they are not art. Despite not being to her taste, it is a nicer place to work than her office in Oslo. His office has a door and—unlike her own office door back in Oslo—has no windows out to a central room filled with young police officers and their irksome optimism.

"Do you know where he went during his time off?" Sigrid asks.

"I know he liked the outdoors. We didn't talk about such things much. He was . . . as I mentioned . . . an adjunct."

"Adjuncts are people too, aren't they?" Sigrid asks.

"You should get that onto a T-shirt."

"Is the department secretary here?" Sigrid asks, hoping that—by now—she has proved to Melinda that Professor Williamson is absolutely useless and knows nothing.

"Mrs. Perlmutter? Yes. She's always here."

"Melinda," says Sigrid, turning to her. "Would you mind getting a copy of the curriculum Marcus is teaching and also a list of his students? It might help."

"You mean . . . now?"

"Yes."

Sigrid sits up farther in her chair, hoping to communicate certainty, authority, and a touch of urgency. Melinda is about to say something when Sigrid adds, "We'll be right here."

Melinda looks at her two elders, who look back at her, and she chooses the path of least resistance by shaking off her doubts and fulfilling the task assigned to her.

With Melinda out of the room and, more to the point, out of earshot, Sigrid fishes for the knowledge she really wants: "Any favorite spots? Places he'd take his classes?" she presses.

Places he might be right now? she doesn't ask.

"Well," says Dr. Williamson, leaning back in his chair. It creaks like a graveyard gate and he doesn't seem to notice. "He takes his class to the Adirondack state park, of course. They go twice a semester for obvious reasons."

"What obvious reasons?"

"It's why we're here," the professor says, leaning far enough back into his chair that Sigrid wonders how close it might be to flipping right over. "It's why we teach these courses at this school. Adirondack is special because it's a state preserve, but a little over half of it is privately owned, which is unique. And I use that word correctly. For this reason, it's been called one of the greatest experiments in conservation in the industrialized world. If you're interested in sustainability and the relationship between man and nature, this is the experiment you want to be watching. And we live right next to it."

"How big is the park?"

"Over six million acres."

"What's an acre?"

"Let me put it this way. It's more than twenty-four thousand square kilometers in area. By way of comparison, that's a bit smaller than Albania and a bit bigger than Israel. It has ten thousand lakes and fifty thousand kilometers of rivers and streams. A man could get lost in there."

"Where was Marcus's favorite spot in the Adirondacks?"

"That's easy. The Saranac Lake Islands is where they'd always go. For those who stayed for the weekend field trip he'd bring them hiking up Redfield."

"Do you think Marcus went there?" Sigrid asks.

"If he did, and he doesn't want you to find him, you won't. It's impossible."

"I see."

"All that grief," Professor Williamson adds. He kicks off his shoes for some reason and wiggles his black cotton toes from beneath the desk. Sigrid resists sitting back farther, but the temptation is real. "Lydia dying. That little boy getting shot like that. So much tragedy for that poor family. I remember when it happened. Marcus was upset too. He knew Jeffrey also."

"What little boy?"

"Lydia's nephew. Jeffrey. Jeffrey Simmons?"

"I don't know about this."

"Oh, aside from the presidential election, that's the biggest news around here. Lydia's nephew was shot by the police. He was twelve years old and was playing in his front yard with some other boys. The police mistook his cap gun for a real one and . . . they killed him. We had protests on campus against police violence, there were sit-ins demanding answers, we've had guest lecturers coming in to discuss race and racism and the politics of . . . Well, anyway. I don't want to intellectualize that tragedy. I didn't see Lydia after it happened. She stopped attending CARE, though I did see Marcus, and he was profoundly changed."

"Did that happen in this jurisdiction? Was Sheriff Wylie involved in—"

"Oh, heck no," he interrupts. "This was the next county over. It was their police, not ours. But after the boy died everything erupted here. I can honestly and shamefully say I never paid much attention to these sorts of things, and frankly these student protests can be more about growing up than the subject being protested, but in this case my eyes were really opened to the depth of injustice here and how primitive our institutions are in protecting the vulnerable. Did you know that in the U.S. we don't even have a database on fatal police shootings? We the people don't even know how many citizens the government kills—justified or not."

"Yes, I did know that," Sigrid says.

"Really?

"I'm a police chief in Norway. There's a lot of talk about America near the coffee maker."

"So we're global news, huh?"

"It's hard to ignore the moose sitting on your waffle."

"What?"

"That might not translate."

"What do you think happened to Lydia?" Sigrid asks.

"I don't want to speculate. But let's say . . . she was a childless woman in her forties who loved her nephew very, very much. And a few months later, she died."

Sigrid writes this down in her notebook and surreptitiously glances at the door to make sure Melinda isn't lurking in the corner making the same notes she is.

"Who knew Lydia best, Dr. Williamson? Who can help us understand this and find Marcus?"

"On campus? Gloria Dillane. English department. Teaches contemporary American fiction. I heard they had a lively discussion going about psychology versus sociology when it came to understanding people's motivations. Took the conversation beyond the more static discussion of individualism versus structure. Even I'm sick of that one. Anyway, the students were enthralled. You should talk to her. She's sad now too. It's contagious, you know."

"What is?" Sigrid asked.

"Sadness."

IT'S EUROPEAN

OUTSIDE ON THE quad there is a large maple tree under which Sigrid imagines young American hipsters in earth tones strumming Nick Drake songs to young women in thrift-store clothing who aren't listening.

This is where she sits with Melinda after they've collected lunch from a nearby deli, as the cafeteria is closed for the season.

American sandwiches, Sigrid learns, are four times larger than Norwegian ones and have bread on both the bottoms *and* the tops. Between the two slabs of starch is enough sliced meat to choke a lion. Sitting on the grass, Sigrid opens the sandwich and evenly distributes the meat onto each piece of bread and then uses her brother's lock blade to cut each of those in half. She eats one while Melinda devours the entire torpedo.

"Hungry?" she asks.

Melinda shrugs. "It's lunch."

If the hipsters with their beards are missing, there is a grunt of young men strolling around in flip-flops and extraordinarily long shorts that droop below their knees. As in the movies, they wear base-ball caps and all have surprisingly thick calves and wide shoulders. Given that America is a multiracial society, it is a wonder that so many people are exactly the same shape.

"Why are they all carrying a large bottle with a straw in it?" she asks Melinda.

"To hydrate."

Sigrid looks up at the blue sky and the cotton clouds. "Is dehydration a special problem here?"

"I couldn't say."

Sigrid wraps the remainder of her lunch into its wax paper co-coon, and sips from a bottle of sparkling water before packing it all up. What she needs to do now, and urgently, is create some privacy for herself to look through Marcus's orange hard drive; finish reading the letters he'd written to her father; better under-stand both the life and death of Lydia Jones; and learn as much as she can about the Jeffrey Simmons case. Getting rid of Melinda for a few minutes was simple enough. Shaking her completely will not be.

"Why did you become a cop?" Sigrid asks as an opening gambit for a longer play.

"To fight crime."

"You could have fought cancer," Sigrid says.

"I think cancer is smarter than me. I stood a better chance of win-ning a few this way. You?"

"I said the same twenty years ago."

"Not anymore?"

"I thought I wanted to fight crime. Now that I'm older I realize that it's injustice that bothers me. Fighting the first one doesn't always solve for the other," she says.

"I can't believe you're not American," Melinda says. "You talk bet-ter than almost anyone I know."

"I have a vocabulary for work. Not for other things."

"What do you mean by that?"

"It means I can talk about police work in English, but I can't talk about love."

"Who can?" Melinda says. "Must be so cool to speak a second language. I can't really imagine it."

"That's because you speak English. You're all terrible at second languages. You, the British, the Australians, the New Zealanders. The Canadians pretend to speak French for national unity, but they're not good either. Do you share your apartment?" Sigrid asks, as though it is not a non sequitur.

"No. It's my own. It's right in town off Main Street by a laundromat. Two bedrooms, one bath, on-street parking. It's nothing special but it's in my budget and it's mine. You know that store called Ikea?"

"Yes."

"You have that in Europe?"

"It's European."

The flip-flop boys with the hydration issues have started tossing an American football back and forth. Sigrid, watching them, can't understand why the Americans call it football.

"It is?"

"It's Swedish. You might have noticed the blue and yellow on everything."

"I thought that was just the color scheme."

"Those are the colors of the Swedish flag. It's why they sell frozen meatballs and everything's in Swedish."

"Never gave it much thought. And Legos are from Denmark, right?"

"You have two bedrooms?"

"Yup. Mine and yours. We're roomies now."

"I'd like to go back and take a nap."

"Seriously?"

"Central European Time is plus six hours from now. It's past ten at night and I've already had a long day. I need an hour or two of rest before going for another stretch. It's a smart choice. It doesn't mean I'm weak."

"I'm on the clock no matter where we are. So . . . I guess. But while we're here, shouldn't we talk to Lydia Jones's people?"

Sigrid stands and brushes herself off.

"There's no one here. We'll talk to Lydia's friends later. Right now I need to rest."

THE DEATH OF
JEFFREY SIMMONS

THIRTY MINUTES LATER Sigrid is alone behind a closed bedroom door in Melinda's apartment. The bed is unusually high off the ground due to what Melinda called a "box spring" under a mattress as thick as her forearm is long. There is also a wardrobe and a desk. Everything smells like the inside of a box. The bedspread is a handmade quilt that Melinda's grandmother had made and presented to her grandfather as a wedding gift and there was more to the story but Sigrid had switched off by then.

"Mi casa es su casa," Melinda told her.

At the desk Sigrid unpacks a Korean laptop, boots it up, and for fifteen minutes she has to stubbornly refuse to join anything, update anything, or connect to anything. She fights past legal agreements that are in no way a "meeting of the minds" but ultimately has to capitulate; otherwise she can't use the computer she allegedly owns.

Her first order of business is to plug in the orange hard drive to the USB port. She listens to it spin to life as Melinda turns on some music in the other room—some teenage girl singing about herself.

Sigrid inserts a USB key into the right side of the laptop.

The condition of his home notwithstanding, Marcus has histori-cally been tidy and organized, and the hard drive shows that he hasn't changed. It contains four folders marked in English rather than Nor-wegian. It would be interesting to know whether he's dreaming in English now, after twenty years here.

The files are marked: DEPRESSION, POLICE, JEFFREY, IDEAS. They are sized 103MB, 127MB, 57MB, and 3K respectively. Sigrid imme-diately copies all four to the USB stick she names Ferdinand for no particular reason. Ejecting the hard drive, she opens the files directly from the UBS key so the original files will remain untouched and the casual investigator will not see changes to the dates they were mod-ified.

This way, no one will know where she's looked, what she's looked at, or in what order. This all feels more criminal than investigative, but there's no law against taking precautions.

The DEPRESSION folder consists mainly of PDF files or screen shots from medical and quasi-medical websites, including blogs and letters from people with depression or some related psychological concern. Listing the files from largest to smallest shows that the file sizes are mostly small— 500K to 1.5MB. A few exceed 4MB and these are gen-erally short movies he has downloaded. She watches two—each a documentary-style interview about living with depression.

In the other room, Melinda has changed the music to something that reminds Sigrid of the Bangles, though it is unlikely Melinda is old enough to have heard of the Bangles.

She should have been more thorough at Marcus's house and checked the cabinet for medication, but she knows not to castigate herself too much. No one can see everything the first time. The source of the guilt, though, is the misuse of the term "evidence"; it confuses too many investigators. As Sigrid has discussed with her colleague Pet-ter on more than one occasion—especially when attending confer-ences conducted in English—the English term *evidence* isn't used in Norwegian, or more to the point it was only lately introduced but not in relationship to crime and law. In Norway, the term is *bevis*, derived from the German *beweiss*, for proof. Still, though, the term doesn't quite translate. It is not proof as the Americans or British mean it. As you search a home or other crime site, an English-speaking investigator does not look for "proof," because proof is that which proves a theory to be true. But when an investigator is wandering around a crime scene the first time, it's imperative not to have a theory in mind and be looking for ways to prove it. Proof is the last thing a professional should be looking for. He or she should be collecting information that might eventually allow a defensible claim to be made—both logically and legally.

It takes time, and effort, and the application of reason to the range of facts to craft a plausible explanation—to craft a story. How can one possibly get it right on the first pass? That bloodied knife sticking out of the butler is likely to be important. But what about that piece of half-eaten toast? Or that the dishwasher is full? Or that it's empty?

The trouble is that few of the youngsters want to hear it. It's dull. They develop a far-away look when she explains that investigation is an iterative process of hypothetico-deductive reasoning. That it isn't magic. That it isn't easy, or sexy, or based on their unique intuition, and that building a reasoned argument isn't for amateurs. "Facts are not evidence," she says. "Facts become evidence when they are mobilized in support of an argument."

Those who survive the lecture might survive the career.

It is the Bangles. Melinda is playing "Manic Monday." How can she possibly know that song?

The POLICE folder contains more complicated and varied documents than the DEPRESSION folder—not that she has read it all. This has images, videos, legal documents, policies, articles from newspapers and magazines, reports from nonprofit organizations and hospitals as well as church, civic, and youth groups. Photos of dead children; a black man with a thick neck and little hair with bruises all over his face and neck and shoulders; statements by police insisting that they had to protect themselves; statements from communities saying the police showed up pumped and ready to kill; gun ownership debates and arguments about the need for black men to defend themselves against the police because of a culture-wide presumption about guilt and violence that makes them all marked men.

Marcus had collected newspaper accounts from across the nation as well as academic studies and policy documents. How any of this relates to Marcus, though, is still eluding her.

The JEFFREY folder is all about the boy: a twelve-year-old boy named Jeffrey Simmons who was a sixth-grader at Lincoln Middle School in nearby Cofield, New York. Jeffrey's mother was a secretary for the regional office of an industrial chemical company that primarily served the timber industry, and his father was a manager at a large do-it-yourself supply store. Jeffrey was in the school band and played the drums, and he was mad for Harry Potter. He'd spend hours, his mother explained, sketching descriptions from the books or copying images from the movies that resulted in extraordinary worlds with castles and clouds, dragons and wizards. He and other children would meet up on weekends and compare one another's creations. He once told his father he wanted to be an engineer or an architect or a writer.

Jeffrey's mother reportedly told the children to stop playing inside and get outside into the sunshine. With Harry Potter still on their minds, Jeffrey and two friends were running around his house with cap guns for the Muggles and wands for the wizards. At 1:26 p.m., a white police officer name Roy Carman pulled up to their house rapidly, removed a Glock 17 nine-millimeter pistol, and shot Jeffrey twice in the chest and once in the head. The other two children, Peter Macintyre and Buddy Sandler, were uninjured. Peter ran away. Buddy stood and screamed for twenty minutes no matter what the second officer tried. News reports following the case explained that both boys were in psychological counseling and suffering from "severe trauma." Their parents all said both children now wet their beds, were afraid to go outside, could no longer sleep alone, were terrified of death and authority, and were no longer able to focus at school.

Peter and Buddy were white. Jeffrey was black. He is survived by his parents and two younger sisters, Elizabeth and Marjorie, and they too are broken.

This was two months ago, in June. It was two weeks ago that Marcus disappeared after writing his cryptic letter, and two weeks ago that Lydia died. That is also, Sigrid learns, when the grand jury concluded there were no grounds for Roy Carman to stand trial for Jeffrey's death.

The final folder is IDEAS. There is a single text file called "The Future." She opens it and finds it empty.

AMERICAN HORROR

A FTER AN HOUR with the material Sigrid sensed she was losing her focus and capacity to reason so decided to take a short nap.

Now, on waking, she is surrounded by a pitch darkness. The disco beats from the living room have become muffled TV voices punctuated by atmospheric music. She raises her left arm into a defensive position to see her wristwatch, but the toxic glow from the hands refuses to arrange them into readable lines and she gives up, deciding it doesn't much matter how long it's been anyway.

Usually, after a power nap, Sigrid experiences a moment of grogginess that makes way for strength and mental acuity.

This time is not like the other times.

The skin on her face feels as though it has slid off her skull and collected into pink and tacky puddles around the pillow she has fallen through on her way to China. No hangover, no regret, no bitter memory has left her this exhausted. No soldier she has ever listened to over the years; no parent of triplets; no caveman awakened from a block of ice has ever felt this tired.

At the corner of her eye, Sigrid can almost make out a thin line of blue light through the curtains proving that there is, still, a world beyond her headache. A land where there might be perambulating life with motive and will.

Sigrid tries to make a deliberate noise. What emerges from her chest, like a breath from an awakened Egyptian mummy, is a minor groan in the key of B.

She'll try again in a minute.

She had dreamed of her mother and can't think of why. Her mother, Astrid, was outside the farmhouse wearing rubber boots with images of Paddington Bear painted on their sides. She was washing the family car with Marcus. They were each using massive sponges dipped into warm and soapy water and splashing them onto the glimmering paint that sparkled a navy blue in the sun. Sigrid must have been about five in the dream and Marcus the same age as Jeffrey Simmons. He was barefoot and his jeans rolled to his knees. After working the side of the car he kneeled by the fender and lathered the chrome around the headlights until they shined as though from an inner happiness only made warmer by the sun. Marcus smiled at his mother and she smiled at him. Astrid's hair was in a ponytail, tied with a green band. She was slender—more slender than Sigrid would ever become except in her late teens—and her cheekbones were more pronounced. She had a look that others might have considered very beautiful had she been worked on by teams of makeup artists and fashion consultants and colorists. But here, in their village, she was plain and blond and familiar.

Astrid had been scrubbing a fender when she stopped washing and turned still and grave. She looked at Sigrid with a neediness parents do not expose to their children. In a growled whisper she said, "My son. Is he OK?"

Sigrid looked for Marcus by the car and could no longer see him. All trace of him—the bucket, the sponge, the water that had collected into a puddle at his feet—was gone.

"I don't know, Mommy," she answered.

• • •

That's when she woke up. She remembers this now and wishes she hadn't.

The distress it causes her, however, releases a minute drip of adrenaline that permits her to lean over to the bedside table, work her right hand up the tapered base of the lamp, around the harp holder, and find the switch on the socket.

She turns it twice with a *click click*, hoping the room will come into view, but it doesn't because her eyelashes have been sutured together with barnacle glue.

Into this comes a banging sound like a troll hammering at the door of a farmhouse.

"What!" groans Sigrid.

Melinda sticks her head in. "You're up?"

"What time is it?"

"About eight thirty."

"Why's it so dark?"

"It's nighttime. It's usually dark."

"What do you mean, nighttime?"

"You've been sleeping for four hours. It's eighty thirty. At night. Wednesday. August 13. 2008. Third rock from the sun."

"Oh dear God."

Melinda crosses her arms and ankles and falls like timber against the door frame with a smirk on her face. "You've got jet lag. I've heard about this. I don't travel much myself, but I went to Paris once when I was eleven, and when I came home, me and my sister would fall asleep around five in the afternoon and wake up at three in the morning and go downstairs to watch TV. But there was nothing on except these scary B movies from the 1950s; which I guess is how we shook the jet lag, because after a few days of that we simply refused to go to sleep at all and that put us right back on schedule."

"I don't think that's going to work for me," Sigrid says, wiping slobber from the corner of her mouth.

"Have you tried Ambien?"

"I don't want to talk about Ambien."

"I know some scary movies, though. Have you seen *Twenty-Eight*

Days Later? I almost pissed myself. Or *Aliens Two*? That was awesome. *Blair Witch Project*? I couldn't sleep. That final scene? Frankly, I don't know why I do it to myself. Why do any of us? Especially zombie movies. They freak me out and I have an actual gun in the house. I don't think a country with so many guns should make so many horror movies."

"It's the other way around," Sigrid says, using her fingers to un-stitch her eyelashes.

"How do you mean?" Melinda asks.

Rubbing her face, Sigrid blinks fast and often to try to jump-start her face in the hopes it will remember how to do this by itself. "We have a lot of new immigrants in Norway. We have to take these classes on culture. Our instructor was an American with questionable taste in movies. She said American culture is all about individualism. It's not just an idea. It's what she called a performance. The way you per-form individualism is through self-reliance. But acting self-reliant usually means acting alone. And being alone is a weaker position than working together. That's America's paradox—your individualism is a strong cultural trait that weakens you as a community and you just can't see it. You worry that working together undermines your myth of self-reliance, so you hyperexaggerate its value to mask the fear. If you don't do this, you lose your sense of being American. You're basi-cally doomed."

"What does this have to do with jet lag?"

"Nothing. We're talking about horror movies. You're the one who linked the two."

"OK," says Melinda. "Explain the horror movies."

"Every horror movie ends with someone being self-reliant and over-coming her own fear or else failing to do that and dying. I can't think of a single one where the horror was overcome through strategy, co-operation, teamwork, or planning. It's a terrible machine you've cre-ated. It's why you all buy guns rather than build institutions. None of it makes you safer, but it does make you more American."

Melinda doesn't move from the wall. "I was issued my gun."

"Try not to shoot anybody."

"You don't talk like a cop. You talk like . . ." Melinda looks to the ceiling, where the answer is usually plastered. "Some kind of college professor who used to sit around thinking about this stuff all the time but now doesn't care anymore because he knows too much about it and doesn't have any questions left."

"That's a pretty good description."

"Thanks."

"Catching bad guys means outsmarting them," Sigrid says. "Knowing how people think, and why, gives you insight into what they might do. Or not. I need some coffee," Sigrid adds.

"You're gonna need to open your eyes at some point too."

Melinda's apartment—when it comes into focus—proves itself to have been tastefully decorated in inexpensive but stylish furniture. Sigrid sees how Melinda has leaned toward the modernist and Swedish side of the spectrum rather than the country cottage style, thereby brightening the small space. Further, she's accented the sofa, tables and chairs with vibrant colors. It creates a sense of being settled and present in her life that Sigrid reads as an unexpected maturity.

"Do you have a computer with internet access here?" Sigrid asks Melinda.

"Are you joking?"

"Why you do keep asking me that?"

"Something about the way you talk."

"No, I'm not joking."

"There's a laptop over there."

Sigrid sits herself down on a comfy chair and starts poking around looking for inspiration that will lead to a plan that will lead to some time away from Melinda, who is starting to make her feel slightly guilty, because she seems like a genuinely good kid in need of a mentor, but the circumstances dictate that Sigrid needs to find Marcus without a chaperone. She does have an idea, if an imperfect one, about how to find Marcus in his wilderness fortress, and she wants to explore that possibility as far away from the sheriff and his people as possible—if only to give Marcus a real chance to explain himself and let the two of them work together to find a solution to the predicament.

"Target is really open until eleven at night?"

"Midnight on Saturdays. Not in Norway?"

"Not exactly."

The shootout at the summer cabin last month began with the murder of a Serbian woman in the Oslo neighborhood of Tøyen. She had run to a neighboring apartment with her seven-year-old son for shelter, and it was provided by an eighty-two-year-old Jewish American—and Korean War vet—named Sheldon Horowitz. The woman didn't make it, but the old man took it on himself to protect the boy by disappearing into the Norwegian landscape. For four days he evaded the city police, the district police, CCTV cameras, a helicopter, and the Balkan mafia. He didn't speak Norwegian, he didn't spend any money, and he left no evidence behind. After the fact, it took Sigrid's team over two weeks to reconstruct his movements. They fielded calls from movie theaters, hotels, restaurants, and from tourists and motorists. She and her partner, Petter, had built out Sheldon's time line until it made sense, and eventually a navy dive team was deployed to locate and photograph a tractor that had been parked creatively at the bottom of a lake.

Sigrid did not know Sheldon. Not beyond the moment they spent together on the grass, clutching each other, outside the summer cabin as he lay dying. She had, however, had the chance to explore his mind and personality—both of which were expansive. She is half the age of the man who did all that. She is unquestionably in better shape now than he had been—the jet lag notwithstanding. Unlike him, she speaks the local language, and her life isn't at risk. Most important, Sigrid doesn't have a traumatized child in tow as she searches for Marcus. There really is no good reason, she figures, that she shouldn't be able to outperform the old man aside from three facts: She has to shake the police with whom she is now living; she was never trained by the U.S. Marines during a war to avoid the enemy as a scout-sniper; and she simply doesn't have the audacity of Sheldon Horowitz.

The first is circumstantial, the second is beyond consideration, and the third . . . well . . . it invites an interesting question:

"What would Sheldon do?" Sigrid asks aloud.

"Huh?"

"I said, 'What would Sheldon do?'" Sigrid repeats.

"Who's Sheldon?" asks Melinda, not glancing away from a doctor show on TV.

"A man who always seemed to find a way."

"Maybe we should hire him," she says.

As Melinda watches *House* on television, Sigrid uses the laptop to find what she needs. Her plan is simple—ditch Melinda—but it seems to require an unusual recipe of information, including satellite imagery, some luck with line-of-sight considerations from Target's parking lot, reasonable nighttime ambient temperatures, train timetables, and a prostitute. This all takes time to look up. In the meantime, she hears Dr. House yelling, "If her DNA was off by one percentage point, she'd be a dolphin!"

After ten minutes her plan has come together: She knows what to do, where to go, and how to get there. All she needs to do now is send a text message to Juliet, which she does.

Melinda laughs.

"Good show?" Sigrid asks.

"I think Hugh Laurie is sexy. Don't you?"

A SLY ONE

WHEN YOU ASKED me what time Target closes," says Melinda from the driver's seat of the patrol car, thirty minutes later, "it hadn't occurred to me that you were actually wanting to come back here tonight."

"Are you paid overtime for this?" Sigrid asks.

Melinda makes a thoughtful if sour face and says, "That's a good question."

"I'll suggest it to Irv."

According to the dashboard, the ambient temperature in the parking lot outside Target at 9:48 p.m. is 18 degrees Celsius, or 65 degrees Fahrenheit, which is about as warm as it gets in the daytime in Oslo. Behind Target is a fence that keeps children and hobos from wandering along the single operating railroad track that cuts across the county, far inland, parallel to the St. Lawrence.

Inside the superstore, staff wear beige trousers with the same pleats no one in Norway has worn since the Thompson Twins were ascendant. Their polo neck T-shirts are crimson red, and though it is night, and though the store is nearly empty, each cashier sports a smile of

unnatural permanence. Above them, the store is lit with a checker-
board of rectangular lights through a dropped ceiling, shining down
on a polished linoleum so clean it could warm the heart of a prison
warden.

Sigrid watches a woman push a red cart holding two flatscreen TVs
and a bag of school clothes.

Another heavy woman with thick ankles dotted with pimples is
holding up what appears to Sigrid to be identical pairs of beige panties, each large enough to cradle a bowling ball. Through a pair of
frameless reading glasses she is reading the fine print on the satin tags.
She looks up at Sigrid to read her face as they pass each other.

A nighttime news program is showing on twenty widescreen tele-
visions. A distinguished man with a deep, calming voice is present-
ing a new NBC/*Wall Street Journal* poll putting Barack Obama three
points ahead of John McCain in the presidential elections.

Sigrid's plan to shake Melinda is subtle and simple, and was proven
effective years ago against a woman who was also smart, driven, but
inexperienced: herself. Nine years back, in 1999, Sigrid was working a
city beat and had slowly followed a woman through the Glas Magasi-
net department store on Stortorvet in the city center across from the
Oslo Domkirke. The woman—a drug addict—had grabbed a Michael Kors handbag and stuffed it with perfume, leather gloves, and
wallets. Sigrid pursued her undramatically through the store with the
intent of making eye contact, telling her to stop, defusing the situation, and taking her quietly into custody.

Sigrid reasoned that as a druggie with money issues—and possibly psychological ones—the woman was probably used to being followed around for one reason or other. And so when she started walking faster through the woman's clothing section in the direction of
the bathrooms, Sigrid radioed to her colleague, Lukas, and told him
to meet her outside the small bathroom hallway on the third floor that
had only one way in and therefore only one out.

"Stay here," she'd told Lukas, who took position at the choke point
of the hallway as Sigrid walked confidently down the hall and into the
women's restroom. After a thorough search, she found it completely

empty: no open windows, stalls empty, no storage closets, no space under the sinks.

"Did she come out?" Sigrid asked Lukas when she emerged.

"No."

"Changed her clothing?"

"No one came out."

"She must not have gone in," Sigrid concluded.

"Or she turned into a bird and flew out the third-story window," Lukas said.

"I don't like either option."

"Let's pretend it didn't happen," Lukas suggested.

"All evidence suggests that it didn't," said Sigrid.

She'd been stupid. She knew that. So had Lukas. But over the years she'd also come to appreciate how pervasive and deep our learning is, whether it is helpful to our condition or not. Now she knows better. And she knows how to put that understanding to use.

Sigrid stands with her hands in her trousers, messenger bag over her shoulder, watching a Panasonic TV that has a sharper picture than the one next to it. Melinda arrives beside her—armed and in uniform —and places her hands inside her own pockets too. Obama's lips are moving. The closed-captioned text says he's talking about hope.

"You have a strange way of looking for your brother," Melinda says, immobile.

"What do you think about this?" Sigrid asks, nodding toward the election polling.

"I think McCain's gonna win."

"Why?"

"Because Obama's black."

"The polls are all saying Obama's going to win."

"I think Fox News is right. I think that in the privacy of the voting booth, white people just won't pull the lever for the black candidate. I wish things were different. But I've learned a lot recently about how things really are. And they aren't good."

"Who do you want to win?"

"I'm on the fence. I like the idea of more local government and less federal. McCain seems like a pretty regular guy while Obama seems like a fancy lawyer with all the right words. But McCain thinks everything's just fine out there all by itself and all we need to do is leave things alone. I know that's not true. Broken things don't fix themselves. Obama gets that part. I guess I'm OK either way."

"Tell me about what happened to Lydia's nephew. Jeffrey."

Melinda averts her eyes. "He was a little boy playing with his friends outside while his mom was doing the dishes. Two cops showed up like they were a SWAT team and blew him away. The grand jury decided it was a clean shooting because the cap gun looked real and the cops acted according to the rules."

"Do you agree?"

"The police union, the commissioner, the departments—they're all saying it was a good shooting."

"That's not what I asked," Sigrid says.

"Irv said it happened in the next county and we're to mind our own business and focus on Lydia."

"That wasn't my question either."

"I think America's screwed either way."

"What does that mean?"

"If the grand jury had decided it was a bad shooting, it would mean we have a police force that can't tell the difference between right and wrong. And if they call it a clean shooting, it means we have a whole country that can't. But no one cares what I think."

"Does the sheriff feel the same way you do?"

"Irv went to talk to Lydia's parents. They're Jeffrey's grandparents too. They've been through hell. He went there to pay his respects and learn more about Lydia. He came back all quiet. And then he talked to the police commissioner. And then Reverend Fred Green. And after all that . . . all he wants to do is talk to Marcus. I guess the situation is pretty . . . well, you know."

Sigrid checks her watch. It's almost time.

"I have to go to the bathroom."

"Again?"

"Traveling upsets my stomach."

"All right."

Sigrid moves briskly toward the bathroom.

"That bad?" she hears Melinda ask behind her.

Sigrid ducks through the aisles and around whirling carousels of marked-down shirts and skirts. She rounds a bend filled with humidifiers and dehumidifiers in equal numbers. She enters the hallway for the restrooms, checks her distance from Melinda — about twenty meters — and makes her move.

Melinda stands watching Obama's lips move as Sigrid turns the corner into the bathrooms. Melinda didn't know Jeffrey Simmons's shooter but she'd heard his name: Roy Carman. Jefferson County is pretty big, area-wise, but the cops tend to know each other and there's a policy of trying to get people to know each other across the county lines. Barbecues, picnics, pickup softball . . . that sort of thing. Roy had attended high school two towns over, and had graduated from the police academy three years before Melinda. Rumors among Melinda's colleagues at the office were that Roy had attention deficit disorder, was known for having a short temper, and liked to listen to right-wing talk radio, which he often quoted. He always banged on about personal responsibility, and law and order, and consequences for actions, and that sort of seesaw thinking that made the world tilt only one way and only so far.

When she listens to other cops talk, every argument about shooting Jeffrey sounds both reasonable and incomplete to her at the same time. Somehow, though, she can't put her finger on the missing ingredient that explains what's wrong with the actions except for the outcome.

Melinda was born in the small town of Harrisville, New York, which has a population of under 650 people. It was clean, gentle, and unassuming, but not the sort of place a young woman could fulfill her dreams or ambitions. It wasn't a town that gave her a national perspective let alone a global one, and life wasn't so much about trying to change history as it was pushing through the day-to-day and trying to hold the line on being a decent person while doing it. This involved fighting the small-time battles of family arguments, alcoholism, and unemployment, and pressing back against the atrophy of all things built by man—car transmissions, truck engines, roofing, potholes. The move to the sheriff's office after the police academy was a godsend for her, and working for a boss like Irv, who not only had a college education but a master's degree to boot in something involving Latin and Greek, well, that turned Melinda into a disciple. Still, for all that, it never much occurred to her that a local police shooting —even one caught on video camera—might actually be noticed by people living in foreign countries across the ocean.

Melinda watches Obama talk about the economy. She can't hear him but she can see him and read along. She feels his confidence, and body language, and sense of purpose. He's a man with somewhere to go and he wants America to give him the chance and come along. He could be holding a flute and skipping through a village.

In Jefferson County alone there had been almost two dozen police shootings that had left someone dead. Eighty percent of those dead were black despite fewer than ten percent of the population being black. Everyone knew something was off, but event by event, every shooting sounded right and reasonable. But how could that be?

A colleague had shown her the footage of the Rodney King beating. It was before her time. She wasn't even ten years old when that happened so she didn't remember it, but the folklore and his famous appeal still floated around the office, and eventually Melinda was pulled into it.

A nice guy she knew—who went by Wilky—tried to explain why King deserved every smack he got. He played the beating in slow motion the way the lawyers had done. At that speed, at that magnification, it all seemed right and reasonable. But when it was over and Wilky left her alone with the video, she played it over and over at full speed and it all felt wrong.

Wilky had made it sound like each cop had been left without a choice, and had a tough decision to make, blow by blow. But at full speed, she simply watched a guy getting the crap beaten out of him by people who were winding up for the nice strike—their batons bouncing off King's pulverized muscles and joints.

Jeffrey's death had really upset her. Jeffrey wasn't a criminal. He wasn't even an adult. And even people who are both aren't supposed to be treated like that by law enforcement. Jeffrey was just a little boy playing make-believe with his friends. And then a man who was sworn to protect him showed up on his lawn and killed him. And after that, the grand jury decided not to even hold a trial to see if there'd been a mistake made, let alone negligence or manslaughter or worse.

It didn't make sense, but she couldn't figure out what part was out of balance. People talked about "institutionalized racism" on TV and seemed pretty passionate about it, but it didn't make immediate sense to her; didn't all that end after segregation? Now that the laws are the same, aren't we all just responsible for our own actions? Melinda didn't doubt that there were racists and bigots. But doesn't it all come down to what they do, not what they think? The angry people on the news sure didn't think so, and every time Melinda thought of bringing this up with one of the black cops, she's lost her nerve. No one wants to looks stupid on purpose.

Now she had a Norwegian police chief looking at the same thing. Maybe Irv was onto something with that Bible stuff; maybe Sigrid could see the world through different eyes and understand something they couldn't. Even if she couldn't, though, it felt strange having a foreigner ask her about Jeffrey. It made her feel uneasy and ashamed. It also made Jeffrey's death feel larger; like eyes from around the world were watching upstate New York through a one-way mirror and judging her and everyone she knew. Maybe it's a good thing; maybe this is what they needed. Witnesses.

Obama has stopped talking and now there is an advertisement for dishwashing detergent. She's had enough with this late-night shopping and bathroom-waiting and babysitting. Irv told her that Sigrid was probably going to try to give her the slip somehow, so her job was to keep an eye on her, but this was taking forever.

You had to sympathize with a woman who had the runs, though. Traveling can be tough on the belly.

Melinda glances over her shoulder to aisle seven. Without taking her eyes off the restroom hall for more than a moment or two, she grabs some Kaopectate, Pepto, and Imodium and heads toward the bathroom. She walks down the short hall and steps into the women's room. There's a line of four sinks on her right and four stalls to the left.

"Sigrid, I've got some stuff that might help."

Nothing.

"Sigrid?"

Melinda bends down and looks under the stall doors for feet.

"Sigrid, come on. Not funny. I'm being a good sport here. I don't want to touch the bathroom the floor or crouch down or anything."

Melinda opens each stall: every one is empty.

There is a small horizontal window on the far wall—big enough for a message in a bottle and little else—that's encrusted with spider webs and bugs. There is no utility closet.

"Well, that's impressive," Melinda says to no one.

Using the radio on her belt she calls in as she exits the restroom and heads back to the main concourse.

"Cory?" she says to the microphone on her shoulder. "It's Melinda. Tell Irv the Norwegian pulled a Houdini at Target."

"Gave you the slip, Mel?"

"She's a sly one."

"I'll tell Irv."

"Roger that."

Melinda climbs onto a green plastic lawn chair and then onto the round matching table, providing her with a commanding view of the store. There are a dozen shoppers. It is late. Several turn to look at her and Melinda gives them a casual wave. She looks toward the emergency exits in the back, but they aren't open. No fire alarm has been activated and the theft sensors haven't been tripped. Chief Inspector Sigrid Ødegård has made her move.

THE ONE PERCENT

T HE MEGASTORE'S PARKING lot is lit by a grid of lamps that turn the asphalt into a glittering game of chess—one entering its endgame, Sigrid hopes, if her gambit proves successful. Without Melinda in tow, Sigrid jogs to the end of the building and turns the corner on her right, leading to the truck bays and dumpsters where the alley lights are switched off.

The passage smells of stale cigarettes, wet cardboard, and burnt clutch. Ahead, partly hidden from view, Sigrid sees Juliet McKenna standing in the same short purple skirt she wore earlier. She is leaning against the wall at the far end and in the shadows—a place most women would avoid yet she commands. As Sigrid approaches her it is clear she followed through with the arrangement; she's holding a new black leather jacket with a price tag hanging from the inside lining, and a square box containing a motorcycle helmet marked down to a very reasonable $59.96 plus tax.

"You owe me two hundred dollars," Juliet now tells her. "Sixty for the helmet, plus tax, one hundred and twenty for the jacket, plus tax, and two hundred for doing your shopping in the middle of my shift.

That's what's called the opportunity cost tax. That's on top of the two hundred you gave me last time."

"That's a hundred and eighty I owe you."

"Fuck you."

"Here's the two hundred," Sigrid says, removing two crisp bills from her wallet. "I wasn't sure you'd come."

"It's called 'work for money,' honey. It's all the rage these days."

"Still."

"You want to tell me why I'm doing this?" Juliet asks.

"No," says Sigrid.

"I don't want to get in trouble."

Sigrid is pressed for time and her internal clock is spinning, but even so, she's certain that her confusion is legitimate. "You spend your time working as a prostitute but in the last twenty minutes all you've done is buy two items at a department store. What are you going to get in trouble for?"

"But I don't know why, do I? I don't know what you need them for. I don't know where you're going. I don't know what your plan is, do I? And where's the bike? Who the fuck needs a helmet without a motorcycle? I don't see Evel Knievel waitin' here in his jumpsuit to give you a ride."

"Thanks for your help."

"Where are you going next?"

"You can keep the change."

"I want to know what your plan is."

"OK."

"I'm not your bitch."

"Thanks again."

Sigrid pulls the tag from the rocker-styled leather jacket and slips it on. It fits surprisingly well. She zips it up to where the collar flares before tearing open the square box, removing the helmet, and tossing the packaging into a dumpster.

The new items look regrettably unused and Sigrid is not unaware of this, but they will have to do; men in bars are not terribly good critical thinkers anyway.

With the sling bag taut to her shoulder, she glances back a final time to make sure Melinda hasn't caught up to her before making her way into the open parking lot and toward the biker bar across the street fronted by a row of Harley-Davidsons.

"I hope you're not going into that bar!" Juliet yells after her. "Those are One Percenters. You're just fresh meat to those motherfuckers!" but Sigrid is out of earshot and en route to the Inferno.

"Dumb-ass foreign bitch," Juliet mutters.

When Sigrid was three months into her first stint as a detective, she was asked if she wanted to get her hands dirty with some "real police work." Hans Andersen was her captain and it was a rhetorical question, because her hunger was palpable.

Hans's office smelled like black currant syrup. Most people drank coffee or tea, but Hans had a sweet tooth and hated caffeine. Oslo's winters were no warmer for him, though, so he'd defrost by pouring boiling water into the *saft* and then pouring that into himself; the scent was in everything.

He called Sigrid in and explained the proposition.

"I've got two cases here. You get to choose. Both are undercover. The first is a Swedish motorcycle gang running cigarettes from Poland into Norway by land. There's some reason to think they might also be filling up the empty trucks over here with stolen goods, including bicycles, motorcycles, and baby strollers and bringing them back to Poland."

"Baby strollers?"

"Three hundred and forty-six baby strollers have been stolen across Oslo in the last ten months."

"That's despicable," Sigrid said.

"So I'm thinking you want this one."

"What's the other choice?"

"Lithuanian diaper smugglers."

"Again?"

"Lithuanian diaper smugglers."

"I'm ready."

"Apparently . . . and this is from a commissioned research study by the Norwegian Institute for International Affairs, or NUPI . . . diapers are much cheaper here than in Lithuania. I do wonder why we needed to commission a study for this rather than just call one of their supermarkets and ask . . ." Hans faded out for a moment. He often did that, hoping the insight would fade and leave his career unspoiled. When he returned he said, "And so the Lithuanians are buying our diapers cheap and smuggling them into Lithuania, where they sell them for a mark-up, which is still at below-market prices and they're not paying the import duties."

"It isn't illegal to buy diapers in Norway. Why is this our problem?"

"It isn't, but the Foreign Ministry has received a request for assistance from Vilnius and we're meant to assist in an international sting operation because tax evasion hurts us all and usually we're the ones with the higher taxes."

"Lithuanian diaper smugglers," Sigrid says.

"Sorry?"

"I wanted to say it once myself."

"So . . . you prefer the bikers?"

"Yes, sir."

Her assignment had been to pose as a corrupt customs official expecting a kickback from the bikers. In order to gain their trust she needed to talk about motorcycles with them at bars.

Sigrid had known nothing about motorcycles generally, and less than nothing about Harley-Davidsons specifically aside from their popularity with miscreant subcultures. In preparation for the assignment she was made to memorize their eclectic names (Glides, Softails, Sportsters), their shapes and engine displacements, years of manufacture, and distinctive repair issues. It nearly bored her to tears. But by the end she could talk a good game.

Her most unexpected observation in studying for her outlaw motorcycle gang exam was how all the clubs adopted American tropes about freedom, individuality, and rebellion and then demanded complete conformity to them. It was her first glimpse into the complex system that organized American culture—even when it was being exported to Scandinavia.

The cigarette runners in question were part of an antiquated club that had survived the Great Nordic Biker War of the mid-1990s, which left a dozen or so dead, about a hundred wounded, and a whole bunch charged with attempted murder across Norway, Sweden, and Denmark. Her undercover work was part of a cross-border task force that wasn't nearly as intense or risky as it had been for the senior officers, years ago, who'd infiltrated the ranks and helped set up new intelligence networks. But it was risky enough, especially for a first foray into undercover work.

Sigrid wraps her fingers around the skull-shaped door handle that will open the Gates of Hell to the Inferno. She does not hesitate so much as pause. Draped in leather and surrounded by beards and chrome, she feels as though she's stepping backwards half a decade into that shithole in Västerås, Sweden, northwest of Stockholm, where she was to meet a Norwegian contact. The main difference here is that everyone is speaking English.

"Oh, Marcus," she says to the skull.

She pulls. The handle not only opens the door but pulls with it a cloud of gray tobacco smoke that rises as it hits the outside air and stings her eyes. The orifice to the Inferno looks less like an entrance than something you'd throw a virgin into to appease an angry god, but Sigrid presses through the sulfur and brimstone—helmet dangling from one arm—as some kind of death metal pounds a dark rhythm around her legs, threatening to pull her into shadow. The door closes behind her, leaving her inside a bar that smells of grease and unwashed, bearded men. Behind the bar, in a frame, is a black piece of cloth with a patch on it that says THE 1%.

Sigrid recalls that expression from reading the Norwegian newspaper. There it referenced the world's richest people. Here it seems to mean something else.

The clubhouse is busy but not crammed. Everyone is dressed in a version of the same uniform, carefully calibrated to blend in rather than stand out. Confederate flags are more popular here than Sigrid might have expected this far north in the United States, but culture isn't bound by location. A quarter of the bikers are women and none of them is young. With her own tired countenance, dirty hair, and glazed eyes Sigrid feels well-camouflaged aside from not showing as much cleavage as seems to be the norm, and weighing significantly less than most of the women. She leaves the jacket on so she doesn't upstage the competition.

There is an empty barstool beside a woman wearing black chaps over jeans and a black tank-top—the ribbed neck cut off to show the tops of her breasts—that reads CHOPPER. Sigrid sits in it and turns to her:

"I need a ride," she says.

The woman pulls from her beer, her eyes dulled by the future she can easily imagine. She glances at Sigrid, sees nothing interesting, and turns back to the television above the bar showing a sporting event.

"I don't do women."

"Someone stole my bike and I think a cop is following me," Sigrid says. "I've got to disappear. I need a ride."

"I don't know you. What kind of accent is that?"

The wrinkles around CHOPPER's eyes become mascara-black as she squints at Sigrid. There is a beer sud parked on her upper lip.

"Sweden," Sigrid lies. "I'll ask someone else." Sigrid places her palms on the counter and has begun to shift her weight when the woman says, "Aryan, huh?"

Sigrid sits back down on the barstool.

"What's in it for the rider?" CHOPPER asks her. "I might know a guy."

"Money and gratitude."

The woman makes a practiced and unflattering noise.

"I'm going south of Malone," Sigrid says. "The cops are in the parking lot. I need to slip out now."

"You might as well stay. This is the last place they're going to look," she says, ordering another beer and a shot.

"They know I'm around here someplace. Aside from Target it's the most obvious place to look."

"I didn't say they don't know where you are. I said it's the last place they're gonna come inside to look."

A DEPRESSING SPOT

SHERIFF IRVING WYLIE sits alone in his 1989 Jeep Wagoneer in the parking lot of Target, sipping from a safety mug filled with coffee and listening to a bluegrass band on NPR. He stares out the windshield into the darkness as the folks at Target start to close the shop up for the night.

Melinda opens the passenger-side door and slips into the beige leather seat beside him.

"Spot her?" Melinda asks, scanning the parking lot.

"Walked right out the front door," says Irv, gesturing. "Jogged along there, and turned into that dark spot at the corner."

"Cory pick her up on the back side?"

"She was in the alley for a bit and then he watched her cross the two hundred yards from the ally to the Inferno," Irv says, turning down the music. "Cory says she's in there right now."

"Maybe we should call the coroner now, save some time," says Melinda.

"I'm not so sure. Cory got a good view of her from his position and says she emerged wearing a black leather jacket and carrying a motorcycle helmet; two things she did not have when she slipped the surly bonds of the parking lot. A minute later, Juliet McKenna walks out of the same alley—here on my side—leans her boobs into a Honda Accord, and drives off with the guy."

"Huh," says Melinda.

"That's what I said."

"How does Sigrid know Juliet?"

"They met at Marcus's place before she came over to us asking for help."

"Hard to see them as friends. Not exactly the same type," Melinda says.

"Hardly," says Irv. "What we're learning about Chief Sigrid is that she plans ahead and plays everything close to the vest. When you called back Professor Williamson while Sigrid was sleeping . . . what did he say again?"

"Said they were talking about the Adirondacks and how much Marcus liked it out there."

"And he specifically directed her to Saranac Lake?"

"Yeah. She's definitely going to the 'Dacks, Sheriff. Can't quite figure out how, though. She still in the bar, you said?"

"Yes. You can see the entrance with the binoculars." Irv glances at Melinda and smiles. "You were supposed to let her get away, but you're telling me she actually skipped you?"

"Went into the bathroom and disappeared like a ghost."

"Which one?"

"By the bras and stuff."

"You didn't go in with her?"

"Waited at the end of the hall."

Irv chuckles at her. "That old chestnut. You figure it out yet?"

"No."

"Keep trying. Oh, look, there she is," Irv says, jutting his chin toward the window and raising the binoculars. "Climbing onto that Roadking. You see her?"

"How can you tell it's her?" Melinda asks, watching a woman in a black leather jacket and helmet settle into the pillion seat on the Harley.

"Three reasons. She walked out the door with the helmet on. No one does that. Next, none of these bikers use a full-face helmet. They all ride in shorties and open-face gear. She's trying to cover her face and probably protect her head, too. And lastly . . . just look at her. That jacket and helmet are sparkling, they're so new."

"That's some real Sherlock stuff, Sheriff."

"The truth is, Melinda, she's got a nice and upscale wiggle to her tush that has never been seen walking into or out of that place before. Don't give me a look. It's nothing the pope wouldn't'a noticed."

"Wouldn't'a mentioned it, though."

"That's probably true," Irv admits.

The biker who owns the Harley is talking with a fat man in a brown leather vest and fingerless gloves. Sigrid is sitting with her feet on the foot pegs, waiting for movement. It is probably her imagination, but Melinda can almost feel Sigrid's anxiety about wanting to get on the road.

"Being so smart and everything," Melinda says, "I'm surprised she didn't see this coming. Us setting her up like this and everything."

"Her mistake was underestimating us," Irv says.

"Why do you think that happened?"

"It's the cowboy boots, Melinda. No one has ever overestimated the intellect of a man in cowboy boots. That's why I wear them. I always liked that Everyman edge Columbo had. You remember Columbo?"

"No."

"Doesn't matter. All right, they're about to head off. Get out of here. I'll see you after I catch up to her."

Melinda opens the heavy door of the Wagoneer and slides to the asphalt. Before closing the door, she says, "She knows about Jeffrey Simmons. She's been asking about him."

"It was bound to come up. It doesn't affect anything. We need to find Marcus. So does she."

"You really think her brother did it? That apple would've had to have fallen pretty far from the family tree if she's any indication. Given her upscale tush and all."

"Marcus and Lydia were lovers during an emotional time. Anything could have happened. That's the whole point of the investigation, Melinda. Now go home to bed. You did good tonight. Aside from . . . you know . . . losing her and everything."

"Drive safe, Sheriff."

She slams the door and walks back to her patrol car under the towering lamps of the parking lot.

Irv fastens his seatbelt and starts up the car, leaving the lights off. The rider is a mountain of a man in short sleeves wearing a Kaiser helmet with a spike on top. He pulls out of the parking lot, the Harley's flatulent pipes filling the night with hostility.

"Damn bikers," Irv says to himself.

He puts some field glasses to his eyes to get a better look at the make and model in case he has any trouble tailing them. It's a custom job with leather panniers on the back and a sissy bar and Sigrid.

Irv puts the Wagoneer into gear, checks that he has a full tank, and urges its V8 after the Harley while keeping at a respectful distance. On his way out of the lot and onto the dark road, he turns up the radio. Gillian Welch and David Rawlings are playing "Revelator." Their harmony is almost unnerving. It occurs to him that if he'd found even a measure of that with his ex-wife they'd still be married.

On the back of the Harley, staring at the white skull painted on the back of the idiot's helmet, Sigrid again asks herself why any woman would choose a view like this rather than just ride the damn thing herself.

Two hundred dollars she had to pay this Neanderthal, and upfront, for the forty-minute ride through back roads to a bus stop in a place called Nicholville.

The biker reins in his hog outside a deserted brick building beside a split-lane road with signs for Greyhound. A cigarette machine and a Coke machine buzz under a corrugated roof nearby. Behind the building is a forest, dense and black. There is no other structure in sight beyond the road itself, the telephone poles, and the drooping wires that even the birds have abandoned.

"Who are your people?" the man asks.

"Thanks for the ride, we're done," Sigrid says, removing her helmet.

"I asked you a question."

"My people have patches on their vests that say 'The Filthy Few.' You don't. You even speak again," Sigrid says, "and it's going to cost you."

The man snorts and looks her over. He's obviously much stronger than she is and could overpower her easily if given the chance, but she's certain she's faster. Sigrid concentrates on his exposed throat. This is what she'll strike if he makes a move. No one fights well with a broken trachea.

Without taking his eyes off her, he starts the bike again, revs the engine a half dozen times for dramatic effect, and peels out leaving her alone in Americana.

Across the road there is a field of black grass that moves to a breeze too far away to reach her. If she closes her eyes, and waits long enough, maybe it will.

In time, when her pulse slows and she allows the coolness of the night to settle her mood, she opens her eyes again and looks across the street to the field. There is a forest silhouetted behind it, and above, a mountain range of clouds lit on their edge by the fiery white light cast by the unseen moon. Streaks of navy blue and cobalt trim the clouds. Sigrid sits alone on the bench, the helmet and sling bag beside her, resting her neck and shoulders. At least now she's alone and free to find her big brother.

"You forgot your guitar," she'll say to him when she finds him.

"I know," he'll answer.

"The one I bought for you."

The clouds create the illusion of mountains but in fact the land around her is flat. Should the weather turn, the rain will fall hard and flood the field. There is a heaviness now. Night rain always feels intimate to her; a chance to be washed by a secret. The sound against the clay tiles on the roof. The drip into the gutter. The soft stream of water outside the window, the rivulets dancing black on the ceiling surrounded by the yellow glow of the streetlamp. Night rain feels to Sigrid like a vestige from when the world was new and there were no people here and the planet had only itself; its own cycles and rhythms and changes, going on and on for a billion years without witnesses or someone to put those experiences into words.

She sits there watching the clouds, waiting for them to break open so the moon—half full—might appear and take her back to her farm with her father and maybe farther back in time to when her family was whole and everything felt complete. But the moon does not come, nor does the rain, and instead a heavy light breaks through the darkness and a truck drives up the road the way she first came. Instead of moving on, though, the truck slows until it blocks the view of everything that was in front of her and finally rolls to a crunching halt.

The window drops on the driver's side and from the shadow of that space comes a talking elbow:

"This is one depressing spot you've selected for yourself."

"You're a shit," Sigrid says to Sheriff Irving Wylie.

"I know it."

Sigrid doesn't move and Irv juts his elbow out the window. "The bus out here doesn't run until five in the morning. It's . . ."—Irv checks his watch—". . . not even one. What were you planning to do here for four hours?"

"I was going to read a book."

"It's darker than a witch's soul out here."

"Not all my plans work out."

"Neither do mine. But I'm on a roll tonight."

Sigrid does not move or reply, and Irv shakes his head. "Want to get some coffee?"

Irv sees that Sigrid does not understand him. "There's a diner up the road near Malone. Coffee's on the menu."

"It's one in the morning."

"It's open twenty-four/seven. They keep the coffee flowing like it's coffee. You don't have twenty-four-hour diners in Norway?"

Sigrid still does not move.

"Don't be like that," he says.

"I don't see how we can work together, Sheriff."

"That's funny, because I don't see how we can avoid it, Chief."

Irv turns on his hazard lights and opens the door but does not step out. Instead he swings his legs around and rests his elbows on his knees. "Here's how I figure it, Sigrid. You probably have a good sense of where your brother is. You figured that out in twenty-four hours, whereas we came up with bupkis after two weeks. So . . . well done. But now we know too. Saranac Lake. Or thereabouts. How, you wonder? I instructed Melinda to give you some space at the university to ask your own questions and then we circled back and called the professor afterward to get him to snitch on you. It was pretty sneaky of me, but I told you that I have faith in your love for your brother, and clearly it wasn't misplaced. What happens now, Chief Sigrid, is we get you a nice Monte Cristo sandwich with local maple syrup to warm you up, and together we find a way to bring him in all nice and easy. Otherwise, the local sheriff isn't going to have any choice but to call in SWAT or an emergency response team to surround Saranac Lake —where there are families on vacation with children—and we hope to God your brother didn't bring a rifle with the intention of living off the fat of the land so he could stay away from ATM machines and their little cameras. Does he know how to shoot?"

"He's not violent and he doesn't care for guns. The crime you accused him of doesn't even involve a gun."

"But he grew up on a farm. I don't know anyone who grew up on a farm who can't shoot a rifle at least. Maybe it isn't true, but it will be a perception shared by SWAT. So it comes down to this: It's you and me working together, or it's SWAT in full crazy mode. Because there are pressures on me you don't understand, and I need to get to Marcus before our little world up here catches fire. It really is more flammable than it looks."

GODLESS COMMUNISTS
IN AMERICAN DINERS

HE DINER IS called Diner if it is called anything at all. In Sigrid's eyes, it is the kind of place where nothing good was ever intended to happen and probably won't. It is set back from the road and buffered by an asphalt parking lot. The façade is fake stone painted white and the roof is rimmed with a white fence that almost but does not entirely fail to hide a giant air-conditioning unit mounted beside an angular sheet-metal chimney. Walking in, Sigrid sees four solitary patrons staring blankly through the large windows at the road, beyond the parking lot from which they came and will later go again—their pasts and futures looking identical from their perches on red Naugahyde.

The patrons are male and the wait staff not. The men sit on stools all wearing beige or blue trousers. Thick belts peek out from shirttails floating above bulging waists. They hunch over food that is making them sicker and older but tastes familiar and comforting and reminds them of happier times when they were not here.

Sigrid and Irv take seats in a booth—their own unique piece of American real estate.

A white waitress without an expression appears with two pitchers of coffee that hug her hips like misbegotten twins — one caffeinated, the other not. Irv raises a finger to the brown one and the woman pours its soul into a cup trimmed with a single red stripe. Sigrid says nothing and the woman pours for her on the assumption that anyone here would need coffee.

Irv removes two maroon vinyl tomes from their pinned position between the ketchup and napkin dispenser and hands one to Sigrid.

"What's this?" she asks.

"The menu."

Sigrid opens it. It contains a thousand options ranging from T-bone steak to blueberry pancakes.

"They have all this?"

"Yes," says Irv.

"At one in the morning?"

"Yes," says Irv.

"How?"

"I don't know."

Irv orders a toasted corn muffin and a glass of apple juice. Sigrid reads about a bagel with "lox."

"What's that?"

"Smoked salmon. I think it's Yiddish. Now it's American."

"Laks, L-A-K-S, is the Norwegian word for salmon."

"Aren't Yiddish and Norwegian both basically German?"

"No."

"OK."

Sigrid orders it and settles into her booth. Irv removes a map from his black canvas bag and spreads it out over the table. It displays the northern region of the Adirondacks.

"How were you going to find him?" Irv asks her.

"How were you going to find him?" Sigrid asks.

"Manpower. Wanted posters, a hundred cops, interviews, show his face around, circle him, surround him at night. Throw in some dogs. We have sweaters from his house. No one ever washes sweaters. Those armpits are like ambrosia to the bloodhounds. But you don't have manpower or dogs. You're alone. How was that going to work?"

"Differently."

"Why don't you trust me?" Irv asks her. He shifts his weight into the corner by the window and lifts his right leg onto the bench.

"Tell me about Jeffrey Simmons," Sigrid says.

"Melinda said you were curious about that. How's that connected to your brother?"

"Through Lydia Jones," Sigrid says.

"OK, but not directly. Jeffrey was shot. It was tragic. Months later, Lydia falls to her death and your brother was right there. And Chuck. And the phone call. I'm not seeing a connection between Jeffrey's tragedy and Lydia's."

"Are you sure?" Sigrid asks.

"I'm sure that I have no reason to think there is."

"Which isn't the same thing."

"True. But I have no reason to suspect that Lydia Jones's death is connected to the missing Lindberg baby either, though I accept that the world has invisible levers and the universe is a vast and complex thing. Why are we talking about this?"

"Whether or not Lydia's death is connected to Jeffrey's might be a secondary issue to whether Jeffrey's death is connected to Marcus's circumstances."

"You've entirely lost me."

"What worries me, Irving, is trigger-happy cops shooting people for no reason. That's the . . ." — Sigrid pauses for a term — "the thing they have in common that connects them."

"The common denominator between Jeffrey and Marcus?"

"Right. You can see why that might interest me in a manhunt for my brother who is suspected of murder."

"That isn't a concern in this case."

"Is it because my brother is white?"

"That's unfair."

"To whom?"

"Been here for two days and you have America all figured out, huh?

That's very European of you, you know that? You aren't the first tourist who's passed through here pissing on the trees."

"I've read about the Jeffrey Simmons case," Sigrid says. "Roy Carman is a racist murderer with a badge. Which happens. What's inexplicable is why the grand jury didn't even consider the case worthy of going to court, let alone did a court find him guilty and get him off the street."

Irv lifts a butter knife and spins it across the thick of his palm the way Sigrid had seen schoolmates do with pens back home. As he performs the trick he stares at Sigrid.

"Jeffrey Simmons may have been young," Irv says quietly, "but he was five foot eight inches tall. That's about your height. He was wearing a black hooded sweatshirt with the name of a rap gang on it, and he was wearing dark glasses. It would have been impossible for anyone to know what age he was without standing right in front of him or talking to him. He was holding a toy gun, yes. But it was not a pink water pistol. It was a realistic-looking object. Roy Carman, something of a hothead, responded to a call from a neighbor saying she saw a black man in a hood carrying—and I'm quoting here—'what looks like a gun,' unquote. Seeing two children running from this mystery figure when he arrived, Roy threw himself into harm's way, burst from the car, and told the perp to drop the weapon. Jeffrey did not drop the weapon, and Roy engaged him with his service pistol. The result was tragic. No question. But it is not obvious where he made an error in action or judgment. It was just bad luck."

"Jeffrey was pretending to be a character from a storybook. His luck would have been different if he'd been white."

"Maybe," he concedes. "But unfortunately Jeffrey was the exact profile of what we arrest around here at a disproportionately high rate: African American males between seventeen and twenty-five wearing either gang or rap-related clothing."

"There's a difference between the general and the particular," she says.

"Yes, there is. But the space between them is a universe of problems."

"Let me tell you what I see when I look at this situation, Sheriff," says Sigrid. "I see a little boy playing with his friends on his own front lawn when an armed police officer bursts out of a squad car only meters away and inside of two seconds—that is an actual measure taken from the video camera—murdered that child in front of his mother, who was watching him play from the kitchen window. What I'm telling you—as a police professional and as someone who has commanded armed assaults—is that Jeffrey was dead the moment Roy hit the accelerator in his car rather than the brake at thirty meters away. Because the only reason to drive that close to someone suspicious is to make sure you don't miss when you shoot them. He drove up next to Jeffrey in order to kill him."

"Norwegian police don't even carry guns. What do you really know about it?"

Sigrid leans over the tabletop and speaks in a hushed voice:

"One month ago my partner and I were taking point on an assault at a summer cabin in the woods backed up by our own emergency response team called the *Beredskapstroppen*. They were under my command. Unlike Roy, I stopped my car more than thirty meters from that cabin when someone came out with a knife and ran directly toward me. And in that time I called halt twice before pulling the trigger because it was my sworn obligation as well as my tactical training to defuse the situation rather than intensify it with the use of deadly force. But he didn't halt and so I put two nine-millimeter slugs into that young man's chest because while we do not normally carry guns, we do in fact know how to use them and sometimes we do. But not often. Norwegian police kill civilians in fatal shootings about once every decade. In America? No one even knows. You have no national database on police-involved shootings. You literally don't count the number of people your police kill. And as a community you barely ask questions about it. You think that's civilized?"

"There is a war on the police out there, Sigrid. America is an armed country and we have hardened criminals. Personally, I'm in favor of gun control because I think the opposite of gun control is gun out-of-control and that seems wildly irresponsible. However, all that's immaterial because . . . there are lots and lots of guns out there. Which means we're sworn to serve and protect in a gun-rich environment that makes our jobs scarier. And we're legitimately scared. Anybody would be."

Sigrid sits back in her booth and crosses her arms. She's had this conversation before. And usually with people who simply do not understand numbers.

"I'm assuming you studied criminology?" she says.

"I studied divinity."

"Divinity?"

"Yes. I have a master's degree in divinity from Loyola. I wrote my thesis on something called Accommodation Theory. Every religion, when it spreads out, has to reach some kind of accommodation with whatever's there already, otherwise it won't really stick. The question is how that works and what makes it work or not. Interesting stuff. I focused on the conversion of the Roman Empire to Christianity."

"How do you go from studying ancient Rome to being a cop?"

"You run for office and win. It seemed like it would be fun, and I got tired of using my knowledge of Latin, Greek, and Hebrew to help name pharmaceutical products, which was the job I had previously. And it was fun being sheriff—that is, until you showed up."

"You named pharmaceutical products?"

"I got fired."

"Why?"

"I was getting punchy because most of the products aren't meant to cure you but make you dependent on the treatment, and that seemed wrong. So I ran my big mouth and gave them a name they didn't like."

"Which was what?"

"Puratoxin."

"There is no war on the police in America," she says. "I recently read an article on this. While we don't know how many citizens are killed by the police, we do know how many cops have been killed by criminals. For one thing, the overall number of murdered officers has been dropping in a nice flattening curve since the 1970s. In fact, the last time there really was a war on the police was in the 1920s during Prohibition. What's also interesting is that since the 1970s there has been a growing number of officers. It's almost double what it was then. That means, if you do the math, that the absolute number has dropped and the relative number has plummeted. It is barely more risky today to be a police officer in America than it is to be a citizen in most big cities. Oh, and the crime rate has been going down too. America is safer than ever. But according to the media, the country is doomed. The fact is, Irving, the war on the police is a fabricated lie supported by a misperception. That fabricated lie is complicit in the murder of Jeffrey, because it planted a false idea in the head of the cop with the gun. It's that same idea that puts my brother at risk."

"I'm sorry about the kid too. I know the family. I've been to their house. They are so destroyed that their pastor, Fred Green, doesn't even want . . . Never mind. Look, this is not your fight. Why are you so angry about it?"

Irv's left hand rests on the table. It is a strong hand, like her father's. He has long fingers with no obvious bruises or scars. The veins run prominently across the back of his hand, and his forearms are muscular and yet they seem gentle; hands that are not inclined to violence. Hands that once raised a daughter and patted her bottom and carried her to sleep.

Why *is* she so angry about it?

"I've stood in that moment between Jeffrey and Roy," says Sigrid. "It wasn't the same, but it was close enough that I can see it vividly. Despite being cleared by my department, I am not convinced that I needed to kill Burim because I'm not sure he was really planning to hurt me. I'm not even sure he was conscious at all. The men inside were hardened criminals, and that went as it had to. But outside, on the grass, in front of my car, I could have done more. I could have looked with different eyes. I could have seen more. I could have understood it differently. And if I had, I could have saved his life rather than ended it. I'm no Roy Carman. I'm not guilty of the racially motivated murder of a child. But I'm responsible. I just can't figure out for what. I don't think I ever learned a vocabulary for it. In any language.

It's possible," she says, "that figuring this out is the next big thing that needs to happen. Not only for me, but for everyone."

"I'm sorry that happened to you, Sigrid. I sincerely am. But it was an ambiguous situation. You had to act. Maybe Roy did too. As you said, it was almost the same."

Sigrid really had wanted Burim to halt. To stop. To come to his senses. To see her as someone there to help him. His girlfriend, Adrijana, had been the one that tipped off the police about the gang. She was born in Serbia and adopted in Norway, having been an orphan from the war. Her Norwegian was native and her countenance was that of a young woman from the wealthier part of town — the west end.

Why would a girl like that, a modern girl, a stylish and educated and trusting girl who walked into her police station to help save a lost child, be involved with a young man whom Sigrid would have to shoot like a rabid dog? It didn't make sense. But there he'd been, running toward her with a knife. The analysis and backstory told her that she was not in danger. These were just suppositions, though. Ideas of the mind. Hopes about human nature, hopes about relationships and the kind of people who love, about female judgment and dating bad boys — all of that came from later in evolution. That wasn't the part of her brain that was firing in that moment. She wasn't building conceptual models and running regressions on probability. She wasn't thinking with her cerebral cortex; this was her limbic system kicking in — fight or flight. Eat or be eaten. She had been looking at a man with a knife charging toward her with the inertia of a bear. How could she have been expected to ignore that? She shot him. The nine-millimeter round was not entirely effective, because it had limited stopping power. So she shot him again and this time in the center of the heart.

She has wondered, though: Am I simply exonerating myself by saying that I didn't have the time or resources to think of something better? Could I have stood aside and let him run past, allowing the backup units to later surround him after he was winded and possibly more self-possessed, and feeling less irrational?

And what about Roy? If Jeffrey had had a real gun, a leg shot would not have ended the confrontation. The need to make a decision had been immediate. Wasn't it fair for Irv to make the case that the police officer was doing his best?

Yes. It would have been fair. Irv was right.

If.

If the very same officer were to ignore the laughter of the other children, and the presence of the woman in the kitchen window casually washing dishes, and the relaxed expression on her face as she watched her son frolic on her property with his friends, and the youthfulness of Jeffrey's movements and body language, and the time between the emergency phone call and the actual confrontation—almost fifteen minutes—during which time nothing bad had happened when that same officer arrived.

If you ignore everything observable that would have contradicted Roy's presumptions, then of course it would have been fair to say he had only been doing his best. Are we really saying that officers should not be held accountable to situational assessment? To specificity? To actual reality?

Ambiguous?

"No, Irv," Sigrid says as the waitress takes a hamburger to a patron who receives it without pleasure. "My situation was ambiguous because Burim was charging toward me with a knife and didn't respond to my calls to halt. There was no time delay and there was nothing else I could have used as a cue. But for Roy, it was entirely different. You know . . . I've heard people talk about institutionalized racism before. It's one of those terms that floats around these days. But they always talk about it like it's a psychological condition or a ghost in the police machinery. I never really understood what people meant. But in the past month I have stared at that idea, from a Norwegian perspective, in terms of what happened between me and Burim, and now I'm looking at what happened with Roy and Jeffrey. And I think I've come to understand something. This is what I think it means: It means that your policies, your doctrine, your training, your classroom education, your academic credit system, your textbooks, your case studies,

your decision-making tools, your final exams, your grand jury procedures, your measures of success for promotions, the qualities you cel-
ebrate . . . all the tools that institutions use to create professionals and
direct their actions . . . all shift the risk of violence during ambiguous
encounters onto the citizens, but it's the moral duty of the state—the
social contract itself—to better manage and better shoulder that risk.
Because in a democracy, Irv, the citizen cannot live in fear of the state
and its shortcomings. It is simply not acceptable. There has to be a re-
lentless commitment to self-improvement. The case of Jeffrey Simmons was not ambiguous because everything that told the officer that
he wasn't in danger was ignored or interpreted through the fact that
Jeffrey was black. It was the officer—not Jeffrey—who should have
read the situation differently. It was the officer who should have been
trained and required to make that situation unambiguous through
careful measures to protect everyone involved, and especially the people he was sworn to serve and protect. And you should know that."

The corn muffin and bagel arrive.

The corn muffin's mushroom head has been lopped off and the
two sections fried in butter on the grill and then semi-reassembled on
the plate, to be served with two additional pats of butter wrapped in
golden paper that glisten with ice crystals. The bagel has been slath-
ered in cream cheese and heaped with thirty dollars' worth of salmon
for a charge of $4.95 plus mystery-tax. The woman returns with fresh
coffee to the depleted cups and says, "Anything else," in a way that
prevents it from being a question, and walks off.

Irv forgoes the extra butter and rather daintily picks off a piece of
the crisp muffin top and eats it. While chewing he says, "I agree with
you."

"What?"

"I agree with you. American police shoot people. We handle ambiguity badly. We have a tendency to make bad situations worse rather
than doing the opposite. We often attract the wrong kind of blue-
collar kids rather than pulling in top recruits. There's too much cro-
nyism and too many guns. We have a long way to go. The thing is,

Sigrid, we're in a diner in the middle of a black hole and our job is to get through it. If you don't help me find Marcus, I'm worried things will get out of hand. Just like you said. I'm not threatening you. Or him. I'm saying . . . Marcus is in more danger than you know. After Jeffrey, there's a lot of tension out there. The streets are warming up. The commissioner wants Marcus for Lydia's death. The Simmons family wants justice for Lydia too. That means Marcus is being hunted."

"He didn't do it."

"If he resists arrest and gets hurt, no one is going to care. Do you understand?"

"That sounds like a threat," Sigrid says.

"It's not. Saranac Lake is out of my jurisdiction. But I have relationships and friends who can help. I'm your only chance. Like you said, the job is to bring the tension down."

Sigrid bites into her bagel. The salmon is surprisingly good, but there's too much cream cheese.

"So anyway," Irv says, sounding suddenly jovial. "I took an interest in Norway while you were sleeping at Melinda's house. Spent a whole hour on the internet. I read the *Economist, U.S. News and World Report,* Wikipedia, and something about stacking wood. I learned that you invented the cheese slicer—so you get a point for that—but Quisling sold you all out to the Nazis, so that's two points off. On the other hand, your resistance stopped the Germans from building a heavy water reactor, so you get three points for that, almost leaving you in the plus column, but—uh-oh . . . along comes A-ha with 'Take on Me,' which is a really bad song that makes no sense. So minus two. So you're back to zero. Meanwhile, America? We invented jazz, rock–'n'-roll, and chocolate chip cookies. Anyway, it eventually occurred to me that I'm a sheriff, so I just called your chief in Oslo. It was late, but they put me through."

"You did not."

"He's weird."

"Oh no. You did."

"I said I was calling from New York, which I guess he took for the city, and he had questions. He wanted to know why Jews had Jewish last names. As it happens, I know the answer. I explained that, in fact, they didn't have last names until the early nineteenth century when the Austro-Hungarian Empire and Russia insisted they start using them. Until then they used Patronymics and Matronymics. So most of the ones they picked are the ones we associate with Jewish names today. Your chief was very impressed and now we're good buddies and have you in common. He told me all about your case with Sheldon Horowitz. Old marine had you chasing your tail."

"Yeah, well. He was a pretty exceptional guy."

Outside the window four semis and their trailers whiz by in rapid succession.

"Apparently you are a very good police officer, Sigrid, despite being a godless communist in an American diner. Work with me. Tell me how you were planning to find your brother in the big bad forest."

Sigrid picks up Irv's pen and draws a circle around Saranac Lake on the unfolded map. "I wasn't going to look for him, because you're right, I wouldn't have found him—even if the professor was right about his favorite spots. I could pass within ten meters and never know it, especially if he didn't want to be found."

"So?"

"I was going to make him come looking for me."

"How?"

"Eventually Marcus'll need supplies. He's resourceful and experienced outside, but he's no survivalist. While he could very well be in Fiji or Peru by now, I'm guessing he's probably in here . . ." she says, drawing a circle three miles in diameter around Saranac Lake. "If that's true, he'll most likely go to one of these seven supermarkets or hardware stores for supplies within a week at most. My plan was to take a bus to the town, put up pictures of myself on all the bulletin boards and telephone poles around there, make an inside joke in Norwegian that only we'd know, proving it was me, and then I'd leave my phone number. At that point I was going to buy a bicycle to get around and otherwise sit back and wait for him to call while also avoiding you."

Irv sips his apple juice from the purple bendy straw provided. "That's a good plan."

"Yeah."

"It'll still work."

"The first half will."

Irv continues: "It'll be easier to get around with the Wagoneer to put up all the pictures. Actually, I think we can get some of the young'uns to do it. Frank Allman's the sheriff out here. He's a bit soft around the middle but he's all right, and his people can work wonders with staplers." Irv finishes his apple juice with a loud slurp. He uses the end of the straw to chase around the last drops that are settled in the irregularities of the glass. "Sounds like we're going to have a little together time, you and me, as we wait for Marcus to get hungry," says Irv. "What do you think we should do with all that time?"

"Isn't it obvious, Sheriff?"

Irv smiles and leans in. "No. Tell me."

"We are going to find out what actually happened to Professor Lydia Jones."

KING CANUTE

RV DRIVES SIGRID back to Melinda's house, chasing the high beams over black asphalt. They leave the radio off.

Melinda meets them at the door at four thirty a.m. wearing a bathrobe and a vacant stare. Sigrid, unlike her new roommate, is wide awake and caffeinated. She steps inside and makes her way to the guest room, where she flings the messenger bag to the bed, kicks off her shoes, and heads to the bathroom to wash the stink of the biker bar from her hair.

Irv slides into the house gingerly and smiles at Melinda, who does not smile. She slams the door closed behind him with a flick of her wrist and a blink.

"So that all went swimmingly," Irv says to her, checking his watch and rubbing his face.

"Why did you come back here?" Melinda manages to say as her robe falls open to reveal an extra-large Go-Gos concert shirt underneath. "You couldn't get a motel?"

"You kidding? It's creepy out there."

"Of course."

Irv pats her on the shoulder and tells her to come to the office at ten rather than eight and bring Sigrid with her. Though Melinda's eyes are almost completely closed, she still manages to squint out a message of confusion.

"She won't pull an O.J. on us," Irv says. "I converted her. She's on our side now."

"How did that happen?"

"I agreed with everything she said."

"And that worked?"

"Isn't that how you win over any woman?"

"Are you planning to stay too, boss?"

"Me? Hell no, I've got a home. I'll see you both tomorrow."

Irv caught four hours of rack time figuring that—as sheriff—he could stretch out his boots after lunch and take a nice power nap like his Western forebears who had the same jobs. When he arrives at the office, Cory is already there and the evidence of yesterday's birthday party has been erased by the overnight cleaning crew. Everything is back to normal except for a bright light on Irv's telephone answering machine that blinks away like a warning.

Ignoring it for now, as he does most warnings, Irv plops down at his desk, powers up the desktop computer, and ventures forth into the unknown by pressing that flashing light and activating the recording that turns out to be a request for a call back by the New York State Sheriffs Association: they want a rundown on the state of affairs in the county and they've asked whether Irv might be good enough to ring them back.

Technically speaking, which is how he typically chose to think about it, Irv didn't have a boss or a line manager. As an elected official the buck stopped with him, and while he did have to account for his actions to the county commissioner—and occasionally speak with the Sheriffs Association and their chums—he didn't actually have to punch any clocks or kiss any real ass; if the voters didn't like him, they could express that disapproval during the cyclical bloodless political revolution America called voting. They don't get to do that, however, for another two years, which is precisely why democracy is not very effective.

But Irv isn't a dummy. He knows that unless he is on proper terms with the powers that be, his own powers would be nullified because no one will return his calls. The whole checks and balances thing plays out in lots of complex ways, but in the end it all boils down to calling people back. Which is also what makes democracy ironic: It's only because it's ineffective by design that it's accountable at all.

The person at the center of the cobweb, as best as Irv can reason it out, is Howard Howard—who understandably goes only by Howard. He is the right-hand man of the commissioner, and whatever Howard says into the commissioner's ear comes out his mouth. It's a neat trick, actually.

Howard is as tall as a tree and has feet like flippers. He should have been a backstroker in high school but missed his calling. His voice is a Barry White baritone that regularly bottoms out Irv's telephone speakers. Cory's dog, Muppet, hurries to Irv's office door whenever Howard calls: mouth agape, ears up, eyebrows in the awe position. Irv suspects that Muppet would chew off his own paw if Howard were to command it.

Irv calls Howard back on the office phone. The sound through copper wires, he notes, is always warmer than the digital buzz through the cell.

"Howard Howard Howard."

"Just Howard."

"How're ya doin', Howard?"

"Sheriff Wylie."

"When are you going to sing 'What a Fool Believes' for me? Huh? People say Barry White, but I think more Michael McDonald."

"I only sing in the shower."

"You could have had two, three ex-wives by now if you'd 'a let your freak flag fly."

"What's new, Irving?"

"The usual, Howard."

"No, I mean it. What's new?"

"Oh. That missing Norwegian? His sister showed up. All the way from Norway."

"That's quite a coincidence."

"Not really. He dropped off their radar too, so she came looking for him. Same as us, mostly. The fun part is that she's a cop. Maybe a good one. She's cooperating. Or she's playing me for a fool. It's definitely one of those."

"What's your plan?"

"It's her plan. She thinks he might come looking for her if he learns she's in town looking for him."

"Unless he hides deeper."

"Maybe. But I'm not going to find him with either manpower or technical know-how. I'm not exactly running the NSA over here," says Irv, glancing at Cory, who is right now trying to open a tape dispenser with the business end of a mail opener, which Irv figures is only going to end in tears. "I'm feeling optimistic about it. For this plan to work out though, Howard, I'm going to need some time."

"What kind of time?"

"The time it takes to get it done. I need you to open that space for me, Howard. I don't want people getting nervous. People usually mistake thinking for doing nothing because they can't see anything. Especially politicians and the media. Which is why we're all doomed, but no one asked me."

"So you already know what the answer is."

"I do."

"And you know why."

"I do."

"Lydia Jones was black."

"She was."

"She was a black woman. And now she's dead."

"She is."

"Not just any black woman. A professor. An intellectual. A community leader."

"By all accounts she was sort of bookish. The quiet type."

"After the Jeffery Simmons case was closed," Howard says, ignoring Irv, "there have been calls—high level and important calls—for greater attention to the use of force by the police, as well as renewed concerns about racism and insufficient attention to cases involving black victims. The Jones family deserves justice, Irving. If the system tries to give you time on Dr. Jones's case, it might look like we're privileging the white perpetrator over the black victim by dragging our heels. I might also add," says Howard, "the white *male* perpetrator over the black *female* victim. A white male who is a foreigner, and a victim who is American. Time is not on your side, and it is not ours to give. I suggest," says Howard, "that we not stand with the arrogance of King Canute, who tried to hold back the waves."

Cory's victory over the tape dispenser is—as Irv had anticipated—a Pyrrhic one, as he is now bleeding. He has inserted his index finger into his mouth and instinctively turned toward Irv, who is now shaking his head at him.

"The thing is, Howard," says Irv, "people always remember that story incorrectly. It wasn't true that Canute commanded the waves to stop out of vainglory only to realize his own limits. It's by a strange twist of fate we think of him as a negative example. It was quite the opposite. He sat on his throne on the shore of England and showed his subjects that the waves would not obey him—quite deliberately and theatrically. He then declared to his kingdom, and I'm quoting from memory here, Howard: 'All the inhabitants of the world should know that the power of kings is vain and trivial, and that none is worthy the name of king but He whose command the heaven, earth, and sea obey by eternal laws.' Unquote. More or less. So I beg to differ, Howard. I say, let King Canute be our guide. We too must recognize that there is but one King who commands over all of us, and we must obey the foundation of His law, and hold fast to our greatest truths. And if unto you, O Howard, the world delivereth a giant shovelful of shit and a fan against which to throw it, you might remind them of the good Lord Jesus Christ and our requirement to be actually good to one another, and not only appear to be so in the media—so says Proverbs 902 . . . 10. And if they are unconvinced by that, you can also remind them that the motto of the New York State Police is 'Excellence Through

Knowledge' and has been since 1917. I do not like the way this case is becoming about optics rather than justice. I believe in my heart of hearts, dear Howard, that if we hold fast to the simple things, we will bring more justice to this world so help me God. You mark my words."

"Who taught you to talk like this, Irv?"

"The Jesuits at Loyola—though you need to load them up on Glenlivet if you want to hear the really good stuff."

"Don't fuck this up, Irv."

"Amen, Howard."

SHOP TALK

RV DIRECTS CORY to put a white board and worktable in the jail cell, but the desk won't fit, so it takes Cory the better part of three hours to unscrew the legs thanks to his cut finger and the stuck screws that probably haven't touched oxygen since "I Like Ike" pins were all the rage.

Once the command center is set up, Irv lays out the map with Sigrid's marks. He's asked Cory to run a long cord for his old mint-green Cortelco, which he's placed on the corner of the desk; it has a pleasing heft and a sculptural certainty that he now uses to hold the map corner in place.

Irv never has liked modern telephones. The built-in loudspeakers deny privacy and also rob him of the tactile experience of being on a phone, not merely talking into one. It's a bit like smoking. Who would smoke if you couldn't hold the cigarette? Waving it around, hanging it from your lips—that's where the fun is. Life has always seemed more real when you're contending with gravity. Because in the end that's what's gonna get you.

He considers using his gun as a counterweight for the other side of the map but thinks the better of it. It's a pity, though. It would have been the first time it proved useful for something.

Sigrid arrives at the station at eleven a.m.—not ten, as Melinda had—and she explains that it is five in the afternoon back in Oslo and she's having some sleeping troubles. Irv nods. It could be the shape of the earth conspiring against her. It may also be worry. He's seen women who are broken from the inside out and watched them apply a thin layer of paint to their lips and eyes and cheeks—not to attract attention but to divert it. Sigrid may be tired but she is unbroken and tries to divert nothing. "We're going to need a picture of you for this plan to work. Something for the flyers we're putting up."

Sigrid nods and asks for coffee, suggesting they revisit that discussion when she's had time to wake up a bit, during which time Irv holds up his iPhone and snaps a picture of her.

"Ah . . . wait a second," Sigrid says.

Irv does not wait a second and instead shows the photo to Melinda, who is standing nearby, and this makes Melinda's face contort to the point where she excuses herself from the cell.

"Let me see that," says Sigrid.

"All in good time."

"You can't use that," Sigrid says, and Irv smiles at her as he says, "What?" while his iPhone says *SWISH!* and the picture of Sigrid is sent into the metaverse.

"What were you saying?" Irv asks innocently.

"Who did you send that to?"

"Frank Allman, out in Saranac Lake. Though maybe, out there in the blue sky, Duane Allman too. We miss you, Duane."

Sigrid sits herself down in the same spot as . . . Was it only yesterday? It feels like a week ago.

Sprawled across the new desk in the jail cell is unexpected proof that Irv has been doing some actual police work in between juvenile pranks like photographing her in her current state. He has—based on a cursory assessment—done a solid job of pinpointing the most likely spots where Marcus will show up for supplies—assuming any of their grander assumptions are accurate.

"Frank's people will do the legwork and put up the posters," he says.

"Before you said flyers. Now you said posters. Posters are bigger, right?"

"Yuge. By the way, I think you have something on the corner of your mouth there. What is that, a piece of muffin? I hope that doesn't show up on the poster."

Irv notices that Sigrid, though plain at first sight, has a beautiful neck. She has a quality he's seen many times in blondes: One moment they are the boring women next door who are as interesting as drying laundry, and the next—as though transformed with sunlight—they become angular and sultry. Sigrid has clearly been spending a lot of time in the wrong light, but her neck is a revelation and invites questions Irv hasn't thought to ask before.

"How did you catch me at Target?" Sigrid asks.

"I bribed Juliet and she ratted you out when you called in for help. Melinda was supposed to lose you, and I had Cory out back in case you went that way, which you did. But for the record, you actually did shake her. And she's totally confused, poor kid."

"How could you have known to bribe Juliet?" Sigrid asks. "You couldn't have possibly known I was coming from Oslo, and I went directly to you after leaving Marcus's house. So how did you know of my connection to her?"

"I didn't. I bribed her before you got to town when we searched his house with the warrant. Told her I'd pay one hundred dollars for any information about Marcus, especially if he came back or anyone came around asking for him. Let me guess," Irv adds. "You paid her something too?"

"Two hundred."

"So she collected your two hundred first and then ratted you out for an additional one hundred from me."

"She's a criminal mastermind," Sigrid says.

"Well . . . that's six pieces of gum she doesn't need to chew," he says.

"What I'm worried about here, Irv," says Sigrid, crossing a leg, "is that you have a very specific idea about what happened and now you're working your way backwards toward proving it. It's harder to be proved wrong that way, and investigators have a tendency for theory-fixation."

"I like it when you talk shop like this," Irv says.

"This is what I can talk about best in English."

"What's hardest for you to talk about in English?"

"I couldn't say."

"Well played."

"What I try to emphasize at home, with my staff," Sigrid says, "is how to take an exploratory approach rather than building a formal hypothesis, testing it, and reformulating it with findings. Investigation shouldn't be an experimental science, both because it's the wrong approach and also because cops aren't scientists trained at falsifying claims. In my experience, if an investigator picks a hypothesis too soon it starts to look like a convenient conclusion rather than a target for refutation. You know Charles Peirce?"

"No."

"Founder of Pragmatism?"

"Sure," he lies.

"He talked about the 'provisional entertainment of an explanatory inference.' It means we have to hold an idea loosely at first and allow new pieces of knowledge to enrich our understanding rather than sum things up too quickly and be wrong too early. It requires an open mind and a comfort with ambiguity that most cops don't have. It also requires police leadership that isn't pushing cops to close cases as soon as possible."

"I'm not the top of the food chain, Sigrid. There is a big and hungry leadership above my head that thinks I like look like a cupcake."

"You need to get us the time we need to learn and act wisely."

Irv gives Sigrid a wide-open and innocent smile that Sigrid doesn't buy for a second but still, and strangely, has some effect on her. He actually opens his arms expansively as if to physically pull Sigrid into his charismatic orbit: "So," he says, "this is the part where I'm supposed to argue with you, and be the tough guy, and put you in your place because you're . . . you know . . . just a woman. The thing is, that's not going to happen. I like women. I think they're swell. And I'm OK with ambiguity. It's the sea in which I swim. So let's break with convention and say that I find you reasonable and articulate. Tell me then, O Wise One of the Far North: How do you suggest we come at a recorded statement that includes the phrases 'I did this, I did this'?"

"As facts in your case for which we don't yet have a basis for interpretation."

"That . . . is actually convincing. You're serious about this investigative stuff, huh?"

"I am an investigator," Sigrid says.

"The pickle that I'm in, Chief—and this has nothing to do with my love for ambiguity or women, because let's face it: they're a matched set—is that I'm worried that your neo-zen-pragmatism is going to slow us down. And I have reasons to speed things up, and it isn't because I'm an idiot."

"Why do you want to speed things up?"

"Put simply, because something is chasing me."

"Doing things right usually speeds things up," Sigrid says.

"You know what? That can be true. But it isn't always true. Because it's most true when people care about the quality of the results. Usually they don't, though. They care about perception, and it's easier to perceive something in motion, and fast is more exciting than slow. My worry, Sigrid, is that the results they want are for themselves. They want conclusions that make them look good. Not everyone wants justice. Certainly not everyone I work for."

"You work for the people who elected you."

Irv doesn't reply. He sits there, quietly, looking at her. He is expressionless.

Sigrid looks away from him toward the ancient green telephone on the desk as though it might ring. It does not.

"Tell you what I'm going to do," Irv says. "I'll follow your lead for seventy-two hours while Frank Allman puts up posters all around the lake and we hope to God Marcus calls in because he wants to avoid getting shot. Now ..." he says, leaning back against the bars and crossing his legs. "What do you have on your brother that we don't? You're too strategic to have given me everything. Please tell me."

"I don't know anything for certain yet," Sigrid says, neglecting to mention the existence of a USB stick named Ferdinand. "But I do have his letters to my father over the past year. I've only skimmed them. But I'm hoping they will illuminate something about his relationship with Lydia, at least from his perspective."

"That will help."

"The only thing is," she adds with a smile, "they're in Norwegian."

RELEVANT IRRELEVANCIES

OR THE REMAINDER of Thursday and much of Friday, Sigrid learns to rely on Melinda, who proves herself to be organized, enthusiastic, and productive. She also follows instructions even though Sigrid has no authority here. At one point Melinda smiles awkwardly at her after completing some tedious but helpful background reading, and Sigrid is forced to ask—again—why she is being smiled at.

"I've never had a woman boss before."

She considers Melinda's age. "How many bosses have you had?" she asks.

"That isn't it," the deputy explains. "There are sixty-two sheriff's offices in New York State and never, in the three-hundred-year history of New York, has a woman ever held the job of sheriff. There have been some women *undersheriffs*, though. I find the title awkward."

Melinda sits at Irv's desk in the jail cell with strict instructions not to answer his phone. Irv himself has returned to the main room so he can attend to a range of topics he refers to as "his job." That has left Sigrid alone with Melinda, and she is starting to understand—to a

point—how the young woman thinks. She visualizes Melinda's process as a work of art. One produced by Jackson Pollack: not so much
drippy as nonlinear, abstract, and impossible to follow even if you like
the results.

"Melinda," Sigrid now says, sympathetically. "America is in the
dark ages. You are not supposed to be excited to work for me. You
are not supposed to be pleased that men might someday let you do
the same thing as them if you're both obedient and twice as qualified,
which is actually the recipe for a mental breakdown, not a productive
life. You need to slip out of this, OK?"

"Snap."

"What?"

"Snap out of it."

"It isn't slip?"

"No."

Colloquial phrases are not the only lessons Melinda has been teaching her, though. Irv, as it happens, is responsible for more than Sigrid had first assumed. Aside from Melinda and Cory and the others
she's met in the office, the wider force has a total of twenty-six deputy
sheriffs, though most of them work elsewhere. There is a drug task
force, a recreation patrol unit that patrols the Canadian border, a K9
unit, a sheriff's emergency response team—much like her own Delta
Force back home in Oslo—who are trained in special weapons and
tactics, a school resource officer, and Irv's jurisdiction swells to a not-
insignificant population of 100,000 summertime residents.

The sheriff, she's noticing, commands all this with the easy posture
of someone running a children's football team. His primary attention,
however, is this case. Lydia's death and Marcus's disappearance matter
a great deal. What she wants to know is why.

Exhausted by Melinda and curious about Irv's commitments, she
asks if he'd be willing to come back to the jail cell with her.

His eyebrows rise like those on a retriever, but without an argument he sends Melinda back to her own desk in the main room and
rejoins Sigrid.

• • •

Across from Irv, Sigrid cups her hands over the headphones to better isolate the sounds and listens to Marcus's 9-1-1 call over and over again, trying to burrow into it and find a truth that might be hidden in the pauses between the phrases. She listens to the background hum and passing noises. She takes notes on what she hears. But it isn't working. She was hoping for a quick fix, a decisive piece of evidence that would turn the investigation around, but she knows this kind of magical thinking is for children. Yes, there is the occasional clue, but more often than not, police work is about constructing plausible stories and, in the end, being sufficiently confident of the story constructed to pass it on to the prosecutors, thereby making it their problem.

When she first started listening to the message she had hoped she could build . . . not so much a competing story line but a better argument, an argument rooted in black earth itself. After what seems like a hundred passes through the tape, though, she still has nothing. Nothing to exonerate her brother, nothing to direct her toward another conclusion. So she changes her tactic. Rather than try to find a new solution, perhaps she can falsify the existing one.

Sigrid removes her headphones. Every time she listens to the events she pictures the scene. The building, the street, the woman's body, Marcus speaking into the phone. She assembles the images from the sounds. Every image is wrong—every color, every angle—because she has never seen this place. Never been there. Never stood where Chuck stood. She is staring deeply into a picture she has created on her own. It is a destructive path, and she removes the headphones and sits back.

"What?" Irv asks.

"Don't talk to me. I'm thinking."

Forget the pauses and the noise. Forget the technical end. What about the human side? Why would Marcus confess twice? *I did this. I did this.* It sounds to Sigrid like a man speaking to himself, not to someone else. Not so much a confession but a self-realization. A statement about causality, the way a child might connect one happening with another.

I did this: But how?

I did this: But why?

I did this: *And I'm sorry.*

He says it in English, not Norwegian.

Why English?

Because he's saying it to Lydia. He was having an epiphany about the consequences of his unintended actions. He is coming to see himself as complicit. And that is not the mental journey of someone who has thrown another person out a window.

All this might be wishful thinking, but it is a worthwhile thought in any case.

In her jail cell, as Irv types away on his computer, Sigrid removes Marcus's final letter from its envelope and reads it again:

> Dear pappa,
> It happened again. You told me the first time that I didn't understand. That I misunderstood everything. Well, I'm a grown man now and it happened a second time and this time I understand it all too well. And more than that. It has forced me to see it all with a line of sight unobstructed by the years and the events and the decisions in between. What I now understand is that it was my fault. It was also yours but you, I forgive.
> Your son,
> Marcus.

What had Marcus done again? Failed a relationship? He certainly never pushed anyone out a window before.

"Can I use your phone?" Sigrid asks Irv.

Maybe her father will know.

"Dial nine to get an outside line," he says without turning away from an academic paper of Lydia's he's been reading. "It's a local call?"

"Norway."

Irv looks up.

"No. You cannot call Norway on our phone. You think I have that kind of power? Budget? Friends in high places? Use Skype like normal people."

Sigrid calls her father after lunch, during Norway's bright and early evening. He answers on the third ring.

She explains her question about Marcus. About the word "again." Her father is not helpful.

"I really don't know. I'm sorry. It didn't make any sense to me either. What are you planning to do next?"

Sigrid tells him that she is—for the moment—trying to take the very approach she has asked Irv to take but admits that being patient and waiting for Marcus to show up is not easy. The entire plan is based on soft information anyway. He might not be there at all. He could be in Vegas.

In Norwegian, and therefore incomprehensible to Irv, who is sitting across from her, she describes the files on the hard drive. She asks about depression and whether he might have it. "I'm looking to link the word with Marcus in a way he would have found meaningful."

"Depression?" repeats her father. "He never mentioned medication. In his letters he always ties up his views in philosophy. He's a private person, your brother. And after everything you explained about Lydia," his voice trails off. "It sounds like sadness. Don't you think there are legitimate reasons for being sad?" he asks.

"Yes."

"Me too. If sadness is normal, it makes no sense to me to treat it with drugs as though the brain is broken. Sadness is normal. Even if it's permanent."

"I didn't mean to upset you," Sigrid says.

"I'm just thinking about your mother."

"I know."

"The problem with arguing ideas with your children," says her father, "is that you start wondering what the conversation is really about. Your child can talk about Kierkegaard but as a parent you start thinking, 'This kid needs a hug and a nap.' The older I get the more I suspect this is true for everyone. It is astonishing the things we think about to keep ourselves from thinking about things."

"I've been going through his files on depression," says Sigrid. "There are hundreds of them. I can't read them all. I read English well but very, very slowly."

"Maybe you need help."

"Maybe I do."

By midafternoon Sigrid admits to having Marcus's hard drive and has Melinda reading through three hundred files on depression. The assignment is affecting Melinda's mood but not in a way that Sigrid had anticipated. Rather than weighing her down—by the sheer tonnage of material, not to mention the nature of the subject matter—it has instead seemed to fill Melinda with purpose and exuberance. This makes Melinda chatty.

"First of all," she says, coming to sit by Sigrid at her new desk with a yellow legal pad, "America is mental. I did not know how mental we are. The National Institute of Mental Health says—and I'm quoting here—'mental health disorders are common throughout the United States.' How common? About twenty percent of all people. So one in five. One in five!" she repeats. "And that's conservative. One in five drivers. One in five people who owns a gun, who votes, who raises children. One in five. And . . . check this. One in twenty has a serious mental health problem—serious as in Coocooville—and that number is conservative. And . . . this is interesting . . . almost thirty percent of people didn't complete the interview during their massive survey and the main reason was that they refused to participate! I'm going to go out on a limb here and say that more nutters chose not to participate than healthy people, so this thing is already conservative in its findings. And in kids? Over twenty percent of children, either currently or at some point during their life—I don't get that part, because they wouldn't be children anymore but . . . OK—have had a seriously debilitating mental disorder. Oh, and ten percent have personality disorders! One in ten. Women, apparently, are far more likely to have mental health problems than men—which doesn't make any sense to me because men are obviously more insane, judging by their behavior—and one in four women is given drugs for a mental health condition, but only fifteen percent of men. And—check this out—almost thirty percent of women are using antidepressants. And women are using twice as many anti-anxiety medications as men, but that one does make sense to me because they're probably married to unmedicated men, which is why they're freaking out. What's happening right now is that drug use is going up and up and up."

"Melinda?" Sigrid says while Melinda is drawing breath.

"Yeah?"

"How are you choosing what to read?"

"I'm reading everything."

"There's a lot to read."

"I read wicked fast. I remember most things, too," she says before she sticks a Bic pen into her mouth and starts chewing on the end of its blue cap.

"You remember those girls in high school who liked to highlight the entire book?"

"Yeah."

"They had trouble separating what was important and what was simply interesting. We don't want to be like them."

"Can I ask you something?" Melinda says.

"All right."

"How'd'ya give me the slip back at Target?"

"You haven't figured it out yet?"

"I've been thinking about it. I can't figure it out."

"That's a lot to admit," Sigrid says.

"Irv knows."

"I believe it."

"Look, you win, OK? Just tell me."

"Think it through in pieces. I went down the hallway. What's at the end of the hallway?"

"The bathrooms."

"Say it again."

"The bathrooms."

"One more time."

"The bathrooms."

"And where did you go?"

"To the bathrooms."

"No. You didn't."

Melinda stops chewing on the pen tap which has become warm and malleable. "I went into the women's bathroom."

"Right."

"But you weren't in there."

"No, I wasn't."

"Because you'd gone into the men's bathroom."

"That's right."

"And when you heard me talking to myself and opening the stalls you just walked right out the front door without a care in the world."

"That's right."

"I'm an idiot."

"No, you're not. A woman did that to my partner and me once. Only she didn't come out at all because he was at the end of the hall, waiting. She just stayed there until we left entirely. Neither one of us even thought to look in the men's room. What I learned from that failure is how hard it is to see the world in a new way and break our own habits. In this case, it really was a two-person job. Alone, you had to check one bathroom first because there was no other way. Only natural you'd check the women's. As soon as that happened, I won."

"I get it," Melinda says. "I gotta start changing my perspective on some things."

"And sometimes we need to ask for help. Oh, and that reminds me. This eyewitness of yours. Chuck. He says he saw Marcus and Lydia on the corner of the street by the building. How is it he happened to be there?"

"I don't know. I mean . . . his story checked out. What he says he saw lines up with the emergency call, so we figured we're good."

"Logically you are. Legally you're not. The two are only vaguely related. You need to find out what he was doing on that corner and why. I'm going to be too busy with other things, but you need to stay on that, OK?"

"Are there a lot of senior women cops in Norway?" Melinda asks.

"Yes."

"That must be something."

"I haven't given it much thought," Sigrid says.

"I can't even imagine that," Melinda muses.

"Melinda," Sigrid says, returning her to the files, "have you noticed anything that might seem relevant to Marcus and his interest in depression?"

"I've found kind of the opposite, actually."

"You've noticed things irrelevant to Marcus?"

"Exactly."

"Like what?"

"Mostly this is about depression in black women."

THE D WORD

D R. LYDIA JONES'S best friend was Gloria Dillane. Irv said she'd been on his to-interview list but he hadn't swung around to seeing her yet on account of it seeming unimportant compared to Chuck's eyewitness testimony, the 9-1-1 call, and there being no suspects other than Marcus.

Sigrid, however, wants to go see her immediately after reading Marcus's queries into depression. Irv is unconvinced. They sit at his desk in the main police room sipping Nescafé from chipped mugs.

"We know Lydia died from a fall," Sigrid says. "We know Marcus was there, and I believe he felt . . . What's the word? It's not 'responsible.' It starts with a 'c.'"

"Complicit."

"Less than that."

"Culpable."

"That's it."

"Which comes from the Latin meaning 'fault' or 'blame.' We keep going back there you'll notice," Irv says.

"Only because you picked the word. Yes, something obviously happened up there on the building. He could have pushed her but what I think is that he failed to stop her from jumping. Maybe the experience of losing Jeffrey was instrumental in her death in ways we don't fully understand. Lydia had deep reasons to be depressed. And maybe she was prone to it, or else on medication. Maybe she was in therapy. All this would matter. Her best friend would know. The reason you thought she was unimportant is because you weren't thinking like Charles Peirce."

"You're a little annoying."

"Yes."

"I'm not saying it's impossible," Irv says.

"Great. Let's go."

"It won't change anything that I have to deal with."

"That makes no sense."

"That's because you don't have enough information to make sense of the situation yet. You just got here. I've been here the whole time."

"I'll wait in the car," she says.

Irv drives and Melinda rides shotgun, forcing Sigrid into the back seat. Irv says there's a New York State regulation that prevents civilians from riding in the front, though Sigrid is reasonably certain Irv just made that up. She doesn't mind, though. It's a tactic she's used often with her own staff. The younger ones always think that the senior officers know absolutely everything. But the senior officers know that no one knows absolutely everything because the rules keep changing without notice. What the senior ones do know, however, is what it was like to be young and look up to the seasoned veterans. So they use that particular insight to simply make shit up that the younger ones are likely to believe. And it works every time.

Sigrid taps on the bulletproof glass as they drive to Ms. Dillane's house. Melinda unlocks it and slides open the glass.

"What's this for?" Sigrid asks, tapping the glass, feigning ignorance.

"Our protection."

"From what?" she probes.

"The crazies in the back seat. You don't have this in Norway?"

"No."

"Why not?"

"Same reason we don't have anything we don't have: we don't need it."

"Why don't you need it?"

"I suppose because there have been fewer than fifty Norwegian officers killed since 1945. None in a police car as far as I know."

"Wow."

Sigrid sits back. "People aren't walking around with guns all over the place to scare the police."

"There are no guns?"

"We actually do have many guns. There's a lot of hunting in Norway. But there's almost no gun violence."

"Why do you think that is?"

"On a fundamental level," says Sigrid, "I think it's because we don't want to shoot each other."

"That could be our problem right there," says Melinda.

Gloria Dillane lives twenty minutes from campus on a suburban back road lined with old growth trees and sensible cars. As the police cruiser ambles down the road with Irv squinting to find the numbers ("They're on the mailboxes, Sheriff," says Melinda), a flurry of bicycles slip into their wake and the kids pump their two-strokes as fast as their sprockets allow trying to keep up with the car.

Sigrid sees Irv glance at the pursuers through the rearview before activating the lights for a second. The kids all whoop. He turns it off before parking on the street outside Ms. Dillane's house. It is painted a dark gray with white trimming along its gable roof. Care has been applied to the small lawn out front. Ferns and purple astilbe line the short driveway. To Sigrid, it exudes middle-income tranquility. Gloria and her husband probably bought into the neighborhood before it became unaffordable for teachers and professors and now use the equity for steady improvements to keep up the value. This tranquility, though, may only be an illusion. If Gloria was indeed close to Lydia and her family, it must be hell in there.

Gloria herself opens the door before Sheriff Irv knocks. She is slight, and her blond hair falls limply to her shoulders. She wears mascara and it turns her eyes deeper and sadder rather than larger and more intense. Irv removes his hat and extends his hand to Gloria. She receives it without any look of interest or curiosity in her face.

"I'm Sheriff Irving Wylie. This is Deputy Melinda Powell. And . . . this is Sigrid Odegard, who is Marcus's sister. Marcus is missing and she's helping us find him."

"Ødegård," Sigrid says. She shakes Gloria's hand. Her grip is weak and dry.

"Come in," she says.

The house—much like Melinda's—is awash in colors. Here, though, the quality of the furniture is finer, the sense of permanence runs deeper, and the home shows a precarious balance between aesthetic preference and the utilitarian solutions imposed by the management of children.

The shoe sizes speak of two boys and a little girl. The silence says they are out.

Gloria leads them into the living room to the right of the hall, decorated for entertaining guests rather than everyday use. It looks the way most living rooms do on American TV shows featuring affluent white people. There is a sofa facing two armchairs across a low and wide coffee table with books not intended for reading. There is a flatscreen television mounted above the fireplace. There are plants poorly suited for this climate.

In Oslo, most homes have modern sectionals pressed against the walls, opening up the space for wandering. The furniture here is similar to the kind Scandinavians used to make: heavy and wooden and built for the ages. Now everything in Scandinavia is modular and treated as modern art, though much of it is designed to be cheap and disposable.

Gloria extends her arm toward the guest seats after settling into her wingback chair. Sigrid positions herself next to Melinda on the sofa.

"Thanks for meeting with us, Professor Dillane," says the sheriff.

"I gave a statement last month to Officer Cory . . . I forget his name," Gloria says. "He was on campus."

"Yes," says Melinda. "We know. We wanted to talk with you."

"How are you?" asks Irv, whose phone buzzes before Gloria can answer. He glances at it and dismisses the call.

"Terrible. And no one will tell me what happened. I spoke with Lydia's parents but they've withdrawn and won't discuss it. I tried speaking with Reverend Green and . . . it doesn't make sense."

"What doesn't?" Melinda asks.

"After Jeffrey was killed, the black community rallied behind the Simmonses. And so did many of us—many of us . . . whites," she says and stops talking. Sigrid watches her face as it expresses a mental journey she is taking alone. On finding a path, she returns to the conversation: "The faculty. The students. The black community in the city and in Jeffrey's neighborhood. Everyone came out to support Jeffrey's parents and also Lydia's parents. Lydia was . . . destroyed . . . but she was as active as she could be. Reverend Fred Green . . . at First Baptist? You know him?"

Irv nods.

"He was central to galvanizing the community for Jeffrey. Before the verdict, anyway. And now . . . Lydia's dead at the side of a building and there's nothing. Complete silence. Her parents aren't talking to the media. Reverend Green is nowhere to be seen, and no one's looking for her killer." Gloria looks up at Irv. "Why aren't you looking for her killer, Sheriff? What are you doing? What happened to her? Why are you here?"

"We are looking for answers," Irving says. His voice is authoritative, deep, and tranquil. In those five words Sigrid does not hear the man-boy and the prankster. She hears an adult who feels and is able to convey the gravity of the matter and is prepared to shoulder it.

"Was she murdered by a black man?" Gloria asks. Her voice is almost a whisper. "Is that why you're not telling me what happened?"

She presses herself farther back into the chair as if distancing herself from the answer.

Sigrid looks out the window. It is unfairly bright for such a discussion.

"Was she? Was she killed by a black man?" she asks, whispering again.

"What makes you ask that?" Melinda says.

"If she was killed by a black man, it would turn the whole conversation away from Jeffrey. It would undermine our moral argument. It would explain why the black community has stopped talking. The police would say, 'Told you so' and Jeffrey's death would be forgotten."

"No, it wouldn't," Sigrid says.

"It would," Gloria says. "People are looking for any reason to justify a police shooting and to vilify and negate anyone calling a shooting into question. Oh, sorry. I meant to say, a police shooting of a black person. A white person is shot and everyone's in an uproar. But someone black? They must have had it coming, people say, or else the police must have had a reasonable fear. So if a black man murdered Lydia in a run-down urban area near a crack house shortly after Jeffrey was gunned down? Well . . . they'd say, sad about Jeffrey, but it's people who look like him who are the cause of the problem. Just look at his dead aunt. And it would all . . . vanish. Like all the others. Is that why Mr. and Mrs. Jones don't want to find the killer? Why Reverend Green is keeping silent on this?"

"We can't discuss the state of the investigation, Professor. I'm sorry," says Irv.

Sigrid expects Gloria to cry at this, but instead she absorbs the emotion and her face becomes strangely calm and devoid of expression.

"Is there anything else you can tell us about Lydia that we might not know?" Irv asks. "Or Marcus?"

"I think Lydia felt that Jeffrey was the son she'd never have," Gloria adds. "She was forty. She was smart. She knew that kids probably weren't coming her way. Jeffrey was much more than a nephew. And he wasn't just a substitute for a son. He was such a nice person! So curious. So empathetic. So interested in the world. There was this . . .

expansive sense of possibility with him. He wanted to know so much. Bugs. Dinosaurs. *Star Trek*. Video games. How you grind glasses. What makes something beautiful or not. It was enriching watching him grow up, watching how one excitement led to another. I think I kept judging my own boys against that. Unfairly, I guess. When the grand jury let that man go and didn't even make him stand trial, she was . . ."

"Depressed?" Melinda says.

Irv and Sigrid both give Melinda a look that silences her immediately.

"I was going to say despondent. I explained this already to . . . Cory."

"Yes, ma'am," says Irv.

"She spent most of her time alone after Jeffrey died. With the grand jury decision, though . . . she was simply done. We didn't talk much after that. Everything that started to build and swell . . . all that momentum that we could have turned into something, something that would have given Jeffrey's death a legacy if not a meaning. All that stopped when Lydia died. Now you're saying Marcus is missing?"

"Yes," says Sigrid.

"I'm not surprised he left. There's nothing here for him anymore."

IT IS ONLY A PAPER MOON

AN AMBER MOON hangs like a plate over the black hills of Hedmark, Norway, during the few hours of night, but Morten Ødegård is uninterested in the glories of the cosmos; he has photographs to find. They are in here somewhere. They have to be.

He sits in his kitchen with his eyes closed, roaming the house in his mind to find them.

He definitely put them in a box of some kind.

Probably.

Not a shoebox. It was something larger. The color gray comes to mind. Not a neutral gray. More an administrative green. This was probably an unwise choice for a box of memorabilia. That is a color for camouflage, a color to aid forgetting. He should have chosen a nice safety green—the kind that decorates every baby carriage and kindergarten class in the winter months here, a color that the brain is unable to ignore. That's how to store something meant to be protected and retrieved.

And there were rivets.

Not in the basement. It wouldn't be there. The basement is an unfinished place. Damp, too. And Dank. And Dark. Not a place for paper, let alone photos of a dead wife.

He's had to do this before—this forensic process of introspection. Call it remembering, but in fact he's studying himself. It's all that works now. Memory as a device doesn't deliver results when you've lived someplace too long as Morten has lived in the farmhouse. Each object, over the years, has been placed in every possible or available spot. And his memory is fine so he can remember them all. It's ordering the memories that creates the confusion. The mind, after all, rebels at chronology. Ours is a pattern-seeking machine, always forming connections and creating webs of associations. It lives. It moves. It morphs. It creates and changes and invents.

This is not what you want your files doing.

So in the end the only solution involves consulting his former self and hoping that he was a reasonable and logical man. If the present you can trust the former you, and anticipate the future you, it becomes possible for all three to engage in a little intertemporal teamwork and select the right place for objects. No, it isn't remembering per se, but the collaboration brings the body to the same place, in this case being . . .

". . . *i soverommet,*" he says aloud.

The bedroom. The wife in the bedroom. Of course the wife in the bedroom. "What a stupid conversation this has been," he mutters to himself. See how you can trust your former self more than the current one? That can't be good. And there's the problem, he thinks as he trudges up the stairs. If you start losing your capacity for reason, then the dance comes to an end because it doesn't matter how helpful the former you was, or whatever you plan on doing for the future you, because it's the current you—now and always—who has to do the legwork.

On entering, Morten tries to estrange himself from his bedroom. It is quite familiar, so it is not an easy task. The bed. The windows. The dresser. The end tables and lamps. The rug. The closet. All where he'd left them and planned for them to remain.

The closet.

He opens the closet.

He closes the closet. He knows exactly what is and is not in the closet, and his wife is not in there.

He turns to the bed.

Their bed. The one in which she died.

Morten works himself downward to his knees, takes to all fours, and lowers himself into the dust like the other humble creatures. There it is, somewhat as he'd remembered it: rivetless and more beige than gray but . . . there.

That amber moon, though, is not as done with him as he'd hoped. It is looking in, lurking about. When he opens the box, alone and on the bed, it casts an unwanted patina of gold across Astrid's pillow and his memory of the face she wore on the night of their wedding. She had been in a rented white gown that had draped itself around her and looked as radiant as her happiness, a radiance that burned out the shadows and struck up the band.

They were married in the 1960s but there was no early rock-'n'-roll for them. They danced their first dance to Ella Fitzgerald singing "It's Only a Paper Moon." And Ella was right; it didn't matter whether that moon was sailing over a cardboard sea or not. Because they had each other.

His right hand was aflame in the small of her back as his thumb found the valley that led to and from everything he would ever want. That hand held the entirety of her as she slid and stepped around the floor, creating a gravity of her own.

He would have followed her anywhere. And he did until he no longer could.

Morten shuffles the wedding photos to the back of the pile and looks over others that have already faded to yellow and bronze on their own. They are the usual fare and surprising only for the amount of plaid worn over the years. There, Marcus. There, Sigrid. The cat, black with a white chest. Astrid had named him Roman. He and his mate produced a litter. Astrid called them Roman's Legions. They dug into everything.

Morten recalls sitting down with the kittens once and explaining how, in Norway, there are seven legal ways to kill cats. He described each one as they mutilated the edges of their sofa. They called his bluff.

More flipping of photos. He looks at the faces of his wife, his children.

Sigrid had said "depression."

No, it wasn't depression they had faced together. It was the other thing.

Morten had told his children that their mother's death wasn't their fault because it wasn't. Marcus had started to blame him, and after that, he started to blame himself. Morten tried to dispel both notions, but children will blame themselves for the rising and setting of the moon, such is their certainty of their own power and centrality. And they will blame their parents for the same, such is their confusion about the difference between power and authority.

What could Marcus have meant by "It happened again"?

Morten replaces the photos and seals the lid. Seeing the faces of his family brings a tempest of emotions but no insights. This is little surprise, as few storms are productive; best to keep a lid on all of it. He slides the box back to its own spot beneath the bed, realigning the dusty edges.

MOST ACTS OF VIOLENCE

OUTSIDE GLORIA DILLANE'S house, the three police officers sit in the patrol car. The bulletproof partition is open. The black vinyl seats bake their thighs and the warm air stifles their lungs until Irv starts the engine and the cold air begins to flow through the vents.

"What kind of contact have you had with Mr. and Mrs. Jones until now?" Sigrid asks. "It is strange that Lydia's death—the second death in a single family that has not resulted in justice—has not made matters worse. And it is very strange that pressure to solve her death has slowed down."

"The momentum for justice has not slowed down," says Irv. "The commissioner wants us to find Marcus and lock him up. It will help calm down the situation caused by Jeffrey."

"Jeffrey didn't cause anything," Sigrid says. "Roy caused it."

"I meant what Jeffrey's death caused."

"What you're describing is pressure from the top. From politicians. I'm talking about pressure from below. From citizens. I don't understand why there's less pressure from below. We have to see Mr. and

Mrs. Jones," Sigrid says. "They're Lydia's parents. Jeffrey's grandparents. They should be central to this."

"I've already spoken to them," Irv says. His voice is barely audible over the air conditioner.

"You two ask the wrong questions," Sigrid says. "I've heard you. I need to speak to them myself. Nothing about this case makes sense. Lydia's death does not make sense to me. Marcus's sense of responsibility and disappearance does not make sense. The politics around all this don't make sense. Call them, Melinda. Please?" Sigrid removes an old napkin from her pocket and wipes her forehead.

Melinda turns to Irv for guidance but he looks out the window. Sigrid repeats herself, and without Irv's explicit objection, Melinda places the call.

Sigrid isn't done with Irv, though:

"Is the police commissioner white?" Sigrid asks.

"Yes. Why?"

"Was he elected like you?"

"He's a civilian political appointee. So he wasn't elected, but he's part of the executive office."

"So he's political, like you, rather than a career professional, like me."

"I suppose."

"Our situation, as I now understand it, is that the white politicians want to lock up Marcus for Lydia's death. But the black community does not."

"Not exactly. They don't know about Marcus. He's still a missing person to the general public assuming they have any thoughts about him at all. We haven't charged Marcus. We haven't implicated him publicly in any way," Irv says. "There's no reason anyone—outside the police system—would suspect Marcus or want us to arrest him. Unless Chuck has started blathering, but I haven't heard that happening yet and I already put the fear of God into him. So the pressure is all from the inside at the moment."

"Who exactly is Fred Green?" Sigrid asks. "Gloria mentioned him."

Melinda's call has been answered and she's speaking quietly into the phone. Sigrid catches the phrase "yes, ma'am."

"Reverend Fred Green," says Irv, "is the pastor at First Baptist. It's a mostly black church. He buried Jeffrey. And Lydia. He's very close to the Jones and Simmons families."

"You know him?"

"Not well. I met him during my campaigns. Handshake, quick chat. I don't think he voted for me."

"You didn't talk to him after Jeffrey's death?"

"I've told you. That was a different county. We didn't do it. I wasn't going to start making rounds and confusing the matter."

"You should have gone there. You made a big mistake."

"All right. Fine. Thank you."

Melinda has removed the phone from her ear and pressed the red image on the screen. She places her face closer to the vent and breathes in.

"Why would they not want justice for Lydia? Even if Lydia was a suicide—"

"We have no proof of that," Irv says.

". . . the black community could reasonably say it was indirectly caused by Roy's killing of Jeffrey."

"You can argue anything," Irv says.

"Not convincingly, you can't. And I would absolutely find that convincing. Wouldn't you?"

Irv says nothing.

"I think any decent person would see that, whatever the law says. It would make sense for the black community to keep pressing for justice because she was, in effect, another victim of Roy Carman and everything that created him."

Melinda makes a small cough. Both Irv and Sigrid look at her.

"I don't mean to . . . well . . . I don't see why this is a black thing," says Melinda. "I mean . . . if cops killed a white kid everyone would be going nuts. If that white kid's aunt ended up dead on a street corner it would be headline news. So why if they shoot a black kid, is it only the black people who are going nuts? I get why it's a black thing also, but not why it's a black thing *only*."

"She's right," Sigrid says. "That's a good question."

"OK, look, people: This is not American Culture 101. You"—he points to Melinda with a rigid finger—"are in the doghouse for providing a leading question to an interviewee. It's like Tourette's with you. And you," he says to Sigrid as he starts the car. "You are not Alexis de fucking Tocqueville here to study America's prison and justice system. I'm not blithely accepting this suicide theory you're pushing in the hopes that I won't notice and it'll soak into my brain. We still have every reason to suspect Marcus aside from the fact that he seems so gosh-darn nice. Well . . . nice people do bad things. This should not be news for grownups," he says. His phone buzzes again and he looks down to see the name of the caller on the screen. "Goddamn journalist parasites."

"My copy of *Democracy in America* was stolen."

"Are you being a smart-ass?"

"My father gave me a copy. I didn't realize that's what the book was about."

"There's no safe place to stand around here," Irv says to himself.

"Here's what I'm thinking," says Sigrid. "Lydia Jones had a nephew who was gunned down by a police officer and denied justice from his country. Lydia was broken. Marcus tried to help her and couldn't, for which he blames himself. She killed herself using an open window. Ashamed and hurt, he runs away to the woods."

"Good story. All neat and tied up. Here's the thing, though. It's complete speculation," says Irv.

Irv flicks the car into gear and rolls them out of Gloria's neighborhood as if pushed by a tailwind. Ten wordless minutes later he turns off at Exit 12 onto a road with franchise restaurants, chain stores, pawn shops, and stores that promise—in neon—to give advances on paychecks.

They turn right onto Allard Road, where they pass wooden houses in various states of disrepair. The lawns are weathered here, and chainlink fences separate properties, not ferns and flowers. It is midafternoon and two Latino men sit on lawn chairs studying the police car for intention as it glides down the wide street. No child waves as Irv squints at the mailboxes for the numbers.

Irv flicks the transmission into park behind a baby blue Delta 88 and sits for a moment, the air blowing, before turning off the engine. The house is painted brown with beige trimming on the windows. There is a faded plastic swing hanging at a slant from frayed yellow ropes in the front yard.

Irv rotates his body to speak with Sigrid and smacks his elbow against the bulletproof glass he forgot was there. He winces, draws breath, and tries again.

"Let's get clear on the play before we take to the field, shall we? Number one: We're going to take a 'do no harm' approach on this one. No theories. No wild speculations. No leading questions," he says directly to Melinda, "and no efforts to outsmart them and make them say things that will help get Marcus off the hook. We're here to get a lay of the land and understand why things aren't adding up. Maybe we learn it. Maybe we don't. But we tread softly. Gently. Gingerly. You know that word?" he asks Sigrid.

"No."

"It means softly and gently."

Sigrid does not interrupt.

"And so we're all clear on my thinking at the moment: I am not convinced that a scholar on race relations or whatever she was would hurl herself out a window after the race-related death of a loved one rather than go fight City Hall. Anyone who knows anything about the history of civil rights in this country knows that people have endured living hell to get where we are today. It does not compute that a woman who has spent her career reading about abuse and self-sacrifice would toss herself out of a window when faced with more of the same. The only hint that she might have been clinical is your brother's files. Meanwhile, he had zero credentials in psychology, and the fact that he downloaded a bunch of stuff from the internet could mean nothing more than he was trying to eff the ineffable. Or, you know, he planted it there deliberately and after the fact to cover his tracks. We'd have to check the . . . metadata or whatever the hell they do on television."

"Irving," Sigrid says.

He raises his hand to prevent her protest. "I don't think he did that. I was making a point. The good money right now says he and Lydia got in a spat because they saw the world differently and something got out of hand and went terribly wrong. It is my experience that most acts of violence are the result of benign situations escalating into tragedy. Somehow he's responsible and he knows it, which is why he's hiding in the woods and trying to figure out what to do next. The part to all this I can't understand is what on earth they were doing halfway up an unfinished building they had no business being in."

Melinda tucks her shirt deeper into her pants as she stands at the corner of the small property trying to decide which door to use. At her left, uninviting, is the proper and formal front door. The lawn has not been cut all summer and the flat stones are obscured by the overgrowth. The pots on the steps are cracked and empty and the doormat is rotted and weather-worn.

To her right is a set of steps leading from the driveway to a screen door. They are shorn of paint at the edges as a thousand ascents have worn them through, exposing the soft wood at their centers and leaving them bare and unprotected.

Melinda looks behind her and Irv nods her up the stairs.

At the top Melinda grasps the aluminum handle of the screen door intent on opening it so she can knock on the wooden door behind. Instead she finds it held in place by a tiny slide lock woefully outclassed by the hostile world it faces.

Irv and Sigrid join her on the landing and stand behind her.

Melinda raps gently on the sheet metal as if to alert the people inside of their presence but not wake any listening spirits.

When the door is opened and the screen unlatched, a tired black woman with a drawn face looks out at them. She does not open the outer door immediately. Instead she looks at the three white faces through the rusty screen. Cops on her doorstep have never had good news for anyone. Her countenance is stone behind the flimsy screen that separates them. She looks to be beyond the insincere use of words and pleasantries now; words she may once have valued for their kindness and civility. Irv removes his hat as the woman opens the door without ushering them in. Melinda crosses the threshold first, her eyes cast to the kitchen floor.

Sigrid walks into the house behind Melinda. She looks at Mrs. Jones as she passes her. Their eyes meet but there is no connection. No unity. Sigrid has met people in Oslo who have lost family members before. But she has not met a woman who has lost a grandchild and — immediately afterward — a daughter. There is a sourness to the air inside the kitchen. Takeout foods, processed and oversalted. The woman's face is gray. Her clothing is gray. The light from the sun through the kitchen window and the door behind her is gray. The truth of this world has leeched away all its color.

They are led through the living room. The air is dusty with an institutional oppressiveness. The ancient shag carpet is worn bare in its trafficked paths. The window curtains are drawn.

A silent glowing television flickers. No one is watching it.

As Sigrid turns into the dining room she sees a table of heavy maple and two photographs in its center — a Christmas photo of Jeffrey and a half-body shot of Lydia in a mortarboard hat and a full professorial gown speaking from behind a podium.

Sigrid has seen two photographs of Jeffrey. One from his mother's Facebook page, which was used extensively by the media, and the other from a birthday party. In this new one he is looking down at a present he is unwrapping. He is wearing black pants and a white dress shirt, but — as with all children — he's a bit disheveled because the shirttail has come untucked. The photo captures him at a moment of recognition; the moment he realized that the present was exactly what he wanted or else was even better. The wrapping paper blocks the view of the object, but it doesn't matter: He is the subject. Behind him are two clapping adults whom Sigrid takes to be his parents—Lydia's sister and brother-in-law. Their empathy is obvious. They are feeling what he feels.

In the other photo, Lydia is standing at a podium before a microphone. She is a slight woman but one hand is braced firmly while the other gestures dramatically. She is smiling and her eyebrows are raised as though inviting her audience to accept her argument. It is the photo of a person aloft, soaring at the full height of her emotional strength and rhetorical power. Her face glows with purpose and the promise of possibility.

A ring of votive candles burns around the photos.

Mrs. Abigail Jones leads the three visitors to the table. Sigrid notices Charles, the father, hanging back in the hall without entering the room. He does not extend a hand to the police or to Sigrid.

They are led to the dining room where they sit around the images of the dead. Sigrid studies the candles and wonders whether they were lit before Melinda called.

"I never thought I'd see you again," Mrs. Jones says, looking at Irv.

"Why is that, ma'am?"

"I think we both know why."

Sigrid touches Irv's leg beneath the table. He is not expecting this and it works as Sigrid had hoped. Instead of responding, his confusion keeps his mouth closed.

"Reverend Green explained the situation to us," Mrs. Jones continues. She leans forward onto the table, her forearms flat against the dark wood. "How do you live with yourself, Sheriff, knowing that you have within your soul and your station the power to make things better, but you choose not to?"

Sigrid has experienced these sorts of confrontations before. Junior officers freeze, and experienced but foolish ones take a defensive stance. They think their honor has been insulted, or the department, or their masculinity . . . something that turns them away from the task and back toward themselves. They forget their reason for being there. In the moment. In the job. Irv, to her surprise, does not make this mistake.

"How can I do more to make things better, Mrs. Jones?"

She sits back and folds her arms. It is Charles, from the doorway, who speaks:

"You don't want to catch who did it."

"Sir?" Irv says.

"Don't 'sir' me. The reverend said you have no suspects. He said you have no ideas. He said you are nowhere on this, and that it is now our job to shoulder the weight of your incompetence and laziness and apathy—your sins—and carry them like Jesus carried our sins. He says that God is once again placing the weight of our community on our shoulders, and that it is only our fortitude as a family that is keeping this city from turning into Watts, or Detroit, or L.A. And I have to wonder, Sheriff: Why is the calm of this country always the result of black people deciding not to get angry? To turn the other cheek? James said to us that to be a Negro in America and to be relatively conscious is to be in a constant state of rage. And yet America is not enraged because we are not enraging it. We are calming it down. Every church meeting. Every town meeting. Quoting Jesus and Martin. Mothers wiping away their own tears. You studied the mind of God, Sheriff. Tell me. Tell why it is that black people's faith always needs to be tested on both sides? Why does God take away from us, and later tell us to do nothing about it? Why doesn't he do that to white people? Deep down, does he hate us as much as America does?"

Abigail Jones does not turn to her husband. She does not rein him in or try to control the situation.

"Why are you here?" Abigail asks them. "You haven't made an arrest. You have no news for us. You're here wanting something. What is it?"

Irv places his hands on the table and locks his fingers together. He does not speak immediately.

"I'm trying to understand," Irv says softly, "what Lydia was doing halfway up an unfinished building. I can't figure it out."

Charles Jones is a broad-chested man in his midsixties. Physically, he has not crossed the line into old age. He carries his weight proportionately and could shift it forward if he chose to lean into his words.

Instead, he settles into them with the weight of iron: "You want us to think our Lydia was weak. I know what you're thinking. What you're insinuating. But she was not weak. She was a strong, courageous black woman. Something you can't understand. So you put her in the only box you have for her. But even in death she fights against it. Look at her. Look at her," he says, finger pointed to the picture. "She was a professor. A scholar. A woman who could look at words on a page and conjure up a universe. She stood on ideas the way people stand on the ground beneath their feet."

Charles Jones walks into the room and places his hands on the shoulders of his wife.

"Whether she took herself into that building or whether she was pulled into it against her will, all you need to know is that my daughter was as strong in character as any person I have ever known. She was full of life. And now, as sure as we sit here, she is in heaven because the Lord God knew that Jeffrey could not be there alone and he needed looking after. So Jesus took our daughter from us to comfort that poor boy in the least harmful way he knew how, knowing that Jeffrey's own blessed mother could not follow to look after him with two other children to raise back here in the dirt."

Charles Jones walks them to the door. His face is fixed and is holding back whatever he might have said next. When Abigail takes hold of the handle, he turns away and retires to the living room television, leaving his wife to see them out.

The volume is turned up. There is an attack ad against Obama, calling him an affirmative action case and a false messiah.

At the door, Abigail Jones takes Irving's hand in her own. She whispers to Irv: "You are a Christian, Sheriff? Under all that? Under the uniform and the politics and the skin? Is that the man you are?"

"Yes, ma'am. I am."

"My children are in heaven, Sheriff. You understand that, right? Both my babies are in heaven."

"Yes, ma'am," Irving says. "They most surely are."

"You leave them there. You leave them together. You leave them with the Lord. You understand me?"

"I do, ma'am. I assure you that I do."

No children parade after the police car as it leaves the neighborhood. The radio crackles without words or news. Melinda watches the city's skyline emerge from behind the sagging rooftops as the cars all speed up and Irv merges them onto the highway.

"Sheriff?" she says.

"Yeah."

"I don't understand why Mrs. Jones was talking to you about heaven."

"Because," says Irv, "if her daughter committed suicide by throwing herself off the building, doctrine says that right now she is burning in hell."

A GOOD BURGER

S IGRID IS STARVING, so Irv turns off the main road toward a shopping mall and pulls the patrol car up to a freestanding restaurant called the Cheesecake Factory. The building looks as new as a child's toy, with design influences from Greece, Sumeria, art deco, and Hasbro. It's as natural as Las Vegas and as welcoming as an airport. The franchise does not exist in Norway.

"Cheesecake is a dessert," Sigrid says. "I need something more savory."

"That's just the name," Melinda says as they lock the car and walk across slabs of sandstone to the glass doors.

As they open the door, an arctic wind blasts through Sigrid's hair and chills the sweat on her neck. A waitress in her twenties who is aggressively eager to please seats them at a round table with wicker chairs woven from plastic. She hands them a menu with two hundred items.

"Is it always like this?" Sigrid asks Irv, flicking through the options.

"Choice is freedom," says Irv, putting on his reading glasses and peering down at a sea of plenty.

"From what?"

"Huh?" he grunts.

"Freedom from what?"

"I don't understand," he says, glancing up from the menu.

"You can be free from something, or free of something. You can't just be free. It's a relational concept. So . . . choosing between the salad and the baby back ribs makes you free . . . from what?"

"Tyranny?" he tries.

"This isn't a quiz," Sigrid says. "I sincerely want to know the answer. It seems to have something to do with everything going on over here."

The restaurant has a split-level floor plan with two steps leading up to a sitting area with a bar. Down below there are more than thirty tables. A quarter of them are filled with families. Children are absorbed in coloring, eating, using iPhones, and spilling things. The adults are either speaking to each other, focusing on the children, or staring—defeated—toward some imagined horizon, hoping that either a new lover or else death itself will come to take them away from this shiny place.

In this sense it is exactly like Norway.

"You should probably choose what to eat before the waiter comes," Irv says. "Service is great in America."

"No. Service has been trained to artificially increase table turnover rates to generate corporate revenue. You've been trained like dogs to think it's good service, whereas it's actually incredibly rude. I'm handed the bill while I'm still chewing."

"You're one of those low-blood-sugar women. I can tell. You're not my first date."

"Irv," says Sigrid, leaning forward to keep her voice down. "Maybe you can't see it because you're inside it, but to the rest of us, America is weird. You have these immediate, ready-made answers to everything and most of them are meaningless and the others were designed by PR firms. Choice is not freedom. Sure, you can choose among what's available, but what's available was decided already by someone or something else. There are no hookers and cocaine on the menu, for example. You can't choose those."

"Not here," he concedes.

"Really. What is this freedom thing that seems to end all conversations with you people? I'm watching the elections on TV and the Republicans are saying they want to give America freedom. Cut taxes for freedom. Abolish government for freedom. Defeat Obama for freedom. I sincerely don't understand. Explain this to me."

"OK," says Irv, rising to the challenge. "I'm going to stick with the tyranny answer. We don't want anything imposed on us. Don't Tread on Me and all that. Being able to choose is proof that we aren't living under tyranny. Choice may not be freedom itself, fine, but choice is proof of freedom because it proves there's no tyrannical imposition. The more choice, the less tyranny."

"But it's an illusion, Irv. The way the goldfish is free to move to the right or the left. The fact is, he's still stuck in a bowl. Laws and policies and doctrine and procedure, and the powerful strings of interests and money and greed—these are what put things on the table or take them off. We live in a world shaped by things above our heads. The freedom you fought for—that we all fought for, by the way—is the freedom to shape those big things together, not to be free from them. We didn't fight to be free of community; we fought to have one. But you Americans chose between the . . ."—she glances at the menu— "Louisiana Chicken Pasta and a Glamburger and you think you're a bunch of cowboys."

Irv shakes his head. "That's not a choice. The Glamburger, all the way."

Melinda nods.

Sigrid ignores them both. "Americans have longer life spans and a lower infant mortality rate than they used to because of the directed hard work of invisible people who built complex systems that resulted in your better lives. It's not because someone cut your taxes."

"You're just saying that because you're a commie," Irv says, putting on his red reading glasses again. "And you're hungry. Girls are always like this when they're hungry. You may think that's sexist, but it's a battle-hardened fact and I stand by it. You should get the burger. Angus beef," he adds, glancing back down.

"I'm not sure if American culture is frighteningly simple," she answers, "or overwhelmingly complex."

Sigrid has nothing left to add. America is not making more sense to her, but its internal contradictions are coming into finer focus. Overwhelmed by the menu, she fixes her eyes on the television screen mounted above the most well-stocked bar she has ever seen in her life. There has to be fifty thousand dollars' worth of booze back there. The massive LG TV is tuned to sports.

Two teams are playing baseball. She doesn't know the uniforms and from this distance the labels are too small to read. She likes baseball to the extent she understands it. It seems a patient game that is skilled and inspired by an agricultural past. She also rented *Field of Dreams* a thousand years ago and liked it: Kevin Costner surrounded by corn. It was comforting for some reason. She wonders whether Marcus has become a fan of the game over the years. It isn't played much in Norway.

"Come on. What are you having?" Irv asks, closing the menu.

"What's chipotle?" she asks.

"No one knows," he answers.

"I think I'll have the fried calamari for an appetizer and then a burger."

Melinda laughs. "That's too much."

"Let her," Irv says. "It's her colon."

They order from a man who does not blink. His job complete, he is sucked back to the kitchen as if by a pneumatic tube.

Adjusting her eyes to the distance, Sigrid can better see the emblem on the baseball uniforms. It is the Cardinals against . . . someone else. She has seen cardinals in films before. They are exquisitely beautiful birds that are colored for the tropics. Nothing like them in Scandinavia.

Melinda hears the lull in their conversation as an imperative to speak:

"Do you believe that?" she says, directing her wonderment at Irv. "That if someone commits suicide they go to hell?"

"No."

"But many Christians do, right?"

"There's a debate, but it's doctrine."

"But you don't think so?"

"No."

"Why not?"

"For the same reason the Catholics believe in the Trinity, Melinda."

The appetizers arrive with a speed that Sigrid finds suspicious.

"Which is . . . what?"

"It's how I understand Jesus's words spoken from the cross," says Irv, taking one of Sigrid's calamari. "Jesus spoke seven times on the cross. In Matthew Twenty-Seven, verse forty-six and in Mark Fifteen verse thirty-four he says, 'My God, my God, why have you forsaken me?' This led to the Trinity," Irv said, sucking cocktail sauce and grease from his thumb. "The thinking is, if Jesus was Lord, who was he speaking to? He was obviously speaking to someone or something other than himself, unless . . . ya know." Irv makes a circular cuckoo motion by his head with a piece of squid. "So perhaps he was speaking to the Father, or to the Holy Spirit. In this act, he distinguishes himself from the eternal and embodies everything that is Man. The fear, the sadness, the tragedy. The longing. The recognition of betrayal. We see him, in that moment, only as the Son, and because of that, as ourselves. As I read it, Melinda, we are not invited in that moment to be cruel to him for his despair, or to mock him. Instead we are asked to feel his pain. When Jesus says, 'It is finished' I don't read, 'Mission accomplished.' I see a person resigned. A person who has lost hope. A person who has taken a step away from this life. And our pity for him grows. And finally he says, 'Father, into your hands I commend my spirit.' Now, I'm not going to equate Jesus letting go with suicide, but any decent and forgiving Christian person would have to admit that we are looking at a person who cannot fight anymore. We are being taught to be understanding of that state of mind and sympathetic to the suffering that might lead a person to it. It does not follow to me that if someone succumbs to that grief we are to treat them with eternal contempt. I just don't believe it."

But Sigrid isn't listening anymore, because as interesting as it is listening to a sheriff discuss scripture, it is nothing compared to the picture of herself now on the widescreen television. Because it is not only a picture of her. It is, unquestionably, the worst picture of herself that she's ever seen.

It is a manipulated version of the picture that Irv took during her pre-coffee haze. The burning fluorescent bulbs in Irv's converted jail cell had been directly over Sigrid's jet-lagged face, and so cast their industrial light down and into her blond eyebrows, which — on television — burn with electric fire. By rights, glowing eyebrows should be stare-worthy, but the tip of her nose was far more interesting, having been, apparently, polished. As the announcer speaks, Sigrid focuses on the nose and, yes, sees a tiny little image of the photographer in there — a little gnome in a sheriff's hat. Beneath her eyes are black triangles; her eyebrows having sucked in all the available light. Sigrid looks at herself. She has never been especially vain or concerned with appearances beyond being neat and clean and properly dressed for occasions. But here she looks not so much bad as . . . evil. The kind of evil that hates children and birthdays and piñatas, the evil that lives in a cabin with meat hooks. And . . . what is that at the corner of her mouth? A piece of gristle? The foam of insanity? The remains of Hansel and Gretel?

"Hey, look," says Irv. "That's you. Melinda, go have them turn that up, will ya?"

Before Sigrid can object, Melinda — uniformed and authoritative — tells the barkeeper to crank the volume up, so now everyone at the bar at the Cheesecake Factory is watching the scary woman on TV and listening to the report as a new video of Sigrid replaces the photograph:

> ". . . sister of Marcus Odd-Guard, who is now missing and wanted by the police, in possible connection to the death of Dr. Lydia Jones, who was found bloodied on Brookmeyer Road on August third. Ms. Odd-Guard is believed to have connections to a white supremacist motorcycle gang — the Vandals — who proclaim themselves to be the descendants

of the original Vandals; the Germanic tribe that sacked a decadent Rome."

The report pops back to an interview with Roger Mandel, whom neither Sigrid nor Melinda can hear on account of Irv's immediate curse-filled rant. Melinda shushes him and Irv dials it back to a steady growl so that the women can hear Roger say:

> ". . . a tip from a reliable source, who provided the video, showing Ms. Sigrid Odd-Guard enter the notorious Inferno bar by Target off the I-37, tells us that Ms. Odd-Guard was looking to—and I quote here—'catch a ride with the gang to avoid the local police,' unquote. Our investigative team has learned that Ms. Odd-Guard was suspended from the Norwegian police force recently for the shooting of an unarmed immigrant. No one knows where she is now, or what her direct connection is to this case, but we are pursuing this new connection between the Odd-Guard family and the Vandals, and Marcus Odd-Guard's own romantic relationship with Professor Jones at the time of her death. So far the police investigators have been unavailable for comment. We're going to be staying with this story, Alison, until we have some answers. Back to you."

Sigrid's burger arrives.

"Melinda," says Irv, seeing Sigrid's condition, "go tell Alan to turn the channel, OK?"

"Yes, Sheriff."

As Melinda carries out her duties, Irv lifts a french fry from Sigrid's untouched plate and chews it. "So I'm thinking Juliet takes your money for a favor. She then rats you out to us for more money. And then—it really is a masterstroke, I have to admit—she rats us both out to the media for even more money. I wonder how much she got from Roger."

"There is no case."

"When you said before, that not all your plans work out, did you mean that some of them do?"

"You took that picture, Irving, and that journalist is part of your coterie."

"That's not true. I hate the guy. But nice word. *Coterie*."

"Fix this."

"I'll do it right now." And true to his word, Irv fishes in his pocket for his phone, settles back in his seat, and—staring at the ceiling— waits for Roger to answer the phone.

"Sheriff!" says Roger. "I've been trying to reach you all day."

"And now I know why," Irv answers, switching on the phone's speaker for Sigrid and Melinda.

"Saw the news, huh?"

"Is that what we're calling it?"

"I wanted your comment, but deadlines must be met. The reason is right there in the term. Dead-line. A line that . . ."

"How much did you pay the industrialist?"

"I can't reveal my sources, Sheriff, and you can't compel me . . ."

"I paid her a hundred bucks to know if anyone came or went from that house."

"A hundred! We paid her three hundred."

"This woman should be running Wall Street. And when, exactly, did you get to her? The time line doesn't make sense to me."

"Not long after you issued that APB a few weeks ago. We went to Marcus's listed address and there she was in pink curlers and one of those freaky green face masks you see in old movies. Told her we'd pay for tips on his whereabouts. We do that sort of thing all the time, so that was no big deal. I didn't think it was going anywhere. Not until we found out about the love connection to Dr. Jones after a few interviews at the Ivory Tower. That's when we learned that we had ourselves a SECRET interracial CAMPUS murder mystery coming shortly on the heels of that Roy Carman judgment. And now with the white supremacist motorcycle gang angle tossed in there with video to show? It's like an afterschool special gone wrong! It's paperback magic, Sheriff. There's gonna be a miniseries about this. You mark my words."

"Interracial? It's 2008. We got a black guy running for president. Ten years ago we had a Jewish Secretary of Defense—from my home state of Maine no less—married to a black woman."

"We did?"

"I think you just made my point."

"Not a campus murder mystery, though. Everyone loves those."

"Hmm. Yeah. Unfortunately, Roger, that's not the story."

"Ingredients make the dish, Sheriff."

"No, Roger, it's the recipe. It really is. For example, using careful observation and solid police work I could tell you that Sigrid *Ødegård . . .*"

Sigrid raises her eyebrows at Irv's perfect pronunciation of her name and Irv winks. ". . . is not exactly a fugitive from the law. We know exactly where she is and what she's doing."

"Oh, really. And where's that?"

"She's at the Cheesecake Factory by the multiplex. She's having herself a Factory Burger, medium rare, and she's barely touched it."

"Really."

"Don't believe me? Ask her yourself."

Irv hands over the phone.

"I'm going to kill you in your sleep," she says.

Irv takes back the phone.

"Her English is really coming along nicely. Thing is, she's working with us, Roger. We're even buying her lunch. Her brother is indeed missing and she came here to the Land of the Free all worried-like and looking for him. Doesn't have anything to do with anything else. It's all in your head."

"And what about the video proving her ties with the Vandals?"

"She's an expert on international drug smuggling and the influence of . . ."—he looks at the round hamburger bun—"globalization. Yeah. On organized crime." He gives Sigrid a thumbs-up. "While here, as a tourist, we asked her to teach us a thing or two given that Scandinavia is so enlightened and everything and we have those villainous Canadians to deal with it. My crew was in the parking lot taking notes at the time."

"And how did Juliet McKenna—lady of the night—come onto the scene with the grainy phone video?"

"Video. Right. Video that was taken from a dark corner by a dumpster. Personally, I think you shot the video. I think you were involved in some Expect-More-Pay-Less activity in the alley with Juliet—the one you admitted paying money to—when you saw something weird and decided to stop taking a home movie of your own shenanigans— which is just icky, by the way—and shoot that instead. Now, I admit I'm only wondering all this, but I find that a common sense of wonder is what brings people together, and I think it might be fun to share my sense of wonder with your wife."

"Oh, come on, Sheriff . . ."

"Bye, Roger."

Irv places the phone back in his pocket and smiles at Sigrid, waiting for her to acknowledge a job well done. He is slightly surprised to find that she doesn't agree.

"You should have provided him with the solution," Sigrid says, slumped in her chair. "If you tell him to fix something, you're at the mercy of his imagination. If you tell him how, you only need to supervise."

"You have an interesting problem, Sigrid," Irv says. "It's like . . . you're right about everything, and yet it never seems to matter. You're a Greek myth of some kind, but I can't put my finger on it."

"You're really annoying me," Sigrid says.

"You should eat. American beef, right there. Perk you right up."

LE SUICIDE

FROM THE COMFORT of a flat-topped rock facing due west, Marcus Ødegård watches the golden crest of the sun drop below the lake. He digs his bare feet more deeply into the sandy bottom of Lake Flower near Saranac.

America, for all its expansiveness and romantic poetry about wilderness, is a nation built by people with a keen sense of real estate and no fear of solitude. Every piece of land with a view of mountains or water is precious here, and someone has always laid a claim.

God is in the wilderness for the American soul. Out here is where you sit to watch the battle rage, the battle that rages both inside and out.

As he'd explained to his class, the officials in the Adirondacks call it "primitive camping" and it is legal. Not that he cares. The park is big enough, the area wild enough, that if he avoids making fires and using a flashlight, he might never be seen. But the problem, as always, is his compulsion to seek out the beauty of the day. It pulls a spirit like his to the very best spots as if by a song. He is not the only one who hears it, though. This is what leads people to gather, unbidden, onto wide streets and boulevards at the close of day—at the end of a war. We saunter like the undead toward the sunset, exultant.

He should have known better. Still, he submitted to the impulse to watch the sunset by the rock and now three young men are emerging from the woods, all drawn, it seems, by the same forces that pulled him here.

They are polite. They too are camping nearby at Pine Pond, they explain. Is he alone? Yes, he is. Sorry to bother you, they say. It's no bother, he is forced to say. Nice night. Yes. And so on. They make small talk as people do in the woods, being unable to avoid one another or break off for another conversation as they might at a party.

There are lights by the rising moon. They are not stars but planets.

The men are playful and young, taken in by one another's company and keeping the mood buoyant. They try to pull Marcus into it. "Have you seen this?" one of them—Jacob—asks him. He's on his mobile phone. In contrast to the simple majesty of the sunset, the phone casts an eerie blue mask across his face, separating him from the natural order. He laughs at the image a second time. The others gather and laugh too. He is the kind of person who is *plugged in* and becomes nervous when he is not. Marcus has students like him. The more they strive to express their uniqueness in those machines, the more conformist they become.

Jacob and his friends speak of *memes* and *viruses* and *winning the internet*. They seem to exist on the crest of an endless chuckle that is both constantly renewed and immediately forgotten.

The phone is placed in front of Marcus. There is an image of a woman. He focuses—the screen is too close—and that quickly, as if through a wormhole, he is sucked in.

Jacob is on some kind of robot service that finds whatever is trending around his phone's location so Jacob can surf the wave of proximate interest. The joke of the moment is from a local network affiliate.

What Marcus is looking at is a picture of Sigrid subjected to juvenile humor and Photoshop. The campers find her hilarious. They call her Mrs. Hagrid. Has he seen this yet? No? This is great.

Marcus does not laugh because seeing Sigrid here is not funny, but he smiles enough to endear himself and convince them that he needs to borrow their phone. The photo links to the news station and a story. Attached to the story is a second picture of her on a flyer stapled to a telephone pole on a street corner that looks familiar. That picture has not been doctored. At the bottom of the flyer is a phone number.

"Do you all mind if I make a local call?" he asks.

Ensconced back at her workstation in the jail cell, Melinda is now free and emboldened to pursue her new interest in suicide. Sigrid can hear the clicking and scrolling of the mouse, which is old and yellowed like a smoker's teeth. Her searches are manic and her findings impressionistic, but she is covering remarkable ground—much like anyone falling down a mountain.

Sigrid plans to let gravity slow her momentum before intervening to direct her course toward something more productive.

Unfortunately, and as always with Melinda, this journey is not going to be a silent one.

"According to the World Health Organization," Melinda says, "suicide is the third leading cause of death in the world for those aged fifteen through forty-four. Men do it much more often, but many more women attempt it. Meanwhile, depression is the leading cause of disability worldwide. Men, at least in America, shoot themselves. Women poison themselves. But in looking for the relationship between cause and effect, the story gets very confused. Wow, now this is cool. Turns out," Melinda says, sipping from a cup of instant coffee, "modern sociology was founded by someone named Émile Durkheim and his first subject of study was . . . get this . . . suicide! It was called *Le Suicide*," she says in an accent learned from a cartoon. "He reasoned that suicide was the one thing you could do that didn't give back any social benefits and for this reason it shouldn't have a social origin. But it turns out, there were patterns. And so sociology was born. I always wondered what people were studying in sociology. Society, I guess."

Sigrid didn't know any of this either. Even if Melinda's information is procedurally useless, Sigrid finds it comforting to learn that her own confusion has roots and a pedigree.

"Maybe you should take a break from the material for a while," Sigrid suggests. Taking the cue, Melinda leaves Sigrid for the main room and passes Irv, who is walking in at the same time. He plops down in his favorite spot in the cell.

"Still not eating?" he asks her, nodding toward her take-home Styrofoam container.

"Your term 'doggie bag' is unappetizing."

Irv explains that it is common for Americans to bring food home from low-cost restaurants, as the portions are so large now that they cannot reasonably be consumed in one sitting—though many try. Sigrid asks why the restaurants don't make the portions smaller and simply charge less. Irv explains that more is better than less for anything of value. Sigrid says this is obviously not true.

"'Dance Me to the End of Love' by Leonard Cohen is a great song," she says. "It would not be better if it went on forever. In fact, the song would be meaningless if it did."

"I've been on the phone with Howard," Irv says, changing the subject. He puts his feet up, locks his fingers on top of his head, and prepares to deliver a message that Sigrid can anticipate because she'd given this speech before after talking with politicians.

"That tall drink of a man has just placed my nuts in a vise. Do you know what a vise is?" he asks. "It squeezes things to hold them in place, unless you just use it for the squeezing property itself. I find myself in the awkward position of all the white people wanting us to throw your brother in jail for killing the black woman and all the black people wanting us to leave her case alone and let the woman rest in peace. The universe has turned inside out, but the consistent part is that whatever I do, I will make lots and lots of people angry at me. I hate this case."

"What are you going to do?"

"Huh? Oh, I'm just here to complain. I know perfectly well what I'm going to do."

"Which is . . . what?" she asks.

"I am personally going to make it my job to ensure that we send the right souls to heaven and not the wrong ones. How about that for a day's work?"

"How about we just solve the case with the facts and let justice have its day?"

"Isn't that what I just said?"

"No."

"I thought it was."

There is an unfamiliar and high-pitched tweeting noise that interrupts their conversation. It sounds as though a small bird is trapped inside the jail with them.

Irv and Sigrid both look around trying to find the source.

"I think it's coming from your bag. Is that your phone?" Irv asks.

"That's not what my phone sounds like."

"Maybe it's the other phone."

"What other phone?"

"The phone you bought explicitly to receive calls from Marcus, Chief Inspector."

"Oh . . . right," says Sigrid, digging into her bag to find the Samsung. She locates the green button.

"Hello?"

"You shouldn't have come, Sigrid."

A NIGHT AT THE OPERA

O N HIS ROCK, staring at the darkening lake, Marcus is uncertain whether it is good to hear his sister's voice. It complicates matters, but he does not regret placing the call. He is obligated through love to send her back to Norway where she belongs.

"Marcus," she says, "pappa said you were missing. I came to find you."

"You didn't need to," he says to her.

They speak Norwegian. It is a cloak that unites them as it secludes and protects.

"There is a manhunt for you. The police think you pushed Lydia out a window. There's an eyewitness who obviously doesn't know what he witnessed. I know you didn't do it."

"How do you know that?"

"I know who you are. Circumstances challenge us. They don't change us. I also found your computer files. I know about Lydia's depression," Sigrid says. "I spoke with her parents. Her mother fears, but won't admit, that she committed suicide. They believe it's a mortal sin and subject to damnation. But they're stuck because if they continue to deny it, they force the case to remain open. The police are looking for a killer who doesn't exist."

"They're looking for me."

"Which is not the same thing. But that's changing," says Sigrid. "There's a local journalist—of a type—named Roger Mandel who has linked your disappearance and the APB to Lydia's death. The sheriff has been avoiding any public connection between you and Lydia, but that's now unsustainable. The good news," says Sigrid, "is that Irving—the sheriff—isn't convinced you did it. He's decent and reasonable—in an unstable American sort of way—but he needs convincing. We know about Jeffrey and how much it pained Lydia. I really need you to explain to them that it was a suicide, how you tried to stop her, and having failed, you foolishly but understandably ran away. I'm sorry for you, Marcus. I really am. So let me come get you. We'll sort this all out and then we should go home. Pappa could use your help. I think everyone needs a rest. Me too."

"I heard you killed someone," he says to her.

"Yes, I did."

"Me too," he says, and hangs up.

Irv is opening the photo album on his laptop as Sigrid speaks to Marcus in that Elvish language of theirs. He flips to the picture of her he'd taken earlier.

"Bastards," he says, loud enough to be sure someone hears it.

Neither Sigrid nor Melinda looks up.

"Bastards!" he says louder.

Sigrid, on the telephone, looks at him the way his ex-wife used to look at him, which is similar to the way his mother used to look at him when she knew he wanted attention. And women in bars, too. They looked at him like that. A lot of women looked at him like that, come to think of it.

No one pays attention to Irv, so he looks more closely at the morning photo of Sigrid.

OK, he knew it wasn't the most flattering picture when he sent it to Frank Allman and—sure—it was a kind of ribbing between cops, especially ones trying to get to know each other better on a case. It wasn't really *that* bad, though. If her nose had been that shiny, her eyes that sinister . . . well . . . he would have noticed and not sent it.

Irv compares the photo he took to the one presented.

No, Irv thought, she looked OK. Even then. Her neck was still regal and sloped elegantly into her shoulders. It was even more obvious in the picture because he could look more closely.

"See?" he says to Sigrid when she hangs up the phone. He holds up the unaltered image. "It wasn't that bad. They manipulated it. You can kill anyone you want. You get even one woman on that jury and they'll never convict."

She doesn't smile at him.

"What?" he asks.

Sigrid looks down at the phone on her lap.

"Come on. What?" Irv says.

"It was Marcus."

"I assumed that given the language. And?"

"He . . . ah . . ."

"What?"

"He was not happy to hear from me."

"I'm sorry to hear that. Where is he and where do we meet him?"

"I don't know."

"That's not going to do. Give me that phone."

Irv clicks and pokes and summons the received calls list. It has one number and he dials it. Four rings later he is connected: "Hi, this is Sheriff Irving Wylie with the county office. You just lent your phone to someone. Where are you? . . . Uh-huh. OK. What kind of phone have you got there? . . . Uh-huh. OK. Open the compass thing and read me your GPS coordinates . . . I'm listening . . . Uh-huh. OK. Listen, if he packs up and heads out, send me back a note to this phone. He's a good guy but he's in a bind and we're keeping an eye on him, OK?"

Irv hangs up and Melinda says, "There's a problem, Sheriff."

"Now what?"

"A whole bunch of blacks . . . ah, African Americans . . . have formed a . . . a . . . bunch. And they're outside the Inferno, and I think we're looking at some impending violence."

"Is this on account of that bullshit from Roger and that fucking video?"

"Just might be, Sheriff."

"And this bunch is blaming the motorcycle gang for Lydia and they're looking to do the job they think we're not doing?"

"I wouldn't want to speculate, Sheriff."

Irv stands up and adjusts his gun, belt, balls, and boots.

"Have Deputy Rhineheart go pick up Roger," he says. "He's authorized to pick Roger up by his thumbs if necessary. Bring him to the Target parking lot. Roger will talk about his rights. We can ignore those." Irv points at Sigrid. "And you. Stay put. I'm not fuckin' around on this one. You go near there, those folks will kill ya because they think you helped murder Lydia, and the bikers will kill you because they'll think you're trying to set them up, and the cops'll kill you a third time because they'll think you're an escaped convict. Furthermore, the blacks hate the whites, the whites hate the blacks, and everyone hates the cops. And generally speaking, cops hate everyone. So it's going to be a delicate triangle of misery and hatred and you're at the center of it. So stay here, please. Do we have ourselves an understanding?"

"Yes," says Sigrid.

"How did things get this way?" he asks rhetorically.

"You blinked," Sigrid answers.

"It's constant politics. Isn't it?"

Sigrid doesn't reply.

"Is it like this for you?"

"I'm on vacation."

"Where the hell is Cory?" he yells.

Cory waves his hand like a schoolboy who has found a lost baseball.

"You call Frank Allman and give him these coordinates here," he says, handing Cory the note. "You tell him that Marcus is there, he probably isn't armed or dangerous or anything, but he should still take it slow. And I need you to call—God help me—Joe Pinkerton on the SERT, let him know about the bunch of people heading to the Inferno and tell him this is not a drill but I don't want guns blazing at the Club House. Oh, and tell him not to use the word 'target' for any reason. It's just that kind of slip-up that can upset the apple cart. Honestly. Who names a department store Target, anyway?"

Irv withdraws his revolver to see that it's loaded and—satisfied that it is—puts it back in its holster, only to remove the entire thing and place it in his drawer. He locks it with a tiny steel key.

"What are you doing?" Sigrid asks Irv.

"This isn't a problem I can fix with a gun. Besides, I'll most likely end up shooting Pinkerton. Melinda?" he says, turning from Sigrid. "Where's Melinda?"

"Sheriff." Melinda's voice comes from his right. Melinda is a lot shorter than Irv and she habitually stands too close. He thinks she sneaks up on him deliberately.

"I hate it when you hide there. Go put on a vest."

"But, Sheriff . . ."

"Do you have a problem with that order?" he snaps, and as the room falls silent he gives her a hard stare, long and deep.

"It's in the trunk, right?" she says, changing her tone.

Irv takes her by the arm and gently leads her to the door and then pushes her out.

"We're going to see Reverend Fred Green first. At First Baptist on I-Thirty-Seven. I'm driving, so you call."

"Is that the place with the big white sign that flickers when it rains?" Melinda asks.

"Yes."

"Get him on the phone and tell him we're coming because I need to talk to him," Irv says, starting up the car. "In fact, tell him we're coming to get him. And tell him to wear the frock."

Irv heads them out of the parking lot with the flashing lights switched on but not the siren, and they ride with force and intent toward I-37.

Melinda turns on the police scanner, and—from habit—switches on the FM radio, too. Queen's "Bohemian Rhapsody" is in full swing about Beelzebub, and Irv tells her to turn it off.

MATTHEW 5:9

A SILVER DRIZZLE FALLS on the black hood of the police cruiser parked outside First Baptist. The church is a concrete affair set a hundred feet behind a macadam parking lot that on Sundays sees a mostly African American congregation in glinting patent leather crunching their way to the gray door above three steps. This is Irv's second time here. The first time, six years ago, was for campaign purposes. His campaign manager—Frida Larkin—had insisted that since he was "open about his faith in God," he might as well use that to attract key voters in the African American community who might be inclined to vote Democrat but could possibly be swayed by shared conviction.

"Open about my faith?" he'd asked.

"You admit it."

"It isn't something to hide, Frida. I don't have lice."

"No. You have faith. For Democrats that's worse than lice. Because, you know, lice can be cured."

"I don't think faith has a political party. Nor does morality. Let's just stick with the campaign slogan I wrote and try and be nice to people, OK?" he'd said.

"Your slogan is too long."

"It's perfect."

Irv had a pile of campaign lawn signs in the trunk. They read IRV WILL BE A GOOD SHERIFF.

Irv had met Fred Green during that visit, but sitting in the police cruiser now, in the drizzle, he can barely remember it. There had been muffins. That part he remembers.

Fred is supposed to come out and meet them in the parking lot. The church door remains closed and neither he nor Melinda is in any mood to rush the reverend or get any wetter than they need to.

Radio off, Irv watches the rain on the hood as it dints and splatters.

He'd read a book by George Smoot years ago about the cosmic background radiation—a relic radiation from the hot primeval fireball that began our observable universe some 13.7 billion years ago. He took a minor interest in cosmology to complement his religious studies. Thinking about both topics felt balancing and expansive rather than contradictory or defeating.

Even in the nearly perfect thermal equilibrium at the moment of creation, Smoot had explained, there were still primordial perturbations in the early matter and energy distributions, tiny fluctuations in matter density. As time passed and the universe grew like an expanding balloon, those irregularities grew in significance too and those dense regions attracted more mass until they became entire galaxies. And our solar system. And the earth itself.

They didn't stop there, though. No. They kept right on going and ultimately resulted in the very imbalances now playing out beyond the raindrops dancing on the hood of the prowler in the Target parking lot, where people are probably not sharing Irv's thoughts about the awesome improbability of being here but instead are thinking about the inevitability given the kind of forces they have to contend with on a regular basis.

There really is no unified theory. There really isn't.

Irv looks at Melinda, who is staring outside too. In a few moments he—Irving Wylie, MA in divinity from Loyola and second-term sheriff in Jefferson County—and she—Melinda Powell, good small-town kid who wants to help people—are to reverse the course of the expanding universe and bring everyone back together so they might find some common ground.

Melinda looks worried, and she is uncharacteristically quiet in her flak vest.

"You OK?" he asks her.

Melinda doesn't answer. She may not have heard him but he thinks she did.

"I told you to stop watching *The Wire*."

"I can't help it."

"That show is not good for your brain."

Reverend Fred Green emerges from the church holding an enormous umbrella with the red and blue logo of Costco. He holds it with both hands, elbows tucked in, as though it is keeping him up and not the other way around. With the rain falling hard he looks like a man trying not to drown. He wears rubbers over brogues and his face is grave, as though he'd never learned to smile. The blue lights from the cruiser flash over his watery eyes as he bends down to address Irv through Melinda's window. As she lowers it he places a hand on the door frame and bends low. The water spills off the front of his umbrella as he leans, and the splattering rain sprays the dashboard and soaks Melinda's pants.

"Turn off the lights, please," Green says.

Irv does as he's told.

"Is this really the best idea you have?" he asks Irv.

"Honestly, Fred, I only have the one."

Reverend Green looks away and out toward a row of trees that separates the parking lot from a construction pit that fills like a quarry in the heavy rain. Irv watches his eyes but they reveal nothing to him about the criteria or calculations, politics or learned wisdom that might be helping him make a decision. Without looking back at Irv, Green closes the umbrella, shakes it, and sits himself in the back of the car. He slams the door closed behind him and the sound itself is what confirms that a choice has been made.

Irv pulls away. The rain and light on the black hood attract every glimmer from the neon store signs as they pass into the commercial zone, but all their messages are distorted and lost in the dark.

They drive a few blocks from the church before Irv turns on the blue light again.

For a long while the reverend doesn't say a word. Irv glances at him in the rearview mirror and sees him staring silently at the wet trees.

"Thanks for helping us out here, Reverend," Irv offers.

Hands on his lap, as though in a pew, Fred Green turns to Irv through the open slot in the bulletproof glass.

"I've never been in the back of a police car," he says quietly.

"What do you think so far?" asks Irv, turning right onto Lancaster Road at the Dairy Queen. A club is having an antique car week in the parking lot. A bunch of Irocs, Corvettes, and Z28s are parked out front, glistening in the rain. They'd probably hoped for a better turnout.

"You can't know what it feels like until you sit here yourself," the reverend says.

The Target asphalt parking lot is teeming with life. The white lines that mark the parking spaces are faded to stripes of gray, as dull as the clouds above. The yellow lamps glow inside a ring of haze. At the edge of the lot, in front of the Inferno, is an angry crowd.

The last protest that required Irv's attention was a peaceful demonstration that started at the university campus when Jeffrey was shot. It proceeded through the city on a five-mile walk. That was a family crowd and the message was unity and a call for social justice. There were speeches at the halfway point and demands for greater protections against police violence and greater accountability for police action, and an explicit appeal to recognize and reduce racism.

Cory was put in charge of directing traffic and did a stellar job.

After six hours, the only drama had involved one case of heat exhaustion in a sixty-four-year-old who overexerted herself and the arrests of three teenagers who'd been zipping through crowds on skateboards and stealing iPhones.

These people who are gathered here together to face the Inferno did not come with their families. They are not interested in unity. They are not protesting at a government building or exploiting a teachable moment at a place of higher learning or community worship. This is a crowd of bitter, misinformed people who want to extract the cold hearts of white supremacists who decorate their Harleys with Confederate flags.

No one is holding a placard.

Irv estimates the crowd at thirty to forty and judges the general mood as dour. There are no children and few women. They form a line, three deep, a hundred feet from the bar. They would probably be closer, Irv figures, were it not for his emergency response team, who are lined up between the crowd and the Inferno.

The bikers hang around by their Harleys pointing at the protesters and shouting well-practiced obscenities and the usual racist epithets from behind the protective barrier of fifteen white and heavily armed police officers.

Irv is surprised to see the SERT in full riot gear with the men carrying military-grade submachine guns as though they're preparing to go door-to-door in Bogotá. Irv authorized none of this, but there are standard operating procedures he still hasn't memorized because of how much there actually is to learn as a sheriff and because, well, this doesn't come up much.

Unless it isn't standard procedure and all this paramilitary shit is Pinkerton's idea.

Pinkerton: the macho weenie who's in charge of the local SERT.

Irv has always been suspicious of Joe Pinkerton. He grew up in a tough part of Brooklyn, was sent to the navy to get straight, turned himself into a SEAL, and didn't so much get straight as master the skills to be a grade-A asshole. He retired from the SEALs earlier than most of them do, but Irv doesn't have full access to his service record so doesn't know the reason. He has always assumed it was because everyone hated him and either didn't want Joe backing them up in a dangerous situation, or because they didn't want to back him up be-cause—well—Joe is an asshole.

In the six years Irv has known him, Joe has always been training for something: a marathon, a triathlon, one of those Iron Man things. He doesn't do it quietly; everyone needs to know about it. For each com-pleted event he's had his finishing time tattooed on his arm—some-place visible so people can ask about it. Like most narcissists he has an insatiable appetite for something that comes from crowds. Irv would fire him, but the guy is part of the union; he's going to have to wait until Pinkerton seriously fucks up before he can get rid of him, and Irv's worry is that by then it'll be too late.

Irv swings his arm over the passenger seat and again whacks his el-bow on the glass.

"God damn it."

The reverend doesn't blink.

"Here's what you need to know, Fred. The Nazi biker dicks over there didn't do it. Whatever happened to Lydia had nothing to do with them. That woman on the news—the mug shot—she's a Nor-wegian cop. And she doesn't look like that. She's actually quite . . . Anyway. I've seen her credentials, I know her, and I trust her. Mostly. The point is, this whole circus here . . ." says Irv, nodding toward the standoff by the motorcycles, "is media created. It's not real. I mean, it is now, but it didn't need to be, because the new reality is built on sand. What I can't figure out is how things built on sand never seem to sink anymore. Sign of the times I guess. So here. You and I need to make sure nothing really bad happens as a result."

"You really have no idea what's happening here, do you," Fred Green says. It is not a question.

"I think I just described it perfectly. I need your help to calm things down. A little teamwork. Church and state, hand in hand."

"You think those people are angry because of one news report?"

"I think flammable things burn when you light them on fire, so yeah."

"You murdered a black child because he was black. Try and think back, Sheriff. Miami after Arthur McDuffie. L.A. after Rodney King. St. Petersburg after TyRon Lewis. Cincinnati after Timothy Thomas. And now little Jeffrey Simmons. Right here. How much more of this can reasonable people take? If black cops were killing white people — beating them to death, strangling them, shooting them when they're unarmed — how long would it take before other white people reacted? Would you have described that as a castle built on sand? A reality anchored on lies? I doubt it."

"I didn't murder anyone," Irv says, "and I'm not here to hurt people, Fred. On the contrary. I'm looking to keep us off the list of federal disaster areas like the ones you just mentioned. And you're going to help me."

"I'm supposed to tell people — black people, and black people only — that violence isn't the way. How long can that message remain credible, do you think?"

"Reverend, we're looking at an imminent problem, right over there —"

Fred Green raises a hand and interrupts: "The police murdered Jeffrey Simmons. I don't know and I don't care if those bikers were involved. What I do know is that there's a line of cops over there with rifles facing black people and protecting those . . ." Green does not choose a word. "Those black people, Sheriff, are American citizens. Their taxes bought the bullets in those guns. Some of those people elected you, Sheriff. Why do you think that is?"

"This isn't a damn game, Fred. Now let's go mingle."

The reverend doesn't move.

Irv holds his temper but his voice is not steady enough to conceal his anger. "Please, Fred. Those people are not gathered to protest police violence. They are there to extract justice from those bikers because Roger Mandel reported that Sigrid is a white supremacist and her brother might have killed Lydia. The facts are, she's a Norwegian cop here to find her broken-hearted brother who probably didn't kill Lydia and definitely has no connection to that gang over there. I take your point about the meta-politics here, Fred, but we don't decide right and wrong at the level of national dysfunction. It's right down here where the people are. So let's go calm people down. Get their attention, say a terrible mistake has been made, and then we can introduce Roger Mandel and throw him right under the bus and let the crowd have at him. Once they're fed and digesting they'll probably calm down."

"And then what?" asks Fred Green.

"Then Melinda is going to go stand up there to try and disperse the crowd."

"Whoa. How's that?" Melinda says, suddenly engaged.

"I think they are less likely to be violent against a woman."

"So why am I wearing a bulletproof vest?"

"I might be wrong. OK, folks, showtime."

Irv opens the car door, but before he is able to slide out, Fred manages to grip Irv's shirt at the shoulder. This surprises him, and he looks at the hand and the arm attached to it. Reverend Fred Green has reached out so far that his face is pressed against the glass, distorting his cheek and muffling his message. "After Jeffrey, and Lydia . . ." he says.

"I know," says Irv, shaking Fred off.

"After Jeffrey and Lydia," repeats Green, gripping him even tighter, "if the police shoot one black person in defense of a white gang—no matter the circumstances . . ."

"I get it, Reverend. And now that you know about Marcus being a suspect too—though an unlikely one—I assume you want me to find him. Get this solved. I know. I'm working on that, too."

"No, Sheriff. I do not want you to find him. Or arrest him."

"That doesn't make any sense. Why not?"

"Because justice lost is better than justice denied."

• • •

Melinda opens the back door of the car and leads the reverend toward the crowd.

Irving does not follow them. Instead he makes a beeline for Pinkerton, who is on the phone looking very pleased with himself, and who clearly wants a chance to demonstrate his skills with leadership and a baton. Pinkerton gives Irv the upward dude-nod. Irv, scowling, is now between the gathering and the SERT, and everyone's eyes are on him.

Someone shouts "No justice, no peace." It sounds less like an analysis than a promise.

"Joe," says Irv to Pinkerton.

"Sheriff. Howard wants a word."

"Don't shoot anybody while I'm on the phone. And turn some of your people around. Face the upstate biker-Nazis."

"I don't think they're Nazis, Sheriff," says Pinkerton. "They're just white supremacists."

"That's what we call a distinction without a difference, Pinkerton. Now: Point some of the guns at the white people. Confederate flags have always made nice targets. That's an order."

Irv looks up into the sky, which glows a celestial green. The mist doesn't cool his skin, and he imagines the acid rain eating him alive like a solvent. Eyes closed, he takes the phone from Pinkerton and presses it to his ear.

"Howard, Howard, Howard. Why are you always in my face?"

"How does it look?"

"Manageable," says Irv, lying.

"You ran your campaign on being hard on crime."

"I ran my campaign on being *smart on crime*, which everyone took to mean whatever they wanted, which is how I won. You're wasting my time, Howard, and I'm going to hang up."

"I know—the commissioner knows—that you're sympathetic to the Simmons family and don't agree with the Carman verdict. Well . . . too bad. That's the law and you're the lawman. If anyone in that crowd breaks the law, you make the arrest and get control. The law is colorblind. No exceptions."

Irv hangs up to keep from saying something he'd enjoy but regret.

Taking a breath, Irv turns to face forty irate people who—against expectations—turn out not to be facing him or the line of cops. Instead, their attention is directed toward Reverend Fred Green, who is now gathering people toward him with slight gestures, the way a guide might draw a tour group tighter to discuss a ruin. His face is passive and relaxed under that massive umbrella, and once a circle forms he starts shaking hands and introducing himself to those he doesn't know.

Irv is too far away to hear him. What Irv can see, though, is that Fred Green is not doing most of the talking. He is not politicking or working the crowd. He is, primarily, listening. And with someone attentive and interested to speak to, they are speaking. One by one: gesturing, explaining, wondering.

Irv turns to Pinkerton. "Shoulder all the rifles, take off the helmets, and tell your men to clean their fingernails. We're deescalating."

"That's not wise."

"That's an order. And I want you to personally go into that clubhouse over there and arrest somebody."

"For what?"

"Something illegal, preferably. But anything will do. Catch and release is fine. Just . . . go catch. I want bearded faces shouting obscenities on the evening news."

"Something like what?"

"Like what?"

No imagination in this guy. Nothing.

"Put your Popeye Doyle hat on," Irv explains, "and find me illegal possession of a firearm, drugs, drunk and disorderly conduct, wearing plaid and fatigues at the same time, or simply picking their feet in Poughkeepsie. I couldn't care less. I mean, shit, Joe, maybe you can get one to hit you and we'll have a win-win. Either way, I want to see a white man in handcuffs in five minutes."

"I thought we were the law, Sheriff."

"That's where the country has forgotten its roots, Pinkerton, but luckily I remember. We're not just the law, Joe. We're the peacemakers. Like the old Colts. We are here to be more than meter maids, Joe. We're here to be the actual instruments of God. Because it was the Lord above who said, 'Blessed are the peacemakers for they will be called children of God.' Matthew Five, verse nine. Now go walk in the way of the Lord, Pinkerton. Make peace. Right the fuck now."

THE NEWS

Two months ago, Marcus invited Lydia to Montreal for a long weekend with the intention of exploring as much of her mind and body as he possibly could. It was only an hour and a half away by car, but Montreal could have been Paris compared to upstate's rural walks and the muddy rills lining the interstate between here and there.

A whole weekend in Montreal? At a hotel? With a bed?

"Yes," she had said.

Marcus had his one and only suit dry-cleaned, his shirts laundered and ironed, his hair cut, and he shaved. He spent sixty dollars on a cologne he would never have considered buying before. Friday morning he dressed in front of the mirror that was steamed at the edges. His skin was shaved and smooth, his clothing crisp, and he smelled like the sea.

"Yes," she had said.

"OK," he said to himself, smiling at the thought.

• • •

He drove his Saab 900 with a rip in the driver's seat. They passed northbound rigs with screaming tires. They listened to NPR until the nation was behind them. They crossed the border north of Brasher Falls State Forest, across the St. Lawrence River, and over Cornwall Island in Canada. The border guard told them to enjoy their stay.

Marcus turned right onto the 401 going east, and from there it was a straight ride into Montreal. That right turn had made everything feel very close, as though the city itself had them in a tractor beam.

Lydia popped in a cassette tape she'd found in the glove compartment. "So," Lydia had said, as Modern English played "I Melt with You" on Marcus's cassette.

Marcus raised his eyebrows. "Yup."

"What's the big plan?" she asked.

"Check in. Clean up. Go out."

"So quickly?"

He had made reservations at a restaurant with excellent reviews. The pictures on the website showed a stylish, modern, cosmopolitan space with beautiful people having lively conversations about fascinating topics that entertained themselves and everyone around them. He couldn't imagine himself at one of the tables and almost didn't book it. But he could picture her there. He could visualize that room reflecting off her eyes. That he wanted to see.

He called from his house in New York. They answered in French. He spoke English. He spelled his family name for the man on the phone. Of seven letters, two don't exist in English. Twenty-eight percent of himself was erased in translation.

Ødegård.

His name is derived from a Norwegian term given to the farms emptied by the Black Death of 1349–50. It is a name that still whispers of absolute despair seven centuries later. It is a name that has no place in a restaurant in Montreal with someone as vivacious and present as Lydia Jones.

Momentarily panicked by this thought while driving, he didn't answer her question and instead asked, "What did you bring to wear?"

Lydia smiled at that. Apparently she had been thinking about something other than the Black Death of 1349–50, because she said: "Do you remember that cat suit Halle Berry was wearing in *Catwoman*?"

The car followed Marcus's thoughts into the neighboring lane. Lydia coughed and Marcus returned, though begrudgingly.

Lydia shook her head at him. "You white boys and that cat suit."

Marcus looked at her forearms and, after, her cheeks. There was copper to her skin. It held sunlight. He tried to open his mouth to answer but had nothing to say.

Lydia ejected the tape and adjusted the radio to a French station playing American music.

After ten minutes of silence, Lydia's bare feet on the dashboard, Marcus said, "I've never been a white boy before."

"What do you mean?" she asked.

"I've never really thought of myself as white. I've just been me."

"That's the essence of white privilege right there."

"I'm not so sure. I'm not American. I'm Norwegian. We don't have the same history. We never had anyone else there to define ourselves against, other than the Swedes and Danes who occupied us. I mean . . . I see we're different. But I didn't grow up thinking about it the way people do here."

Lydia smiled at him. "That might be why this works." And then she tilted her head to the side. "We'll see."

The hotel was stylish and glowed lavender by the reception desk, where a perfectly quaffed Moroccan man in his late twenties smiled and took their passports as he clacked away at the keys with the lightness of Art Tatum.

Lydia wore jeans, a powder-blue button-down, and a faded corduroy jacket snatched from a secondhand store, giving her the look of an off-duty model from 1978. In his memory of the day the world seemed to wrap itself around her so that everywhere she went was a perfect fit.

They were issued two plastic cards for keys. A green light, a downward push, and they were in.

Lydia's suitcase was a rolling garment bag small enough to use as a carry-on. He had packed a leather gym bag. Behind him, Lydia slipped wordlessly into the bathroom while he opened the folding suitcase rack and placed his own bag there, only to find that it drooped between the two nylon straps. He removed the bag, folded the rack, and studied the room for a new plan.

That is when Lydia walked out of the bathroom smelling like Ivory soap and wearing nothing but satin blue panties. She slithered between the bleach-white sheets like a princess, rolled onto her belly, and gave him a look.

Canada was not Mars. It was not an alternative dimension or the far side of the universe. The prevalence of French notwithstanding, Montreal was firmly North American and not the Europe many pretended it to be. And yet, to cross an international border was still a statement — even an achievement of a sort. It was to stand in another history. A place unlike the one on the other side. A life apart. Here, the rules of order, the experience of cause and effect, the very memory of continuity and change were different. Not all the differences were better. But the awareness that the difference existed — that difference was possible — was a kind of freedom. It was a freedom that empowered him. That aroused him. That gave him confidence to put away the fears he'd been building up in himself over the previous month.

He joined her in that indefinable place between the sheets while it lasted. His hand felt enormous on the small of her back. His thumbs settled into those dimples by her spine. The longer he stared into her skin the more he wondered why humans — his humans — ever migrated from Africa to the Arctic; the ones with such a chronic sense of discontentment that they were led directly into Lutheranism.

"What are you thinking about?" she asked from beneath the sheets.

"Happiness."

Afterward, Lydia slipped out of the bed for the bathroom and sooner than expected reemerged in a black dress — "Zip me" — and he tried to match her in his casual navy blue suit with brown shoes.

They walked three blocks toward the restaurant and decided, thanks to her new shoes that chafed her heels, to flag down a cab. Lydia spoke the French she had learned during her doctorate as a research and credit requirement. Her accent was imperfect and her phrases dated. The Quebecois were charmed that an American would even try.

The restaurant was larger than Marcus had expected. It was a converted industrial space. The ceilings were vaulted and the ash pillars were concrete and square. Interspersed were rich fabrics of bold and geometric design that contrasted with the polished steel surfaces. The bartender was a beautiful brunette in a sleeveless black dress that plunged to her sternum. Her face said she was uninterested in her own beauty.

They both ordered the lamb shank.

Lydia selected a Brunello di Montalcino and ordered carpaccio with rocket, parmigiano, and capers for a starter. When it arrived she picked off the capers and used his lemon.

The bread was baked in the kitchen. It was hot on arrival. They ripped the crust and steam rose between them.

Marcus is remembering Montreal from Saranac Lake. The other men have retreated down the coastline a few hundred yards and have started a fire. It is the only one nearby. Marcus watches the smoke rise and the orange light flicker off the still lake. He is focusing on the point where the smoke dissipates and becomes part of the vast nothingness beyond; dissolution but also a unification with the infinite. The boy-men by the fire are scorching marshmallows for s'mores and roasting hot dogs that bounce precariously from the tips of twigs. They are enacting a ritual from childhood that has specific rules and expected outcomes. They are also defying the traditional social order —civilization itself—by making the savory and the sweet simultaneously. Rebellion too is part of the American frontier experience.

Marcus sits against a tree in the darkness. The clouds are matte black to the west. Someone is getting wet somewhere. Maybe someone he knows.

The woods here in the Adirondacks are not unlike home—that place where Sigrid used to follow him around, everywhere, when friends came to his house and they'd all run off into the woods, or go for a swim, or cross-country ski or go sledding. He liked having her around more than he admitted. That stopped when their mother's cancer came. Sigrid was too young to understand. Five years old. He was almost eleven when it started. It irked him that she didn't feel what he did. That feeling — that distance — only grew.

"She isn't very sad," he'd said to his father on one especially bad morning for his mother.

"No. Not really."

Sigrid was having a conversation with a stuffed camel. She looked perfectly normal and he wondered which of them was broken.

"That's because she doesn't know what love is yet," he'd said.

His father pressed him closer but neither had more to say.

Astrid was dead in a year. That battle was lost. He had not said the right things. He wanted to say the right things with Lydia. He wanted it at the beginning of their friendship so badly, he was willing to steal the exam and cheat on the test. After their first kiss — more a declaration of intent than an act of passion — Marcus started to obsess. He wanted to understand and be deserving of this smart and pretty and vivacious and driven woman, this woman who read books on Saturday nights. Who liked hiking in the woods. Who could talk for hours about history and ideas. Who was passionate about justice but also forgiving in character. A woman — he soon learned — who knew how to turn a cloth napkin into a chicken and make it sing and dance to *if you want my body and you think I'm sexy* . . .

The day after the kiss Marcus collected all her publications from the library and set about the task of understanding this part of her mind. With the crooning chicken still fresh in his memory, he was surprised to find her analysis of the American experience to be powerfully pessimistic. Most of the work was targeted to academics in peer-reviewed journals, and he tried to make sense of the citations and scholastic shorthand but he wasn't able to place the debate and so couldn't fully understand it. What he did find as a guide to Lydia's mind was an interview conducted by a student journalist for the school paper. Lydia had had a piece accepted in *Daedalus*, the journal published by the American Academy of Arts and Sciences. Barack

Obama's showing in the polls was getting stronger, and the journalist —a nineteen-year-old junior named Darren Farley—wanted to understand why Lydia's central thesis in the *Daedalus* article seemed to run counter to the optimistic and popular mood.

DARREN FARLEY: Professor Jones, your central thesis is that America is not so much ignoring racism as much as it's inherently incapable of addressing it. How can a country be inherently incapable of something?

LYDIA JONES: I don't recall using that phrase, *inherently incapable*, but I did say that the primary structuring ideas of American identity—the ones that sustain us as a culture through time—orient us away from dealing with racism, not toward dealing with it. That's not quite the same thing, because it leaves open the possibility for learning, but for regular people it will feel the same.

DF: Which ones orient us away from it? I mean ... most people would think that liberty and justice for all, and equality and civil rights and all those superhero values are the ones that are most American. Aren't they?

LJ: In my view, all those wonderful values are reposed on something else. We think they're core, but they aren't. If you take all the words you just used—all those superhero values, as you call them—and cluster them like a little galaxy on the blackboard, you can ask yourself a helpful question, which is: 'What's the gravitational center that holds those ideas together? What is the organizing principle, as it were, that keeps them in orbit?' If you spend time on it, you'll find that a productive answer is 'individualism' and the worth of the single person. In one way, that is very beautiful. But it's also pretty unyielding. If you are entirely focused on the individual, you end up with blinders on for other things. Conservatives—and a lot of white people generally—cling to the idea that we're all racially free now and we're equal and there's no more work to be done. Some say this because they're racist. But a lot of them aren't in my view. They do it because of their cherished belief in American individualism. When liberals or people of color draw attention to race, it sounds to conservatives and libertarians and individualists like we're splitting people into groups, rather than helping them overcome the condition of being born into a group. Individualists claim to be aspiring to unity. In a twisted way, they think that focusing on and addressing racism is itself a kind of racism because it subordinates individuals to group status.

DF: So individualism is the problem?

LJ: It's not so much a problem as a paradox, isn't it? It's both the problem and the solution. What we're up against now is a conservative movement anchored in a way of seeing Americanness that says that any attention to group problems, or trying to actively support diversity through representation is actually divisive and discriminatory itself. This, by the way, is why they call liberals un-American. Any attention to group suffering or group needs is divisive in their view. People of color cry out, saying that we're in pain, but they deny the pain and say it's an individual pain, not a group one. They see the entire world through this *individualism prism*—or that's what I call it in the article, anyway. It negates discussions of race and racism. In my view, this perspective is overpowering and insurmountable maybe because it's deeper than race. It's deeper than politics. It's a culturally organizing system. It's how we achieve Americanness. It's how we do Americanness. It's a kind of performance. If this is true, America can win battles against racism in court or in passing new laws and adopting new policies, but we'll never win the war on history and circumstance because it requires people seeing with different eyes; eyes that would force them to unravel and redefine their American selves. And that's the one thing we can't do, because it's the only thing that binds us all together. One can't escape the observation that America historically enslaves groups, but only frees individuals.

He sat on this knowledge for weeks like it was a guilty secret—as though he had stolen a furtive look at her diary and knew more about her than she would ever have told him. It felt as though any look in its direction, any admission that her conclusions were real—any attention given to their racial identities—would wake them from a dream or break a spell. He wasn't delusional about the depth of their bond, but he needed to find a way of overcoming what might be the cause of their future ending. He couldn't look past the obvious irony: He wanted to elevate their uniqueness by negating the very history that Lydia had argued was essential to their condition.

But . . . he was Norwegian. Did American race relations extend to him? Is whiteness contagious?

"How is everything?" the Canadian waiter had asked.

Marcus didn't answer. He was watching Lydia sprinkle flaked salt on a piece of bread.

"Fine, thank you," Lydia had said.

That is when her phone rang. The ringtone was old-fashioned, the way home phones in America used to sound. Their main courses had not yet arrived. The waiter cleared the table as she reached into her purse and checked the number.

"It's Karen," she whispered, the candlelight reflecting off her eyes and the phone.

Her sister. She needed to take this.

Jeffrey—with whom Marcus had played chess twice and lost, with whom he'd played Battleship once and won—had been shot by the police. He was dead.

Marcus could hear Karen choking on her grief on the phone. The sounds were pre-verbal, pre-human. Anguish.

Lydia's impulse was to make Karen's pain stop. As she opened her mouth to speak, though, the breathlessness entered her too. It swelled inside her, silently, and her eyes filled with tears as her free hand moved—not toward Marcus—but to her own throat. When she finally gasped for air it sounded like a valve opening and a cold wind rushed into her, filling her, and remaining there.

Marcus led her to the parking lot. In the car—in time, and once the engine started to cover the sound, she sobbed. He raised his hand to place it on her back but he didn't dare.

In the dark, smelling of fine cologne and perfume, and rent from all capacity for speech, they drove back to the United States across the border, where the guards asked, again, if they had anything to declare.

The boys with the melted chocolate meals would be gone tomorrow, they'd said. It is just as well. It is only a matter of time, Marcus thinks, before the police arrive here; before the black helicopters appear through the rain clouds and pierce the night with their blinking red and green lights—an orange shadow aglow in their cockpits, their pilots soaring over the water like mystical demigods, whirling their blades for divine justice with no sense of its value.

It would be best if Sigrid didn't come, Marcus thinks as he pushes forward the cylinder release on his Taurus .38 revolver and counts the rounds. She doesn't need to see this. He knows what it looks like when a story is over and he understands how the parts must fulfill their dramatic promises. Lydia's parents need her story to end in a way that removes all doubt. The police need a villain. The black community does too. And it's fine. He deserves it. He did then, and he does now. It is better this way.

Still. It would be better for Sigrid to hear about it all later. Like the first time.

THE SOFA

THIS MOTEL, SIGRID learns, doesn't even have an ice machine. It crouches in the woods behind a black pool of asphalt that shimmers in the rain, the oil rising to the surface and distorting the inverted letters mounted on the roof—L-E-T-O-M.

Her brief internet search for Saranac Lake back at the police station had made the town look picturesque. This motel was not in those photos.

The window is open and Sigrid sits on the edge of the bed. The colors inside are warm but uninviting. Burnt umber in the bedspread. Yellow from the aged bulbs. A red carpet worn to the white threads at the door. She is the only one staying here tonight aside from the fat man in the office watching a game show.

It had been easier getting here than she'd expected. Irv's people are helpful and accommodating, but their willingness to drive her out here without his sign-off confirmed her suspicion that they are too officious and overly yielding to authority—whether real or imagined. If it were her team she would start demanding more critical thinking.

The main office at the sheriff's station has a television mounted to the wall on a swing arm, and Sigrid had been able to see it from her jail cell. The news report from the Target parking lot had been broadcast live. She watched a well-dressed black man carry a colorful umbrella and talk to the crowd of people as Melinda exited the patrol car. A ticker ran across the bottom of the screen telling of the deescalating tensions.

There was no more drama to watch and, she realized, no more reason for her to remain at the police station. The time had come to move on.

Setting out for the Adirondacks alone felt right. Irv could catch up later. Or not. At this point, finding Marcus was more important.

She may not have needed Irv but she did still need a ride. Taking another American bus deliberately was not going to happen. That smell of rotting processed meat and stale cigarettes, the whiff of urine from the platforms, the exhaust fumes, the sweaty feet up on the armrests . . . there had to be another way.

Leaving her jail cell, she found a young deputy out in the main room named Eddie Caldwell. There was something in his face that made Sigrid believe he had never experienced pain.

"Irv wants you to drive me to Saranac Lake," Sigrid had said. "We have to leave now. You know who I am, right?"

Eddie looked skeptical but also impressionable, so Sigrid leaned into the lie. "I'm Chief Inspector Sigrid Ødegård. And we're running a little late. I wouldn't mind a bit of hustle."

Eddie grabbed his jacket and told a woman named Alice he'd be back in a few hours, and off they went.

Sigrid's first motel visit had been shared with two bottles of second-rate blended whiskey and a gigantic bucket of ice. She'd spent her time wiggling her toes and staring at them. This time, Sigrid wants to do better.

Tomorrow she plans to visit Frank Allman, the local sheriff, as soon as the station opens at nine in the morning. It is her assumption that Frank will be there and Irv will not. This should give her time alone to apprise Allman of the situation with Marcus and to see whether he's inclined toward a thoughtful and considered approach to finding him or—in the vein of Irv's SERT commander, Pinkerton— he's preparing to burn the forest to find Marcus. If it's the latter, Sigrid will have to put her new plan into motion.

This new plan, unlike her failed biker-bar plan, is going to work. All that's required is a map, Marcus's GPS coordinates, and—if the situation turns dire—a lot of alcohol. In a few minutes she'll have everything she needs.

She takes the key and leaves.

The motel is a dump, yes, but its saving grace is its proximity to an all-night liquor store. Outside, along a path worn into the grass by the side of the road, Sigrid draws in the evening smells of warm pavement and fresh rain before entering a surprisingly well-stocked freestanding garage of a liquor store. An electronic *bing-bing* announces her entrance, but no one inside acknowledges it. She collects a green plastic basket with two stainless handles and swings it from her arm while whistling a new song by Maria Mena.

In Norway there is only one store for alcohol and it can be found in cities all across the country: the Wine Monopoly. It is state-owned and taxed beyond reason, and the cheapest bottle of fermented Austrian sludge costs around seventeen dollars. Here, though. Oh . . . here it is different. Here is where a plan comes together at the right price.

When Sigrid and Marcus were children they would find discarded soda and beer bottles in a creek that ran through the center of the village. They'd soak off the labels, wash them off, and then—in the deepest, darkest, deadest of night, way, way after eight o'clock—they'd balance the colored bottles on upturned flashlights, casting an eerie green aura across the room, turning their cozy home into a flickering cloud of nuclear mist. Into that toxic cloud they'd tell ghost stories until someone—usually Marcus—freaked out.

All those bottles are here. And so are all those blended whiskeys for people who can't afford or appreciate the single-malts in aisle three. And, yes, there are her friends from the Isle of Skye, and the Highlands, and a few Lowlands, and—look!—a sale on almost-properly-shaped whiskey glasses.

She doesn't need whiskey, though. She first needs the clear stuff. Aisle two has that, and she finds four bottles that she's going to need later and places them in her basket. They have a fake Russian name and are bottled in New Jersey, but they are one hundred proof, and that's value for money.

What she wants for herself, though, is rum.

Rum is not so popular in Oslo. Ron Zacapa 23, which is good, has more or less completed its world domination and now colonizes the upper shelves of all the Vinmonopolets, leaving the lower shelves for Bacardi, which is less for drinking than spilling on the floors of bad clubs. Here, though, is a bottle she once bought at a duty-free in Brussels. The El Dorado 21. And it is only a hundred dollars.

That same bottle would have been over three hundred in Oslo.

"Excuse me," Sigrid says to the man at the counter, who resembles a leather-clad bear. "I'd like that bottle of El Dorado Twenty-One, please. It's in the locked cabinet."

It is ten o'clock at night. There is no music in the store. A quartz clock ticks behind the man.

"That's a hundred bucks plus tax. You know that, right?"

"It's a bargain, believe me. You should try it."

The man snorts through his fur. "I can't afford that," he says, collecting a cabinet key attached to a giant plank of driftwood so that, she assumes, it won't be lost or stolen or carried off by someone smaller than himself.

When he returns with the rum and starts ringing up the sale, he looks down at the vodka she's stockpiled like artillery rounds.

"You know these other bottles are garbage, right? Even the Royal Gate is better than those."

"It's what I need."

As she waits for the man to charge her credit card she watches the silent television playing above his head. A portly middle-aged woman is standing on a ledge in front of four enormous red balls mounted over a pool of water. As Sigrid stares, trying to figure out the purpose of this game show, a massive wall swings into view, slapping her from behind and sending her hurtling over the top of the first ball before she falls headfirst into the gap with the second ball and then sort of ricochets between the two until dropping face-first into the pool below.

"What is that?" she asks as he hands back the card.

"*Wipeout.*"

"Why would people put themselves through that?"

"For your viewing pleasure. And money."

"What channel's it on?"

Back at the motel, on the bed, the television tuned, Sigrid pours a generous portion of rum into her bathroom's tumbler. Shoes off, toes out, she closes her eyes and sniffs, allowing it to transport her to places where the colors are primary and rich, the sea is turquoise and white, and the sunset creates a new kind of evening warmth in the company of people who could talk for hours and hours about forensics, criminal investigation, and comparative methods of violence reduction. With some great music playing, of course.

She touches her lips to the rum and draws the tiniest of sips.

The phone rings and she ignores it.

She takes another, longer, and more languorous pull, allowing it to roll across and around her tongue for the duration of two, three, and finally four rings before swallowing. The warmth of the Caribbean glows inside her and for a brief moment she is young and hopeful and possibly someone else.

She answers the phone.

"Hello?"

From the phone comes a cold bitter wind that blows from the lips of Sheriff Irving Wylie.

His tone is the message, so she holds the phone away from her ear. Whatever he's ranting about, an arm's length away, now sounds like a couple of bumblebees in divorce court.

During a pause, when Irv stops ranting to inhale, Sigrid places the receiver against her face and says, "Everyone knows where I am, Irving. I wanted to get an early start when we look for Marcus tomorrow. Have a few moments alone with Frank Allman. What else did you think I was going to do, Irv? Really. I flew here from Norway. I'm not going to sit around in your jail cell until your schedule clears up."

Irv grumbles in what might have been Hebrew, Latin, or Greek.

"How'd it go tonight?" Sigrid asks, pouring more.

Irv says something about no one getting shot.

"Come on," she urges. "How did you deal with the protesters?"

"It was a mob with pitchforks going after innocent monsters, but monsters all the same."

"Is that how you treated them?"

"No. I treated them like legitimately angry citizens and members of my constituency who deserved to be understood, in the hopes it might calm things down."

"You talked to them?"

"No. I sent the local reverend. Or, more to the point, I asked for his help and he begrudgingly obliged."

"That was either very cowardly or very wise," Sigrid says.

"It might have been both."

"So why do you sound like your puppy died?"

"You alone?" he wants to know.

Sigrid isn't sure why he is asking. "Yes."

"I've come around to the idea that maybe Lydia committed suicide and Marcus . . . I don't know, failed to stop her or something. The thing is, Fred Green doesn't want me to arrest Marcus."

"Why doesn't Green want you to arrest Marcus?"

"Because we might let him go."

"Perhaps because it's late, and I'm drinking, Irv, but I'm not following you."

"I've been rolling it around in my head and the best I can land on is this: It would be worse to arrest Marcus and then let him go than to not arrest him at all."

"But the alternative to murder would be suicide, and that would be a bad conclusion too."

"Yes. But an unsolved crime is better than a solved one where justice is denied. In the first instance the police are simply uncaring or incompetent. In the second, we're actively racist. Which is what releasing Marcus would look like. Assuming he gets released. Which he might not. This is all making my head spin."

"Are things that bad out there?"

"Clearly, some people think so."

"Maybe there was no crime, Irv. As you said."

"In which case . . . Lydia's parents live in torment forever thinking of their daughter in hell."

"Religion is cruel."

"Procedure says I have to bring Marcus in, Sigrid. You know that. The 9-1-1 call, the eyewitness, the disappearance, the golden triangle of motive, means, and opportunity . . ."

"We don't have a motive."

"There's love involved, Sigrid. You can always impute a motive. And this happened blocks from Marcus's house. And he was there. So something happened and it was something emotional. Clearly. But . . . let me finish."

Sigrid can hear him adjust the phone and she uses the moment to take a sip and reconnect with the Caribbean.

Irv continues: "Here's my worry. If you're right about Lydia's suicide, it means that Marcus was a nice guy in the wrong place at the wrong time. He runs away from guilt and grief. We bring him in, but then we let him go. That's the law. But not the optics. Because from outside, all we see is a black professional woman who was the aunt of Jeffrey Simmons murdered by a white man with supremacist connections who is soon released without charges by a police department a town over from where Roy Carman was exonerated by a grand jury. You'll notice how the inside voices don't sound the same as the outside voices, and the same facts sound very different depending on what you emphasize."

"The facts of the case remain the facts of the case," Sigrid says, "whatever they sound like, and whatever language you use. I accept that you have a communication problem, and a race problem, and a political problem. But you don't have an evidentiary one. I'm not going to let you lock up Marcus because your country can't get a grip on itself. Your job is to solve the case," says Sigrid. "Not fix America."

"Maybe not, but I don't want to burn it down, either. I live here."

Sigrid pours herself another and, thanks to a highly attuned ear for that particular sound, Irv asks what she's drinking.

"It's a twenty-one-year-old rum. I haven't seen this bottle in four years."

"How much have you got left?"

"Why do you want to know?"

"For the same reason I want to know how many clean glasses you have left."

"There's one wrapped in paper in the bathroom."

"You have plans for it?"

"I usually just use one," Sigrid says.

"I'm coming over."

"I didn't invite you."

"I'll knock."

By the time Irv arrives, Sigrid is asleep. As promised he knocks gently on the door and she, groggily, walks barefoot across the threadbare carpet near the door. She opens it and he stands outside with his hat in his hands, looking more boyish than she remembers him.

"You actually drove all the way here?" she mutters. "At this time of night?"

"We need an early start, like you said. And I can't drink in the morning."

"It's easier than it looks," she says.

"I have some strong stuff in the car. Should I bring it in?"

"Why did you get divorced?" she asks him, hand on the door and pinching sleep from her eyes.

"We didn't have any questions left for each other. Why aren't you married?"

"When I was young I thought it was me. When I grew up I started thinking it was them. And then I stopped thinking about it entirely."

"How about that drink?" Irv asks.

"You're sleeping on the sofa, Irv."

"There's a sofa?"

"Not all of your plans work out either, huh?" she says.

Sigrid flattens her palm against the door. Irv lowers his head and slips inside the room, placing his hat on the dresser to his right, below the mirror that faces the bed. Sigrid releases the door and allows the natural forces of the spring to do the rest.

FALLING

I T WAS AN epithelial ovarian carcinoma. Sigrid's mother, Astrid, was under thirty-five years old and otherwise in excellent health, so it was caught late, during stage three, when her chances of surviving five more years were twenty-nine percent. There was no familial link. No genetic predisposition that might have warned her. Cancer cells had spread from the ovaries to the lining of the abdomen. Morten was the first to know, and so the first to hold the secret. They ordered themselves along two fronts—managing the cancer, and managing her decline in front of the children.

She told her husband everything. They only spoke about it in their bedroom so as to keep the plague contained and so that the place where life was created—where the children were conceived—could counter the forces of death. They did not say this. Words were immaterial. And yet, together and with a shared understanding, they cordoned off the topic from the wider world and locked it in a private place.

Astrid's doctor was named Gunnar Nilsen. He was calm and precise. In his early fifties, he had no talent for putting her, or anyone else, at ease. Astrid would later learn, through discussions with Dr.

Nilsen's secretary, Hilde, that he was tired of his job spent with suffering innocents. His own father had suggested he take up architecture as it was more suited to Gunnar's disposition. To his father's mind, such a job would be creative, solitary, and less socially or emotionally demanding. And so Gunnar went into oncology to spite his father while secretly resenting his own success. Astrid asked Hilde if she should see someone else. "No," she explained. "He's very good. His spite runs very deep."

Astrid met him in a rotation of examination rooms. She peed into cups and submitted to blood tests and waited for human contact that never arrived.

She sat on the crunchy rolling paper on the elevated table with her feet dangling childishly when Nilsen came in on a Tuesday. He smiled weakly and sat down. They did not shake hands. He opened a brown folder. He explained what stage three meant, what stage four looks like, and, to some extent, would feel like.

Morten later learned that there had been a great many studies and debates and codes of conduct written to control the information and tone of conversation between doctors and patients in response to the question of longevity. The professional consensus favored a stance of managed ignorance. Oh, there are many factors at play, they would often say, and a lot we still don't know. There's diet, weight, attitude, prior history, age, support systems, and dumb luck that you may label miracle. All these factors factor in, one might say, and there are many possible outcomes. For your case . . . we can't really know, so let's focus on the treatment. That is a common approach. It was not Dr. Nilsen's.

"Mrs. Ødegård," he had said, "you have a twenty-nine percent chance of surviving five years. Those five years will be declining years, and they will be hard for you and those around you."

And then—because his son was taking drugs and he and his wife were strained to the emotional breaking point and couldn't believe that all their education and experience gave them no edge over common folk, and because their failure seemed to prove that his own father might have been right—he continued beyond the point of necessity or even utility. If he had stayed with convention he would have told Astrid's husband first. But he strayed: "Your family will likely react in one of two ways. They will either start to distance themselves from you now, imperceptibly at first and not at all consciously, but genuinely and significantly to protect themselves from their eventual loss, or else they will redouble their love and commitment to you, making your death that much more unbearable and excruciating. If you love your family, I suggest you think about this."

This is what Astrid conveyed to Morten later that night in their bedroom when the children were asleep. They drank a white wine that was dry and cold. He now has no memory of its taste.

It was not a twenty-nine percent chance of a cure. Or surviving for a full life. It was twenty-nine percent of lasting five years.

"You're suffering from perspective," he said to her.

"That's what we say about Marcus," she said. Her voice was weak.

"He asks very big questions," Morten said.

"All children do," she told him.

"Yes," Morten replied, "but they don't all lose sleep over it. He does."

"I'm dying, Morten."

"I know," he said. They did not lie about this.

"I think I know what it's going to be like," she said in the dark. That night she wore a flannel robe of blues and blacks. Crosshatched and boxy. She often slept in a scarf. He bought her one of fine cashmere. It held the heat she produced that much longer.

"Tell me," he said.

She turned her head and looked out the window. A waxing moon. A sliver on the edge of a black ball.

"Where was I before I was born?" she said. "That's what they all ask."

"Who?"

"Children. Adults. All of us. Where was I? Before there was a where. Before there was an I. It is inconceivable," she'd said, "for there to be no self and no place to put it. That's what it will be like. Like falling backwards into a pocket of space that constricts and then pops out of existence."

He said nothing.

"Where am I now, Morten?"

"Here with me."

"What's the difference?"

"Between something and nothing? Quite a lot."

"It's not enough, though, is it?" she'd said.

"Actually, it is." He raised himself higher onto his elbow. "You know what the secret to death is?" Morten said.

She smiled at that. He had made her smile. He remembers that.

"Tell me the secret to death," she answered, mocking him.

"You have to back into it," he'd told her.

"What does that mean?"

"You stop staring ahead into the void. There's nothing to see. You need to turn around. Watch life. Watch it like a rabbit about to come out of a hat. Keep your eye on it the whole time until — like that — the seeing is no more. That's the trick."

"What made you such an expert?" she asked.

"I've never once taken my eyes off of you," he told her.

She remained still.

"Do you remember our song?" he asked.

"Yes," she said. But she didn't name it. Instead she looked at the moon through the frosted window. "The children," she finally said. "Marcus won't be able to do this. My death," she said to Morten, "will change him. But my dying . . . my prolonged act of dying . . . that will destroy him. We need to do something about that. We need to make the prolonged part go away. Can you do that for me?" she asked.

"Yes," he'd said.

Astrid nodded as though the conversation was over.

From the vent above their bed came a scuffing sound — the sound of an animal trapped inside. A mouse, a bird, a squirrel. Everything that could fit had been lodged in the chimney at some point, and this sound was usually the first indication. They looked at each other and before Morten could comment there was a loud crash from inside the house.

Morten swung himself off the bed and ran into the children's room —found Sigrid fast asleep with a stuffed camel—but he didn't see Marcus.

"Marcus?" he called out.

"Here," came a weak voice, a voice that was fighting back tears.

In the downstairs bathroom Morten found Marcus curled up in the fetal position, clutching his left arm tightly against his body. He wore mismatching pajamas of red bottoms and a blue T-shirt top, and both were too small for him. His face was awash in tears from pain, but he held back his screams. Morten heard his son biting for air as he rocked back and forth on the gray-slate floor, pressing his forehead into the stone and starting to wail over what would prove to be a broken arm.

Marcus often used this bathroom when they ran out of paper upstairs. How he broke his arm, though, was a mystery Morten planned to solve later but never did.

"It's going to be all right, Marcus. Everything will be OK," he said, crouching onto the floor and wrapping his arms around his son. "It'll be OK."

But Morten was wrong.

He took Marcus to the hospital, where they confirmed he had broken his radius and needed a cast. It was an over-the-elbow type that mercifully left his thumb and fingers exposed. "Six weeks, come back," the doctor told them, and sent them home.

Astrid had to stay behind in the house with her sleeping daughter. She curled into bed with her and placed her open palm on the girl's chest. The window was cracked open because the room smelled like acrylic paint. She had seen a picture in a magazine of a red tree with butterflies and decided to enliven the children's room with color and whimsy. Astrid could hear the wind in the trees outside and Sigrid's slow and peaceful breathing. A glorious, living heat radiated from her body, and her arms swept comically across the bed. Lying there, Astrid absorbed Sigrid's youth and her health and tried not to think. The boys would be back soon. Marcus would be exhausted. She knew he'd fall asleep in the car on the ride home. Morten would carry him in and put him to bed on the sofa downstairs to avoid the stairs. There was a blanket on the sofa, and a pillow. He would sleep well.

Soon after, a soothing summer rain started and Astrid listened to the drops on the roof and windows; the heavier drops falling from the gutters to puddles collecting below. She took comfort in knowing that the children would listen to that sound too. Her job—her duty—was now to cast their ship as far forward as possible into the sea without holding on to it for too long, thereby delaying their journey.

After putting the photos into the box last night, Morten found a bottle of very good whiskey and drank as much as he wanted. In the morning he ate eggs, sausage, and toast with two cups of coffee, which he rarely does. Afterward he drove to the church.

It is a small and white building in a pool of grass. It is austere, as they all are in the Lutheran north, but it is not unwelcoming. The doors are closed this morning; there is no one else there.

He has not been to visit Astrid's grave in . . . it must be some four months or so now. The last time was in April after the snow had retreated, leaving only small pools like cream collecting in the brown hollows on the dark sides of hills. The days, then, were already appreciably longer, and what had been hard ice on the path through the gravestones had melted. Left behind were millions of pebbles the community council had used to keep mourners from slipping. Now, the snow long gone, each stone digs into the soft soles of his leather shoes. There is truly no point in dressing properly in this country. The expectations don't require it and the physical conditions don't allow it. That too is something to lament. And yet he trudges on, stubbornly, defiantly, dressing properly and wearing good shoes.

When he reaches her, Morten bends low but does not place his knee to the ground. He arranges the small bouquet of flowers in the holder at the base of the grave.

Astrid had wanted to be cremated and her ashes scattered in the hills, but Morten had begged her not to. It was too much, he'd said. "I can't take the thought of fire. Just . . . spare me that. A place—somewhere to go. Do that for me."

"You know I won't be there," she'd said to him.

"No, but I will."

True to analysis and now true to fact, here he is. The August winds are picking up and the first smoky scent of the coming autumn is already in the air. "It's warmer where the kids are," he says to her. Morten doesn't feel closer to her here, nor does he feel more at peace, but her grave gives him something to tend to. Something to do with his hands: something to husband.

Morten removes a small white cloth from his pocket, wraps his finger inside it, and traces the letters of her name, returning them to a sharp white.

"I had thought they could help each other," Morten says to Astrid. "I didn't know Lydia died. He hadn't said. I sent Sigrid there because I thought he could help her. They were so close, those kids. I remember that morning over breakfast—you remember the one—when you were watching them paint with watercolors and you realized they loved each other more than they loved us. I was a bit jealous, I admit," he says, "but you said it's better that way because they'll have each other the longest. That was the first time I understood that you and I had created something together. We created the children, obviously, but here we had created things that loved each other completely and independently of us. It was like watching balloons dance together as they rise up to the clouds."

Morten stops talking and looks around to make sure he is still alone.

"Balloons," he says, appalled at himself. "I'm talking to ducks now too. Ferdinand. We haven't had a pet since the cat. I figured I was done. To be honest with you, I'm a little lonely.

"Astrid, the reason I'm here is that something is wrong with our son. When you died, Marcus fell apart. It was worse than we could have imagined. He became a shadow of the boy he had been before. I feel as though you already know this, but I need to say it anyway. Since then, one way or another, I believe he has been looking to return to the magic of those early days with the watercolors. When he was safe in our presence and joined in every way with his sister. Undistracted. Now . . . he roams the world looking for something, which is always elusive or denied to him.

"As much as I lost Marcus," he continues, "I gained Sigrid—I gained her in ways I didn't deserve. I feel as though I didn't earn her affections; I simply lost or sent away everything else she loved. We are so close now, and it means so much to me, that I feel guilty. I think our bond is too tight. I hold her too close. We closed up the space where other people might belong. She has no husband. I thought by sending her to America to be with Marcus, we could bring him back somehow. Bring us all back together at just the right moment. Time seems to be running out though. I joke with her, but I'm concerned."

Morten puts his hands into his pockets to fish for his pipe but it is not there.

"He wrote me a letter. He said it had happened again. At first I didn't know what he meant. But now," he says to Astrid, "I'm wondering if it had something to do with you."

MY MOTHER

S IGRID WAKES TO the sound of Irv in the shower bellowing out a song she doesn't know. It involves somebody knockin' and whether Irv should let him in. And then something about the devil and blue jeans.

He is quite committed to the tune.

It has been a long time since Sigrid has shared a bottle and talked for hours. She tried with her Ambien-recommending friend Eli after the Horowitz case last month but it didn't work. Unfortunately, Eli isn't very good at drinking. She doesn't understand that as a bottle drains, it does not become empty so much as it becomes filled with the room around it; its moods and emotions mix with whatever remains in the bottle so that every subsequent drop expounds greater truths and erstwhile beauties.

But only if you can hear it. And Eli, poor Eli, simply does not have the ear.

Irving does.

This morning Irv sings and Sigrid lies against the pillow, beneath the warm blanket. The first cars of the day make their way across the dew-soaked asphalt outside. Across from her is the old cathode-ray television and a cream-colored hotel phone with a key pad that looks ancient today. This room hasn't returned to the 1980s but has stayed there. Shabby as it is, there is a comfort in the familiar.

In Oslo, Sigrid lives alone. She is accustomed to solitude. But there is a new quality to solitude here in America—one that is less about being alone and more about standing beside time itself as though it is a river you can watch flow past from the bank. In Norway, she always feels the presence of the city, the country, and government, the grand agendas of politics and continental debate. Even in her solitude there, she feels connected—not emotionally, perhaps, but factually, as if the shared journey is always a character in her life.

Not here, though. Not in this motel that is separate from the flow of time. Here she is an individual. Classic rock songs on the radio sound current and cowboy boots are tomorrow's fashion, not just yesterday's. And unlike anyplace she's been in Europe, here she feels . . . separate. She can slip into oblivion if she chooses or rend her clothing from the top of a building and demand the attention of the world. The choice, though, is hers.

Until this moment she's always thought of America's lack of interest and sophistication about Europe—and the rest of the world, it seems —as a kind of ignorance and inferiority. But lying here, she has the most unexpected sensation of *destination*; as if here is all that really exists and is the only place she is meant to be. It isn't a wonderful place, or even special. But it is present and vivid, the way life was as a child.

Beyond the American shores—from that television on the dresser —come stories about life and events elsewhere. But they feel removed and abstract and safely, even inherently, far away. Sigrid does not feel cut off from the wider world so much as she feels it doesn't really exist. Is that what it feels like to be American?

The singing stops and the water with it. He starts to whistle. He's terrible. This becomes a hum when he brushes his teeth and then —surprisingly—blow-dries his hair. He appears in the doorway in a towel with the smile and swagger of a man who's won a prize for something made in his garage with a spot welder.

"Howdy," he smiles.

"OK."

"It's gonna be a good one. I can feel it," he says, whipping off the towel and dressing as if they were married. "We're going to go out there under that warm sun in a rented canoe, we're going to shimmy up to your brother, who's going to be so glad to see you that a tear comes to his eye, you're going to convince him to come back and tell us the story, and then we're going to bring the stakeholders to this nightmare together and see if we can't find a smart way to ease us all back from the brink of a new race riot—oh yes, we are. And later, when President McCain pins that Medal of Freedom on my chest, I'm going to accept it with all the humility that befits my station . . ."

"Good God, Irving. What is it with you people and all the words?"

"I'm as energized as that little pink bunny this morning."

"We didn't have sex last night."

"And yet I feel like I did. Isn't it fantastic?"

Irv buckles up his pants as Sigrid walks in her panties and Marcus's T-shirt to the steamy bathroom. Kicking Irv out, she showers. When she emerges Irv is not in the room at all. Alone, she applies more than her usual amount of makeup, in part to remedy her late night of drinking and not sleeping, and also because the memory of her face on television is still fresh.

Irv returns twenty minutes later with three local newspapers and a bag full of muffins. He is balancing two cups of coffee in a cardboard holder, designed for a nation on the go.

"It's seven," says Irv, handing her the coffee and flopping down into the chair by the window. "I realize you got here first and this is your call, but for my two cents, I say we first visit Frank Allman, learn what's what and take stock, and then we'll see if the police have a boat on the lake. I figure they must. We're out of our jurisdiction, but these guys won't mind if we take a peek. I bought Marcus a blueberry muffin. Does he like blueberries?"

"American blueberries are different than Norwegian ones."

"What's the difference?"

"Ours are smaller and blue on the inside. Yours are bigger but aren't blue."

"Our blueberries aren't blue enough for you?"

"No."

"Don't tell Maine."

"It was nice of you to bring my brother your inferior muffin."

"Like I said, it's all going to work out just fine."

By nine o'clock in the morning the three young men who had been camping near Marcus had waved their goodbyes to him, packed their canoe, and left behind a patch of flattened thistles and a black char of ash. Marcus—finally alone—walks among the stones and fallen marshmallows and stands in the spot where they'd laughed last night. Hands in his pockets, he takes refuge in the absence of those same sounds.

Nearby, two black crows are tussling over the remains of a hot dog coated in dirt. The tube of meat splits into uneven pieces and each crow takes flight with its own share.

Marcus kicks through the needles and leaves at the campsite. Raucous they may have been, but the campers didn't leave behind anything that wasn't biodegradable. They were, ultimately, good kids.

The lake is dimpled by a breeze, as gentle as a confession. The sea birds bob with their backs warming, their feathers dry and glowing. The rain did not reach here last night. The thin mist on the lake is only the morning's haze. It will burn off. There is a deep blue above that will soon scorch the world when the angle is right. For now, though, he breathes in the morning.

He could be done with it immediately and he knows this. Guns are good that way. In the eye, the mouth, the temple. Painless and instantaneous. It isn't even scary, really. The brains are blown out before the sound wave of the bullet even reaches the ear. Which doesn't matter anyway, because by then there's no brain to process it.

The Taurus .38 revolver is in the same orange backpack he brought to America eighteen years ago; it was that and his guitar. It is a pity not to have it here too, but he left it behind in his room because he knew it would make him too melancholy and possibly rob him of the courage for what needs to be done. The sound of picking a C chord and transitioning to an A minor using the C/B note is simply too beautiful to be halted and replaced with a gun. Leonard Cohen's "Hallelujah" begins this way. Marcus knew he didn't have the fortitude to move from that sound to death. The distance would be too great.

So: The stage is set. All that is required now is for the player to perform his part. It is a one-man show without an audience. What, then, is he waiting for?

A completeness. A sense of the whole. A resolution. A return to the tonic. A way to close off this life before ending it. This is what he doesn't feel yet. There is something left undone.

Marcus would laugh at the idea if he could. How remarkable that a need for aesthetic balance can fend off death itself.

He was told once that the wavelength of a note is precisely half as long when played one octave higher. This makes music a physical presence, not only a learned convention. The mind actually rebels at sonic discord; the absence of harmony can cause actual physical pain. Could that be true for a story, too? And if for a story, what about a life?

Jeffrey's? Lydia's? His own?

The gun is heavy. It is beautifully made.

He is surrounded by harmony and balance and composition. It is why he has always liked it here. Remembering makes him part of that.

Karen called Lydia when they were in Montreal. Jeffrey had been dead for four hours before she had been able to dial.

Lydia was alive for two more months.

During those two months—from the distance at which she kept him—he watched her decline.

It was different from his mother's decline. In their house, when he was a little boy, Astrid was calm and quiet and withdrawn. Her motions and activities were ritualistic and mechanical. The way she washed dishes. Washed the clothing. Corrected his homework. Marcus watched Lydia suffocate under the pressures of injustice and hopelessness around her. It was a suffocation born of history but felt in her throat. This was not his mother's death. That was only personal. She had been in charge, despite the cancer. She had chosen to emotionally remove herself from life. For Lydia, life was being ripped away and torn out.

Sigrid—little Sigrid—had barely noticed. Sigrid hopped into her mother's arms in the mornings and complained and demanded like little children do; she rattled off stories as she turned herself into a mannequin with clothing flying on and off—this matches, this doesn't, where's the one with the flowers?—as her mouth produced a flurry of ideas, each featherweight and irrelevant on its own, but together becoming evidence of a contented child living a present-minded life. Growing. Alive.

Marcus does not remember himself that way. He was older. His arm was broken and wrapped in a cast with a blue coating. He understands now that he projected the literal feelings into a metaphor and came to see his mother like a statue, as immobile as he was—the cancer a calcification working its way outward, her skin hardening into a moon-pale stone. She would occasionally ask him about his broken arm but he said only "It's fine." He visualized the cancer that he'd heard about in the bathroom as a coldness inside her that was spreading; the way ice crystals form on still pools of water in the early winter. The crystals were so cold, they were almost black. He remembers hearing the ice inside her freezing. It hardened in her veins and arteries and seeped into her organs, threatening—and then promising—to constrict her heart until it stopped.

Lydia always hated Marcus's house, but he had tried to keep it clean for her between the time of their first post-lecture coffee conversation and the Montreal trip. They usually went to her place—a two-bedroom on the upper floor of an old Victorian converted into a condo. There were some rare times, however, when she would come by and stay over. As their relationship deepened and stabilized in those formative weeks, she eventually commandeered a drawer and brought a few toiletries. He, in turn, stocked the fridge with the best he could buy, which was not much. Under these conditions she periodically stayed at his house. After Jeffrey, though, this stopped.

When they returned from Canada she pulled away from him. There were no more visits and he let the house go. They would see each other on campus and talk, but the connection—the sense of a love developing—was gone. She didn't end it yet, not explicitly. He tried to reel her back.

"Let me take care of you," he once said.

This is when she explained what his house "signified" to her. They were at her office. It was after hours. The janitor was buffing the floor with a giant metal polisher while listening to his iPod. The building was desolate.

Hers was a small office in a modern building. It had one large window that partly faced a green courtyard, but it was obstructed by another part of the same building. She there—the teacher—waiting for him to say something. He stood behind the chair reserved for the student. He wouldn't sit. Wouldn't play the student. He was her lover. He was here for an appeal, not a lecture or a grade. There were black-and-white photos on the wall of African American faces. He could recognize only a few: W.E.B. Du Bois. James Baldwin. Maya Angelou. Richard Wright. A black woman astronaut with a sweet face he should probably have recognized but didn't. A dozen more portraits or busts in small frames collected from yard sales and antiquing trips. He wanted to ask them: "What do I say?"

He didn't come for a lecture, but that is what she delivered. And not one that was heartfelt; not one that cried out from the vastness of her heart about loss and grief and anger. Lydia, instead, doubled down on academic and Latinate words of the intellect that seemed, to Marcus, inadequate and confining. The fancier her vocabulary, the more infuriated he became.

"What, Lydia?" he said after she started to explain calmly why, no, she did not want to visit him anymore. "What exactly does my apartment 'signify' to you?"

"Someone who couldn't even keep what he was born with," she answered.

"Which is what? We're not rich. We aren't powerful. My dad works on a farm. My sister is a cop. It was a little Norwegian farm that—"

"Your skin, Marcus! Your skin," she said finally.

Was this a truth revealing itself, or was it simply the most offensive thing she could think of in that exact moment because she was so hurt and there was no one closer at whom she could lash out? Are we most truthful during our anger or just the most creative in finding ways to hurt people?

"Your skin is a shield," she said. "My skin is a target. That's it. That's where the shovel hits the stone, don't you understand? It isn't some abstract discussion about inequality or indignity or history, Marcus. It's about being born into danger. It is *dangerous* to be black. To be *called* black. To be *labeled* black. To be singled out, specified, categorized, compartmentalized, and ultimately treated and shelved as black. Jeffrey was born with a bull's-eye for a face. And eventually someone shot at it. The end."

"I'm not a symbol, Lydia. I'm a person."

"You're both."

"I love you."

"I don't know what I was thinking," she said aloud but clearly to herself.

"Are you kidding me?"

"No," she said, immobile behind her desk.

Marcus was flailing for direction. Should he have been apologetic? For what? The past, the present, or the future? He was angry and defenseless and he felt wronged. Unable to think of how to defend himself, he chose to attack. This was the day of her death. These were the precipitating events. This is what he needs to relive and replay to settle on an understanding of this moment that will satisfy him while he sits by a pond in a forest in the soil of an America that will become his grave.

"You're blaming me for this?" he asked. "For Jeffrey? For . . . my God . . . America?"

"No," she'd said. "You're just some foreigner. I absolve you, Marcus. But I look at you and I think about it. I look at you and it reminds me. I look at you and I . . . Your skin, your hair, your penis. I don't want it near me anymore."

"I didn't do this," he yelled at her in his defense. "I don't want to let what's most random about us matter most. It's all so . . ."—he looked at her, he looked at the faces of the chorus on the wall, and through it all still said—"arbitrary!"

"It might be completely arbitrary that my skin tone makes my life dangerous and not yours, Marcus. But once it's true, it stops being arbitrary. It becomes very consequential."

And then, pathetically, he appealed the decision with the nothing that remained. Not as lover, not as an adult, not as a man. But as a child overwhelmed by impending loss and the final recognition that he was letting it all happen again; that words were failing him again. That if only he'd spoken his mind properly he could have saved it all. Again.

"My mother," he'd said.

She looked at him with pity but not comprehension. And he knew immediately that she wasn't going to. She had lost Jeffrey. A sister to heal. A family. A community. Students who were facing this . . . this . . . for the first time. He was a casualty, yes, but a lucky one. He was only walking wounded.

Even thinking about this is so embarrassing that he wants to vomit into the lake. Forty-six years old, and he was saying "my mother" to save a relationship that was only months in the making. They weren't married. There were no children to suffer from this. "My mother," he'd actually said. And he'd said it because there was a musical note to this. A tone. A shifting earth below the surface of their conversation that maybe hinted at another reason why she wanted him to go away. Was he hearing it or creating it? Was it an echo or a new sound? Was Lydia only sad, or was it deeper? Was she finished with not only him, but all of it?

It would have been better if she had quietly stood and taken him by the arm and led him into the hallway, saying nothing. But that isn't what happened. She folded her arms and acknowledged that he had turned this moment onto himself.

"What about your mother?" she asked.

"She had cancer. I had to watch her die," he said.

"I know, Marcus. And I'm sorry for you."

"I knew she was going to die."

"I really am sorry for you."

No, that isn't what he meant. He had meant something more specific than that. But he'd failed to find the right words. Again.

A HOT ONE

S HERIFF IRVING WYLIE'S Jeep Wagoneer chugs merrily into
the town of Saranac Lake. When they arrive, Sigrid feels as
though she has finally stepped onto the movie set of the small-
town America she had always imagined. The green forest wraps
around wooden homes that stand impervious to time and change. The
main street is simple, welcoming, and unmarred by the brand names
that litter the interstate and bordering towns. Saranac Lake is not
overwhelming in its beauty or aware of its own charm. It feels to Sigrid as though the town has discovered a way to live in harmony with
its own American self, and the source of her attraction to it comes
from its integrity. It is a proper destination; a place to experience a
way of life and an invitation to perform it correctly.

The lake itself is not called Saranac.

"Lake Flower," Irv tells her.

It is, at least today, a vision of tranquility, and its blue is less a reflection of the sky above it than a melody inspired by it. Beyond the lake
are distant mountains that ring Lake Placid, where the Olympics had

once been held—back when they were held every four years and were therefore interesting.

Sigrid looks out the open window as they drive. A dozen middle-aged women and pension-aged men have erected small easels and are painting the town and scenery. Two children wave at her and she waves back.

"It's delightful here," she says.

"You're surprised," Irv replies, turning toward the police station.

"This isn't what I've seen so far."

"You haven't seen us at our best. The whole area out here is inspiring and relaxing at the same time. A lot of celebrities and artists and famous folks have summer places out here. I've had the pleasure of meeting many of them, even became friends with a few. I used to set them up with security companies for their big parties, and help them manage the press. You might say I have fancy friends out here."

Irv drives down Broadway and through the intersection of Main Street.

"It's actually called Main Street?"

"Yeah. Why?"

"I thought that was a metaphor," Sigrid says, as a cyclist in Spandex and a helmet passes them briskly on the left.

"What?"

"Main Street. I thought it meant the primary street."

"It does."

"But it's also the actual name."

"Yes."

"Like . . . Watertown."

"Sigrid, I have no idea what you're going on about," Irv says, crossing an intersection marked as Route 3, passing a convenience store on the right, and then slowing to a near crawl as they pass over a bridge that abuts the lake on their left, which is due east. The sun breaks through the trees there and broils the car.

"Gonna be a hot one," Irv mutters.

He parks outside a low brick building that is tucked discreetly behind trees that separate it from the town.

Irv parks in the shade and proceeds into the station, but Sigrid lingers outside and walks the short distance to the edge of the lake, peering outward toward the distant forest and hills.

"Marcus," she whispers.

Of all places for us to end up.

In Oslo, like the smokers outside her office building, she too would often stand with her eyes closed to feel the heat—finally—upon her face. The entire city would loiter on street corners or between shops where the light broke between buildings and they would bask, for precious moments, as urban flowers of unwavering reverence.

Her colleague, Petter, used to mock her for the metaphor. "Flowers don't turn to the sun because they love the heat," he once said. "The sun is actually burning off the moisture of the cells on that side of the stalk, so the flower is collapsing in the direction of its tormenter," he explained.

"Sounds like love to me," she answered.

This New York sun, though, is vastly hotter than her Norwegian sun. These people talk about being upstate as though it means north. But it is not. It is barely 43 degrees north latitude. Compare that to Kristiansand at the southernmost tip of Norway, she would like to tell them. That is already 58 degrees north.

Even Venice is farther north than this.

No, this is south. And the sun burns like a southern sun.

Sigrid's solitude ends when a black van with SWAT markings rolls to a halt in the space beside the Wagoneer. Behind it, on a trailer, is a black Zodiac raft with an enormous engine.

Five men, unhurried, hop down from the back in helmets and full assault gear. The leader, emerging from the passenger side, is no one Sigrid has seen before, and the five other men look task-oriented but neither excited nor grave. Together with the driver, they set about off-loading the raft and gliding it into the lake.

Sigrid leaves them and steps into the cool hall of the police station. A clerk smiles at her so Sigrid makes a face much like a smile in return, which stops the clerk from smiling. Sigrid turns to the left through a closed door and finds Irv talking to a portly white policeman in an official POLICE baseball cap that is too small for his round head. Irv stands in front of the man's desk. He is speaking quietly but waving his hands dramatically. The officer—Frank Allman, according to the brass shirt pin—is taking Irv's rant in stride.

"What's going on?" she asks, not sitting or introducing herself.

The local sheriff stands and extends a hand, which Sigrid shakes. His palm is moist and his face looks innocent and helpless.

"Sigrid Ødegård," says Irv, "this is Sheriff Frank Allman. Frank . . . Sigrid. She's the police officer from Oslo I talked to you about."

"You're much prettier than your photo," he says.

"What's going on?" Sigrid asks.

"The commissioner has called," Irv says. "Not Howard. The actual commissioner."

"What does that mean?"

"It means," says Frank, sitting again, "that a number of decisions have now been taken over our heads, and events have been set in motion, as they say."

"There's a SWAT team outside," Sigrid says. "With a commando raft."

Irv melts into the visitor chair across from Frank's desk.

Sigrid does not like his body language. "Talk to me about the SWAT team," she insists.

"The commissioner," Frank says, "heard about the standoff by the biker clubhouse last night. He has gone on television to allay any fears that the African American community might have that the death of Dr. Lydia Jones will be ignored or sidelined. He has made a statement from an institution with marble steps saying that catching the killer of Dr. Jones is now a top priority for his office."

Sigrid looks at Irv, who is looking down at his boots.

"There is no killer of Dr. Lydia Jones. What little evidence we have suggests suicide."

"There is now," says Frank.

"That's not how evidence works. Or facts. Or truth. Or reality."

"It is, however, how politics works in this crazy world of ours," says Frank.

"If you send six men into the woods with guns after Marcus, they will go in with the idea that the job requires six men with guns. And they will act as if they are on a job needing six men with guns. And the chances of them hurting Marcus will be disproportionate—it will be unrelated—to the job they should be doing."

"I don't disagree with your analysis, ma'am, but there is a chain of command and I am not at the top of it."

"So this is now politically driven—is that what I'm to understand?" she asks.

"They were elected," says Frank Allman.

Sigrid places two hands flat to the desk and leans far forward toward Frank's ruddy face.

"A month ago I was leading a manhunt that ended violently. This one is not going to end that way. That is my brother out there. Who is not violent and never has been. I need you to look into my eyes and promise me this will end gently and peacefully."

"Ma'am," says Frank, leaning backwards to gain some distance. "I cannot promise you that."

Sigrid stands. "Irv," she asks quietly. "Do you have anything to say?"

Irv looks helpless for the first time since they've met. "No," he says.

"I see. I'll be outside," Sigrid says. "I need a minute to myself."

"I understand," Irv replies, though Sigrid knows he understands nothing about what's coming next.

The SWAT team members are chatting amicably to one another about a movie the SWAT leader saw last night about a man whose only way of communicating was by blinking, and he ended up writing a book that way.

"I'm more of an action-adventure or comedy kind of guy myself," he says, but his wife had made him see it because she thought they needed to break out of their usual patterns. "Ten-year anniversary coming up," he says. "I guess she's feeling a little jumpy about it so I went along. I'll tell you though . . . it was beautiful. Really was."

The other five men nod their heads until one of them erupts into sobs and the others laugh.

"You're such assholes," he mutters.

They talk while stacking gear behind their van as Sigrid strides purposefully but inconspicuously to Irv's car, where she had earlier placed her bag with the four terrible bottles of one-hundred-proof vodka. When she bought them, and even when she brought them with her, she did not actually think the circumstances would require her to use them.

As she assembles the Molotov cocktails in the trunk of Irv's car, she tries to remember the name of that film the guy saw. She had seen it too. Something about a butterfly. He was right; it was beautiful.

She rips a motel towel into four strips and shoves them into the bottles. She soaks the wicks. She feels for the lighter in her pocket.

According to the comprehensive report about her last case, Sheldon Horowitz had bullshitted his way into a room at the finest hotel in town and had fooled a rural cop into thinking he was German. He had stolen a boat in plain sight but without witnesses. He broke into a house on the fjord and spent the night there with the boy, having left nothing behind except a sink full of dishes. After that he jacked a tractor, and later, alone and eighty-two years old, he assaulted a mafia stronghold with an inoperable rifle after demanding their surrender.

Not all of Sheldon's plans worked out either, but she couldn't help but admire his moxie.

Leaving the bombs in the Wagoneer, she emerges from the side and yells to the commandos: "Hey!"

All six men turn to look at her.

"Frank needs you out back. You need to wait there for him. He's coming out after he talks to the commissioner again."

The six men turn toward one another for some piece of knowledge none of them has, and so Sigrid provides it. "Move it."

And so they move it.

Alone by the water, she walks to the floating black raft and examines the controls. A steering wheel, a lever that adjusts the speed, a red button to start it, and—helpfully—keys in the ignition; they dangle from a fuchsia-haired troll.

There are two other small boats by the pier. The first with a Yamaha 75 HP engine started by a pull cord. The second boat has an old Honda engine that starts the same way.

Snapping open her brother's Buck knife, she hops into the first boat and takes ahold of the plastic handle on the starter. She pulls it out of the engine as far as it will stretch and slashes it off. She hurls it under the dock and out of immediate view.

As quickly as possible — glancing back toward the building for signs of an enlightened SWAT team — she performs the same trick on the second boat. Their navy effectively sunk, aside from the Zodiac, she jogs back to the sun-drenched parking lot, removes the bottles from the Wagoneer, and enters the black raft. Throwing off the mooring line, she starts the engine by turning the troll head. Once she knows it is running smoothly, she lights three of the bombs.

With a nice arc, the first bottle lands a tad short of the SWAT truck, smashing glass and spewing liquid fire over the stacked gear bags. A thick black smoke quickly rises. If the team wasn't on their way back before, they will certainly come running now. She has to hurry.

She presses the throttle forward and pilots the Zodiac away from the dock, bringing the bow into line with the open waters of Lake Flower. She and the troll pull away from the pier, the sheriff's station, and what will soon be at least eight angry men.

She putters slowly past the two disabled boats; she tosses firebombs into those, too.

Certain of her lead now, Sigrid shoves the throttle into the forwardmost position and hauls ass away from the police station, leaving behind her a small war zone.

In her rearview mirror Sigrid sees Irving Wylie standing with his hands on his hips as the SWAT team and three other officers from the police station douse the fires with extinguishers retrieved from the van. That is all she can make out, though, because in a moment Irv and the others become nothing but wiggly lines and clouds of color in her vibrating mirror that become indistinguishable from the smoke and flames.

· · ·

The boat is easy to maneuver. At high speed it skims over the surface of the lake like a stone tossed by a restive god.

Steady now, and on course, she familiarizes herself with the controls and sees that the commandos have helpfully mounted a dedicated GPS unit inside the windscreen of the boat. There is also a map of the lake district inside a waterproof plastic shield. It illustrates how Lake Flower orients almost due south and connects with something called Oseetah Lake; probably an Indian name she can't pronounce.

The wooded edges of the lake blur into a wall of greens and browns as she speeds along. The night's storm clouds have broken into billowing mountains. They cast patches of shadow on the land below. They blanket the green hills like spilled paint.

There is no reason not to do this, she tells herself. Only she can prevent Marcus from being harmed now. And the best way to do it is by getting there first.

Sigrid watches the GPS coordinates draw closer to the number Irv was told by the camper. Marcus is—or was, anyway—camping near a place called Pine Pond. The pond is inland and not connected to another body of water. She needs to reach the southernmost point of Oseetah, secure or scuttle the raft, and head into the forest by foot if she stands any chance of reaching Marcus before they do. She presses the throttle forward as far as she dares.

The Zodiac is stunningly fast. She has never been on a boat like this. She is partly protected from the wind blast by the screen, but her hair is lashing. A woman would have designed it all differently.

She opens the throttle farther when the lake turns from blue to black. If the boat had wings she would be flying. Each ripple on the water lifts the boat and slams it back to the surface. She thinks of concrete. Of Lydia's fall.

Sigrid takes her hands off the wheel and ties her hair into a bun to keep the strands from whipping her eyes. She snakes the arms of her brother's aviators over her ears and the lenses cut the glare. More comfortable, she glances down to the map to take her bearing.

If the map is any good—and belonging to the SWAT team, it probably is—there is clearly no place to land a helicopter close to Marcus's last-known location; no bare spots, no roads into the woods, no field wide enough to accommodate the diameter of the rotors.

Even if they do manage to call in an airlift, they will have to fast-rope down into the forest, but that would be tricky and dangerous for anything but a properly trained team. Which they are unlikely to have available in the next hour. This is Saranac Lake, after all, not the Helmand province.

It is more likely, she reasons, that the team will get a new boat. They'll follow her route and—like her—make their way by foot through the forest at the edge of the lake.

She looks at her footwear. They're stylish and Italian.

She should have worn combat boots.

THE SILENCE OF THE
HUSH PUPPIES

RV STANDS, A bit forlorn, with his hands on his hips as the other officers put out the flames. Surveying the impressive damage done by one angry Norwegian woman, he watches one of the six black-clad men pick up the remains of a bottle of truly terrible vodka with a fake Russian name. Irv had always wondered why people bought it. Now he knows.

He probably should have locked the doors to the Wagoneer. That's all it would have taken to avoid this.

Frank Allman shuffles up next to Irv and wipes some sweat from his face with a napkin he used earlier to blow his nose.

"Holy shit, Irv."

"I know. I didn't see this coming."

"You realize this could be considered terrorism. Don't you?" Frank says.

"Oh, knock it off."

"I'm just saying."

"She's trying to slow us down so we don't kill her brother. Besides, the Feds never get to visit nice places. If you call that in, and if you bring them down here, by the lake, in the wealth of summer, they will not leave until the last leaf falls. Imagine the joys of federal involvement for a few minutes."

"You got to admit, though, Irv," says Frank. "This really flips things around. I'm not going to say 'turns up the heat' or anything dumb like that but . . . it does."

"The facts of the case are the same as they were before she went all postal on us, Frank. I'm assuming no one's hurt?"

"No," says Frank. "I should at least call the state police. And the insurance company. Hard to write this off as an accident."

"I shouldn't have let go of the reins," Irv concedes. "This is my fault. Goddamn politicians are going to have to learn that the people closest to a problem are the ones best suited to dealing with it. That's why I became a Republican in the first place, but that's not how things are working anymore. This election has got people all fired up. Now everyone's pushing us locals around from up high. Democrat, Republican, makes no difference anymore. Fuckin' Howard."

"It's a job, Irv," says Frank.

"Yeah," he agrees. "Listen, Frank, let's go calm down the men with the machine guns. I don't want them getting riled up over—"

"Being firebombed?"

"She sent them away first."

"I know, but this is not Beirut, Irv. It's Lake Flower, for heaven's sake."

"There are no lakes in Beirut."

"What do we know about Beirut?" Frank asks.

"Nothing," snaps Irv.

They watch the smoke.

Frank takes a piece of wintergreen gum from a white packet in his pocket.

"So. Now what?" asks Irv.

"Well . . . same thing as before, I guess, only slower," Frank reasons aloud. "If we can't make those boats start working again we'll have to go over to Calypso Marine off the Three past Bloomingdale and see whether they've got a Zodiac in stock and whether we can take it on credit. Mr. Vance is not the kind of man who likes working with credit, so we may have an issue, because I don't have a budget line for something like this and God knows I'm not plunking down my own Visa. And then, well, I guess these guys'll go do whatever they were gonna do before."

"I'm going with them," says Irv. "I'm not leaving this to Hogan's Heroes over here. She may have gained some time on us, but now she's got us mad, and that goes in the other column."

Frank pulls up his gun belt so that it nestles nicely under his gut in the way that annoys Irv. "I really don't see why a normal person would do something like this," he says, looking around at the smoldering boats.

"She doesn't trust us, Frank."

"Why doesn't she trust us, Irv?"

"I think it's the cowboy boots, Frank," Irv says.

Frank looks at his own feet. "I'm not wearing cowboy boots. I'm wearing Hush Puppies."

"She may not understand Hush Puppies, Frank. She's from a foreign land across a great ocean."

Sigrid's phone rings in her pocket as she nears the far end of the lake.

"Hello?" she says, without looking at the screen.

"Sigrid," says her father. "How are things with you and Marcus? You haven't called."

"I've been rather busy."

"What's that sound?" Morten asks.

"I'm on a boat. This isn't a very good time."

"I've been doing some thinking since your last call. I need to ask you a question."

"Can this wait?"

"Over the years, has Marcus talked to you much about your mother's death?"

"Pappa . . . this does not sound urgent."

"You know Marcus took it very hard. Very, very hard. Has he talked to you about it at any length?"

"She was my mother too, pappa. I took it hard also. I was a little girl when she died. I really need to go."

"He took it harder."

"Yeah, yeah," she says, agitated. "I'm not simply on a boat, pappa, I'm driving it. I'm also running from men with guns."

"I think the correct term is *piloting*. You're piloting the boat. Though I might have to look it up. Nautical terms in Norwegian are quite extensive and specific."

"Goodbye, pappa."

"I'm wondering if his last letter was alluding to your mother. I'm wondering if Lydia's death isn't somehow connected—in his mind, of course—to your mother's. He said in his last letter that it was all happening again."

"It's not relevant right now."

"If it's relevant at all, Sigrid, it's relevant to everything and definitely right now. If Marcus blames himself for Lydia's death, the way he blamed himself for your mother's death, he may be in a very delicate frame of mind. You are in a fragile situation."

"You may have a point, and I am impressed you can see all this from the farm. But I really am on a boat running from men with guns, so I've got to go. OK?"

"Try not to antagonize them."

"For that you should have called an hour ago." And she hangs up.

The edge of the lake approaches her like a green wall. The natural run of the lake is to the east, where Oseetah splits like devil's horns into Kiwassa Lake to the north and Second Pond farther south, but she isn't going either direction. Instead, she runs the raft over the green algae that grows heavy and dense from the still water by the lake's edge. She presses on at speed toward the line of trees where the land begins and hopes that the raft doesn't run aground too soon, because her shoes are not waterproof and there is a walk ahead.

Near the shore the weeds slap the rubber hull and a cold mist splashes over the Zodiac's prow. Fifty meters from the edge she cuts power to the outboard and slows to five knots, easing the craft into a dark nook behind a clump of trees. A meter from land, she guns the engine and jumps the boat's prow onto a patch of coarse grass that serves as a beachhead. Convinced the boat is secure, she turns the engine off and waits for the moment to settle.

Behind her, the lake is still clear and blue. Her wake is already dissipating and mixing with the new ripples created by the easterly breeze. Her tracks through the weeds and algae will be visible if the police are attentive—especially by air—but there is still no sign of them and of course Irv has the same GPS coordinates that Sigrid does, so he doesn't actually need to find her at all; he can go straight to the meeting point. She has the lead, though. Perhaps no more than minutes, but maybe long enough to find Marcus and move him to a new location. If she can talk sense into him, there might still be a way to turn him in publicly and without incident; maybe at a diner in the town or in a playground full of little human shields. Someplace the police wouldn't risk a spectacle or scaring the locals.

Not in a town as white as this, anyway.

The SWAT team for Saranac Lake is commanded by Lieutenant Alfonzo Plymouth, who is nothing like Irv's SERT captain, Pinkerton. Irv met Alfonzo once before—at a regional police convention a few years ago—and remembers liking the guy well enough. On the scorched pier by the police station, Alfonzo is wiping the sticky residue from the fire extinguisher onto his trousers as he calmly directs his men in taking inventory. They rummage through the black bags that were recently burning and now smell terrible.

Calypso Marine confirms to Frank that it does not have any Zodiacs in stock. Thanking them, and hanging up his cell phone, he tells Alfonzo they'll need to get the two remaining boats—such as they are—seaworthy again. Al steps gingerly onto the first and larger of the two boats. He hops up and down a few times on a blackened spot near the stern to test for integrity.

"How does it look?" Irv asks.

"Seems OK," Alfonzo says. "I'd risk it. We won't set any speed records, though."

"So . . . off we go, then. Right?"

"Well . . . no," says Alfonzo, examining the motor. "Your friend cut off the starter cord."

"Take it from the other boat?"

"Cut that too."

"That can't be a hard fix," says Irv. "You take off the cowl, pop off the choke linkage, and wrap another cord around the motor. Bob's your uncle."

"Yeah," says Alfonzo, unconvinced. "Anyone got any cord?"

"Can't you use a shoestring or something?" Irv asks. "I think I saw that in a cartoon once."

Alfonzo looks down. "Mine are tactical boots. Zipper and Velcro. Why, what have you got?"

Irv wordlessly looks at his cowboy boots and so does Alfonzo. Neither comments.

"Frank?" Irv yells. "We need a starter cord from the hardware store."

"I got it, I got it . . ." Frank says, waving as he opens the door to his police car and wedges himself in like a cupcake into a packed lunch box. Rumbling up his eight-cylinder he sets off to find the missing component to modern law enforcement.

Alfonzo instructs the men to spray some kind of magical glop on the bottom of the blackened boat that supposedly will harden up and help prevent a leak from forming. They scale back their gear to raw essentials—including walkie-talkies and firearms—and set to the task of turning the small fishing boat into a small fishing boat filled with a tactical SWAT team.

Frank returns thirty-five minutes later with a nylon cord and lunch.

A FEW SMARTLY
CHOSEN WORDS

THE BRASS BELL above the police door at the sheriff's station rings, crisp and bright, before Howard Howard's towering head muffles it with his coif. Howard has never visited Irv's police station—at least not since Melinda has worked here—and no one knows him by sight. But when he opens his mouth to speak, Muppet the dog knows him by sound.

"I'm looking for the sheriff," says Howard, gliding into the office like a specter.

Muppet, who's been resting after an exhausting nap, springs from the floor of the kitchen, stumbles on the waxed linoleum, runs to the front door, and skids to a halt in front of an imperial God of a man who hovers above him with eyes of puppy-dog brown and eyebrows as expressive and inhuman as his own.

"Who are you?" Howard asks the dog.

Melinda can see that Muppet does not know the answer because Muppet does not speak English. But he wants to know. He wants to answer Howard.

"Woof," says Muppet.

"And where's the sheriff?" Howard asks the office more generally.

Melinda had been in Irv's office typing up numerous warrants for the county that have to be issued by the end of the week, and she stops working as soon as Howard starts to speak and Muppet shuts up.

"I'm Deputy Melinda Powell, sir," she says, rising and extending her hand. Standing close to him, she is dwarfed. While Irv has broader shoulders and generally more heft to him, Howard's Lincoln-esque height, raised chin, and lowered gaze make him far more imposing. It's like looking up at an angry Gandalf.

"Where's the sheriff, Deputy Powell?"

"In Saranac Lake. The town, not the body of water. We believe that Marcus Ødegård may be in the general area based on a call we received. Irv is there with Frank Allman and the regional SWAT team."

"How many men is that?" he asked.

"Maybe half a dozen, sir. I'm not sure."

"How many do you have under your command here?"

"We don't have SWAT, we have SERT under Pinkerton. They've got fifteen including him, sir."

"Pinkerton."

"Yes, sir."

"He's the one who successfully broke up that mob last night?"

"No. That was Reverend Green . . ."

"But it was Pinkerton's team on site that was the thin blue line between order and chaos. Yes?"

"I think that's the wrong question."

"I beg your pardon?" Howard steps forward. The door closes behind him, trapping everyone inside with him. The bell that had been resting on his head now slides off and finishes its ring.

Howard's voice possesses a deep and chambered resonance like a Howitzer being loaded. She looks around the office for support but everyone, including Cory, has bunkered behind a desk.

"All I mean, sir," Melinda clarifies, "is that Reverend Green was the one who deescalated the situation. The SERT stood down on Irv's instructions after Green solved the problem. I mean . . .

there are still problems, obviously, but he averted an incident. It all worked out OK."

"Maybe we should send the Reverend Al Green—"

"Fred Green, sir."

". . . to apprehend the foreign fugitive who pushed an Afro-American woman out a window to her death. Is that a good idea?"

"We're wondering if it wasn't a suicide," Melinda says.

"A few blocks from the Norwegian's house? A suicide by an aunt over the death of a nephew? When does that happen? It wasn't a suicide. Our job is to arrest the man and hand him over to the prosecutor, who—with his juris doctorate degree from Fordham, and his membership in the Bar Association, and his sworn duty to the state of New York—may be as philosophical about such matters as he likes. But that's not our job. Is it, Deputy?"

Melinda looks at Muppet. Muppet looks at Howard. Melinda gives the dog the evil eye and the dog doesn't care.

"The commissioner wants to send our team to Saranac to assist. That's why I'm here. Seven officers is not enough. And they're SWAT, not SERT, because they don't have their own team like we do."

"Yes, sir. Or, no, sir. I'm not sure."

"Saranac Lake is . . . Gregg Allman?"

"Frank Allman, sir."

"Get him on the phone. And Irv, too. I want a word with your Supreme Leader."

Alfonzo's magical boat-repair gunk needs thirty minutes to harden. It's as good a time as any to eat, so they do.

When Frank's phone rings Irv is finishing off a Kiwassa Burger from Blue Moon Cafe.

"Hello?" says Frank.

It is Howard Howard. Howard is going to send them a team and they'll be there soon. How are things going? Howard asks.

Frank muffles the phone with the heel of his palm and speaks to Irv: "Howard is sending your SERT to help. He wants to know how it's going."

"Same old, same old, you can tell him," says Irv, reaching for a napkin.

Frank finishes absorbing instructions from Howard and eventually stops his nodding and starts his frowning. Irv doesn't like the look on Frank's face and shows this by mimicking it.

"Howard wants to talk to you," Frank says.

"Tell him I'm not here."

"He knows you're here."

"How?"

"He can hear me talking to you."

Irv takes the phone and watches Alfonzo tap the repaired hull with the pommel of a fixed-blade knife. From this distance it sounds like glass. Alfonzo gives a thumbs-up to the rest of his team. They half-heartedly return the gesture as they eat.

"What do you want, Howard?" he shouts into the cell phone.

"I'm sending Pinkerton," Howard says.

"Pinkerton is a fascist with little testosterone-deprived testicles looking to put lead into something because he's unable to produce semen. There might be a need for people like him someplace, Howard, but not on Lake Flower. I have seven guys here who constitute a crackerjack assault team. I'm watching them prepare right now and it's like the Harlem Globetrotters with guns. You send a guy like that over here and you'll throw a wrench into the works."

"I'm not only sending him. I'm sending your whole team. Give me the coordinates," Howard says.

"You don't have the authority to do that."

"The commissioner agrees."

"I'd like to talk you out of this," Irv adds more quietly.

"I will not let this fugitive of yours get away and complicate matters in New York State even further."

Irv calls Howard something other than Howard and says that he is going to need a moment to find the exact coordinates that are "here someplace."

There is a small notebook in Irv's side pocket with addresses—an old-fashioned little book with tabs for each letter of the alphabet. He skips to the W section to see if a friend's number is there and, finding it, decides that now is the time to take a hint from Sigrid and boldly grasp this shitty situation by the short ones and turn it right around.

Irv had been taught in a business course once that all strategic action has four components: a goal, resources you'll use, methods you'll perform, and—at the center of it all—a theory or argument about *why* using those resources a certain way will bring about the desired goal. In this case, Irv's strategy to deal with Howard and the commissioner and Pinkerton is held together by a simple theory that Irv thinks is rock solid: *People in government are assholes and will always sell out others to save themselves.* So the question becomes *What resources do I have, and how might I use them to get all these people fired in one go?*

It is quite an ask, but he's an innovative guy and he has an idea.

Irv finds what he needs in his address book, pulls up a bit more information from his phone, and reads the GPS coordinates to Howard with resignation. He hangs up without wishing Howard a nice day.

Frank stands and brushes about half of his lunch from his shirt, which has collected on his belly.

Irv stands too, adjusts his Magnum, and strides out onto the boat with the rest of Alfonzo's well fed and slightly bored team.

Frank unties the rope for them and tosses it ahead of himself and into the boat. He's not coming. On the dock he hooks his thumbs into his gun belt and watches the men ready themselves for an extremely slow and relaxing cruise across the flat lake.

"You know, Frank," says Irv as they pull away, "if you lose the belly you might find your pockets."

"Doesn't seem worth the effort," Frank says.

"All right, Lieutenant," says Irv, "let's go get our man before this thing gets out of hand."

With a confident yank on the repaired pull cord, Alfonzo starts the outboard that produces a gentle *put-put* sound not unlike a lawn-mower.

"Things aren't out of hand yet?" asks Alfonzo.

"What, this?" Irv says, scanning the wreckage behind them. "This is nothing."

With a twist of the throttle on the tiller, the team sets off to find Sigrid, their stolen boat, and Marcus Ødegård as Irving Wylie places a call to a certain Ms. Weaver.

THE LOST BOYS

T HERE IS NO path beneath Sigrid's ruined shoes. Her feet occasionally disappear entirely beneath heavy ferns, and the massive leaves batter her legs. She holds her mobile phone with its compass and GPS coordinates before her like a divining stick. She follows its direction through the scruff and scree of virgin woods and clouds of gnats that swarm silently in beams of yellow sunlight breaking, periodically, through the upper canopy. Below, here on earth, Sigrid walks among the splays of sunlight that punctuate and light the forest floor.

Sigrid is no tracker and no scout-sniper like Sheldon Horowitz. She can't tell whether someone has been here a moment ago or never. She looks for telltale signs within her urban skill set: maybe a discarded Kvikklunsj bar wrapper, for example, or a whiff of Gillette aftershave. That would be the kind of evidence she could use.

She decides that all those natives squatting down to taste the earth must have been full of shit, and she raises the phone higher, putting her full faith in the technological power of the satellite constellation system.

Periodically her messenger bag snags and she yanks it free. She yanks it hard. She yanks it because she is angry at Irv.

And she is angry at Marcus.

And she is angry at her father.

She is angry at men. All men. For their stupidity, their lies, their egotism, their irrelevant words, their aggressive personalities and hairy backs. She is angry at them for what they did and didn't do. For what they say and leave unsaid. For the timbre of their voices and the length of their strides, the ease by which they open jars and their inexplicable incapacity to return even the smallest objects to their rightful locations. She is sick of investing in them without dividend, trusting in them without reward, and pouring her guts out in motels—with words, emotion, trust, nostalgia, laments, confessions—to wake up the next day—feeling good, feeling closer, feeling unburdened and more earthy and connected and natural and complete—and be abandoned at her own moment of need, and set free, once again, to solve everything herself.

"No," he'd said, when asked if he had anything to add. "No." Nothing more. Nothing to explain himself or apologize or come to her defense.

And maybe a small part of her is angry at her mother, too.

Sigrid kicks through the understory and follows her compass toward some arbitrary spot on this earth. And on finding Marcus—if she does, and so help him God—he had better be there with open arms, a smile, and an apology.

As on the university campus, she can hear the conversation they are clearly not going to have. For some reason she imagines him—like a toad—sitting on a log:

"Oh, Sigrid, it's so nice to see you. Thank you for coming for me," he won't say.

"It was a major pain in my ass, Marcus. I should be at home in Hedmark reading a bad romance about a bellboy and a duchess. And instead I'm . . . Where the hell are we, anyway?"

"Over there"—he'd point to a spot between three trees—"is the actual middle of nowhere. Not only in New York or America. But the entire galaxy. We're about eight meters away from it. The actual thing."

"You couldn't be bothered to sit there for the simple poetry of it?"

"There's nothing to sit on in the middle of nowhere. I don't think the universe wants us to loiter for too long."

"I'm being followed," she'd explain, "by Friar Tuck and the rest of the merry men, and when they get here, I'm going to stand in front of you so they don't kill you on sight for a crime you didn't commit, OK? Because they tend to shoot citizens on sight, I'm learning."

"Dad thinks this is about Mom. He's right. Don't you remember? Didn't you know?"

"Know what?"

"Remember!"

"There's nothing to remember. She had cancer, she died in her sleep. It was terrible, but I've come to realize as an adult that it was the best we could have hoped for given the circumstances. There was no cure. There still isn't. There's no regret here, Marcus, only sadness."

"You are lucky," he'd say to her, as he would always say to her.

It rather annoyed her.

Luck?

She kicks through the woods. She kicks at the woods. She hates this. And she hates hating it, because she used to love it. Absolutely adored everything about it. They used to do this; they'd play hide-and-seek in the woods behind the farm. As far as they knew, the woods there extended eastward all the way through Norway and Sweden to the Gulf of Bothnia, which was—in their juvenile imaginations—populated by Caribbean pirates and Arabs in dhows bringing spices and lanterns and magic from the southern realms into the uncharted lands of the world's northern domains. There, in the hills, they'd walk together; they would search for evidence of ancient civilizations and cultures colliding to make new languages and poetry that could unlock doors in the trunks of trees that would lead them down spiral staircases to where they would spy on teams of Vikings carving new navies with glittering swords illuminated by magical orbs that would circle around, overhead, each one representing a planet or moon from an alien sky, proving to her, and her brother, that the universe was deep and vast and unknown and full of possibility.

In the south, Sigrid learned in school—in Kenya, in Congo, in Brazil —the equatorial sun would plummet like a burning rock into the surface of the earth, spreading its fire wide over the horizon to burn the day and relent before the night. Every season the same. Every day the same length. A ritual that devoured time. But up north, in Norway, the summer sun would pilot through the clouds to make the softest and slowest of gentle landings, and if the summer was at its peak, that pale and weak orb would only skim the surface before rising—slowly, almost imperceptibly—back into the sky, rising on its own reflected warmth off the distant snow, to take its place—where it belonged— above them.

She and her brother traveled with an old army compass from the war found in a box in the attic. Marcus carried rations in a Spiderman knapsack. They each had green Fulton flashlights that looked like tiny periscopes and they would flash each other messages using the little black button over the switch, messages through the trees in a Norwegian Morse code they invented themselves.

Where had that boy gone? How does such an open and free child become reclusive and withdrawn and solitary and later holed up in a decrepit house by an off-ramp that absorbs all natural light?

Their mother's death. Yes. But now? Some thirty-six years later? What is it that has caught up to him?

Sigrid emerges from the woods at the end of a large pond that is empty of boats and dotted with lily pads. The sun glistens with an intensity that blinds her as she pulls herself out of the darkness of the forest with the realization that she is hot and sweating and thirsty. But she does not bend to the pond to wash and drink and replenish herself, though it invites her. Because there, sitting on a rock with his feet in the water, surrounded by the dense copse, is her brother, Marcus, dangling a revolver between his knees.

F-U-N, FUN

THIS IS PINKERTON'S first visit to the swanky towns of the
Adirondacks, out here where all the rich assholes take their trim
to summer homes. He is cruising down Route 3 at breakneck
speed with the rest of his team. The sun is shining, a heat is pound-
ing down the way it always has in war zones he's been in, and he has
a green light—no, an order!—to form an iron fist around a foreign
killer on American soil.

OK, no, fine, this isn't Afghanistan. It's Lake Placid or whatever,
but the mission is the mission and the stage is just a stage.

He bounces along on the back of the pickup and feels giddy. Today he has a role in the world and a chance to play his part. His only
regret is that he doesn't have a cigar to hold between his teeth so he
could spit out the soggy bits before giving his big speech to the team.
But . . . well . . . heck. Life is still good and Irv the limp-dicked sheriff isn't here to get in the way. What he concludes, as they pass a Mer-
cedes C-Class going the opposite direction, is that this town they're
headed toward is going to provide a nice place to launch an amphibi-
ous pincer assault.

The team is divided up into two Ford F-150 flatbeds that are breezing along Main Street past the Lumberjack Inn. Fifteen guys still pumped from the standoff last night and feeling like warriors on their way to an alien invasion, boxes full of tactical nukes and a weapons-free directive to light things up. That might not be exactly how it is, but it feels close enough for this chickenshit job that has never given him a chance to pull the trigger. He smiles at the five other guys swaying along beside him and they smile back. They are going to have this fucking foreigner surrounded and on his face in the dirt with his hands behind his back within the hour. And if not? If he resists? He'll die of lead poisoning the way they did when the West was won.

Pinkerton doesn't care one way or another. This is a milk run in a nice town and he is going to come out looking good, good, good, especially after having broken up the black mob last night. That's two stripes in two days in a place where, frankly, very little happens and his team has grown flabby and complacent.

Back in Afghanistan he learned that a good kill can help morale and fill a team with purpose. It helps focus their minds on what's real, and mints them as a deadly force. Eventually word gets around and those words sound like fame. No, something better: glory.

If they capture or kill this wiener-dick, Pinkerton might even be able to get out of here and into some real action in a big city or else join one of the FBI teams. Pinkerton has always fancied himself a hostage-rescue guy. Especially in this whole post-9/11, terrorist-soaked biscuit of a world they're living in now. Back in earlier years hostage rescue was a talky-talky profession; lots of gabbing and negotiation and takeout pizzas. But today? When the Muslims are there to kill people? Oh, no. Now you put together an assault plan and you kick in the fuckin' walls and go full Call of Duty on those jihadist motherfuckers right at the start.

Pinkerton wants a piece of that.

And—he thinks, as the wind blows through his hair—maybe a chance to go mano a mano, too. Yeah. He's fit these days. And this guy they're up against is . . . what? A Norwegian bachelor farmer or something? Whatever. He wants the reputation of taking one down with a knife. Guns are guns, but a good knife kill? That's the kind of solid street rep that doesn't follow you around: It leads.

And what a douchebag! Who throws a woman out a window? A coward, that's who. Not someone likely to put up any resistance to a team like his.

Pinkerton knows it's a good thing he was called in. The local guy —Alfonzo something. Who is he, anyway? OK, SWAT, so maybe he's got some game, but no way he's seen any action up here.

The Ford arrives at a large intersection and turns left onto Route 30 south along Tupper Lake.

And a name like that. *Alfonzo.* He should be fixing Fiats in a dusty garage at the edge of town.

"Hey, Ricky," Pinkerton says to the guy farthest away on the bench opposite near the back. Ricky is the misfit of the group who ended up in the SERT accidentally. He was a U.S. Army Ranger and allegedly knew his stuff, but he wanted to be a police officer after his service, and only ended up on the team because there was a space and he only took it because of the pay. His wife had a baby four months ago and her loss of income had prompted his transfer from a city desk where he wrote up policy documents or some damn thing. Pinkerton wants to either draw this guy out of his shell or transfer his ass back.

"Ricky—who's this Alfonzo guy? And what the fuck are they doing with a Puerto Rican upstate anyway? What is he, lost?"

"His mother's Italian," Ricky says. "Father's from Vermont. Runs an apple farm and antique shop I think. He's a really nice guy," says Ricky. After he says this, and seeing the horror on Pinkerton's face, he looks down at his own boots again.

Ricky doesn't like Pinkerton any more than Irv does.

"Whatever," Pinkerton says to no one in particular.

Bored with Ricky, and typically unimpressed, Pinkerton whacks the side of the pickup and shouts for the driver to put on the sirens. "I want to be back at the bar telling war stories before happy hour is over, you got that? I don't see any reason we all need to be paying more than three bucks a beer tonight. How much farther? We don't want little

Alfonzo getting all the glory, now, do we? No, we don't. No, we absolutely do not. What's our ETA?"

The driver screams out his window. "Twenty-two more miles, sir."

Pinkerton calculates. At sixty miles an hour, which is about what they are doing, that makes it twenty-two minutes to the destination. Fifteen minutes maximum on site. And then they flash the lights again on the way home. It will have to do.

"What kind of place is it?" Pinkerton asks.

"Some kind of compound in the woods, sir. The satellite photos show a house on a little peninsula."

Right. Good. A real and proper operation. A cabin in the woods. Like the Unabomber and the Evil Dead.

Oh baby, yeah.

With the wind battering his head, Pinkerton calls the Alfonzo guy on the phone. It rings twice before it is answered.

"Plymouth? This is Pinkerton. You've been informed of our assistance?"

There is a brief pause, which Pinkerton finds odd. This is a serious mission. What's this guy doing, thinking about the answer? He expects compliance, attention, focus, and some attitude.

"Ah . . . yup. Howard called Irv. I'm not convinced we need a twenty-five person assault team to apprehend a guy sitting quietly in the woods, but . . . OK."

"Yeah, well, we've got one. Iron fist, baby. We're going to circle him and move right in. What's your ETA to the rendezvous?"

"Well, with the new boat we're not making the greatest time, to be honest. I figure twenty to twenty-five minutes to cross the lake and then another twenty or thirty through the brush by foot."

"According to my map," says Pinkerton, not looking at one, "this place is right on the water. Why the long walk?"

"Well," says Alfonzo, "I don't consider that a long walk. Do you?"

"I think we're going to get there before you," says Pinkerton, shaking his head at the wop's cluelessness and lack of drive. "I'll bet you're right, though. My guys are probably enough. In which case, we'll have to secure the location first. I'll keep you informed," he concludes, and pushes the red button on the phone, which really should launch something rather than simply end a call.

Keep him informed, my ass.

Ricky, trying to ignore Pinkerton's mood, feels his own phone ring in his breast pocket and so he answers it, putting a stiff finger into his left ear to block out the wind.

"Hello?"

"Ricky, it's Irv."

"Oh, hey, Sheriff."

"Ricky, listen. I need you to stay close to Pinkerton on this one. I can't tell you why, because it would put you in something of a spot, but let's just say I want a nice, calm approach over there. You're not soldiers and this isn't a war zone. You're police officers hired and sworn to serve and protect. Uphold our laws. Think friendliness. Kitty-cats and trees. Bake sales. Car washes. Teaching kids to wear helmets and use reflectors on their bicycles. Remember that stuff?"

"Vaguely, sir. Though . . . fondly."

"I know you do, Ricky. Because under all that shit you're wearing you're a nice guy, unlike . . . you know who."

"Yes, sir."

"Keep an eye on Pinkerton. Don't shoot any civilians. Or any women you happen to see. Women who might already be there, for example. Women who might also be civilians. And friends of mine. I guess what I'm saying, Ricky, is this: If things get bad, you just shoot Pinkerton. OK?"

"Yes, sir."

"We'll just carve out the slugs, chuck him in the lake, and shrug in boyish wonder when we're questioned later."

"I got you, sir."

Ricky looks at Pinkerton, who looks back at him.

"Who was that?" Pinkerton asks.

"The sheriff. Wishing us luck."

"He didn't call me."

"It was more . . . advice for me, I think."

"Yeah. I don't need any."

The route is smooth and gently curved. The lesser people in their vehicles part the way to make room for the alpha males in their trucks, the way nature intends.

The private driveways for the bankers start coming into view and Pinkerton does have to wonder who this asshole is that they're about to apprehend and how he could possibly be holed up in a place around here, but it's just as likely he's broken into a summer house and made himself comfortable after dissolving the owners in a tub full of acid and lime. Either way, his team is going to slide in like ninjas with a personal grudge and bring this guy back to town the same way the big dogs do it in the cities.

Pinkerton looks at the houses they are passing and indulges in a moment of optimism. He'd like a big house someday. That's for sure. Maybe start a private security company. Everybody seems to be doing it. Escort the executives to the helicopters, close off roads for the VIPs, clear the rooms, take home the big money, tips in cash, and attract the honeys. Today could be day one in making that dream come true. Just last night he'd found a Maserati on eBay for under $30K.

This is going to be F-U-N, fun.

If it weren't a workday, Irv thinks, this gentle cruise on the lake would be really nice. He hasn't taken a boat ride in . . . man, a while anyway. He'd forgotten how pleasant it is. Back at the office, the idea of riding a boat around a lake with no particular place to go might have once seemed pointless. It was not the sort of activity he would have chosen for himself. He would never have seriously considered a cabin on a lake. That's real money. These were, however, the kinds of things his ex-wife wanted him to do. Not just do them, but understand the intrinsic value of wanting to. She wanted him to *want* to take boat rides on lakes and daydream with her about a porch overlooking a body of

water at sunset where they could sip champagne for no particular reason and maybe drop strawberries to the bottom and watch those little
bubbles form on the dimples.

The entire vision seemed expensive and sappy at the time.

That and the bugs. You never see that on TV. The gorgeous brunette leaping up from her Adirondack chair and running around like
a lunatic with thrashing arms trying to keep the mosquitos off. The
smell of DEET overpowering the lemon sole and Chardonnay. And
of course the asshole across the lake who decides that ten o'clock at
night is exactly when he needs to get to work on that downed tree with
his chainsaw.

Hopefully a tree, anyway.

But out here, two fingers dipped into the chill water while they
chug along—his fingers being a little water-skier that he moves back
and forth as they zip along—he feels . . . good. He has a sense that
maybe he made a mistake in that relationship. Maybe these irrational
and quiet moments she wanted in a place like this are actually what
God wants for us by commanding us to keep the Sabbath Day holy.
To stop. To rest. To pause from acts of creation and actually admire it
and revel in the joy of the thing for one-seventh of a week. Maybe if
he'd kept the Sabbath holy he'd still be married.

Maybe. But she was such a monumental pain in the ass and water-
front property is so friggin' expensive. Honestly. How hard should a
guy need to work?

Now, though, there's this Norwegian woman. A crazy lady with a
guitar who has turned out to be a portal to another world. Maybe he
can look past her firebombing of upstate New York and qualification
as a terrorist. Maybe, together, they can bring this whole thing to a
successful landing the way Charlie's Angels always seemed able to do
with giant passenger planes after the pilots had disappeared. He never
could quite remember those plots.

Alfonzo, the low-wattage SWAT commander with little to say, sits
across from Irv on the boat. Unlike Pinkerton, Alfonzo has no tattoos
on his forearms and he wears a wedding band on his left ring finger.

His hair is short but not cut to military standards. He has a calming effect on his men and they all seem relaxed on the boat despite their annoying habit of giving the thumbs-up to virtually everything that is said about anything.

"You got a call?" Irv asks.

"Pinkerton."

"I'm sorry about him," Irv replies. "He came with the job. Like the hat."

"It's OK," says Alfonzo. "I understand how it works. Are we actually expecting trouble?"

"No. And I want to avoid escalating something that is actually under control at the moment, despite appearances. I know the woman who set us on fire. She's scared for her brother, whom I suspect is harmless. I want to go in first. You can hang back a bit. You have a radio I can borrow?"

Alfonzo hands Irv a Motorola and tunes it to the proper channel. They perform a radio check and Irv clips it to his belt on the left side, which counterbalances his .357 rather nicely.

"My thinking," says Irv, wiping his wet fingers on his pants, "is that I go into the forest and have a chitchat with Marcus. You guys hang back a little. I'm guessing Sigrid will be there too. Once I have a sense of what's what I'll call you and give you all a sitrep. My idea is for Sigrid to come out first so you'll see her and know things are OK, then Marcus will come out—and you won't shoot him—and I'll take up the rear. If there's no trouble we can probably avoid the cuffs, but it's your call, Al. The thing is, if we cuff him we have to arrest him, and I'm not sure I want to do that, because we're trying to avoid the catch-and-release scenario here."

"That all sounds fine to me," says Alfonzo. "But I'm a little worried about Pinkerton and your team. If he gets there first everything'll be out of our control."

"No. I sorted that out. You've got nothing to worry about."

"I don't see your meaning, Sheriff," says Alfonzo. "He's almost there and we're not."

"Well, here's the thing, Alfonzo. Pinkerton is almost somewhere. But it isn't where we're going."

Pinkerton's driver turns them off the main road onto a private drive that snakes through the woods. They slow and cut the flashing blue lights on their approach to the gate.

The house looks to Pinkerton like a set of a James Bond movie — one that is going to get the shit blown out of it by the time everyone's done. It is a surprisingly modest affair given the impressive piece of land that supports it. They are on a small peninsula, as shown on the map, so unless this guy has a Miami Vice cigarette out back with a thousand horsepower, there is no way he is getting out of this.

The house is a natural trap.

What kind of asshole, what kind of moron, would hole up in a place with no exit?

The kind of guy who pushes women out of windows, that's the kind.

The thin steel gate is set between two stone pillars. To either side of those pillars is a hedge for privacy, though it offers little actual protection. There's no broken glass on the top, no barbed wire, no spikes.

The gate is wired with an alarm system and a camera.

"Out, everyone out," Pinkerton yell-whispers. They all stand to the side of their vehicles, weapons readied.

"We're going to rip off the gate with the winch, flow inside, break into three teams. Tommy has A-team and you're going left around the house. Franco has B team and you're going right. I'm taking point with Charlie Team and we're going in the front door. Now let's take out those cameras and get this gate open. I want the lead vehicle in there in case we need cover. Go, go, go!"

Tommy and his silenced nine-millimeter sub-machine gun shoot out the camera by the gate as Gary Simkins pulls the winch line from the front of the pickup, wraps it around the gate, and signals the driver to back it up, which he does, snapping the lock and pulling the gate open as ordered. They disconnect the winch line and the F-150 rolls in with A-team staying close and low beside it until they are almost at the front door.

This is how Pinkerton wants it: Quantico quick and deep-space silent. Urban warfare by the numbers.

It's a stylish house but it isn't garish. The frame is a three-story custom timber peg with an inviting entrance, but it isn't extravagant. The car out front is a Ford Mondeo in dark blue, not a Porsche or Land Rover. Someone is keeping a low profile, Pinkerton figures. Drug dealer? Mafia boss? Terrorist financier?

"After me, after me," says Pinkerton, crouching down and moving slowly to the front door. Gun up, knees bent, he turns the knob on the front door and is confused to find it open. Pushing it gently inward, he releases the knob and presses his gloved finger to his lips.

Not a sound, boys, not a single goddamned sound.

When the door is a quarter ajar and all his men are behind him, he gives the countdown—five . . . four . . . three . . . two —and on the final beat, he rams the door with his shoulder and careens into the front hall with his rifle raised. Seven other men flood the room, weapons up, shoulders low, ready to take down the devil and his minions if that's what they are called on to do.

With the skill of former military personnel, they proceed to the living room, dining room, kitchen, the rest of the lower floor and the bedrooms on the upper.

No one's there.

When Pinkerton descends the staircase after declaring the second floor "secure," he finds Ricky standing with his rifle shouldered, hands in his pocket, looking at a wall of framed photographs.

"What the fuck are you doing?" Pinkerton asks.

Ricky is leaning close to one as if at a museum. "I think that's Ang Lee."

"Who's Ang Lee?"

"You kidding?" Ricky starts counting off on his fingers: "*The Hulk. Brokeback Mountain.* The *Crouching Tiger* thing. *Sense and Sensibility,* obviously . . ."

"Have you lost your mind?" Pinkerton asks.

At that moment, and before Ricky can answer the question, a woman walks through the front door. The police officers are pressed aside by the force of her gaze as she steps into the living room that—apparently—belongs to her. The woman is tall and in her late fifties, with enormous and stunning brown eyes, a somewhat severe jawline, thin lips, and an expression that puts her in command.

"Well, well," the woman says, "I just lost a bet. Do you realize yet that you're in deep trouble or are you still processing?"

"On the floor, down!" yells Pinkerton, raising his weapon.

Instead of following his directions, though, she cocks her weight to the side, striking an architectural pose. "Put that down right now, you imbecile," she says.

It is Ricky who immediately places himself between the woman and Pinkerton's line of fire and says, "Sir, you need to put that down right this second."

"Why?" Pinkerton says, still training his weapon on the defiant woman through Ricky's chest, which he uses as a shield.

"That's Sigourney Weaver, sir."

"Who?"

"Sigourney Weaver, sir. *Ghostbusters*? *Aliens*? *Galaxy Quest*?" Ricky turns to Ms. Weaver and addresses her over his shoulder. "You were wonderful in *The Ice Storm*, ma'am. I'm married too. I know what it can be like."

"Thank you," she says to Ricky. "Now tell your monkey that I'm going to call the lieutenant governor now and have him fired. You should take the gun away too."

"Yes, ma'am," says Ricky, "and we—the police—will leave right now, and we look forward to getting the bill for the gate and the camera."

Pinkerton lowers his weapon but he doesn't look convinced.

He doesn't look entirely present, either. It seems as though he has withdrawn into a dream that is, before Ricky's eyes, floating away with Pinkerton in it. And as it rises higher into the atmosphere, it pops.

"Sir?" Ricky says to Pinkerton. "Can you hear me? Sir?"

DEAD WOMEN

"Marcus," SIGRID SAYS, trying to place the person she is looking at into a frame of reference she can comprehend.

"You shouldn't have come," he says to his sister in Norwegian.

"You've said that three times. Throw that gun in the water."

"I need it."

"Marcus," she says, stepping into the clearing by the lake's edge. "Do you have any idea the hell you've put us through? You can't be seen with a gun. There are police coming."

Marcus does not move.

"I'm here to make sure that you don't get shot. You're making that more difficult right now."

"I want you to know what happened," Marcus says. "I'm tired of you not knowing. I think that's why I haven't . . ."

"First the gun. And then we can talk all you want."

"You look tired, Sigrid. And also changed. Killing someone can do that to you, can't it?" Marcus turns from her and looks at the lake. "I look tired too."

"Gun in the water."

Marcus considers his .38 revolver. He moves it up and down. The weight and balance are a revelation, the product of centuries of refinement.

"Do you remember when I broke my arm? We were kids and Mom was still alive."

Sigrid glances back to the woods at birds and bugs, shadows and breeze. There is no one there. She probably has a few minutes before she has to charge him and wrestle the gun away, which she wants to avoid because when Marcus retrenches into an oppositional mood he can stiffen up and there's no telling how well he might—or might not—handle a loaded weapon. She has no reason to believe he has any experience with them.

"Yes, I guess I do. I remember the color blue. Why?"

"Maybe you didn't know this, because you weren't old enough or tall enough, but if you were in the downstairs bathroom, like I often was, you could hear Mom and Dad talking in the bedroom through the vent above the toilet."

"Why are we talking about this in upstate New York in 2008?"

"Because your life—the entire world as you know it, Sigrid—is a lie."

"I don't know what you're talking about."

"You grew up strong and self-confident, and determined, and you became a success. I didn't."

"You teach at a—"

"Please don't. Don't. Just don't," he says, waving the gun carelessly, his voice agitated. She can see he has no real consciousness of the weapon. No sense of its power or the immediacy of its consequences. There is no stepping forward to take it. The gun could go off at any time. The bullet could go anywhere.

"I never had a serious relationship," he says. "I've been in love but only from a distance. I didn't gain the confidence to let someone in until I met Lydia. In my midforties. Can you believe it? She was different enough from me to let me feel like she wasn't intruding. She was a foreigner, but she spoke the same language, and she laughed at the same jokes and I couldn't figure out why. She also had this . . . glow. The way nice people make you feel at ease when you're around them. You know how you can pass someone on the street and—unlike the hundreds of other people you passed that same day—that one person looks at you and you feel a connection? Like you could be friends? Like in another life you were friends. There's some . . . recognition. Because that feeling is clearly mutual. She was like that. And it calmed me. We could sit in a room and read and sip wine and not talk and it felt good. And the sex . . ."

"Marcus . . ."

"The sex was sort of . . . friendly. It started off friendly and cute and only in the middle did the need kick in, but that felt life-affirming because it seemed to prove that even people who liked each other could grow intense sometimes rather than needing to start that way, and I felt so completed . . . assured . . . from that. And she was so damn pretty."

Sigrid thinks she hears something in the woods. A quick scan reveals nothing but she does not take this as proof. Would she have heard Norway's *Beredskapstroppen*? This is an American special weapons and tactics team. Even with Irv stumbling along beside them, there is every likelihood she and Marcus are surrounded already. There is no way to know.

"I heard Mom and Dad talking," he says. "You were sleeping. I went downstairs because I wanted a piece of chocolate and they said I couldn't have one because I'd already had an ice cream earlier, but I was feeling defiant so I went to get some anyway. The Freia kokesjokolade. I think that's what I miss most about Norway. That and the *brunost*."

"Marcus. They're coming."

"Mom only let me have a single square of it each time, but this time I broke off four squares . . . a whole row. I felt like I was making off with the Crown Jewels. No one had ever been so bold. I went into the bathroom to eat it so I wouldn't get caught. And that's when I heard them talking."

"About what?"

"Mom killed herself, Sigrid. And Dad helped. Or let her. Either way. I don't know."

"Marcus, you're imagining this. This was thirty-five years ago. You are distraught now, and you were a little kid then."

"Mom had come home from the doctor. She found out the results of her biopsy. This was the early seventies. No chemotherapy. No realistic surgery that wouldn't have been devastating. The chances of survival now are only forty percent at stage three and that's for five miserable years. I don't even know what they would have been then. The doctor told her she was going to die. It was a matter of when. Mom and Dad decided that if she died sooner, you and I wouldn't have to watch her suffer and we'd get through it all better. That's what really happened, Sigrid. You were five and I was eleven. And you did get through it better. That's what you never knew. And you still don't understand. She sacrificed her life for yours and it worked. Look at you. Chief of police at forty years old. But not for me. Because I heard that conversation. For five months between that moment and her actual death, I sat there knowing what was going to happen and I couldn't stop it. Every day I woke up wondering if she was dead. Because it had to happen at night. I felt like I was being crushed to death inside a paper bag and no one could hear me suffocating. But I didn't say anything. I was too afraid.

"I felt like I'd swallowed poison and all I could do was wait for the effects. I would look at her every day and think, Maybe tonight. Maybe this will be the night she dies. And when I woke up the next morning and I found her there, I wasn't happy. I was shaking. I wouldn't let her near me. I stopped eating. I barely made it through school. And then, months later. It did happen. The moment I learned it, I understood I should have said something. I should have run to her and screamed and told her not to. I should have told her how much I loved her. I should have used every single moment of time with her to express that, and I should have traced her face with my fingers and memorized every curve and every line from every emotion — in her eyes and the corners of her mouth. This knowledge came like a wind through my soul the moment she died.

"I blamed Dad, of course. He must have given her the drugs or at least condoned it. I blamed him because I couldn't blame her. I couldn't mix the anguish with the hate. I needed to separate them. But it wasn't until I was older—when I'd moved away—when I realized the worst part of all. The real truth, Sigrid, is that I actually made her do it. It wasn't their fault. It was mine. Do you see it? She was going to take the morphine at night to save us from the pain, but she was on the fence about it and that's why it took so long. What happened was that I pushed her into it. Every day she must have woken up and seen my own pain getting worse and worse and she must have thought to herself that she needed to do it now. Do it faster. To save her son from suffering even longer. Of course, it was the opposite that was true. I needed to know she wouldn't do it. I needed her to tell me she'd stay with us as long as she possibly could and fight to the end, and be there to say goodbye. She didn't know that I knew her plans, though. And she never said goodbye.

"All I had to do was say I knew. I'm certain of it. They couldn't have gone ahead with it if we'd known. It would have been too cruel. It would have undermined the point of it. She wouldn't have lasted long, but she would have lasted longer. But I said nothing. I killed her. So that was the first woman I killed."

Sigrid had not noticed before that Marcus's feet were in the water. He was still wearing shoes, now submerged to the ankle. Above those, a faded pair of jeans, a blue and white striped button-down shirt that seemed too big for him or else was an "American cut," wide across the back for what they euphemistically call an athletic build. His arms look thinner than she'd remembered. He seems gaunt, physically withdrawn even from himself. He is sweating terribly.

Sigrid stands in the shadows, where it is cooler.

"Even if you heard that, Marcus," she says, "even if they considered it, there is no reason to believe they went through with it. Five months later? It makes no sense. She might have been despondent," Sigrid says, "on hearing the prognosis. I can imagine that. I can imagine a couple of Norwegians in a farmhouse drinking too much and discussing cancer and suicide. Anyone who's been to Norway can imagine that. But actually doing it? No. That isn't how the world works. It is, however, how a little kid makes sense of it."

"She died," Marcus says, emphatically, "because I kept my mouth shut out of cowardice. But this time—with Lydia—I tried talking. My failures with Mom were at the forefront of my mind. So I did the opposite. I pleaded. Argued. I used intellectual words, emotional words, appeals, admissions. I begged her not to leave me. This time I stood too close and said too much. That's how I killed my second woman."

"You didn't kill anyone, Marcus. Lydia killed herself."

"What? That's what you think happened?"

There is a sharp snap behind Sigrid and she turns to see Irving making his way across the forest floor with his eyes to the ground to avoid a misstep. Glancing up he notices her and smiles before wiping his head.

"I should arrest you immediately for what you did back there. I realize we don't have exactly the same legal systems, but I'm pretty sure that arson and destruction of government property is just as illegal in Norway as it is in New York. Am I right or am I right?"

"Yeah. Listen, Irv . . ."

"Did you manage to find . . . hey! There he is. The man of the hour himself! Marcus Odegard, you have put us through quite a bit of trouble ever since . . . Drop that fucking gun right now!"

THE EDGE

RV PLASTERS HIMSELF behind an oak, unbuttons his collar, and breathes. The wool and polyester sheriff's duds aren't helping with the flop sweat. Sticky, grumpy, and in slow pursuit, he'd spent twenty minutes imagining a nice dip in the lake after finding Marcus and the joy of drip-drying in the sun while waiting for Alfonzo and the rest of their team to join them.

Now, though, Marcus has ruined all of that; ruined a chance to cool off, to bring him in easy, to make Irv's life the straightforward and linear affair he deserves. Irv rips the sheriff's hat from his head, chucks it to the ground, and stomps on it—up and down—grinding it into the black earth while shouting, "You said he wouldn't have a gun! You promised me! You said it was all in my head. All in my deranged American mind, that I was making things up, that you know better because you come from some perfect little Utopia, and now here I'm behind a goddamn tree with my dick in my . . ."

"Irv, please, calm down," Sigrid says, but he doesn't calm down, because he feels not only rage but a burning and righteous indignation. She might have raised her voice, but she can't deny that he's justified in feeling this way. The only consolation, as she listens to his diatribe, is that he probably won't shoot Marcus while he's yelling. Americans have always preferred separating their talking from their violence; it seems to be a sequential thing with them.

Eventually Irv regains a measure of control. The calm is not necessarily comforting. He may not want to shoot Marcus, but he's unlikely to risk his own life to prevent it. What he says next she believes:

"Marcus," Irv says from behind the tree. "I will not let you point that at me. So help me God, if you do, I will draw on you. When I became sheriff I spent hours in front of the mirror learning to quick-draw. So know two things. First, I am very, very fast on the draw. And second, I am a terrible shot because I never pulled the trigger. So if you think I'm going to shoot the gun out of your hand or put one in your knee, you're wrong. You point that at me, I will go for center of mass and let the chips fall where they may. And if by some chance I don't hit you, there are six guys behind me who will pepper you until you are dead, and all they do is shoot things. They will not miss. Do you understand me?"

Sigrid has been standing at the edge of the water, and from her angle she can see most of Irv behind the tree. She can also see Marcus on his rock, his feet still in the water, the pistol between his legs hanging in his right hand as limply as a sandwich that has lost its appeal but has nowhere to go.

"I understand you," Marcus answers quietly.

"So throw the gun into the water and throw it far so I can see it fly and watch the splash. If you are very, very lucky and very, very convincing, I might—and I mean might—pretend I didn't see it."

"No," Marcus says. "I don't think I will."

Irv momentarily emerges from behind the tree and he hurls something into the air. As it arcs toward Marcus she hears him yell, "I even brought you a goddamned muffin!"

Irv's toss belies his claims about not being a good shot, because it smacks Marcus in the side of the face and bounces off into the water, where it is immediately devoured by a dozen quacking, snapping, and flapping ducks. Marcus doesn't flinch.

Irv removes his radio from his belt and calls Alfonzo. He explains how there is now a "situation" and he and his men should surround them at a distance and make sure they have a clear shot at Marcus in case events go pear-shaped.

From his angle behind the tree, Irv cannot see Marcus. But he can watch Sigrid. He studies her face the way an infant watches a parent to know what to feel. What he sees is a woman who does not know what to do. He has known her for less than a week, but even so he sees it as an expression that rests uncomfortably on her face. Her eyes and body seem purposeless. She stands there, disassembled.

As all three wait for something to change, the sunlight continues to shift through the canopy. The wind arrives as heat against their necks. It pushes away the breathable air.

Irv looks at the water, as pure and cold as runoff from a glacier.

Hatless and annoyed that he doesn't have any new ideas, Irv decides to repeat the old one: "Throw the gun in the water, Marcus, for the love of God. If for no other reason than to let me have a drink," yells Irv. "How do you think this is going to end?"

"I think we all know how it's going to end," Marcus says.

"What does that mean?" Sigrid says in Norwegian.

"You know what needs to happen," he answers.

"What are you two going on about?" Irv yells.

"He wants you to shoot him," Sigrid says.

"You had better think of something fast, Sigrid. Because while I don't want to shoot him, I might be the last person who doesn't and I'm feeling mighty lonely about it."

Melinda pulls up to First Baptist in her squad car, parks by a lamppost, and dodges puddles in the parking lot, sizzling in the midday sun like tidal pools. There is a rank smell floating up from the parking lot from last night's rain.

Twenty feet away, out of the pitch-black entrance of the church's open door marches Reverend Green. He approaches and shakes her hand. He wears a cordial smile and smells like an amber cologne.

"Why are we meeting again, Deputy?" the reverend asks her.

"Sir, Sheriff Wylie has a few questions he wanted me to ask you as a follow-up to your meeting the other night, and he also wondered if you might accompany me to the crime scene, where we might have a chance to talk about what happened. He's really hoping that the facts of the case might do something to break through the problems we're all facing."

"What do you mean by 'what happened'?" he says, his voice flat.

"To Dr. Jones, sir."

"And you think the facts are going to help us break through the problems, huh?"

"I wouldn't know, sir. "

"No," he murmurs.

They ride in the patrol car with the reverend in the front seat, the lights off, and the windows open from First Baptist to 86 Brookmeyer Road. It takes nearly fifteen minutes, during which the reverend says nothing. The silence is more than Melinda can stand:

"You watching the elections, reverend?"

"Of course," he says, looking out the window.

"I know most cops vote Republican, and I know Irv's one so maybe we can keep this between us, but I've decided to vote for Obama."

"I see," he says.

"How do people at your congregation feel about it?"

"You mean how do they feel about a brother being elected president for the first time in a country where people like him were once slaves?"

"Feels like maybe America's going to take a big step forward, don't you think?"

"Maybe."

"You think he can win?"

Melinda doesn't hear Green's answer. If he said anything it was no louder than the wind battering their clothing through the open windows, his black blazer flapping at the collar.

Eventually and long after the moment had passed, she hears him say—but not to her—"Maybe."

"This is probably none of my business or anything," Melinda says, "but . . . you don't sound very enthusiastic about the prospect."

"That's because if he's elected president of the United States," Reverend Green says, "they're gonna shoot him."

Melinda parks in the no parking zone in front of 86 Brookmeyer Road. They both exit the car and look up before going in.

Eighty-Six Brookmeyer is a steel and glass office building that is still in the making but is no longer being made. It rises from a street corner in a depressed and depressing neighborhood with lowering property values; the kind of structure permanently locked in litigation, bankruptcy filings, and battles for money that leave the physical structure open to the social and natural world to atrophy and rot.

Whatever hope for urban renewal and employment its erection might have once promised, 86 Brookmeyer is a setting for a dream that no one has or wants. And yet despite its irrelevance, there it is: as shiny, as bright, as unfulfilled and overconfident as the people who planned it.

It rises twelve stories and has no organic lines. To Melinda it looks like it was designed on a budget or with a kit; it seems identical, to her untrained eye, to every other glass and steel building she's ever seen. Irv once told her that the population boom, the gas crisis of the 1970s, and bad taste had all collided to create the ugliness of America's "upward expansion," he called it. He told her it was a pity America hadn't decided—after conquering the West—to burrow downward rather than reach upward. "Would have made more sense," Irv had said, "considering that underground buildings retain heat better and are more likely to survive a Soviet missile. And on top, we could have built parks!"

"Have you been here before?" Melinda asks the reverend once they are out of the car, eyes trained on the spot where Lydia died. It is no longer roped off. It is no longer a crime scene, and nothing of its past remains visible. Melinda looks at it; she stares because it has a life force of its own and she wants to scrape her foot over the surface and see whether it is indented or not. It seems crazy to her that a person can be killed and vanish forever without leaving a trace of any kind.

"No," he answers. "I don't understand why we're here, Deputy."

"Irv said we needed to talk and this seemed like a good place."

"Have you been here?" Fred Green asks her.

"I drove by once when the tape was still up. Irv didn't put me on this case until after that."

"Where are we going?"

"Up. To the crime scene. Which . . . now that you mention it . . . I need more information about. Can you hold on a second? I need to ask Irv something."

Alone, Fred Green removes a white and green packet of Newport Kings from his pocket and lights up with an orange Bic. Melinda leaves him to his ritual as she waits for the sheriff to pick up.

Irv is leaning back against the oak trying to convince himself that he isn't cowering, per se, but rather taking a reasonable and defensive position, at least for one with the military training and instincts of a theology student.

As he rests there dreaming of bodysurfing in Maui, the phone rings. He answers it, keeping his eyes on Sigrid as his proxy for Marcus, who doesn't seem intent on going anywhere but heaven.

"Hello?"

"Sheriff? It's Melinda. How's it going?"

"I'd rather not say. What's up?"

"What floor did she fall from?"

"Huh?"

"What floor? I'm with Mr. Green now at the building. The file says it was at least the third because of the injuries, but I didn't see a floor number."

"Yeah. We looked for evidence. We don't know."

"So we've never been to the crime scene, technically," Melinda clarifies.

"We've been to all the floors. So we have, technically, but not knowingly. Hold on a sec," Irv says, and holding the phone away from his face, yells out to Marcus, "Which floor were you on when you killed Lydia?"

"Sixth," says Marcus.

"Thanks."

Sigrid starts to object, but Irv sticks his finger into his ear to hear Melinda better and Sigrid worse.

"Sixth," Irv says to Melinda.

"How do you suddenly know that?" she asks.

"I asked Marcus."

"Is he in custody?"

"He's . . . with me. Is there anything else, Melinda?"

"I know I'm supposed to ask Mr. Green about his relationship with Lydia and his thoughts on our latest theory about her committing—"

". . . diplomatically . . ."

". . . but is there anything else?"

"Well, yes, Melinda. If Marcus really and actually did it, we'll all be fine. But if he didn't, and it's suicide, you and Green need to work out a way to keep her and her parents from living in eternal hell." Irv switches the phone to his other ear and looks at Sigrid, who is sitting on the ground, hapless. "Roy Carman. The grand jury. Jeffrey. Lydia. The parents. The race issues. This stuff is real, Melinda. And the only thing I'm absolutely sure about is that I'm out of my depth. You two need to come up with a way forward to keep the sky from falling. OK, that was a poor choice of words, but you know what I mean."

"There really is a lot to this job, Sheriff."

"Would you just get on with it? I've got problems of my own."

Melinda watches the reverend drop the remains of his cigarette to the ground and twist off its cherry with his black cap-toe shoe. When he's ready, she leads him through the aluminum scaffolding outside the building, through the remains of green canvas sheeting that once served as a door, and into the skeleton of a lobby. They proceed up a steel staircase covered in dust and wood chips, splinters and trash.

The reverend is in no kind of shape to walk up six flights. They stop on the fourth floor landing so he can catch his breath. Melinda waits for him a few stairs up.

The sixth floor is partly encased in glass and partly exposed to the elements. The day is listless in the heat and the open floor feels like an abandoned stage. Melinda walks through plastic sheeting and across exposed wires that lead both to and from nothing, to a spot that overlooks the corner where Dr. Lydia Jones was found contorted and broken.

She is not acrophobic, but there is a pull from the void beyond the edge and it scares her. She had always imagined a window, but there was no window when Lydia fell because there was no window frame because there was no wall. If Lydia leapt to her death, it was easily done here, and if she was pushed that would have been just as simple. Not wanting to look fearful in front of Reverend Green, Melinda walks closer to the edge. But it isn't really the embarrassment that drives her forward. The pull reaches further into her gut and for a moment Melinda thinks she can feel what Lydia felt. Seeing the edge. Almost wanting to stand there. Down below, the street, is what took her life. But here—this was the beginning. The place where it might not have happened. Melinda starts to breathe faster only a meter from the edge. She cannot step backwards, not yet, but she needs to hold something. To do that she needs to stand even closer—to brace herself against the steel strut and anchor herself.

Melinda turns her head and looks at Reverend Green. He is stationary and expressionless and as she looks at him—at his height, at his weight, at his long arms and patent leather shoes, his dark skin and white eyes, his crisp white shirt stained yellow at the collar—she becomes terrified. If he wanted to, with an outstretched hand, he could send her over the edge.

"Are you all right?" he asks her from the middle of the room.

"What?"

"You appear ashen."

"It scares me to be up here," she admits.

"Why are we here, Deputy?" he asks.

Melinda cannot remember Irv's instructions. She cannot contain the enormity of the problems in her mind right now, and all she can think about is Lydia. Of actually being Lydia. Standing here.

"Did Lydia come to see you?"

"Why do you want to know?"

"Did she take her own life? Did she . . ." Melinda tries to turn and face the reverend, but that will leave the edge behind her. He could push her. But the edge could pull.

"I don't know," he says.

"But you suspect. You must suspect something."

Reverend Green walks closer to Melinda. He stops a few feet away and looks down at her feet. There are footprints everywhere. She looks down briefly but her eyes fix on his face. He looks passive and calm, but this only scares her more.

"What does all this tell you?" he asks her, delicately moving a cheeseburger wrapper three inches to the left.

"Nothing," she says.

This limbo—this space between Green and the edge—is too unstable, and if she does nothing she'll have to collapse to the floor and crawl out, but she doesn't want to do that. Taking a sharp breath, she backs up another step and grabs ahold of the girder that separates her from an almost seventy-foot drop. When her hand touches the cold metal she becomes Lydia. She can see through her eyes. As in a vivid morning dream she is fifteen years older, and black, and accomplished. She is dressed in elegant clothing and she's wearing heels, not a beige deputy's uniform and boots. She's lighter and not weighed down by a gun.

Does the world look different to her this way, or does she simply look different in the world? There is a difference, but what is it?

She cannot release the girder. She is stuck there. To calm herself she looks up. Away from the ground, out into the city as though there is a window; something protecting her from the world, not exposing her to it.

"Isn't that Jeffrey's home?" Melinda says.

"What?" says Green.

"Over there," she says, hugging the beam tighter. She doesn't lean out but with her remaining courage she points to a white church steeple with a broken cross at the top. Below is the rooftop that is the same color as the house they visited.

"Yes," says the reverend. "It is."

"Do you think that means something?" she says to him.

"I can't imagine what," he says.

Melinda hears Fred Green's feet shuffle toward her. She turns her head and sees him extending his hand to her. His palm is open. "You're too close to the edge, Deputy. Take my hand, please. Come on back. It's dangerous."

REBORN. AGAIN

AST MONTH, IN the small town of Glåmlia near the Swedish border, Sigrid's own team of *Beredskapstroppen* took a similar position around their target. They were under her command, and her order was to attack. These men—around her now in a crescent —can end Marcus's life instantaneously and with a twitch of a finger. She will see him die before she hears it. They are out there. They must be. She can feel them.

She steps toward Marcus.

"Back!" he yells. He doesn't raise the gun. He only raises his voice, but it is effective. She holds her ground and before she can speak, Irv —the talking tree—lays it out plainly:

"Option one, Marcus. You raise that gun and we kill you. Option two, you toss it far into the water and we arrest you for this specifically and then we see what we think of the Lydia Jones situation separately. Because at this point, you are threatening the lives of police officers and I have cause to lock you up. In fact, I have cause to do whatever I want. Option three is you sit there too long and we all start getting ants in our pants and start making bad decisions and this whole thing becomes subject to human nature, which is not a pretty thing. So what's it going to be?"

Marcus reaches down to the lake water between his feet, cups his hand, and pulls up the water to wet his face and neck. "Option three."

"Fuck you, Marcus."

"Yeah," he replies.

"How about," says Sigrid, sitting down on the dry floor of the forest, "you tell us about Lydia. Tell us what happened."

"It was me. I did it."

"I've heard all that," Sigrid says. "I want the details. What were you doing at Eighty-Six Brookmeyer Road? What is that place, anyway?"

"It's an unfinished office building a few blocks from my house. It's supposed to be boarded up but the neighborhood kids broke into it years ago."

"How is that place connected to your life or Lydia's?"

"It isn't."

"What were you doing there?"

"She was trying to make a point."

"What point was she trying to make?"

"Something about perspective," he says. "I don't know."

"Tell us all about it."

"I told you that Mom committed suicide and you still want to talk about this?"

"I don't think Mom did commit suicide. I think the men with the guns are here and they don't want to hear our family history. I'd like to stay on topic."

Sigrid runs her hand over her face and wipes away the first beads of sweat. Irv looks like he's suffering from the heat. His uniform doesn't look like cotton. That kind of discomfort can affect a person's judgment.

Irv wishes he hadn't ruined his hat already. It would feel great to use it as a fan or for slapping Marcus. "Hey, Al!" Irv yells. "I'm parched. Throw me some water."

From a cloud, from a shadow, from a wormhole straight from

Maine, comes a flying bottle of Poland Spring that bumps between Irv's feet, somersaults, and lands upright.

"Thanks."

He picks it up and drinks it all.

"Marcus," Irv says, wiping his face and flicking the sweat from his head to the ground, "this is that moment when you tell us what happened. And I'll tell you why. It's not because every bad guy has to confess his sins. It's not because we need some deep sense of resolution. Personally, I'm just as happy not knowing and going back to my dozen other cases. It isn't even because you owe it to Lydia, though I think you do. You want to know the real reason, Marcus?"

"No."

"Because talking about it feels good. Talking, Marcus, is the American way. Talking is how you become reborn. Are you ready to be reborn, Marcus? Are you ready to be spiritually renewed?"

"No."

"Of course you are, who wouldn't be. Sigrid was reborn last night, weren't you?"

"Who, me?"

"Yes, you. Sigrid was over at my place last night—"

"No. We were at—"

". . . and we talked and emoted and shared war stories and cried to Bob Seger songs and wondered where the years had gone. She told me all about putting two slugs from a semiautomatic into a semi-innocent kid and how she feels like she did something wrong, something painful, something unnecessary, maybe even sinful, but her higher authority, the institutions she believes in, said she did not. And as a result she does not feel better but feels worse, because the hearts and heads of this world are not aligned. Your poor sister felt like she was being torn apart by horses like poor Saint Hippolytus. You remember that story?"

"No."

"Doesn't matter. And while we talked, Marcus, a mighty weight was lifted from her. Have you taken Jesus Christ as your personal savior, Marcus?"

"No."

"That doesn't matter either, because here's what I learned by studying theology. I learned that we were not studying God. I learned that we were studying the study of God. And now I am a master of that, according to Loyola. So while I still know nothing about God per se, I know a few things about the people who tried to come to terms with God before me. Want to know what I learned, Marcus?"

"No."

"I learned that when faced with the maker of the universe, when faced with the bringer of the moral order, when faced with a force beyond the wildest reckoning of the human imagination, which is itself barely a whisper in the symphony of the cosmos, we are—at some very fundamental level, Marcus—out of our depth. We, in our puny and meek state of sweaty bipedalism, are in no way equipped to understand the mind of our maker. I, Sheriff Irving Wylie, am a very smart man. I'm even smarter than your sister, who's pretty damned smart—"

"No, you're not."

"Yes, I am, and I have concluded that if Saint Augustine and Thomas Aquinas couldn't crack the nut on some of the divine comedies that had Dante giggling in his highchair, then I sure as shit can't do it from my seat of power here in upstate New York. So has it all simply been an orgasmic waste of time? No. Because what I learned from the Jesuits—which is not exactly what they intended for me to learn, but so be it—is one big ironic conclusion. Want to know what that irony is?"

Marcus does not answer.

"The irony, Marcus, is that we came to know nothing about God but a great deal about ourselves, which is precisely what God told us to do all along, but we got too distracted by the messenger to hear the message. Attend to one another, Marcus. We have to be good to one another. You need to be good to Lydia Jones. You need to be good to your sister, and also not shoot anyone here with that thirty-eight of yours. So tell us your story, Marcus. And be reborn in the way that

God meant it most—not by finding Christ, but by recovering your spirit and your place among us; not there in heaven but here in the dirt of upstate New York, where everything that was once in motion finally comes to rest. So speak, Marcus. Speak your piece, and then baptize that gun in the lake and let's go the fuck home."

WHAT HAPPENED

YDIA ARRIVED, UNEXPECTED, at his front door. She had not
been there since before their trip to Montreal. They had not
slept together since then. They had barely spoken since she explained how she felt after hours at her office on campus. And yet, there
she was. Her face was stone.

He invited her in. She stood in the living room looking at the ab-
ject decay of Marcus and his home in the intervening two months. It
was disgusting in there.

The grand jury had not found grounds for concern about Roy Carman's actions. There was not enough reasonable doubt, they had decided, to advance the matter to trial, let alone convict him. He had
done nothing wrong, they said, and there was nothing else to discuss.
Sad, so sad, that the boy was dead. But the specific details of the actual
case were all they had been instructed to consider by the judge, and
the facts were all there, and the law was the law. He was indeed tall
for a child. And that cap gun looked real. And those white children
looked scared of him. And blacks commit more crimes around here.
What else would a reasonable police officer have done? As a point of

fact, Roy Carman had acted very bravely facing down an armed thug like that.

The city apologized to Roy for the hardship that the grand jury process had inflicted on him and his family, and after concluding their affairs, the city sent Lydia's sister Karen a bill for $420 for the ambulance ride that took their dead child to the hospital.

Marcus did not see Lydia often after Jeffrey was shot, but he did see her. A café off-campus. The stone edge of a fountain with a sandwich from Subway. They mostly sat together. She didn't have the strength to grieve and break up with him simultaneously. It was easier for her to accept his presence. This was before the grand jury.

That woman—that Lydia Jones who had lost a nephew—was a person bereft by the loss of love and the universe that constituted a person she knew. But after the grand jury: that was something else. That was a woman who wasn't struck only by an emotion but by an understanding. What had once been theory, had been words, had been conclusions, was now Truth. She had encountered the edge of what her life could be in a way that she had never actually experienced before.

Lydia Jones had been smart and she'd studied hard, and earned her degrees and finally published enough—been lucky enough, focused enough—to have landed a solid academic position in a time, and in a subject area, where competition was fierce. She had studied race, she had experienced race, she had taught race. But until that moment she had not been entirely consumed and nullified by it.

She came to Marcus's house—by then a dump—to collect her few items and create, for herself, a proof of finality. She stuffed them into a brightly colored duffle bag, forcing the items into the bottom as if she were a piston. T-shirts, nightgowns, three dresses, undergarments, and a pair of jeans. Two pairs of shoes. She entered the bathroom. Marcus heard the sounds of perfume jars and beauty implements being tossed in with them.

It was a beautiful day for leaving his house behind. The sunlight glinted off the windows of the passing cars from the off-ramp, and each time it did the bedroom burst into Technicolor. The palette of the bedspread—green and yellow and red, colors he'd been attracted to in the shop and later forgot existed in the oppressive dark of the house—roared into view with each passing car.

The staccato strobes from the bus windows were blinding. In the light, Lydia appeared and disappeared—there and gone. There and gone. There and gone.

Marcus told Irv and Sigrid about their discussion while she packed. What he said at the top of the stairs. How he became aware of the color of himself—not what he looked like, but what it meant to be "white" in relation to her "black." How there, then, his whiteness drowned out his unique and personal voice and in being so negated, he finally had some basis for imagining what Lydia must have been feeling every day. What she must have been feeling then. Negated, not by a person she loved, but by her entire country. And with that new knowledge, that new insight, there was absolutely nothing he could do about it.

When she was finished packing, Lydia swung the duffle bag over her shoulder with the grace of a dancer and descended the staircase to make for the world outside.

Marcus watched from the top of the stairs.

He could have shouted something, but his Lutheranism ran too deep. His edges had been filed off and the stumps worn down by a culture that didn't know how to sin and then repent and so suppressed everything and hoped that God wouldn't notice.

The screen door slapped the doorframe.

Whap.

And he was alone.

Out the door, down the street, Lydia humped her duffle bag like a soldier who was pissed to learn what the war had really been about.

Marcus stood outside the front door to his pathetic house looking over his poor excuse for a lawn as he watched her grow smaller, with each futile step she took in an effort to get away; futile because there was no escape from what she was fleeing.

Her flight, however, was not about distance but the pure expenditure of energy. She needed to burn everything off. She needed to make tracks. She needed to assert her existence through movement and separate herself from all that was static and unchangeable and inevitable around her. It didn't matter what might be accomplished. All that mattered was her commitment to the effort.

Marcus was uncertain whether to follow her or not.

He stood there wanting to yell. It would have been inane. What could he have yelled? "Stop"? "Hold on"?

He acted on impulse. He followed her without intent or a plan. He simply felt that their connection couldn't be allowed to be broken. Not this way. She was walking in the direction laughably called the Financial District. All that was there now, other than the carcass of buildings, was a taxi stand where foreign drivers stared into their smartphones listening to TV shows in their native languages through tiny speakers that made the voices they missed only seem that much farther away.

She trudged down Fourth Avenue like someone fighting against a river, and Marcus pursued. Pale, torn, shredded, and fixated, he walked fast enough to overtake her but he did not run; running seemed wrong, running would have turned him into a pursuer—it was too literal and direct and aggressive. He needed to catch up to her and change her mind about everything, using words he didn't have and hoped would magically appear, the way they did not with his mother.

He caught up to her outside an unfinished building at 86 Brookmeyer Road.

"Don't leave like this," he'd said.

"Leave me alone, Marcus." Her voice was low. There was nothing conflicted in her tone.

Traffic was light. The glass tower rose and merged with the steel sky above them.

"I'm afraid that if you leave now you'll never come back."

"That's right."

"It's because of the verdict. I know, I understand that. But we can't destroy everything—"

"Everything?" she asked, dropping her bag from her shoulder and waving her hand between them. "You mean us? That's the 'everything' to you?"

"I'm afraid to talk to you. I'm afraid of your anger. It's bigger than us, and it comes from a place outside of us, and I can't find a place to talk to you here on the inside."

"I don't care," she said. "I don't owe you that. You don't get a 'safe space.' You have a country of your own, Marcus. Go home. Go to where you belong. Consider yourself lucky that you have someplace else to call home that isn't here."

That is when he threw down the gauntlet and decided that—instead of him leaving Lydia to try to come to terms with the seismic implications of the grand jury decision—they should hold hands and, to save their relationship, declare war on injustice.

"We can fight this!" he'd yelled to her.

He actually said that: *We can fight this.*

What he thought he meant, at the time, was that they could choose to be together, independent of the injustices of the wider world. They would not be the first couple since Romeo and Juliet to try it, and there was a very good chance they'd wind up better off than those two did. An interracial couple in 2008 was a less impossible scenario than the pursuit of romantic love in 1597.

But Lydia wasn't trying to save *them*; she was trying to save some part of herself.

By the time Marcus recounted all this to Sigrid and Irv from his rock on Lake Flower, he had come to understand that his declaration to "fight" sounded different to her than how he'd intended it. She heard it with different ears. To her, his proclamation had been a declaration of war against time and history and gravity.

We can fight the winds and the seas, he might have said instead. *We can fight against the spread of the continents and the pull of the moon. Let's fight against the elements, one by one, until we have dominion over them all, and let us establish a kingdom of righteousness and liberty and tolerance and human kindness and give it a name unspoiled by other names. We will speak of our victory in a new language unshaped by power, and sing to each other in poetry untainted by robbery or theft of one culture by another. We'll do that together,* he might as well have said. *Just you and me. And we will wash away the old world in a great flood and renew it. Adam and Eve, naked on the Ark. A stateroom for two—the only animals here on a mission from God.*

"I want to show you something," she said in reply to his own emancipation proclamation.

If she'd walked away, if she'd shaken her head in dismay as she should have, if she hadn't looked at him as someone who needed to be enlightened—if she had simply told him to fuck off and leave her alone—she'd still be alive.

But she didn't do any of that.

She dropped her duffle bag to the ground and walked directly into 86 Brookmeyer Road and started climbing the stairs, two at a time, like a high school athlete scaling the bleachers.

Marcus considered collecting the duffle, but she had already vanished into the building and there was no way he'd catch up to her if he were carrying it. Something else, something important, was happening.

Why was she going in there? It had never even felt like a place before—only something irrelevant and characterless in his geography that he passed by on his way to someplace else.

Marcus was bigger and taller and stronger than Lydia, and he had a broad chest. He weighed about 190 pounds and stood over six feet tall. He was not athletic, per se, but he lived a clean life and he walked most places out of an aversion to public transport. He caught up to Lydia on the sixth-floor landing, which was already higher than most of the other buildings around it.

"We aren't supposed to be up here," he'd said to her.

"Because the authorities won't like it?"

"It's private property."

He had said this! "Private property"—moments after suggesting they reverse the spin of the Earth.

Lydia swung around and stepped from the landing through the plastic sheeting that helped keep the dust from one side from mixing with the dust on the other, and she entered the unfinished space that was—and was not—the sixth floor; a space without purpose or definition or a future.

"Lydia, come back, please," he implored.

He remembers how there was a wind that collected pigeon feathers from the floor, creating small twisters at her feet. She was wearing a pair of brown shoes with a small heel. Size eight. Nine West.

The wind outside was constant and promised a storm but there was no smell of it yet; only the waft of car exhaust and the permanent sweat of vanished workers, the sweet aroma of rotting wood and sawdust.

There was a sense of height, too. There was no glass where the walls or windows should have been. Neither of them was naturally afraid of heights. Together, he and Lydia had hiked to the top of Mount Marcy, and even taken some rock-climbing classes at Cascade Lakes on grades of 5.3b and 5.4a. He wrote his father about it once in a letter. This place, though, scared him immediately. Marcus did not want to follow her closer to the absent wall, but he couldn't talk to her if he didn't. He needed to convince her. Of something. Somehow.

Even then he didn't know what. But it was Lydia who had the plan. Lydia who had brought them there.

"Don't make me do this anymore," Marcus says to Sigrid. He looks up at her, craning his neck to keep his shoulders low, the gun hanging and heavy in his long fingers—"piano fingers" his own mother used to call them. "You can reach an entire octave," she had said to him when he was nine. "Not your father's hands. Not the hands of a farm boy. You are going to solve mysteries and problems. My little boy with the long fingers."

Sigrid is still on the ground with her legs crossed. She is hot and exhausted from the long night, the hangover, the long day, the jet lag, the long memories, the stretch of time behind her.

"Irv is right," she says to him. "You have to say it. I don't know about reborn this or reborn that, but you need to do this for yourself, Marcus. You were on the landing. You followed her."

"I thought you came here to protect me," he pleads like a child.

"I did. And I'm now fairly certain that the only way to save you is to help you face yourself. If you don't, if you pass this moment without speaking up the way you did last time, you will—in a very real sense —never truly live again. You followed Lydia. What happened?"

Lydia approached the empty space where the wall should have been. There, far above the city, she was exposed to the air and the light and the urban sprawl around her. Marcus saw her squint against the harsh light from the glowing smog above them. Her hands, he remembered, were twitching as if they were meant to be holding something. They looked to him like the hands of a sleeping child, grasping for a parent's hand.

"Lydia, come back. I love you."

Her neck jolted as though recoiling from a pungent smell.

"Look, Marcus," she said, in as soothing a voice as she could manage. "Look at what you want to fight. Come here. It's easy to see from here. We are not only us. We are part of more."

Marcus crossed the room that was not a room to the window that was not a window to look out on the city he lived in that was becoming more unfamiliar by the moment.

She waved her arms and pointed. The city was still racially segregated, keeping people separate and unequal. She mapped out the voting lines and called out the streets by name.

Yes. He knew all this. So . . . what?

Was she demonstrating that America was economically divided and racially unfair? No one denied that. It was the analysis about why it persisted that was at issue. And surely the answer to that couldn't be gleaned by a view over the rooftops.

If they had been standing on a hill in Alabama, wouldn't they be able to look at rich whites and poor whites? Mansions and trailer parks? There's economic inequality in America because America likes it that way. That's how he always thought of it as a Norwegian. How can the winners prove that they've won if they can't have more than the losers? That's an American problem, he wanted to say. This is a place that has convinced workers that foregoing a holiday is noble and impressive rather than foolish and destructive. And honestly, what did any of this have to do with the grand jury decision against Roy Carman anyway? he wanted to ask. A black man might become president of the United States. Isn't that evidence of America's progress, promise, and potential?

"Lydia," he eventually said, clearing his mind of these tangled ideas. He stepped closer to her and reached out his hand. "Lydia, you can't abandon us. You can't leave me behind. Lydia, please. I don't want to be alone anymore. I can't be alone anymore. I need you. I love you. I love you so much. We can get through this together. Please," he said, reaching out both arms to embrace her, "please come to me."

Marcus did not know how close to the edge she had been. There was no frame behind her to judge the distance. There was an illusion of endless retreat. Lydia had not known either. She couldn't have known because she was not facing outward but toward Marcus and his needs and his approaching mass. If she had known she would not have extended both of her arms and tried to shove him away with all the force in her diminutive body, a body that weighed so much less than his, that was so much less planted to the ground, but she wanted him away so badly, and she was so intent and focused on not being crowded and overpowered and ignored by everything he was and everything she imagined him to be in that instant, that she slipped.

She had lunged with her palms out and arms straight and used all her weight, but Marcus had more; she only succeeded in pushing herself backwards to the edge. The sawdust and debris denied her left foot its needed purchase and, off-balance, she slipped and fell.

Marcus's own arms had been extended to embrace her, and hers had been extended to push him away, and in the moment when she lost her balance and her eyes became wide and aware, she tried reaching for him and taking hold.

The nails of her long and slender fingers scraped the tops of his arms, and before he could grasp her she was gone.

Marcus froze there. He heard Lydia slap the pavement.

"I ran down the stairs," Marcus says from his rock. "I ran out the door and picked her up. She was . . . destroyed. Her head . . ."

"I understand," Sigrid says to him.

"Her eyes were open. Exactly as they had been while she was falling."

"You're done, Marcus."

"She didn't call out or scream on the way down. I can feel the fall. The wind of it."

"You're done, Marcus."

"Irving," Sigrid says. "Don't shoot."

"I'm not making any decisions while that gun is in play."

Sigrid stands, brushes herself off, and walks to her brother. She lays a hand on his head. She reaches down and takes the weapon from his hands, presses the cylinder release, and removes the bullets. She throws the gun into the lake, as far as she can, so Irv can see the arc and hear the splash.

She walks to Irv behind the tree and hands him the bullets.

HANDLE WITH CARE

SIGRID TAKES MARCUS by the hand and walks her big brother back through the woods to the Zodiac that she had beached on the edge of the lake. The assault team emerges from the surrounding woods and lowering and shouldering their weapons as they fall in line behind them. Irv can't decide whether or not to cuff Marcus because he isn't sure yet whether he wants to arrest him. But there is time for all that later. Fortunately, though, the danger of being shot is over and no one is going to have to carry Marcus out of the forest.

On the boat, Irv watches Sigrid sit herself beside her brother, who looks spent. He hangs his head and seems resigned and passive. Sigrid holds his hand and together they are silent. She does not try to speak with Marcus and instead looks out at the distant mountains over the shimmering water.

The wind in Sigrid's hair looks good. The sun has added some needed color to her face.

"You need a vacation," he shouts to her over the roar of the outboard motor. And, for the first time, he hears her laugh.

• • •

At Lake Flower, Sheriff Frank Allman is waiting for them. He is standing in the same spot and pose in which Irv left him—hands in his pockets, dropped shoulders, utterly put upon by events beyond his control. Alfonzo tosses the mooring line to Frank, who misses it, collects it, and ties off the Zodiac.

"Welcome back," Frank says to Sigrid as she steps out of the boat. Sigrid pats him on the shoulder. He's had a hard day.

Irv and Frank retire to the police station, where, she's certain, phone calls are being made and political matters are being deliberated. Sigrid sits beside Marcus on a bench close to the van she set on fire.

"You did this?" he asks his sister.

"Yes."

"We are masters of disaster."

"Yes, we are."

Ten minutes later Irv emerges from the police station. He claps his hands like a soccer coach. "All right," says Irv. "We're going back. Marcus is with us."

"He's free to go?" Sigrid asks.

"He's free to go with us. And we're all going to consider ourselves very lucky."

They transition to the squad car and make their way back to Irv's own jurisdiction across the invisible lines that turn one place into another. On the way NPR's *All Things Considered* begins its broadcast, but Irv is not in the mood to consider all things and switches over to a jazz station playing an Art Blakey special celebrating fifty years since the release of the album *Moanin'*.

They listen in silence for more than a half-hour until Sigrid breaks it with a question:

"What does 'the one percent' mean?" she asks. "I saw it on a patch at the biker clubhouse."

"It refers to the myth that ninety-nine percent of bikers are law abiding, but one percent are outlaws. People who call themselves One Percenters consider themselves above the law and are invariably assholes. You should have called a taxi."

When they arrive, Irv locks Marcus into the cell for the night. There's no better solution and Sigrid does not object. She has spent plenty of time in this jail and knows it to be the cleanest and safest place he has been in a long time. They don't even bother to remove her desk.

"I thought you'd insist he stay with you tonight," Irv says to Sigrid as they leave the station for the Wagoneer.

"I have other plans tonight," she says.

"When did you have time to make plans?"

"You were pretty good back there," Sigrid says.

"You're talking to me?"

"Yes," Sigrid says.

"This would be the wrong time, I suppose, to tell you that I was right all along and if we'd worked together from the start all this could have ended the same way but without the SWAT team, the pyrotechnics, paperwork, or tears."

"I think," says Sigrid, "you need to decide how you want the rest of this night to go."

"I take your meaning," Irv says, starting the Wagoneer.

It is seven o'clock in the evening, but Deputy Melinda Powell decides not to go home quite yet and instead sit with Marcus as she finalizes some work. After all, it took so long to find him; seems weird to just leave him there.

Irv has only told her tangentially what happened at the lake and she's hoping Marcus will open up and share the rest, but the longer she sits at Irv's desk—still in the opposite jail cell—the more certain she becomes that the likelihood of Marcus uttering even a single word is very low.

"Do you like Thai food?" she asks him.

Marcus looks up.

"Thai food. Do you like it?"

"I guess so."

"You must be hungry for some hot food, living out there in the woods like that for a week or more. What did you eat, anyway?"

"There was no Thai food."

"Well . . . you're in luck then. Because they deliver. The Thai people. Who I think might be Irish."

Melinda orders a few appetizers and three main courses. It's much more than they need, but she can put it on the station's tab and squirrel away the leftovers in the fridge, which is now working again.

When the food arrives she makes Marcus a plate and hands him chopsticks from her adjoining cell.

"Irv says the Thai don't use chopsticks; they use a spoon and sometimes a fork to push the food onto the spoon."

Marcus nods as he uses the chopsticks.

"I don't want you killing yourself with those or trying to make a prison break or anything, OK?"

She accepts his silence as agreement.

Melinda makes small talk as Marcus eats. "I doubt a lot of people —even the most highly motivated—have what it takes to off themselves with chopsticks. They're quite brittle," she says. "I guess you'd have to bunch them together and then hold the sharpened tips against your chest right between the ribs and have a good fall on them. Impale yourself through the heart. That would be the winner."

Marcus stops chewing and looks at her.

"You didn't hear it from me, though. In fact, give them back when you're done, OK?"

Melinda notices that Marcus, who had been utterly expressionless since being placed in the jail cell, now has something akin to a smile on his face.

"What are you getting all hysterical about?" she asks.

"Your sheriff was right. You Americans keep talking, don't you? I'd never really noticed."

"You're just used to us by now, that's all."

Sheriff Irving Wylie surrendered his three-bedroom Victorian in the divorce with an understanding that—when the house was eventually sold—he'd receive half the sale price. He didn't mind moving out and liked the idea of his daughter having the stability of the home she'd been living in since they moved there fifteen years before.

He bought a two-bedroom in a modern building with an elevator and a decent view of the distant hills from his fourth-floor balcony. The condo is tastefully furnished. The living room has a blue area rug, an indigo velvet chair of a modern design, a tan leather sofa, and a wingback armchair in a green patterned fabric. The coffee table is glass. There are bookshelves along the walls filled with both novels and academic tomes. *A Soldier of the Great War* by Mark Helprin. *On Law, Morality, and Politics* by Thomas Aquinas. *Santaland Diaries* by David Sedaris.

Sigrid reaches for the Sedaris book but stops when her eyes fall on pictures of his ex-wife and their daughter at all different ages. There is a Yamaha acoustic guitar in the corner of the room slightly askew on a steel stand.

Taking her shoes off, she picks up the guitar and flops onto the sofa with it, laying it across her lap. Irv pours two glasses of red. She strums her E chord. "You planning to wear that gun all night?" she asks him.

"That's got to be the sexiest question I've ever been asked."

Irv walks over and hands her the glass. He places his on the coffee table. He slips off his shoes, his gun belt, and his outer shirt. His white T-shirt has seen better days. He sits on the velvet chair and crosses his legs.

"To a job well done," he says, raising a glass.

"You're not done," Sigrid says.

"What does that mean?"

"You told Melinda and Reverend Green to come up with a plan. She said they did."

"Oh?"

"You're going to go back to that church and tell the people there what really happened. And you have to be humble and respectful and make them believe you."

"You mean the black church?"

"I mean the church filled with your constituents. Reverend Green says they need to hear from you. They're in pain and, he believes, only the truth will help. You're going to tell them what Marcus told you."

"Swell."

"Can you play this thing?" Sigrid asks.

"I can almost play 'Handle with Care' by the Traveling Wilburys. Do you know it?"

"No. Are you going to press charges against Marcus?"

"No."

"You believe his story?"

"Turns out that it doesn't matter. Apparently you told Melinda to find out what Chuck—our one and only eyewitness—was doing on the street corner when he saw Marcus run over to Lydia. As it happens, he was selling crack."

"How do you know he was selling crack?"

"She asked him. Oh yeah, and she wanted me to tell you that sometimes the investigative question and the interview question are actually the same. Does that mean something?"

"It means she's growing," Sigrid says, smiling. She hands Irv the guitar and slips her feet beneath her. She sips the wine.

"The assistant district attorney says we can't use Chuck. Melinda has also been up to the sixth floor of that building and she couldn't find anything other than a lot of footprints. And while we could probably match some of them with Marcus's and Lydia's shoes, he's not denying they were there. What we can't do is prove that Marcus pushed her and since no one here has Smilla's Sense of Dust, those footprints aren't going to tell us what happened by themselves." Irv gently strums the D-C-G chords of the song. "That, and Melinda probably stepped on some of them. The ADA says the case against Marcus is too weak. Ambiguity favors the defendant because of the presumption of innocence."

"It didn't for Jeffrey."

"That is not lost on me," he says, trying for the tricky B7 chord.

"I leave tomorrow," Sigrid says.

"I know."

"I'm going to take a shower. How about you bring that guitar into the bathroom and sing your song to me?"

"You won't regret it," says Irv.

FAITH

THE NEXT MORNING, at the station, Sigrid makes her rounds and shakes the hands of various officers by way of good-bye as Melinda leads them to the jail cell in the back, which smells like peanuts on account of the pad thai. Melinda explains that Sigrid's mentorship has meant a lot to her and has really changed her thinking about investigation, her own career path, women in the police, and how best not to lose people in bathrooms. Melinda says she wants to be like Sigrid when she gets "old" and she hopes they can stay in touch. Sigrid makes her rounds and shakes the hands of various officers.

In the back, Marcus is sitting on his mattress with his feet up and arms crossed and does not stand when the cell door is opened.

"You are free to go. According to the sheriff you are not provably guilty and should go away. And never return."

Marcus looks to Sigrid, who explains that they do indeed have tickets for Norway and should now go. And they need to get moving because they have to take a bus and then three planes.

"You're carrying the guitar," she says to him.

"Everything here is the same as it was when I was by the lake. Nothing's changed. If they release me, now that they have me, there will be riots."

"The sheriff and Mr. Green have a plan to solve all of that."

"What kind of a plan?"

"A good one."

"How do you know?"

"The sheriff stopped talking for a while and was really listening."

Irv waits in the parking lot for Reverend Fred Green. They both decided, this morning, that it would be best if they rode in Fred's car for a change. A sensible light blue Toyota Camry pulls up beside Irv, who is dressed in his sheriff's outfit but without his sidearm. It may be a violation of a rule not to carry it while on duty. Luckily he doesn't care.

Irv pops open the door and settles into the passenger seat. The interior smells like Newports and aftershave.

"Is this a 2005?" Irv asks.

"No, 2004," Fred says. "Same front end."

"Toy-o-ta," Irv says to the passing trees outside as they head toward the church.

They drive without the static of the police radio or the pleasure of the stereo. At a long light Irv chases the quiet away by pointing to a CD sticking its silver tongue out of the slot.

"What are you feeding that thing?"

"Bill Withers."

"Did you know," Irv says, "that 'Ain't No Sunshine' is only a touch over two minutes long? That's half the length of your average pop song."

"Goes to show what a man can do in two minutes if he does it right," says Fred Green.

"I was just making small talk, Fred."

"You should be thinking about what you're going to say."

"It'll come to me."

"I'm not playing, Sheriff."

"I know perfectly well what I'm going to say, Reverend. I just don't know how I'm going to say it. It'll come to me. Always does."

Sunday Services at First Baptist are scheduled for nine-thirty in the morning with a Bible study class at eleven. Normally these early-morning services draw around fifty people unless there is an occasion. Today, with a few calls from Fred to key people in the community, there are more than triple that number.

Jeffrey Simmons and Lydia Jones were both baptized here and both laid to rest here too; beside each other in the cemetery three and a half miles to the northeast. Lydia's parents had bought plots for themselves years ago to save money. Their daughter and grandson used them instead.

Fred and Irv crunch into the reverend's personal parking space by the door. They are forty minutes early but the parking lot is already a third full. Irv sits in the car and looks out at the entirely black congregation making their way inside past a half-dozen men, smartly dressed and smoking like high-schoolers by the trash can. Others mill around outside talking. There is a thick pane of glass between Irv and what they are saying to each other.

"A lot of kids," Irv says, more to himself than the reverend.

"It's a church, Sheriff."

"Yeah, I know—I just had this picture in my head of a room full of adults with stern faces ready for a serious discussion about politics or something."

"Maybe the pictures in your head need to be adjusted."

Irv whistles. "Wow. Did you and my ex-wife attend the same course or something? I mean . . . damn, Fred."

"All those kids out there, Irv. You're their sheriff. Go meet them."

Irv looks at them running around, skidding about on the tiny pebbles of the parking lot, their shirttails coming out and their mothers trying to tuck them back in while they're on the move.

"They're all so short," Irv says.

• • •

Fred Green leads Irv inside, and together they sit in the pastor's office as the parishioners file in and silence themselves. The reverend leads the service as Irving sits to the side in the chancel like a choirboy. While Irv waits for his turn to speak it occurs to him — the proverbial pebble dropping — that perhaps he should have prepared what he was going to say and maybe Fred was right.

A lot of people do that, he's read. Prepared people. People who go home afterward feeling good about themselves for what they'd said rather than what they might have said, which they think about to avoid the actual memory of what they did say. As Fred speaks to the congregation, Irv imagines what it might be like to be one of those people.

And then he stops thinking about it because it's never going to happen.

Reverend Fred Green wiggles two fingers at Irv, indicating that he's to step to the lectern now. Irv removes his hat and leaves it on the chair behind him.

He shakes Fred's hand and Fred whispers, "John Eight: thirty-two, Sheriff," as Irv trades places with him. "And you will know the truth, and the truth will set you free."

"Yeah, I was thinking that too," Irv says.

Irv looks out at them without speaking. The audience is silent. They are waiting for something. He rests his hands on the edges of the lectern and slides them back and forth and back again, feeling the space where Fred had, moments earlier, done exactly the same thing. The edges are still warm from the reverend's hands. In the audience, in the fourth row to Irv's right, sits the Jones family. Beside them, the Simmons family.

And that is when Irv figures out how to begin:

"If you ever get the chance," he says to the packed room of a hundred and fifty faces, "to place your hands on this podium here, you can feel how the edges are slightly worn down. You can't see it from where you're sitting because of the angle. Can't really even see it well from here. You have to feel it. They've been polished smooth by speaker after speaker in preparation and practice and worry about what to say. The wood is worn down by the emotions of people trying to talk meaningfully from this spot. I didn't have this thought or know this until right now. That's because . . . well . . . because I've never placed my hands here before. Which is, in a roundabout way, what I'm getting at. Despite being your sheriff I have never been here before to try and say something meaningful like everyone else who's worn this thing down over time. And as I stand here, I have to ask myself, Why? Why didn't I come here earlier?"

Irv pauses. The children are fidgeting. Older women are fanning themselves. The air conditioning is on but it is no match for the high summer sun, the worsted wool, and the full room.

"I remember thinking," Irv continues, "that Jeffrey was killed across an invisible line separating one county from another, which meant it wasn't my jurisdiction. There were so many emotions around it that I didn't want to touch it, and I was glad my people weren't implicated. Two months later Lydia died. That was on my side of the line. But somehow I didn't let it touch me. I treated it as a mystery to be solved while keeping my distance. That made it a second time I didn't come here to talk to you. I find this painful to admit, but I think the reason I didn't come talk to you is because I was afraid to. I mean . . . I didn't think anything bad was going to happen, but I was afraid of all the emotions. The anger. The grief. The way that people who speak from their hearts can sometimes say some pretty mean things and lay some heavy blame, and sometimes the wiser move is to avoid the conversation because it'll only make things worse. I went through that in my marriage. But I also know that my marriage failed, so I obviously did something wrong.

"I don't think that being afraid of all those emotions makes me a bad man, but I do think it might make me a coward. I feared walking in here and being treated like a villain in a story I didn't write. My mistake, my failure as your sheriff and as a man and as a Christian, was thinking I had a choice. That somehow it might all go away and blend into all the other noise. What my cowardice proves to me is that I lacked faith. Faith in God, and faith in you. Because what

I also learned from my failed marriage is that angry people, people who shout at you and accuse you, and vilify you, often do it to try and change you. Which means they think it's possible. Which means they have faith in you. Which means they can imagine the New Jerusalem. And to avoid that, to walk away from that, is to turn your back on the Kingdom of God.

"I can't help but wonder," Irv says, "whether I might have made a small difference to Lydia if I'd have come here when Jeffrey was killed, or maybe when that grand jury verdict was read out. I wonder if, had she seen me here trying to serve this community better by being a part of it, whether she might have had more hope. I don't know. But what I need to do now is tell you truthfully what I know.

"Lydia Bethany Jones, Ph.D.," Irv concludes, "was not murdered. She also did not commit suicide, if anyone has that thought. It is my conclusion—backed by the evidence we have collected—that she accidentally fell off an unfinished building from the sixth floor. The reason she was there at all was to try to help a friend understand something about Jeffrey's world and what that verdict meant to her. Something that was, for him and at that moment, beyond his capacity to understand. In trying to explain that world—with an actual view above it—she lost her footing and fell. The man she was with tried to save her and he failed. He is, right now, devastated to the point of self-destruction, because he loved her even if he didn't understand her —though in my experience that's often the way it is for the lot of us.

"It occurs to me now, as I'm telling you all this, that Professor Jones died as she lived: as a teacher. In her last publication, which I've read, she expresses a loss of faith in what the future might bring for this country. In her head, she was not convinced that we can fundamentally change. But in her deeds, in her actions—and to me, that means from her heart—she risked her life to bring understanding and grace to the world by giving everything she had to change one single mind. And that is not the action of someone who has lost faith. It is the essence of faith itself.

"I'm sorry I didn't come to see you earlier. For what it's worth, Lydia sounds like she was a remarkable woman. I wish I'd known her."

A MISUNDERSTANDING

ORTEN ØDEGÅRD'S CHILDREN haven't been in his car
together in more than thirty years. He can't help but enjoy it.

Sigrid sits up front with him and Marcus sits in the back, the opposite of how it used to be. Before they arrived, Sigrid had written
him a long email—and called to be sure he'd received it—before they
boarded the plane in America so that Morten would understand and
be prepared for the gravity of the situation they now face as a family. His role, as father, might have been to collect them at the termi-
nal and receive them gravely while transporting them to their childhood home for a period of reflection and reconciliation. But Morten
Ødegård is a single parent with his healthy children in his car beside
him and he cannot remember the last time he has been so uncondi-
tionally happy.

On the E6 they zip along pleasantly at eighty-five kilometers per
hour and at one point Morten actually reaches out his hand and places
it on Sigrid's thigh and smiles at her.

Sigrid looks at his hand and his smiling face and assures herself that he is OK and not having a stroke or asking for help. Uncertain of what is happening, however, she manufactures a smile and pats his hand a few times, hoping that will make it go away, but it only seems to make him happier.

Morten can see Marcus in his rearview mirror.

"How do you feel?" Morten asks.

"Like a child again," Marcus says.

"There was a time when you were very happy as a child."

"I don't remember," Marcus says.

"I do."

Morten tunes the stereo to NRK Klassisk and fills the car with Ravel.

"Some things have changed since you've been gone," Morten says, turning into the hills.

"I figured," Marcus says.

"The troll population has surged. They're issuing hunting permits."

"Pappa, he's not in the mood," Sigrid says.

Marcus is returned to Norway through the language coming through the radio. The temper of the presenters is as lighthearted as their American DJ counterparts, but the production is not as polished, carefully timed, or aggressively commercial. In this way it is comforting. But they show no reverence for the music. In the hourlong drive to their house they pass through two news cycles. Each time, the news presenters switch the music off on the hour no matter what piece is playing. A woman named Rachel Podger was playing Bach's Sonata no. 1 in B Minor. Bach's music, passing through her violin, made the world a vivid and memorable place; layered and more possible than it had been only moments earlier, both taking Marcus away from the hills of Norway and yet planting him more firmly in the moment. This is what they end with the casual brutality of a fishmonger wielding a cleaver.

On comes the news. The NRK news sounds authoritative and calming. Norway listens — as Americans once listened in the 1950s —

to one voice. And it both unites them and deceives them in equal measures, but the deception is delicious and the unity appreciated.

Outside, on the road, other cars let them merge.

They drive the speed limit and think nothing of it.

In town, on the way to the farm, almost everyone they pass in the street waves to them. They know Morten; they know his car.

Their waves are not grand swings of the arm as if to flag down a spouse or encourage a helicopter to land. They are short and to the point. There is a nod, or an upturned head, an open palm. Marcus is returning to the land of his birth and these are the people who have buried the last five generations of his family. He had forgotten they existed. It feels as though they have not forgotten him.

The driveway to the farm is still gravel and the pebbles pop as the Subaru makes for its port. The sky is as blue as a daydream. The farmhouse is red and the grass around it is still green and all of this surprises Marcus because he thought time would have faded all the colors.

"I stocked up the refrigerator yesterday," Morten says to his children, leaving their suitcases in the front hall. "I don't know what you're eating these days but I took a few guesses beyond the staples. I started with the four Norwegian food groups of brown cheese, waffles, hot dogs, and beer. I then bought a few frozen pizzas, which I remember you kids eating. I also bought some fruit and vegetables, salmon, pasta, juices, and a chicken we can roast in case your tastes have evolved. Marcus, your bedroom remains unchanged and I asked Agatha to dust it when she was here yesterday."

In America, Marcus did not have a picture of his mother. He did, however, have an excellent memory of her. He also saw her face in his own. Her hair was blond like his. Her eyes were blue and dark like his own. Her neck was long and graceful like Sigrid's, and she had excellent posture and graceful limbs.

Piano fingers.

She had them too.

There are no pictures of her here, either. There never were. His father was never one for family photos on the walls. He has always preferred landscape art; the occasional Ansel Adams–inspired black-and-white of a forest or a fjord, the bucolic countryside, the flea market art from estates. None has moved from the spots where he left them. The farmhouse is preserved. His father either didn't want to change anything after Astrid died or didn't know how to.

Change things into what?

For all the philosophy and verbiage, the growth and the pain, Marcus stands in the hallway by the kitchen and realizes that his life has never quite matured beyond these rooms.

Marcus opens the downstairs bathroom and looks at the vent over the toilet.

From inside that vent he heard a story. His mother and father were speaking. He listens carefully. There is only a whisper of air.

Marcus leaves and closes the door too quickly and as he does the wineglasses in the cupboard rattle as the swinging door creates a pocket of air that swells the entire house.

The family eats dinner together at home that first night. They talk about the farm. Marcus asks about the financials. Morten explains how the farm is working as much as it needs to and the expenses are low and his pension is coming in, so he has no trouble making a living wage that will ensure a stable retirement. He could probably stop now but . . . why bother?

To Marcus, Sigrid sits at the table like an adult—not a large child, which is how he feels. She has been here during the intervening years and has grown into her place. She eats her salmon and potatoes like a forty-year-old adult. Marcus is still eleven.

In his bedroom, after dinner, Marcus lies on the freshly laundered sheets he slept in as a child. Sigrid's room, next door, was once decorated with rock posters and pop stars. No more. She grew in hers. His remained static. The only decoration on the wall is a poster of a U.S. Navy precision flying team called the Blue Angels. On the poster the pilots stand on the tarmac, straight as pines, beside their F-4 Phantom aircrafts. It is 1967. Their uniforms are yellow and blue. After his mother died he would stare at them. He'd imagine his own hand on the flight controls, watching the instruments and picturing the other men flying around him in perfect formation against a cobalt sky. They were high above the earth, working in unison, speaking only when necessary. They counted off the beats before a turn, completing a fleur de lis, leaving behind them white pillars of smoke as they rose ever higher into the sky. In 1973 — the year Astrid died — the Blue Angels suffered a midair collision, killing two pilots and a crew chief. But Marcus did not know this. To him, everyone in the poster was immortal.

Lying there, Marcus decides it is time to take it down.

They remain on the farm, leaving only for provisions. Their daily routine involves more sleep than Marcus might have expected — part of which he attributes to jet lag. Conversation among them is calibrated to avoid upset. All three prefer reading to TV or films. They drink after dark and go to bed early. They do not "catch up" the way Americans do. They are present with one another again.

The market is far enough away to require the car and usually it is Sigrid who does the shopping, leaving the men alone. Marcus isn't sure how much Sigrid has told their father about the events in America, and so far Morten isn't asking, but Marcus assumes he knows most of it. Sigrid would have prepped him somehow. But the uncertainty, on this occasion, is what makes their relationship tolerable.

The days are bright and long but not warm. Not in the way New York is warm now. There, in the woods, the days pull moisture from the trees and earth. The air is so saturated it chokes you, and the only remedy is to plunge yourself into a lake and wash the sweat from your skin with the glacier water that collects in the Catskills. He liked to swim under the water there until his lungs begged for mercy; he'd resurface slowly and deliberately and draw in the cool air that hovers an inch above the surface. He'd drink it in, blue and nourishing.

He and Lydia camped one weekend. Marcus emerged from Lower

Saranac Lake feeling like a Roman god, and he wrapped himself in a thick terrycloth robe. She had smiled at him as she lay there smelling like coconut.

Today, in Hedmark, the day is dry and the light is crisp. Summers here are brief, but they promise a perfection of balance that exists nowhere else. A Scandinavian summer day is a miracle; dry and endless. Full of woodland scents and optimism. Not a bug, not a mosquito. Beneath it, like a melody, is a subtle sense of melancholy because everyone knows it won't last. So they breathe it in and relish it and hold on with the knowledge that they can't.

As kids, he and Sigrid would run to the river every day through woods that were wild and unowned and uninhabited and they would dip their toes in and dare each other to go farther.

He would dive in and the water would hit his chest and constrict the muscles and force the air out, making it impossible to inhale. You could drown in open air, the river was so cold.

Every Norwegian child knows this feeling. Every child knows the feeling will pass.

"Is it warm enough yet?" he'd yell. Because Sigrid was always the first one in the water.

Downstairs, in the kitchen, Sigrid is fixing herself a snack of dark brown bread, herring, and sour cream. After she settles at the table with her food, Marcus silently shuffles into the kitchen and begins to rummage around in the drawer to the right of the sink.

He feels her watching.

"Have you talked with your boyfriend since you've been back?" he asks, his back to her.

"What makes you think Irv is my boyfriend?"

"I watched you say goodbye to him at the airport."

"Hmm."

"How's that going to work?"

"It doesn't have to work," she says, taking a bite.

Screwdrivers. Tape. Stamps. Swedish coins no one needs. A calculator from the eighties. Glue. A red balloon. Layers of junk upon junk. He pushes it around and it makes a grinding noise.

"So it's over, whatever it was?" he asks.

"Irv may have mentioned something about vacation time owed to him. Frequent flier points. You're looking for batteries, aren't you. For those old American flashlights."

"How did you know?"

"I saw you playing with one."

"I want to get them working and I can't think of why."

"We used to explore with those."

"Yes," he says.

"You're ready."

"For what?"

"Exploring."

"I'm just getting the flashlights working."

"I'll come with you when it's dark enough."

"Where?"

"We'll take a walk," she says. "See if we remember our secret code. Do you remember it?"

"I haven't thought about it since visiting here in 1977."

"Me either," says Sigrid.

At ten o'clock, when they are both tired and would normally be in bed, Sigrid and Marcus leave the farm behind and walk into the forest. Marcus pushes the small signal button located above the switch and tests the light. Sigrid, twenty meters away through the trees, flashes back, and they diverge in the wood on two separate paths. The moon is up but the sky is not dark. Even now the horizon is a palette of pastels. They walk softly to hide from each other—from the enemy forces, from the aliens, from the Nazis—and succeed in disappearing into a memory.

Marcus breaks the moment with an encrypted message flashed from his hidden position inside a bush. She reads it:

Put the dog in the bucket and don't tell the monkey.

One of them does not remember the code.

Sigrid is leading them in a direction that Marcus does not quite remember.

Marcus abandons his post with the Resistance and connects with Sigrid, who leads them through a thicket he vaguely remembers. At the end of the path there is a simple white church and Marcus immediately realizes where Sigrid has led him. What surprises him, though, is that his father is waiting by his mother's gravestone with his hands in his pockets and his pipe in his mouth.

"I've been ambushed," Marcus says, turning off his flashlight and clipping it to his belt.

"Sigrid told me everything, Marcus."

"Told you what?" he says.

"About what you heard when you were eleven years old that caused you to fall off the toilet you'd been standing on to overhear our conversation. Which you shouldn't have done."

"You're going to say I misunderstood."

"No. You didn't."

The moon is a sliver of white above the steeple. From where Marcus stands, it looks like a replacement for a missing cross.

"You heard correctly and I'm sorry. But you still don't understand. She did say that. And we did have that conversation. We even considered it. But in the end, she didn't do it, Marcus. She died in her sleep months, months later. You have it backwards. You didn't kill your mother, Marcus. Your silent fear didn't convince her to kill herself to save you. You're the one who saved her. We had that conversation, but we never returned to it because of you. You and your little broken arm. You needed us both for as long as you could have us. It struck us as obvious after that. There was no leaving you. Every day she lived after that was a blessing that you gave to her and to all of us. But in return—if I understand correctly from Sigrid—you were waiting for something to happen that wasn't going to happen precisely because you prevented it, if it was ever going to happen in the first place. People say dark things in the dark of their rooms. Sometimes the talking helps. But I assure you it never came up in conversation again. I can never explain to you how sorry I am for what you went through. But I never knew."

"I don't believe you."

Morten placed his hand on his wife's gravestone. "I promise you."

"You're asking me to see my entire life as a lie. My entire life as a mistake. My entire life has been lived in the cloak of a misperception?"

"A misunderstanding."

"I don't believe you."

"I think you do. I think you need to make room in your heart for how much your mother loved you and how much I did too. You were angry at her for dying and me for letting it happen. But you blamed yourself. Your letter about Lydia proved that. It is my opinion that your guilt has prevented you from mourning. It may have also prevented you from fully living. If you can accept what you're hearing, you might be able to come home again. I would like you to come home again, Marcus. I miss you."

Marcus reads his mother's name and the dates on the stone.

"I can't stay here alone," Marcus says to Sigrid.

"I'm staying for a while." Turning to her father, she says, "I'm thinking I might resign from the police force."

"You don't want to fight crime anymore?"

"Criminal investigation is about solving riddles from the past when the damage is done, and it is already too late," Sigrid says, looking at Marcus. "What I saw in America made me want to get ahead of things rather than show up behind them. Maybe step into the fray. See things from another perspective. Make things better."

Morten smiles at her. "That's the spirit."

ACKNOWLEDGMENTS

Special thanks to Lauren Wein and Pilar Garcia-Brown at Houghton Mifflin Harcourt for their editorial assistance, ideas, and good humor. Thanks to Alison Kerr Miller, and also the entire team at HMH including the late Carla Gray, who believed in my writing. Thanks to Bill Scott-Kerr and the Transworld team at Penguin Random House, who embraced this book with open arms and hearts. Thanks, as always, to my UK agent, Rebecca Carter, for her uncompromising judgment and professional guidance, and also my American agent, PJ Mark, for his support and outstanding (or possibly just similar) sense of humor. Thanks to the full team at Janklow and Nesbit.

Thanks to Dr. Lesley Inker and Dr. Howard Stevens for their guidance on how to set up and address Astrid's cancer. All errors are mine. Some are even deliberate.

Thanks as always to my wife, Camilla, my son, Julian, and my daughter, Clara. It is not always easy having a writer for a husband or a father. It is a little cool, though, isn't it?

Irv was singing "Somebody's Knocking" by Terri Gibbs (1980).

The quote from *House* is from episode #202. That aired in 2005, not 2008 as Melinda was watching it. As a novelist, I occasionally take some liberties with reality. I consider this fair because reality has taken some liberties with me.

I have messed around with the geography but not—I hope—the essence and feeling of upstate New York. Sometimes one needs to pull back to see more clearly.

Morten's duck was named after Ferdinand from the movie *Babe* and, later, *Babe: Pig in the City.* That was one funny duck.

The SWAT team members were discussing the film *The Diving Bell and the Butterfly* (2007), directed by Julian Schnabel.

According to the Bureau of Justice Statistics at the U.S. Department of Justice, only 7 percent of full-time sworn law enforcement officers in medium-sized sheriffs' offices were women in 2007. In small offices, this dropped to 4 percent (www.bjs.gov/content/pub/pdf/wle8708.pdf). In Norway, some 45 percent of employees in the police force are women and the number of female managers and leaders is going up. Thanks to (Senior Norwegian police officer) Cecilie Lilaas-Skari for answering important questions for me. Any errors here are clearly her fault and you should probably call her directly.

In 2014, Jefferson County, New York, elected the first woman sheriff in the history of the state.

The motto of the New York state police really is Excellence Through Knowledge and has been since 1917. I think it should be adopted nationally and used as a beacon for progress.

Sigourney Weaver: Please forgive me.

Q & A WITH THE AUTHOR:
A SELF-INTERVIEW

*This is a self-interview. That means you're interviewing yourself. You're
comfortable with this?*

> Not really, no.

Why not?

> What if the White House starts doing this sort of thing?
> Have you considered the implications?

Listen, I'm the one asking the questions here.

> Are you sure?

*I'm going to get started. Try and focus. People might want to learn some-
thing from you, or about you, anyway.*

> God help them.

Sigrid and her father, Morten. We met them in Norwegian by Night.
What made you want to continue with these characters?

> At first I didn't. Don't you remember? You have a terrible

memory. I wrote a whole other, critically acclaimed novel before this one.

If they want the other book, they can find it. We're talking about Sigrid and Morten now.

Norwegian by Night ended conclusively for Sheldon, and I needed to step far away from that intense story. That's why I went off and wrote *The Girl in Green.*

[Interviewer scowls. Interviewee continues.]

After . . . that novel . . . I entertained the idea of circling back to Sigrid and her father because it felt very comforting. I liked their relationship and I wanted to be around it more. Around the time that *The Girl in Green* came out, I had the idea of bringing Sigrid to America. I liked the idea of a companion piece rather than a proper sequel. I wanted the themes to connect rather than the stories. In *Norwegian by Night*, Sheldon went to Europe and we saw Norway through the eyes of an old Jewish-American man. Here, I had a chance to invert Sheldon's experience by bringing a young Norwegian woman to America. That wasn't a story, but it was a premise to explore.

How does your vantage point as an expat inform your writing?

That's a big question. I'm something of a professional stranger in this world. I was trained as an academic in international relations, and I moved to Europe for my studies at Oxford in 1996 and haven't moved back (yet). Twenty-two years of life overseas, travel through some fifty countries, and a decade with the United Nations, have all provided me with a wealth of impressions and understandings that are resources for my writing. I have a predilection to see the world as something unsettled and in motion at all times, coupled with a compulsion to make sense of what I'm seeing. For *American by Day,* this means that I see America in a way that other Americans don't and possibly can't. For this reason, I have a footing in a story like this that is unique and that allows me to explore it dramatically in distinct ways. That, in turn, results in a special reading experience. With Sigrid as a guide, we can become defamiliarized with received ideas and assumptions, thereby making America into something strange and new and again.

Why did looking at America through a Norwegian investigator's eyes appeal to you?

> That's not the right question.

What's the right question?

> Through whose eyes were we seeing America in this story?

That's better. I don't know if it's right, but it's better. Answer that one.

> I was most interested in seeing America from the outside, from a European's point of view and also from a professional woman's point of view. I don't think Sigrid being Norwegian *per se* was an initial selling point for me as much as her outsider status as a European. Her Norwegian-ness was something I needed to back into to find value. Eventually I did.
>
> Norwegians don't come laden—in American literature or pop culture—with the baggage of some other Europeans. If Sigrid had been French, she'd have been weighed down by everything Americans think they know about the French. Whether or not they are represented fairly, the French have a big personality for Americans. The same can be said for the Germans. And the British. And the Irish. And possibly the Spanish and Italians. If I had written about a character from Central or Eastern Europe, there would have been a cultural frame around her, informed by World War II and the Cold War. But Scandinavia is different. It's not part of the Great Powers. It wasn't even part of the Ro-

man Empire, for the most part. It was late to industrialize. The Danes and Norwegians and Swedes aren't bursting with character and caricature for most Americans, and they don't hold a massive fascination for the American imagination (sorry, Scandinavia).

To an American reader, Norway will feel almost neutral. Almost familiar but still foreign. An exotic Canada, if one can imagine such a thing. But here's where it gets interesting: when someone you think is most similar to you finds you utterly bizarre, it is especially unsettling because it's unexpected. We assume the French will find us bizarre, but we've been shrugging that off since the 1700s. We assume the Germans will find us bizarre, but we'll raise an eyebrow to them and say, "Compared to what, exactly?" The British will say we are bizarre with an ounce of love, a dash of ridicule, and a twist of envy, so we'll just ignore them or laugh it off as we always do. But if someone Norwegian finds us bizarre? This is a group of people who aspire to be the planet's working definition of "normal and well-adjusted." When that happens, it gets our attention. That's Sigrid's power. The power of a normal person telling you that you've lost your mind.

Sheldon Horowitz is a tough act to follow. Were you trepidatious about trying?

What I absolutely did not want to do was compete with Sheldon. Sigrid is not a mirror or a literary doppelgänger. I needed to find a story where she could come into her own.

Sigrid's a different character in a new universe entangled in an ensemble cast telling a story with a very different tone. *American by Day* is a story about a woman looking for her brother who has gotten himself into a heap of trouble because he never came to terms with his own pain as a child. This story is narrower than *Norwegian by Night*. Sheldon's rabbit hole is his pain and his memories in the face of old age. His challenges are mostly internal, despite being chased through the Norwegian wilderness by the Balkan mafia. Sigrid's rabbit hole is American society. It's mostly external. These books invert one another and—for that reason—they are linked.

Also, Sigrid doesn't carry the burden of this book alone. She does it with Sheriff Irving Wylie, whom I absolutely adored writing about and getting to know. He's an old-school Republican sheriff with a master's degree in theology from Loyola, a wonderful sense of humor that is entirely unlike Sigrid's or even Sheldon's—or mine for that matter, and don't ask me how that works—as well as some very unorthodox views of Christianity, science, and suicide. I think he deserves his own novel. Let's see what happens.

You set this novel in upstate New York. Um . . . why?

Yeah. That's a good question. I set it there, in part, because it brings almost nothing to mind. In fact, it brings so little to mind that my first thoughts go immediately to Richard Russo and his novels set there because it's as if it only became a place once he bothered to notice it. The fact that he turned around and read *American by Day* later—and liked it—means the world to me. I really didn't see that coming. At first I thought my publisher said Rene Russo liked it, which obviously would have been even better, but Richard's great too.

Now, saying it brings nothing to mind is a little unfair. Cornell is there. And a bunch of wonderful state parks.

That's it?

Well . . . there's an Arby's. A Dunkin Donuts. Lots of trees. Moss. Rocks. Some hubcaps off the 81 north of Syracuse. So, you know, tons of stuff.

Nice.

Okay, fine, maybe I'm a little hard on it because I'm a New Englander, which is morally, culturally, intellectually, aesthetically, and historically superior. But that's no reason not to be magnanimous.

Of course not.

Speaking as a storyteller, Sigrid needed to come from a place that wasn't too laden with preconceived notions for the reader—Norway—and she needed to go to such a place, too. One regular person looking at a bunch of other regular people in a regular place and concluding they are all off their rockers. That's what I needed. That's what we got. Upstate New York fit the bill.

Now that we're done with this interview, Do you still find writing your own questions and then answering them a bit awkward?

Yes, I do. In most societies, talking to yourself is a sign of mental illness. Here, it's a pathway to professional advancement and already that should give us pause. Personally, I think we should be erecting walls between sanity and insanity and fact and fiction these days, but . . . I'm just happy to be here.